Long Road Home

Brand of Justice
Book 7

Lisa Phillips

eBook ISBN: 979-8-88552-195-6

Paperback ISBN: 979-8-88552-196-3

Published by: Two Dogs Publishing, LLC. Idaho, USA

Cover Design by: Sasha Almazan and Gene Mollica, GS Cover Design Studio, LLC

Edited by: Christine Callahan, Professional Publishing Services

Chapter One

Friday, 7:55 p.m.
Door County, Wisconsin

A closed front door kept secrets from the world.

Kenna's job was to kick the door in and drag the truth to the light. Today though, she knocked.

"It's almost like we're partners." A glint of humor laced the tone of the woman standing beside her on the concrete doorstep.

Kenna had parked her Subaru behind the Mercedes and the Mitsubishi at the curb. Charlayne and Betty were already here. Forrest, her "partner" had hitched a ride, which made sense given Kenna was currently squatting in her garage.

Only the woman beside her knew the whole plan.

Kenna wanted to say she wasn't in the market for a partner. Or she could tell Forrest not to get used to it.

Neither sentiment left her mouth.

Forrest Crosby was just a few years older than Kenna but didn't wear it so well. The past two years had aged her, except when she smiled. Even then, the glint in her eyes didn't touch her mouth above the scarf wrapped around her neck. She wore insulated jeans and tennis shoes, an oversized sweater under her jacket. Hair pulled back.

They both wore heavy coats, but Kenna's had fur around the hood. She'd left the base layer off from under her jeans since they'd be inside Marion's house tonight. Then home to Forrest's house where Kenna's RV was parked in her garage out of the cold, snow, and wind.

The same wind that froze her fingers as she knocked again on Marion's front door.

Forrest held a tray. Under the lid was a selection of meats, cheeses, nuts, and fruit that Kenna was going to make sure they took home if this went sideways and no one ate.

The door swung open.

Kenna pasted on a smile. "We're here."

Marion frowned very slightly.

Good.

Marion should be nervous, but seemed to push it off quickly. "Come in. The others are already here."

Forrest went first, so Kenna could cover her back. The snack tray went to the coffee table in the living room, passed over the back of the couch to Betty, who'd turned when they came in. Charlayne sat in the armchair with a glass of something sparkly she'd probably brought herself and hadn't offered to anyone.

Kenna unzipped her coat, but wasn't about to take the time to unlace her boots. They might have to run out of here.

Forrest did the same. Kenna had given her a full briefing.

Over the last six weeks or so, as Kenna had been living in

her RV garage, she and Forrest had discovered some common ground. Forrest was a mystery writer but hadn't typed a word of fiction into her computer since her husband and son were tragically killed in a traffic accident on the highway late at night, coming back from a movie.

Two years ago.

Instead, she was currently researching a true crime book on a local legend, a serial murderer no one had caught. Kenna had peeked into the office and studied the collection of papers and case files Forrest had managed to compile. So far she'd resisted the urge to call Maizie and get her on the case.

The grieving wife and mother might need to solve it herself.

"Coffee? Tea?" Marion wandered down the hall to the kitchen, which connected back to the living room. The hall rug needed vacuuming, and a thin layer of dust had accumulated on the bookshelves. She set her jacket on the arm of the couch beside her.

Forrest took a folding chair in the corner, which left Marion on the hotseat—a padded piano stool in front of the cold fireplace.

Kenna leaned back against the couch just to feel the pistol at the small of her back.

Maybe she wouldn't need it.

Since before the holidays Kenna had been tracking a serial kidnapper who had stolen girls between the ages of six and nine. Eight girls had gone missing over nearly thirty years. Long enough the community grew numb. Leads dried up, and people forgot.

No one ever found a single body.

Plenty of folks around the county had ideas about the kind of man who would do this kind of thing.

Kenna had ideas of her own. Kind of like Forrest and her "partners" idea.

"Let's get started, shall we?" Marion settled on the stool, which creaked under her weight. Though she looked thinner than the last time Kenna had seen her—a month ago, at the last book club.

Betty lifted a mug from the coffee table. "Who finished reading the book?"

Kenna smiled. "I liked it a lot." And she was going to like this even more.

Forrest made a face. "Yeah, I don't know that I *liked* it. Anton wasn't a good guy."

"Like that made him any less attractive?" Charlayne snorted into her bubbles. "Bad boys are hot." Coming from a sixty-year-old woman, that was interesting. Forrest grinned. Charlayne lifted her glass in a salute. "She knows what I mean."

Kenna frowned.

Forrest shook her head. "I've written a few bad boy stories in my time."

All Kenna could think about was Jax. "I prefer good guys, I've gotta say."

Some guys had an edge. Jax had smoothed his out with exercise, healthy living, and being an FBI special agent for years. He'd invited her to spend Christmas with him at his mother's house, but in a way she knew he understood there was no way she'd have said yes. They were somewhere as a couple...but they weren't *there.* He'd flown out to Colorado and spent New Years with her, Stairns and his wife, and Maizie, who was basically Kenna's teenage ward. Then they'd all gone back to work on January second.

Marion tried to smile. "Sounds like there's a story there."

Oh, she had no idea the stories Kenna could tell. They just wouldn't be about Jax.

No one in this room besides Forrest knew she was a private investigator. Kenna had made sure they didn't know, and most people didn't run a web search on every new person they met.

Betty and Charlayne were friendships of convenience, but they'd figure out pretty soon why Kenna had invited them to begin a book club with her. They would get a front row seat to a real-life story that would clear their husbands of suspicion for good.

"We're here to talk about the book." Kenna grinned. She really wanted some of Forrest's cheese tray but didn't want to be the first one to flip off the lid and look like she had no self-control. "How about the fact he lied to her about who he really was? And she had no idea, so it's kind of mistaken identity since she assumed who he was and ran with that. But it's also the fact he never admitted the truth."

"He wanted to believe the lie," Betty said. "Maybe she knew. I got the feeling a few times that she might've known but didn't want to admit to herself that the truth was right in front of her."

"I think we do that, too. Don't we?" Kenna stared at Marion, more convinced than ever that she was right. "Refusing to see what's right in front of our faces, because it's easier to not stir things up. We like the status quo." She glanced around, then said, "You have to wonder, if he wanted to be someone else, why not just make the change? Why stay with his family when he could leave with her and be the man they both wanted to believe he was?"

Forrest tipped her head in agreement.

"Because they liked the danger. Both of them." Charlayne saluted again with her glass. "There's a rush in the risk and worrying about getting caught. Good guys, schoolteachers, doctors, or ministers aren't risky. They're boring."

Kenna eyed her. Charlayne's husband was at least twenty years older than her, and she was midforties. She kept herself painfully skinny but not a result of limiting alcohol intake. Her husband had retired but played golf in the summer and indoor sports this time of year. He had a tan—most likely from a membership that gave him unlimited tanning bed access.

Kenna turned to Marion. "What about you? What do you think about Anton?"

"Men aren't worth it, but I can see the appeal of a *bad boy*. Someone who does whatever he wants because he can. That's power."

Forrest stood, finally. "I need to use the bathroom. I drank too much coffee today." She smiled and made her preplanned exit.

There could be no accusation without evidence. But a confession would be even better.

Forrest might have a point about their being partners. It was just that Kenna hadn't had one in a long time, and they usually didn't end well.

"Is that why you take them?" Kenna stared at Marion, feeling the rush of knowing she was right like a hum that energized her. And Charlayne and Betty would be her witnesses to whatever Marion said next. "Because you can? For the rush of power."

Marion stared at her, a pinched expression on her face.

Betty said, "Kenna, what are you talking about?"

Kenna locked her eyes on Marion.

The older woman shifted on the piano stool. "Yes, what?"

Kenna shrugged. "I was just thinking about Marcus in the book. Getting into his head, you know?"

Marion cleared her throat. "He was bad."

"But he didn't care. He jumped on opportunity and did whatever he wanted." Kenna stared at her. "She didn't care who she hurt."

Charlayne smacked her lips. "You mean *he*."

"No, I don't," Kenna said.

Forrest came back in. Kenna took her gaze off Marion for a second, long enough to see her friend—her partner—nod. Kenna stood, ready to get this settled. But was she ready to admit that working with someone was better than being alone?

She wasn't so sure about that.

Charlayne uncrossed her legs and launched up. "What are we doing?" She swayed forward off balance.

Marion grabbed her, spun her around, and pointed a revolver at the underside of her chin.

Charlayne dropped the glass, which shattered on the edge of the coffee table and hit the dingy carpet. The lid of the piano stool was open.

Betty gasped. Kenna drew her weapon and held it pointed at Marion.

Charlayne screeched, "What is going on?"

Forrest said, "I found a stack of dirty dresses that would fit a small girl the age of the ones who disappeared. They're old, waiting to be washed."

Betty stood. "I'd like an answer to that as well."

Kenna saw the gun in her peripheral vision. Betty had a .22 she'd pulled from her purse.

"I'll kill her!" Marion's white-knuckle grasp on Charlayne's arm and the gun to her throat spoke loudly enough.

"Put the gun down." Kenna held her aim on the child kidnapper, but there was too much risk of hitting Charlayne to fire. Marion probably knew that. "Put it down, and we can talk about this."

Let her think there was a way out other than prison.

"Talk?!" Marion yelled. "You shouldn't have said anything!"

"If you knew who I was," Kenna said, "you'd know that's not possible."

Forrest crept up behind Marion with a double-fisted grip on an umbrella.

Kenna couldn't react, even though she wanted to tell the woman to stand down. Then again, maybe that was the way to resolve this.

Forrest swung with the umbrella, clipping Marion on the side of the head.

Charlayne screeched.

Marion whirled back from the blow to bring her gun up, aiming at anything in her sights.

Kenna had already moved. She grabbed Marion's wrist, jerked it forward and brought her knee up. Marion's face cracked against Kenna's knee, and she howled. Kenna got the gun, aimed Marion in the direction of the armchair, and handed Marion's gun to Forrest. "She doesn't get up." Then glanced at Betty. "I don't want any accidental shots. You hear me?"

Betty was focused entirely on Marion. "I hear you. What's going on?"

"Marion Wells is the person who has been kidnapping girls." The last one was two years ago. But considering the first had been the younger sister of a former colleague, this one was practically personal.

Betty's expression darkened. "Is that right."

"I know you won't kill her before justice is served." As tempting as that might be for Betty to end Marion's life—and the suspicion that had been cast on her own husband. Or Charlayne's. Then again, over the years nearly every male in the county had been accused in the court of public opinion.

Charlayne had the bottle of bubbly. She took a lengthy swig, then wiped her mouth on the back of her hand. Her manicured nails flashed in the light, and she cocked one hip. "I can get a knife from the kitchen. We can cut her. Just a little bit."

"I need to look around the house. Forrest, call the police and get them here." Kenna strode out of the living room, rolling her shoulders as she walked. Everything she'd found pointed to opportunity, and everything about Marion's life said she was exactly the type of person to do something like this.

The last child had been taken two years ago.

Marion Wells wouldn't be kidnapping anyone else.

Kenna searched the bedroom and bathroom. She didn't want to toss too much, or the police would end up with their evidence tainted. But she had to take a look for herself. The police had never suspected a woman was the perpetrator, always falling back on assumptions about sexual crimes. Not a bad theory, but it hadn't helped them solve the crime. In the end, all it did was leave them blind to what was going on in front of their faces.

But Kenna almost always saw the truth.

An amateurish-looking embroidered verse hung on the bedroom wall. A smudge of dried blood on one corner of the frame. *Pride comes before destruction.*

Kenna frowned. That hit a little too close to home. She'd come in here sure of herself, ready to enact the plan to force the ugly truth of Marion Wells' actions into the light.

A better person—a better *Christian*—surely wouldn't be all puffed up with their own ability. Full of her own surety and self-importance.

Surely, they would...

She didn't know what a better Christian than her would be feeling right now. She only knew her own heart, and it wasn't where it should be. Or needed to be. She hadn't been a Christian long, but she had another question to ask. Whether of Jax, or the local preacher.

But either way, justice would be done here. The missing girls would have voices once again.

Kenna rifled through the closet, enough to see a seam on the back wall. The bathroom was to the left, so what was behind this?

She swept the clothes aside, and the hangers clacked together. A door, barely shoulder height.

A padlock.

Kenna turned around. She shoved her foot back and slammed beside the padlock with the sole of her boot.

The door flung in.

Kenna crouched to look inside and choked on a gasp. "Forrest!" She ducked and crawled into a storage space, a thin mattress on the floor. A couple of old dirty dolls with missing eyes. A plastic sheet had been laid on the mattress, and a too-thin girl lay on top.

Practically gray. Cool to the touch. An IV bag hung from a nail on the wall above her head, nearly empty now.

Forest ran into the bedroom. "What is—"

Kenna touched two fingers to the girl's neck. The last one kidnapped. *Two years ago.* A lump caught in her throat. Thready. Barely there. "She's still alive."

Kenna ripped the IV bag off the wall so the hospital would know what she'd been given.

Forrest threw her a threadbare blanket. "Cover her with this. I'll tell the police we need an ambulance."

"We can take her. It'll be faster." Kenna covered the girl,

gathering the blanket around her. She'd been working on arm strength and prayed now that she would be able to do this. She saw the soiled rags between the girl's legs but refused to think about that. "Let's get out of here."

She crawled through the closet door and gifted the girl with freedom.

Praying she would live long enough to know.

Chapter Two

K enna hit Send on the text.

Suspect in custody. Girl alive.

She set the phone on the chair beside her so the persistent buzzing of notifications for the group thread with Charlayne, Betty, and Forrest didn't get annoying. She needed a breather when she spent too much time with people, and her mind was spinning still about the pride thing. Destruction was more than a trip and fall. She didn't want pride to cause her to lose what she had.

Things were good. She had a man in her life, and she'd found a family in dear friends—people who understood her and still cared.

Forrest weaved through the hospital waiting area holding two cups of coffee. "Confession, I drank a full one and then ordered these two. It's terrible, but it's hot."

Kenna took the one Forrest handed over. "Thanks, *partner*. I'm freezing."

Forrest snorted. "I rescind my offer. I don't think I want a life of fighting crime."

Kenna smiled over the rim of the cup.

"You think it's adrenaline, not just the cold?" Forrest settled a seat over, leaving an empty one between them. She stretched out her legs in Kenna's direction and crossed her ankles.

"I don't know." But she didn't like it, because it felt entirely too much like the person she had been. Not who she was now. "I was in Mexico for a few weeks at the end of last year. Maybe I haven't acclimated to winter yet."

"You wanna acclimate to Wisconsin, you've gotta stay longer than just a case. Thankfully, it was summer usually when your dad was here for that writer's conference."

Kenna ignored the comment, lifted her phone, and checked the thread. "Betty says the police have taped off the house as a crime scene. She overheard one of the deputies talking about a cadaver dog." She wanted to know when they'd be doing that. Finding those bodies was the priority now, so the families could have that huge part of closure. Not that she would stick her nose in—the local cops didn't want a private investigator hanging around, as though she was ensuring they did their jobs correctly.

"So we're gonna talk about work and not personal stuff, I see?" Forrest's question had a tone.

Kenna glanced over, since she'd said pretty much that exact thing to Forrest more than once.

"You knew your dad better than I ever did." Forrest shrugged. "Why would my experience of him make any difference?"

"It's complicated." Like...Vegas Mafia, trust funds, Washington state cults, secret societies, and murder complicated. It almost seemed like every time she turned over a rock in her father's past, there was something under it she would've rather not known.

Forrest snorted. "Yeah, it's *family*. Of course it's complicated. When you live with someone, you see their mess, their bad habits."

"Then why does anyone ever get married?" Her friend wasn't making it sound appealing.

Forrest laughed. Which in itself was progress, even if it was short-lived. "Thank you. It helps to remember the good times."

"It was good?" Kenna hadn't asked her about the husband she'd lost.

Forrest nodded. "He was a good man, and he was good to me."

"I can say the same about Bradley, even if it wasn't 'right' according to God's idea of right living." Kenna had reconciled that one, and concluded she hadn't known better. Ignorance had both hurt her and given her an incredible gift. Things she would cherish in her heart and grieve for as long as it beat.

Partners.

Lovers.

"None of us are perfect." Forrest sighed.

"But it seems like we're expected to do the right thing." Like not being prideful about solving a case when no one else had been able to.

"What's the point in expecting that of us when we're just going to fail?"

Kenna shrugged. "I'm figuring it out."

"I can see why you do what you do," Forrest said.

"And you're good?" Kenna eyed her friend.

"Someone's child came home tonight. That's a good thing. Like I said, I can see why you do it."

"I'm not going to retire and write ridiculous novels, so you don't have to worry about the competition."

Forrest laughed again. "We can dissect one of your father's bestsellers if Charlayne and Betty ever invite us back to book club after what we did. But that's for later."

A dark-haired man in a lined denim jacket, jeans, and tan boots strode across the waiting area. "You're the ones?"

Forrest got to her feet slowly.

Kenna stood. "I'm Private Investigator Kenna Banbury."

His craggy features hardened. "Why did it take you so long to find her?"

Kenna hadn't interviewed him or his wife. She'd had copies of the case file notes with the interviews done years ago, when everything had been fresh in his mind. Hours after his daughter went missing. Two years later, it would only have dredged up his grief.

"How is she?" Kenna wasn't going to answer the question he asked. This man just needed someone to blame.

"She's alive. No thanks to you." He practically spat the words.

A nurse on the other side of the waiting area looked over from her computer.

Kenna felt Forrest's shoulder touch hers so that they stood side by side.

"That's wonderful news," Kenna said. Truthfully, she'd considered the child to be dead. Whatever led her to check for a pulse had meant they could save the girl before she let go for good and took her last breath.

Forrest said, "We will be praying she fully recovers."

"So she can be in therapy for the rest of her life, traumatized by every second she was captive." He scoffed. "Who knows what happened to her."

"But she survived," Kenna pointed out. Unlike so many

others. "She has time to heal and live her life." Like she did every day.

Like Forrest was working on doing.

And the same thing she prayed every day for Maizie to realize, and take hold of.

Kenna wanted to tell him that if it wasn't for her trying to find answers for Ramon Santiago as to what happened to his sister, no one would ever have found his daughter. But she wasn't sure what a Christian who wasn't tainted by pride in what she had accomplished would say right now.

Forrest filled the silence. "Your daughter will probably want to see you. As soon as she wakes up, she'll want to know her dad is there with her. You don't want to miss being the one to tell her she's safe now." It was an effective dismissal.

He whirled around and stomped out, as though late for an appointment.

"We know she's alive," Kenna said.

Forrest nodded. "Let's go." They'd finished their coffee, and it was nearly eleven.

Kenna had parked all the way across the lot in the only empty space. They walked through the parking lot only scattered with cars, and mounds of plowed snow now covered in soot and dirt from cars. Nothing fresh had fallen in a while. Dark shadows left by the streetlights created far too many places someone could hide.

Forrest said, "I always think it could be a trap. Which is why I'm still alive."

Kenna chuckled. "I regret watching that ridiculous movie with you." Even though she didn't. Not really.

She hadn't had a real friend in a long time, and any time Forrest spent not up in her own head was good—unless she needed to be there to work on her book. Kenna had been in high school when her father started writing books. Now she could barely picture the old man hunched over a laptop. Did Forrest share his process? The two of them had met here in Appleton at a big conference for authors of their genre. Her father had been teaching about private investigation.

After Kenna found Forrest's unique short-term rental ad offering storage for anyone's RV or trailer, she'd had Maizie run a full background check. When they'd discovered a connection between Forrest and Kenna's father—where he'd supported the beginning of her author career—that had given her a connection to talk about Kenna staying in the RV during the storage.

They'd made a deal, and wound up becoming friends. At least, as much as each of them was capable of in a few weeks of knowing each other.

Kenna parked on the drive-in front of the RV bay garage door. Forrest dug out her keys, and they jangled in her hand as she walked. She stopped six feet or so away, and Kenna spotted what had stalled her.

She left her friend there with a swipe of her hand. "This is my department."

Kenna tugged the taped note off the front door. Most likely it was nothing, just a scribbled message from a neighbor.

She wasn't even thinking about whether a fingerprint might have been left on the tape when she opened it and read, "Your families deaths were no accident."

Forrest practically shoved her off the stoop. She jabbed her key in the lock and swept inside. Down the hall.

Kenna heard a door slam.

I guess you don't want to talk about it. She secured the front door and threw the dead bolt, then checked around the house. Forrest hadn't wanted Kenna to put up surveillance cameras, but now she might not have a choice. If someone was going to be lurking, Kenna wanted to know.

She left the light above the oven on, then headed through to the garage.

Boxes lined one wall alongside Forrest's car. Three bikes hung from hooks on the wall. Two adult size, and one for a boy. Kids shoes had been discarded by the mat, kicked aside. They were practically falling apart, still caked with mud.

Kenna stared for longer than necessary, thinking about kindred spirits and trying not to dwell on the fate of people who knew her father. Forrest would be fine. Nothing was going to happen to her here in her own house. Neither was Kenna going to babysit the woman 24/7 for the rest of her life. She also wasn't going to allow danger to show up here.

If there was something unknown about her family's accident, Kenna would figure it out.

She didn't need to stay when Marion Wells was in custody. The bodies would be found in due course, by local police. If not for the note, she might have pulled out tonight and headed back to Colorado before the next winter storm rolled through.

She pulled the latch on the door and stepped up into her RV. The interior still smelled like new carpet, and the chrome shined a little too brightly, but she was working on making it home. The stripped- down AR-15 on the dining table helped with the balance of the decor.

Kenna grabbed a Sharpie from her junk drawer and wrote ALIVE under the photo of the kidnapper's most recent victim on her fridge door.

She packed the weapon away now that she didn't have to distract herself to pass the time waiting for book club, then dialed Maizie on speaker and listened to it ring while she latched the case and put the weapon in the bedroom closet.

"Hey."

Kenna stepped out of the bedroom. "I'm here. One sec," she called out, then grabbed her earbuds and slipped them in. Sometimes they talked for a few hours, and Kenna would work out. Or Maizie played music over the open phone line, and Kenna took a nap. This time she grabbed her laptop. "I'm logging on."

"Did something happen with Marion?" Maizie asked. "Is the victim okay?"

At times Maizie sounded like the seventeen-year-old she was, though she would turn eighteen in a few weeks. Other times she sounded like someone who had lived a lot longer. On occasion she might sound like a scared child. With the life she'd lived, she could be whoever she wanted if she found peace.

None of those had shown up when Maizie hid away nearly all of Christmas Eve and most of Christmas Day. Something Kenna still hadn't got an answer about. She didn't know what to make of it, and Maizie didn't seem to want to talk about it.

"The victim is alive," Kenna replied. Few people understood how much of a win that was. "And the suspect is in custody. This is about a note left on Forrest's door when we got back. I'm uploading pictures now." She took them with her phone, which sent them to the cloud without her doing anything. Maizie would see the images almost immediately.

"Not a scholar, whoever wrote this."

She'd noticed the same. "Any indication in the police reports that their deaths were other than a tragic accident?"

"Huh." Maizie went silent. "I can look over everything again, and have Stairns do the same. I read the report, but I didn't think about it at the time."

"Good idea," Kenna said. "Between the two of you, if there's something to find, it'll get found."

Stairns had been Kenna's boss at the FBI. Now retired, he helped Kenna while his wife continued her therapy practice on a limited basis—with Maizie her number one client, and everyone else online.

Maizie lived in Kenna's father's Airstream, the one she'd parked behind Stairns' cabin in Colorado, and the teen was a survivor. Almost an adult now, she'd rescued herself from the man who held her captive since nearly the day she was born. Her upbringing had been written on her soul. Which might prevent her from becoming a functioning adult, or she might survive yet again. Either way, it wasn't going to be easy.

But life never was.

Kenna had surrendered herself and her future to God. And she was praying Maizie would do the same.

Maizie said, "Anything from the kidnapper, Marion Wells, about where the bodies are buried?"

Kenna said, "I hope she tells the police."

"Me, too." Maizie sighed audibly over the phone line. "And I'll look into the accident."

"Run down what you have so far."

"Good thing I downloaded it all months ago before you made the booking, or you'd have to wait five minutes for me to hack the police department network."

"You think it would take you that long?" Kenna said.

"If I was inclined to engage in illegal activity, perhaps it might only take me three minutes."

"If." Kenna didn't like the methods Maizie sometimes employed, but Stairns had written out an honesty code between the two of them and both had signed it. If there was anything he didn't feel comfortable with, Kenna would know.

Maizie rattled off a date in late October two years ago.

"They were traveling back from a football game in Green Bay when a semi coming the other direction veered across the double yellow center line. Forrest's husband swerved to miss it and lost control. There was never any collision. Their car flipped, and both were mortally injured. Though, the coroner thinks it took longer for the child to die."

Alone in the dark. Upside down, hurt. Fighting for breath and wondering what had just happened. Empathy wasn't always a good thing. When it came to children, Kenna's boundaries were a thing of their own. She didn't know if they were stronger than steel, or non-existent. She saved children whenever she could, but otherwise tried to stay out of their lives because if she lost one it hurt too much.

"You think someone might have caused the accident on purpose?" Maizie said.

"There might be someone out there who believes it." Kenna paused. "But the police went over the vehicle, right?"

"There's a report in the file about the car. Nothing to indicate anyone messed with it. But if they were looking for an explanation as to why it flipped, maybe they weren't thinking sabotage. Could be they were only considering contributing factors."

"And the car now?" It had been two years, so it wasn't likely to be anywhere Kenna could go look at it.

"There's a note in the file that it was scrapped and compacted after the insurance company made their final assessment."

The semitruck driver had gone to prison. Kenna could go talk to him and find out if he knew anything. After all this time, he might be inclined to open up.

"Are we making this a case?" Maizie asked.

Kenna didn't want to stir anything up for Forrest when she was working so hard to put it behind her. At least most of the time. The rest of the time she was barely hanging on—which was how grief worked. "I'll keep you posted," she replied.

Kenna needed to find out what Forrest knew.

Then she'd decide if she was going to stick around and investigate a double homicide.

Chapter Three

Friday, 9:35 p.m.
San Diego, California

Special Agent Oliver Jaxton stood in front of his ASAC. He laid the stack of printed images on the desk between him and Assistant Special Agent in Charge Bill Clarke. "She should be warned."

Clarke had loosened his tie hours ago. His gray combover had gone limp, and no matter how late it was, the guy didn't seem to want to go home to his wife. Everyone in the office knew their relationship was colder than the Alaskan tundra. She loved her pug more than she'd ever loved him, even generating side income from the dog's social media channels. Meanwhile, Bill punched a clock every day and carried his gray cloud around the office.

Clarke studied the top image. "Do you believe Kenna Banbury to be in imminent danger?"

"No." That didn't mean she shouldn't be warned. "I

believe the serial killer we've been tracking is trying to bait her into coming after him and using us as the middlemen."

Clarke's saggy cheeks shifted, covered with three days of stubble. "We don't need her help to catch this guy. Sooner or later he'll slip up."

Jax didn't look at the pictures of Kenna. He'd stared at them longer than was necessary already. "I don't like us being in the middle of it either, but if he's got eyes on her, she should know to be careful."

"How 'bout you catch him before anything happens...if you're so worried about her."

"We're still processing physical evidence from the last body. The one that dropped in Hemet." Jax sighed. "I need to nudge for those test results as soon as they can get them to me."

So far it almost seemed as if their suspect had killed someone and between each murder paid a visit to Wisconsin, where Kenna had been for a few weeks, then came back to California to murder the next victim. While he was there, he took stalkerish photos of her.

Jax continued, "I'd rather get him before the next kill occurs, and if Kenna knows to be on the watch for *the Walker*, then we'd be using all the resources at our disposal." Not tying their hands together by excluding her.

"You're gonna have to be careful with that, Jaxton." Clarke laced his fingers on his stomach. "Running to a private investigator every time you can't solve a case."

They knew exactly who they were hunting. Where he'd been. What kind of victims he chose. But Jax didn't think that was what his boss meant. "It isn't like that."

"No? You'll end up with a reputation regardless. Separating yourself from her, at least professionally for some time, can only help you build trust with the team."

Because Clarke thought he needed to?

His boss continued, "Otherwise you're the guy who runs to the PI he's loyal to. Instead of being a team player, loyal to the FBI."

Jax figured loyalty to the FBI might be part of the problem between Clarke and Mrs. Clarke, but he kept that thought to himself.

"Far as I can see, he's just baiting her," Clarke said. "Trying to get a rise out of her—if we passed on the information. So why don't we show him what *we're* made of instead."

"Yes, sir."

Clarke tapped the file. "Your request to inform her that our suspect has eyes on her is denied."

Jax collected the images and left the office, trying not to let the irritation show on his face—or the way he closed the door.

Whatever is lovely. Whatever is of good report.

Not a lot of that in tracking serial killers, so he had to go outside the FBI and his work as a special agent. Which brought him to Kenna. Her family. His family. Faith. The strong foundation he was building, and had been for years, laying each brick with reading the Bible, praying, going to church, taking communion. Simple, but effective.

As he walked back to his desk, he rolled his shoulders. The left side had remained stiff since Mexico, and he'd been working with a physical therapist. Mostly now it was only aches and pains, scars and old injuries that were healing.

The past faded.

He preferred to live in Christ in the present and look to the future. Not something many of the people he worked with understood, though he'd started attending a weekly Bible study in the office here run by one of the agents from financial crimes. And a men's breakfast at the small Calvary Chapel offshoot he attended.

Until something changed, or God said differently, this was where he'd been planted. He worked with two of the agents who'd come down to Mexico and helped rescue him and Kenna, and Maizie. They were tracking the associate of Kurt and his sheriff cousin, a man who had murdered many young women and young men. The killer his friends knew as "Parker" and his victims knew as "the Walker" or *El Caminante* had grown up in a border town in Texas. He joined the US Army so he could kill, and it was sanctioned, and now he operated in Southern California and the west side of Arizona.

El Caminante showed no mercy, and he killed regularly.

The Walker needed to be caught soon.

But Jax couldn't get Kenna's help on this one.

"No dice?" The agent he usually worked with, Farnes, settled his backpack strap over one shoulder.

Jax shook his head.

"I'm out for the night. See you in the morning."

"Night."

Farnes knocked on his desktop. "Get some sleep."

Jax nodded, then packed up his things and grabbed his cell. Halfway to the elevator, his phone started to ring, vibrating in his suit jacket pocket.

The screen of his watch read *M*, which meant it was Maizie calling.

He pulled out his earbuds and answered the call. "Hey, kid." He jabbed the button for the parking level and leaned against the side of the elevator as it descended.

Maizie launched in, barely taking a breath. "The kidnapper was arrested, Marion Wells. The latest victim was in this secret room in her closet, and she was barely alive. Kenna saved her life."

Jax smiled to himself.

"She was hooked up to this slow-drip IV thing so Marion could kill her without getting her hands dirty. She just left the girl in there to die. Can you believe that?"

"She's alive?" It sounded like Kenna got there just in time.

Another case solved.

But his was barely treading water.

Maybe she would consider coming to San Diego and looking at the case files, since she had closed hers. Not that the FBI needed the help of a private investigator. At least, not officially. It didn't look good for them to be asking for help all the time. But fresh eyes, and fresh ideas? Regardless of what his boss might've said, sometimes they needed a little out-of-the-box thinking. She might see something they never would because, while she might've been an FBI agent at one time, Kenna Banbury wasn't one now.

She'd probably never thought *in* the box when she'd been an agent.

Jax needed the medical plan that came with his job. Going freelance would be way too expensive considering how often he got hurt. He could understand why Kenna never wanted to be seen by a doctor. She had a trust fund and a past that meant she distrusted hospitals and doctors. Thanks to his mother, Jax had been cut off for the egregious choice of becoming a cop, and couldn't afford his own plan.

Until something changed, or God said differently.

Maizie said, "She's alive. The girl should make a full recovery."

He headed for his car. "That's amazing." After it had connected to his car Bluetooth system, Jax headed for the apartment he rented.

"Now she's got me looking into the deaths of the lady she lives with's family. You know...the car accident?"

"Sure." He knew about that. Maizie had told him that before.

Now, she mentioned a note and the suspicions surrounding the accident.

His brows rose. "Someone thinks it was murder? Or knows it was?"

"I'm gonna find out what's up with the accusation, and Kenna is going to make sure the kidnapping case is all wrapped up," Maizie said. "I can send you a copy of the note."

"You should probably not, though." He had enough work with the FBI and didn't want to cross streams—or get in trouble. "Just keep me posted, and let me know if there's anything I can do to help that doesn't involve using FBI resources."

"Copy that."

Jax slowed with the freeway traffic. "You okay, kid?"

Maizie didn't speak right away.

"Something on your mind? About the case, or something else?" He tried to tread carefully given her past, and the fact she was technically a minor and he was a grown man. Though, there was nothing childish about Maizie. She'd started updating him on Kenna's whereabouts and how things were going after Mexico. He hadn't shut it down because he wanted to know. But it hadn't ever delved past work into personal with Maizie, and how things were going with *her*.

"What was Christmas at your house like?"

Jax frowned at the ocean of brake lights in front of him. "Holidays at the big house. Right. Ask my mother, she'd say it was *perfect*, which means the decorations are so beautiful you're scared to touch them. Too much alcohol consumed by several family members, who then have to be escorted to a separate sitting room by the housekeeper. My father fell asleep in his easy chair with an empty glass beside him. My mother fussed the entire time, and so did my sister's baby, but she didn't help with that. She also didn't sit down.

"This year my sister's husband was called to the hospital to perform an emergency heart valve replacement before we even had dinner, so she and I snuck up to the media room as soon as we could and watched a couple of terrible small-town romance Christmas movies and ate too much pie."

"So it was good?"

"It has things I love, things that are nostalgic and I'd miss them if they were gone, and things I'd like to see change." Jax bit the bullet and asked, "What about you? What was Christmas like?"

This most recent holiday season had been her first one out from the control of the man who had held her captive her entire life—until last year. She'd been terrorized, brutalized. And that was just what he could imagine that evil man had done.

"He never did that," Maizie said. "Decorations. Dessert."

No, I don't imagine he did. But what Jax did imagine made him sick to his stomach. "And Christmas with the Stairns family, and Kenna?"

"It wasn't that either. And I just..."

When it didn't seem like she would continue, he said, "I'm sorry."

She had been robbed of a childhood. Had her sanity shredded. And she'd still managed to escape far enough Kenna could find her and help her.

Maizie was nothing short of amazing.

So who cared if Christmas made no sense to her because she'd never experienced anything like it.

Jax continued, "Who knows what Kenna's childhood Christmases with her dad were like, on the road in your trailer." They had all been careful to reinforce the fact it was *her* space now. She was the one in control of it. "And she was kidnapped by that serial killer. With Bradley. I don't know what that was like for her. I can't even imagine what she went through, but she keeps moving forward and it's miraculous. And it's beautiful to watch. She stands up for the people she loves."

"Like not backing down and finding me," she added, heartbreak in her voice.

Jax nodded. "Now it's your turn to do the same. Figure out what you like, and what you want your life to be. Find happiness. Drive a car—or a motorcycle. Go on a cruise. Slap somebody in the face. Argue with someone you love, and end it in tears, hugging and laughing about it. Get a stomachache because you ate too much cake."

She gave a gentle chuckle.

He smiled. "You'll bleed a little, but it'll heal. You'll meet a boy we all dislike and get your heart broken. You'll love. You'll lose people, make friends, maybe get married. Have a baby—or a houseful of them. You'll know what joy is, and how to find peace in your soul. All those empty places inside you will fill, and the memories will fade a little every day. Until one day you wake up and realize you haven't thought about him in years."

Jax heard a sniff.

The line went dead.

Chapter Four

To Kenna, the morning air smelled like snow, though no fresh powder had fallen overnight, which was pretty disappointing. Her nose had turned numb after mile two, and thankfully she'd remembered to bring a tissue on her run today.

Bare branches reached over power lines into the road. From behind her sunglasses she spotted a red painted barn before the next corner. One of those geometric quilt patterns on the siding above the doors identified the family—like a crest.

Through the open phone line in her earbuds, under the hem of the beanie keeping her head warm, she heard Jax say, "Sure?"

Kenna slowed enough to turn in a circle and jog going

backward for a few seconds, before turning forward again. "Yes, I'm sure. There's no one following me. I've seen some farmers out breaking ice for their cows. One car. No weirdos."

It was kind of cute that he was worried. But not so cute as to *why*, given she'd come here to find a different killer.

"I should get a motorcycle with rearview mirrors," she added. "Then I'd be able to see if there's someone behind me."

Why would she want to run in a place where she might encounter other people? Forrest might have brought up the idea of partners, but Kenna really did operate better alone— even if she was alone and also on the phone with Jax.

Jax chuckled. "Kind of defeats the purpose of exercise if you're sitting on a bike."

"But I would look good."

"So much it's a little terrifying."

Kenna laughed, inhaling a mouthful of frigid air. "Geez, it's cold."

"I'm in shorts and a T-shirt."

Mmm. Speaking of looking good. She'd jump at the opportunity to be his partner—if all the connotations of that didn't land her morals in hot water given enough time. Thank goodness she was nowhere near California.

"It's seventy-five degrees already," he added.

"Yeesh, no thanks." Kenna smiled to herself. "I prefer this high of twenty-eight and clear skies, thanks." Plus insulated tights, handwarmers in her gloves, and two pairs of socks in her sneakers, as well a base layer, T-shirt, and sweater under an insulated running jacket.

"Your face is numb."

"But I'm not sweaty." Kenna raced around the corner into Forrest's neighborhood. "So what else did Clarke say?"

Jax sighed. "It boils down to him not wanting someone

else to solve our case. He likes his numbers to make him look good."

Kenna had asked him questions through his story of yesterday's workday. She hadn't gone so far as to make him wonder if she was interrogating him, but he was definitely not saying something.

He was holding back.

She'd decided a long time ago that if a man needed to keep his own confidence, then that was his decision. They'd been through enough since they met that if he felt he needed to not tell her something, then she wasn't going to get butthurt about it. What would be the point in inventing a problem when she could just be understanding?

God had been plenty understanding with her.

"The FBI doesn't need help," Jax said. "And my boss definitely won't ask for it."

Kenna snorted at his tone. "At least not from someone without a badge."

Which was why she'd left the Walker case to the FBI and come to Wisconsin to find Ramon's sister. Her former colleague might have been written off by the rest of the FBI. But so had she. The FBI didn't want her on their team, so what was the point trying to be picked? She'd rather fight for the people no one fought for.

"You know I don't agree with that, right? You'd run circles around these guys—and me."

"Maybe not *you*."

"Pick a case." He gave a warm chuckle. "We'll go head-to-head."

As she ran onto Forrest's street, she spotted a police cruiser in front of the house. "Huh. There's a cop here." She slowed her pace instinctively, not all the way sure why.

Every run-in with a cop was different. How would this

one feel about the fact she'd left Marion Wells' house with the victim, rather than stay with the suspect? How did they feel about Forrest's family's accident, and the note suggesting it might have been intentional?

Did they know?

Jax said, "I'm back at my car."

Their hour-long run was over.

Kenna slowed to a walk. "Have a good day at the office, dear."

Jax chuckled. "Right back at ya."

She removed her ear buds and stowed them in her jacket pocket.

Just then, Forrest opened the front door to the officer, who stood in front of her on the stoop. He was probably five eleven. Down jacket, tucked behind his gun, which sat on his left hip rather than his right. Kenna was too far away to hear what Forrest said, but the look on the woman's face spoke loudly enough. Blood seemed to have drained out of her skin, leaving her olive complexion almost sickly. She spotted Kenna, turned, and went back inside, leaving the door open.

Kenna cleared her throat. "Something I can help you with, Officer?"

He turned to her. "It's *Deputy* Kobrinsky. Jerry. And you're Kenna Banbury." At least the cops in this county did a web search looking for background on strangers and newcomers.

"I'm guilty of that, at least." They shook. "Forrest might try and ignore this, but I'm looking into what happened with her family. If that note was right and the accident wasn't an accident..." He needed to know she might intentionally step on some toes. Would his boss mind, or would the sheriff dismiss her like Jax's Assistant Special Agent in Charge?

Jerry frowned. "What? That's not... I'm here about Marion Wells."

"Right, I should've come by and made a statement."

He folded his arms across his chest. "I'm the one who informed Forrest that her husband and son had been killed. You're really dragging all that back up and making her go through it again? You might've done the county a favor finding that girl and detaining Marion Wells, but that's the only thing you need to be worried about. If the accident wasn't that, I'd have informed Forrest when I told her what happened. No one needs you digging up something that isn't there."

She wanted to fold her arms, too, but mirroring his body language would only make her look defensive. "Regardless of how you feel about private investigators, you said you came here to talk about Marion. Correct?"

So what if he got the wrong end of this stick. She didn't have to explain herself or the note. It wasn't like she'd convince him she wasn't doing this to be self-serving, or thinking there was a case where there wasn't one.

Kobrinsky nodded. "Everyone is glad you prioritized saving that girl's life."

"How is she doing?" Kenna shivered. "Let's go inside. You want some coffee?" He closed the door behind him, and she dug a couple of pods out of the box in the pantry—the flavor Forrest didn't like for Jerry's coffee and the one she liked for hers. "Black? Milk?"

"Black is fine."

She set a mug in front of him, then leaned her hips back against the countertop, clutching her own mug. "How is the girl?"

"Awake." He swallowed a mouthful and winced. "I got the chance to talk to her early this morning. Marion had her cleaning and cooking, doing all the household stuff. She said Marion called her Cinderella and laughed about it."

"So what changed?" There had to be a reason Marion had decided to get rid of the girl. She had a theory, given what she'd seen in that room, but wanted to know what the deputy thought.

"She told us she got her first period. Marion told her it was time to go to sleep."

Kenna blew out a long breath. "That's why she needs a new girl every few years."

He studied her. "While I appreciate your assistance in saving this girl and allowing us to arrest Marion, no one needs you digging up something so painful for Forrest. I think you of all people would understand things need to fade into the past rather than being dragged up."

"So you've got me figured all out." Kenna took a sip of her coffee.

"Not hardly." He set the mug down. "Marion Wells isn't talking. At least not to us. The bodies of her victims need to be unearthed so the families can lay their loved ones to rest."

"You've searched the house and the area around it?" Marion had a modest backyard, and no other properties. Maizie had checked into all that, but the deputy didn't need to know. "What about her car?"

"Her property is being processed, but local search and rescue brought in cadaver dogs. There were no human remains found on her property. We believe the victims were transported in the trunk of Marion's car. Whether that was bringing them to the house when she kidnapped them, or taking them to where she disposed of them, we aren't sure."

"You'll find them." If he thought she was going to be a nosy private investigator, then she would change his mind by not interfering with this part of their case. "If you want my help with anything, or an extra set of hands, I'm sure you won't hesitate to ask."

A muscle in his jaw flexed. "She said she'll talk to you."

"Who?"

"Marion Wells said she'll only tell you where she buried the bodies."

Oh...he didn't like that at all. Didn't want her in the middle of his case, key to getting information. And the ASAC in San Diego didn't want her to try to help them find Walker. She'd be inclined to develop a complex if this continued.

Sure, private investigators weren't usually revered by law enforcement, but she'd proven herself, hadn't she? She'd closed some serious cases in the last year plus.

Kenna studied the hill in the distance. "Is that right?"

Jerry sighed. "Are you going to come and talk to her, or are you going to make this difficult for everyone?"

She was pretty sure she could do both without much effort, but didn't point that out. "Let me change into my work clothes." She glanced at the clock on the wall that Forrest hadn't adjusted with daylight savings. In a few months, it would tell the right time again. "I'll be there at nine thirty."

He strode to the door and let himself out.

Kenna found Forrest in the room she used as an office, staring at papers arranged on a huge piece of poster paper that she'd affixed to the wall with a sticky strip along the top.

"Apparently, Marion will only tell me where her victims are buried." Kenna leaned against the doorframe, not wanting to intrude on Forrest's space. "So I'm headed to the police station to talk to her."

"That's good." Forrest didn't look away from the papers.

Kenna didn't mention the note, or Forrest's husband and son. If Maizie found something or this went anywhere, there would be reason to bring it up. Forrest had to carry enough.

Especially with just finding the note and just now opening the front door to the man who'd told her the tragic news.

If she wanted to write a book about a serial killer who had never been caught, rather than face reality, that was her business. And not too far from exactly what Kenna did. Justice was how she'd survived. Burying her head from reality and getting on with her life—the one she wanted.

Kenna said, "Okay, see you later."

It wasn't Kenna's job to fix this woman. Even if everything in her wanted to try, Forrest wasn't her case. She was a grown woman who could live her life and make whatever choices she wanted, and it wasn't on Kenna to convince her something wasn't healthy.

Kenna asked the people who cared about her to respect her choices. No one got to tell her that the way she lived was wrong, or not good enough. That she should have as many friends as possible and share all the intimate details of her life with them. Too many people didn't have contentment, and living in one place didn't appeal to Kenna. She wasn't going to suddenly settle somewhere, start attending church at the same place every Sunday, and quit living on the road. The nomadic way of life was written in her DNA.

She considered her life to be pretty good right about now —battling the fear every day, growing her relationship with God, and being a voice for the lost and forgotten. So what if Deputy Jerry Kobrinsky—or Jax's boss—didn't think she was as good as a cop?

Maizie had sent a video of Cabot, Kenna's dog that she'd left with the teen. The dog had been through illness and surgery and didn't need to be on the road all the time. Kenna watched the video as she dried off from the shower, then dialed the teen's number and put the call on speaker so she could dress.

The teen answered. "Hey."

"Cute video," Kenna said. Her dog, Cabot, had bounded over the lawn to greet Stairns, Kenna's former boss at the FBI. The dog had raced to greet the retired man as he came out to sit with his morning coffee. She'd sat to be petted, then lie down by the man's boot.

"She keeps getting bolder."

"Stairns looks like he's good. Healing." He'd been shot in Mexico a few months ago.

Maizie sighed.

"What?"

"Everything doesn't have to be about that."

"The dog?" Cabot had gone through surgery for cancer. Maybe everyone in Kenna's life was healing. Maybe everyone in the world was.

Maizie snorted. "You know I don't mean everything doesn't have to be about Cabot. Maybe everything *should* be about her."

"But we can't only talk about the dog," Kenna pointed out. "Sometimes we should talk about work."

"Nah." Maizie chuckled. "You should just pay me to make dog videos."

Kenna chuckled as well. As she layered up to go out, she told Maizie about the deputy's visit.

When she was done, Maizie said, "I can't find any other properties under her name, or the name of anyone in her extended family—alive or dead. No cabins she visited as a child. No favorite places to vacation. I have *no* idea where Marion buried her victims."

"There are entirely too many open stretches of land up here. She could have found an out of the way spot and buried them nearly anywhere." Kenna would walk the whole country if that's what it took, but she would rather have an idea of where to start.

"She doesn't have a boat, so that nixes my idea that she dumps them in the lake."

"That would be a good way to dispose of them." Kenna paused. "Although, I wouldn't want to be on the water when it's so cold."

Marion worked at the elementary school, which was terrifying but had given her access to the children. She'd also been overlooked as a suspect by the police.

She didn't own a boat.

Deputy Kobrinsky had every right to be angry that Kenna had solved the case rather than the police, but he should be angrier that his department hadn't figured it out. That so many kids had been victimized and murdered by that slow-drip IV bag.

"That's what Forrest's serial killer did," Kenna added. "So maybe Marion heard about it and figured it was a good way to make sure no one found any of her victims. Or she figured anyone who found one if they washed up on shore would believe they belonged to the serial killer Forrest is writing about."

That killer was more of a local legend, a man who carved a J into his victims, and had been dubbed "J. Pierce" by the media. He'd been dormant for years, and most presumed he was dead now. Unlike Marion, every one of his victims had been found. Washed up on the shores of Lake Michigan, up here on the Wisconsin peninsula.

So much death.

Maybe Kenna needed to go see that girl in the hospital, just to look at the life in her eyes rather than remembering the way she'd looked. Like she was already dead and gone.

"I wanna know," Maizie said.

Kenna smiled. "Me too, Maze. You good otherwise?"

"I'm fine."

"Good. Get back to work."

She hung up to the sound of Maizie laughing and saying, "Yes, ma'am!"

All of them were navigating life together. It was messy, but they cared. Things weren't always perfect, but she knew one thing.

They were a family and always would be.

Chapter Five

The Door County Sheriff's Department had one dispatcher. The entire office took up two floors that were both the size of the coffee shop next door. Interrogation was upstairs at the back, behind the bullpen. They had four deputies on day shift, two on nights permanently, and a boss who'd run unopposed for fifteen years. By all accounts Gingrich was a decent sheriff, but Kenna had no interest in rapport or cooperation.

She took the file with her into the interrogation room, having left most of her weapons in the car. The deputy had noticed she wasn't wearing her gun on her hip and waved her in after letting her know where she could hang her coat. No one had patted her down, searched her, or asked her what else she was carrying.

Marion Wells' hands were cuffed to the table. Her thin sweater didn't provide much protection.

Kenna stuck her head out. "Turn the heat up in here, Deputy. It's freezing."

"Sure thing, boss." Kobrinsky made a face.

He'd better not pump the heat and make them sweat, as if

that might induce Marion into talking. Kenna just didn't want the temperature to be so cold it could be perceived as inhumane treatment. Marion's lawyer would be able to use that, and anything else the police or Kenna did, to argue her case.

If Marion believed Kenna could command the police here, at least to an extent, she might see Kenna as an authority figure as well as the PI who had exposed her deeds.

Kenna pulled out a chair and sat. Whether the deputies or the sheriff were watching didn't matter. She wasn't here to put on a show. "You've been read your rights, and declined counsel, is that correct?"

Why not confirm—and sound official at the same time.

Marion stared at her, the pale skin and dark circles under her eyes more pronounced than yesterday at book club. The lines on her face had deepened. Now that Kenna knew why this woman had taken each of the eight girls, and why she eventually disposed of them, it didn't reassure her of anything other than that she'd done the right thing coming here. This woman had effectively hidden her crimes for decades.

No one in town even suspected her.

If it wasn't for Kenna, one more girl would be dead.

She didn't show Marion the file. Only stared down her nose as though Marion was beneath her. "You said to the police that you'd tell me where the bodies are buried. So where are they?"

"Maybe I just wanted to waste their time."

"And mine." Kenna got up from her seat, shifting the file slightly with her fingers and hoping Marion would take the bait.

Her hands shot out, the cuffs jingled, and she grabbed the file.

Kenna watched her reaction. The eager way she flipped through pages, soaking up a chance to see each of them again.

As if obsessed with just the memory of them, and what they had meant to her.

"This is blank!" Marion cried. "Where are they?"

Kenna leaned down, one fist on the table. "You don't get to see the lives you destroyed. But you *are* going to return them to their parents."

If it was up to Kenna, Marion would never again see even images of the girls she took in a newspaper or on TV. If it was up to Kenna, Marion wouldn't even be able to remember what they looked like.

Even though God could do that, since He could do anything, she didn't ask. It was a little self-serving, since it would only be out of anger and a need to take from Marion after she'd taken so much from the people in this county.

"I bet you're pretty proud of yourself." Marion paused. "Catching the notorious kidnapper." Her expression hardened. Trying to get a rise out of Kenna?

Rather than take the bait, Kenna stood there. Completely still and silent.

Long enough to hear the air vent in the ceiling begin to blow warmth down.

No reaction.

"Bested me," Marion spat. "Like you best all the others."

"It's a shame you didn't see me coming," Kenna shot back, before she could think it through.

A better Christian than her would have managed to stay quiet. She might've felt pride at Marion's house, knowing she had the answers and would be the one to finish it. Now, there wasn't much of that left. Just a whole lot of sadness over the tragic loss of life.

"You'll go to prison for the rest of your life," she added. "I'll head out on the road to another case and another set of victims who need justice. I doubt I'll think of you, except as a stray thought. You'll barely be a memory."

"Ask me why I did it."

"I don't care."

Marion didn't like that. "Ask me why I chose *those* ones."

Kenna shrugged. *No big deal, right?* She hoped her expression indicated as such, anyway.

Marion seemed to want to get a rise out of her. What she didn't know was that it would take more than this to get her to go beyond speaking without thinking. Did Marion want her to get angry, or threaten her?

Kenna did want answers—everyone who had lost someone wanted to know *why*. Before she found the perpetrator, she often told herself she didn't care. Sometimes even after. Occasionally, she viewed that need to know as a weakness.

Now that Marion was in cuffs, if she wanted to confess and offer up information that Kenna would be able to pass to the families, that was one thing. It might help in some small way to give them a semblance of peace. But all the closure in the world wouldn't bring back what they'd lost.

Finding out that Forrest's husband and son had indeed been murdered wouldn't make them any less dead. She would still have to live with the loss.

Maybe that was why Forrest didn't want to deal with the note and what it meant.

"Ask me!" Marion screamed.

Kenna waited until she'd taken a breath. "Where are they? That's all I want to know." They weren't building a rapport or getting to know each other so Marion would tell her everything. All she cared about was the location of the burial site.

"You'll never know!" Marion laughed like a horror movie villain. "They'll be mine forever!"

No, they wouldn't. "The latest one isn't. What was her name?"

"Riley."

"She's back with her parents. They say she'll make a full recovery." Physically, at least. The rest was up to Riley's strength and the support she was given. Like Maizie, there would be days when things seemed good, days when it was too fresh in her mind still, and baby steps of forward progress in between. "She's not yours anymore."

"Good riddance!"

"Marion, the screaming is getting old." Kenna slumped into the chair at the table like she was over it all. "Calm down, okay? Quit screeching." She let out an overly loud sigh. "Just tell me where to find the rest. You have no leverage with me. You only want to jerk me around, the same way you're jerking around the police. Get a clue, Marion. It's done. You've been caught. You're going to jail, and your reign of terror is over. For Riley, and for everyone else."

She hadn't had much time to get to know Marion after she figured out who had taken those girls, and Maizie found the evidence in Marion's online purchases. But what she did know of this woman said Marion wanted to feel superior because she got away with it for so long.

"So you wanted someone to cook and clean for you. The kids at the school often included one you thought was malleable." Kenna's stomach flipped. "So you kept each one for what—a year or two? Maybe longer. Then you ordered IV bags of poison from overseas, and let the drug do the dirty work."

Maizie had found the transactions on a credit card in an anagram of Marion's name.

"After all, why face the consequences of what you did yourself and look them in the eyes while you take their life?" Kenna said. All she needed to know was where the police could find the victim's bodies. "What convenient method of disposal did you use?"

She was honestly surprised Marion hadn't found someone else to dispose of the bodies. But a co-conspirator hadn't come up in the investigation. Marion had been alone for decades, with few friends and no discernable life outside her job as librarian at the school.

"I gave them dignity," Marion replied.

Kenna stared at her, wondering if she actually believed that or if it was part of the delusion she'd been living under. "Because you knew it was wrong, and at least a tiny part of you thought it was a way to redeem yourself."

If Marion admitted she knew her actions were wrong, there was no way an insanity plea would hold weight. She might try to argue she wasn't mentally fit for trial, but Kenna would write to the judge herself if it helped. Marion needed to be tried and convicted of her crimes. The justice system wasn't perfect, but it was a whole lot better than it was in many other countries.

"Where are they, Marion?"

"Backforth Trail. Mile marker fourteen. Behind the oak."

Kenna pushed her chair back.

"You can't leave."

She took the file of blank paper and stepped out into the hall.

"We're not done here, Kenna!"

Jerry stepped out of a room halfway down the hall. "Did you mean for me to sweat you out? I wasn't sure."

"I wasn't in the mood to freeze." Marion had been uncomfortably chilled, and Kenna had needed a way to establish her authority.

"You think that's what got her to tell you where they are? Compassion, or something?"

Another deputy appeared behind him, along with the sheriff. The older guy had GINGRICH on his name badge, even though everyone in town likely knew his name. They had probably been watching and listening to the conversation on a computer screen. Kenna acknowledged all of them. "Does it matter? She said where they are." She wasn't going to give them a seminar on all the interrogation tactics she'd used over the years.

"You're going up there to take a look, I suppose?" Sheriff Gingrich asked.

"Nope." She took a step back, watching the surprise flash on their faces. *Enough with the assumptions.* "Not my case anymore, but I would like to know when you find them all. So don't delete my number just yet."

If she hung around to see them unearth the oldest body, someone might eventually put it together that she had a connection to the victim's big brother. Ramon Santiago had been a ghost since Mexico. She might be here to clear this up for him, and work a case everyone had considered cold, but his name didn't need to be splashed over the news again. His departure from the FBI as a supposed traitor—or the fact that had come after his betrayal by a female agent who had been Kenna's roommate at Quantico—was something no one knew. Cecilia Warren would find the same justice as Marion Wells.

In due time.

She checked her surroundings outside, scanning the parking lot behind the sheriff's office and the surrounding area while she walked to her Subaru. Just another car. Nothing special. As much as people seemed to refuse to believe it, she didn't seek out attention. If the Walker—the serial killer Jax and his team were hunting—wanted to bait her into coming after him, then he was going to have to show his face.

Make a move.

Hopefully a mistake, as well.

Kenna drove through the town. For the first time since she arrived in Wisconsin, she wanted to leave and go home, rather than simply to the next town or the next case. She'd spent a chunk of time at Stairns' cabin before the holidays. Then she'd come here, so she could have work as the legitimate excuse not to go and meet Jax's mother or the rest of his family. Forrest's idea of Christmas hadn't been much to speak of, and that suited Kenna just fine. She and her father had never made a big deal of it, though she had watched a certain Christmas-themed action movie nearly every year then and since.

Right now, rather than contend with the police here and their assumptions about her intentions, she found the desire to seek solace in something familiar.

Why was that?

Maybe becoming a Christian had changed her in that way as well, so that she was more prone to want to go see the people she cared about. Visit her friends. For better or worse, she had more than just work to keep her going these days. Her life had shifted. She was changing—hopefully in ways that were better, even if they weren't so comfortable.

She spotted the local favorite spot two streets over. After the deputy had been there when she got back from her run, she hadn't eaten anything. She'd just showered, dressed, and come straight here. They hadn't even offered her coffee.

The bell above the door jingled when she stepped inside.

Across the diner she saw Betty slide out of a booth and stand. Charlayne slid out after her, and both women met

Kenna by the hostess stand that had probably been there since the mid-'80s. Their husbands, in a heated conversation at the table, didn't seem to have noticed their exit.

"Care to explain why you didn't tell us about Marion?" Betty furiously whispered the words, her face close to Kenna's. "How we had to find out someone we thought was our book club *friend* is the county kidnapper?"

Kenna took a step away from the hostess and glanced between the two women. "You're as surprised as I am that she had a kid in her closet. I'm just glad we got to her in time."

"We?" Charlayne set a hand on her hip. "Marion nearly cut my throat!"

"You should've told us you knew what she was up to," Betty said. "Not keep us in the dark and string us along like chumps."

"I'm sorry I didn't tell you," Kenna said. "But if all four of us were pretending, she'd have seen through it." She paused. "Both of your husbands were suspects."

"That's why you gave us a front row seat to nearly getting killed?" Charlayne ran her fingers across her neck.

"I'm sorry if you were scared."

Charlayne huffed away, back toward her husband and Betty's while Kenna tried to figure out what else she could say. The two gray-haired men made as interesting of a pair as the two women, opposites who had become friends. Kenna was about to apologize to Betty when one of the men said, "Why do I even bother?" and sat back.

The other tossed a water glass at his friend. "I'll kill you myself for this."

Chapter Six

Without stopping at the booth, Charlayne grabbed her huge gold purse and headed back to the front door. "I have an appointment at the salon." Her face remained completely impassive. Whether about the men fighting, or the situation with Marion and the fact she'd nearly been seriously hurt. Could've been killed. Kenna didn't know which was foremost in Charlayne's mind as the woman stepped out into the chilly afternoon air.

Betty, still standing beside Kenna at the hostess stand, was more of a schoolmarm type. Charlayne looked like a Manhattan mobster's aging wife. Betty didn't leave, but she also didn't go to the table.

The two men seemed at odds, when Kenna's impression so far had been that the two women were friends because of their husbands.

She blew out a breath. "Is this going to escalate into more than throwing water?"

Betty shrugged. "You're the professional. Why don't *you* try and get them to figure it out?"

Maybe because she wasn't a shrink.

While the men continued to argue, Kenna said to her, "I'm sorry I couldn't tell you the whole truth about Marion Wells. With all you've been through, having your husbands accused of kidnapping those children, I knew you'd want to help even if I couldn't tell you that's what book club was about." She paused. "I still liked talking about books."

A saltshaker hurtled across the room.

Betty said, "Maybe we can do book club on a video call after you leave town."

"I'd like that." Kenna squeezed her shoulder.

The waitress turned away from the two men, rolling her eyes as she headed back to the coffeepot. No one else in the diner gave them much attention, though a couple of people left quicker than they probably would've after bills were paid.

Kenna headed over to stand at the end of the table facing both men.

They quit talking as soon as she neared.

"So you're the PI?" The man on the left had a scar on his chin on the right side and military-short gray hair. Betty's husband.

The other clearly dyed his hair black—and she'd guess he was Charlayne's husband. Like a lot of married couples, they matched styles. Though, Betty's Sunday school style was contrasted by her husband, who looked like he could probably beat the tar out of anyone who bothered her. Charlayne's husband tried way too hard to reach his wife's level, and to their credit she seemed to have stuck around long enough to make it work. The same might not be said about their friendship.

"Why are you guys causing a disturbance when people are trying to eat?" Kenna asked.

Betty's husband huffed what might've been a laugh. "Theodore Campbell, nice to meet you."

"Don't call him Teddy. It's Theo." Charlayne's husband stuck out his hand. "Alonzo Bernstein."

"Kenna Banbury."

"Yeah," Theo said. "Heard all about Marion Wells." He spat the woman's name.

"But that's not what sent a saltshaker flying across the room. So talk." There was a reason their wives steered clear of the fight, and no one else intervened. Or called in the sheriff.

Theo sat back against the bench with an exaggerated sigh, all his attention on his friend. "I can't believe you lost it."

Alonzo wiped his mouth with a napkin. "It's been so long, I didn't think to check."

"You just assumed it would still be there?" Theo countered.

Kenna glanced between them. "What is it?"

"A book." Alonzo threw the napkin on his plate. "That no one in the world cares about but us."

"And maybe one other person," Theo added.

"Could someone have taken it from where you hid it?" Kenna suggested. There were only two options: The book had been either stolen, or misplaced.

"Right." Theo looked at her. "The PI can find it."

She stared at him, feeling nosy enough to push it. "Tell me everything. Who you both are, what the book is. All of it."

Theo's expression shuttered, but she caught a slight curve of his lips.

"Never mind." Alonzo shook his head. "I'm sure it'll turn up."

They shared a look, and neither said anything else.

That's what I thought.

These two men had some deep secrets, and they weren't about to share them with her—or anyone else. She wondered if their wives even knew. That could be why both women had reacted the way they did about being kept in the dark over Marion. Maybe they were entirely too used to secrets. Or felt they should've let their husbands know their lives might be in danger going to book club.

Kenna didn't like the implication that she'd been prideful about keeping them safe, but it seemed to be coming up a lot lately. The time she'd spent in Mexico had stripped her strength and control down to nothing, and she'd finally surrendered to God. But this was the real test. Back in her normal life—where she liked to call the shots and fall back on her abilities and her strength—that was the proving ground. Could she live a life that represented the choice she'd made to be a Christian, or would she trip and fall at the first obstacle?

She could figure that out pretty quickly, but it could also be a lifelong journey.

I'd rather this didn't take years to settle. If I get a vote.

"Heard about the arrest you made," Alonzo said. "Big deal, so good job saving that girl."

"Thanks." Kenna grabbed a chair from a nearby table and sat with her boot on one knee so her bent leg touched the end of the table and she faced the two men. As she moved, she'd clocked Betty, who sat at the counter, drinking a cup of tea and talking to the waitress behind the bar. "Neither of you has to worry about being implicated anymore."

Alonzo eyed her. "We're not paying you."

"This isn't about money."

Theo made a *huh* sound. "She means that."

Alonzo said, "Interesting."

"So who is the person that might want this book of yours?" Kenna asked. "I can have my assistant locate them. Make sure they're nowhere near here. That should take some of the worry out of it."

"I'm not worried." Theo didn't meet her gaze.

Alonzo sat stiffly. "It's just a whole lot of old information that wouldn't mean anything to a young broad like you. We'll find it."

"Right." Kenna nodded. If they wanted to give her the person's name, they would. Or one of them would contact her later and do it on their own. She didn't particularly need another case right now, but some simple legwork wasn't out of the question. What she should do was ask them about Forrest's family and if they knew anything about the accident.

Were either of these two men the person who had left the note on Forrest's door?

Kenna set that worry aside for another second. "Would you rather I asked you where you had it last?" That was what her father always said: *Where were you when you had it last?* Most times retracing her steps did help locate something she'd lost.

Theo stared at Alonzo.

The mobster looking man with the pinkie ring lifted his chin. "Inside a hollowed-out book on my shelf."

"Could Charlayne have moved it?" Kenna suggested.

Alonzo shook his head.

"Anyone been through that room?" She paused. "Workmen, contractors, or the cable guy? A guest who visited, and it seemed odd. Anything like that?"

Alonzo's dark brows drew together. "Huh."

At the least it gave him some trees to shake. *Good.* Figuring that might be enough for now, she switched up her line of questioning. "Can I ask the two of you about the accident that took the lives of Forrest Crosby's husband and son?"

Theo shrugged.

Alonzo sat quietly.

"Did you ever have reason to believe the accident was

anything other than exactly that?" she pressed. "Driver error, or mechanical failure, or a tragic combination?"

"Accidents happen." Alonzo paused. "It's sad, but that's life."

Kenna couldn't argue with that sentiment.

Theo asked her, "Why do you ask about the Crosbys?"

She explained about the note on the door. "Any idea who might want her to believe it wasn't an accident?"

Alonzo used a colorful word to describe the type of person.

Theo nodded his agreement. "Other than the killer she's writing that book about, she's not exactly a threat."

"The killer everyone figures is dead?" Why would the killer leave a note, even if they were alive? "Could be a way to prevent her from writing the book, but there's no way to tell that's why the note was left unless I can figure out who left it."

Which might mean figuring out the killer's identity.

Theo glanced at her. "Why aren't you out there making sure the cops do their jobs right with Marion Wells?"

"Do they need a babysitter?" Kenna said.

"I just figured you'd want to be there to see them find the bodies. She told you where they're at, right?"

"Small town?"

Alonzo turned his phone and waved it at her. "Emergency dispatch app. They called in a local search and rescue cadaver dog over to up by the state park."

The waitress came by and poured them all coffee, refilling theirs and giving her a mug. When she'd walked away, Theo said, "So why aren't you up there helping?"

It was the way he said it that gave Kenna the feeling this guy might've been law enforcement at one point. She eyed him. "I'm the one who asks the questions."

Theo chuckled. "You think we're just old men."

Alonzo joined in the chuckling.

Kenna wasn't going to tell them she wasn't so sure. "You think I always do what I should?"

Both of them snorted.

"I hope not," Alonzo said. "Otherwise, you'd be another pushover woman who does what she's told. *Boring.*"

Theo seemed to agree but said nothing.

Kenna didn't want to get into the intricacies of what feminism should mean, the role of strong, independent women in society, and the rest of it. She settled on, "This is a more complex issue than not being bored. I'm not sure I want to be the one to unpack it for you."

"Good," Alonzo said. "Because that would be *boring.*"

Kenna drank down the coffee and set the mug on the table. "You guys have a good one."

Theo grunted. "Yeah."

Kenna got in the car and called Ramon's number. It rang through the speakers as she pulled out of the parking lot toward Forrest's house. "Come on." *I might've found your sister.* "Pick up."

No one needed to know that the brother of the first victim was an associate of hers.

As soon as the call went to the canned voicemail service, she ended the call without leaving one.

Forrest's car was parked in the garage by Kenna's RV.

Kenna blocked herself in by parking on the drive, hit the button to close the garage door, and went into the house. She called out, "It's just me."

"Office."

Kenna strode in, ignoring the fact she normally stayed by the door, and flopped down on the armchair that was Forrest's "thinking" chair. She wouldn't be here long enough to warrant taking off her Converse. It took too long to lace them back up.

Because after telling nearly everyone she wouldn't be going up to see the police unearth all the bodies, Kenna planned to get a look after the fact. Just to be sure they found them all.

Forrest stared at the papers pinned up all over the walls. Her desk had nothing but a laptop on it. Cluttered mind, clear surfaces. Kenna liked that about her—including the way she almost obsessively cleaned. She loved to tidy and wipe things down. Forrest had told her that the rote movements helped her think through problems. And procrastinate when she didn't want to do something.

Kenna had never seen Forrest work out, and she was on the slender side. She probably should eat more protein. Then again, when they hung out, they ordered pizza. So it wasn't like Forrest never ate. Life was about balance. And not being miserable or feeling guilty for enjoying something.

Forrest tipped her chin. "Looks like they'll be pulling out bodies soon."

Another civilian with one eye on the police department. Usually it wasn't more than interest. Unless it turned into a problem.

"You have that app as well?" Kenna asked.

"Of course," Forrest said. "It gives me ideas."

"Part of me thinks she was lying. That she might've given up the information a little too easily."

"Maybe it was a lie, and she wants to keep giving y'all the runaround so she can be in control." Forrest glanced over, then looked back at her wall.

"She has more leverage before they find the bodies. After that, her fate is pretty much sealed."

"Maybe she wants it to be over," Forrest said. "She's been caught."

Kenna had met plenty of killers who lost the will to fight the moment their power was stripped away and they were put behind bars. "Maybe we should talk about that note."

"Leave me to my misery." Forrest shook her head. "Your dad said that to me. Pretty sure it was just about how to finish the chapter he'd been trying to write." She glanced over, the tiniest of smiles on her face. "I don't want to talk about it, drag it up, or think about it. I just want to do my work."

And that might be the whole reason for leaving that note. As a way to stop Forrest from writing the book. Would she figure out the identity of the killer before she was done? Someone out there might be worried she already had.

"I know how it feels to have the past dredged up again," Kenna said. "And you know nothing will bring them back." Kenna had lost the man she loved and the child they would've had together.

"I read everything about you, so I know what happened," Forrest said softly. "After your assistant sent the application, I dug up all the information I could find. I don't need help, Kenna. I'm not a danger to myself or anyone, and I don't need a boyfriend...as much as Charlayne thinks that will fix things."

Kenna rolled her eyes.

"Agreed."

"What about church tomorrow?" Kenna asked.

"We'll see."

That might be about as much enthusiasm as she was going to get. Kenna stood up and headed for the door. "I'm gonna get something to eat, then swing by the site and see how it's going."

She was at the door when Forrest said, "You know, if you ever want your story told, I could write it for you."

Kenna glanced back at her. "Who would want to read a book about me?"

An hour later, she pulled over on the highway, behind a red compact and a white SUV with the sheriff's department decal on the side. Both were empty, so she followed dirt road. Probably fire access to this area of dense trees. Not well-known, so Marion had chosen it because few people came this way. Maybe a few hunters in season. Hikers. People with their off-road vehicles. Dog walkers.

Killers.

Kenna found the Backforth Trail and followed it, looking for an oak. She found a clearing with a lone tree in the center. Where was everyone...or anyone at all?

Kenna took a deep breath and called out, "Hello?" as loudly as she could.

A dog ran into view, wearing a vest. The dog barked at her and lifted its front paws off the ground as he did it a second and third time. This was the working dog.

"Hello?" she called out again, looking around, but saw no movement. No people.

Where were they?

She'd have dispatched more than one cop and a K-9 handler. Maybe the sheriff didn't believe Marion had been telling the truth, so he'd only sent one deputy. Or they simply didn't have the resources to go out in pairs.

Kenna heard a faint sound, beyond the dog in the trees. She jogged over uneven grass that crunched under her feet. Thankfully, there weren't inches of snow on the ground But still, digging up bodies would be hard work with the frozen solid ground.

The dog ran between trees ahead of her. Desperation in his movements. Alerting her, bringing her to...what?

Kenna followed the trail the dog took. "Is someone out here?"

"Watch your step!" That was a man, maybe Kobrinksy.

The dog stopped at the edge of a hole in the ground and crouched down, looking in. Whining.

Kenna approached with easy steps. "Who's there?"

Kobrinsky had blood on the side of his face. Beside him a blonde lay with her hair over her face, not far from him. Her body twisted at an uncomfortable angle—if she was awake to feel it. They'd fallen into a hole in the ground that had apparently been disguised.

A trap.

And it was up to Kenna to get them out.

Chapter Seven

Kenna shook her head. "I can't lift her."

Kobrinsky stared at her, thunder in his eyes. "We have to lift her out. *You* have to lift her."

She didn't want to explain about the injury she'd sustained years ago. But if he knew who she was, then why didn't he know about that? "Where's your stuff? We need rope, and I'll call it in."

Was there a helicopter available in this part of the state? Remote areas usually had some form of Life Flight.

His jaw flexed.

Kenna said, "Are you hurt?"

"My leg. I can walk." The way he said it made it seem like sheer determination rather than an assessment of his physical ability.

"Rope?"

"Back of the rig. I was gonna get the evidence bag after we actually found something." He motioned with his fingers. "Give me your phone. Mine is shattered, and she must not bring hers on searches because it's not on her person."

"I'll call. And I'll be back." She looked at the dog. "Stay."

Kenna ran to the deputy's vehicle, paying a mind to where she stepped. Off to the side, she spotted an area she thought might be another trap. A hole in the ground that had been disguised, which would leave her broken like that K-9 handler.

Once she was sure she didn't have to worry about falling into a hole and being another victim, Kenna called 911. She explained about Kobrinsky and the dog handler, then requested a helicopter. It would take firefighters longer to get there, as they were all volunteers in this county.

She told the dispatcher, "I'll get them out of the hole."

Somehow.

She swung a coil of rope over her shoulder. The dispatcher told her it would be twenty minutes. Kenna said, "Tell them to hurry," and ran back to the hole.

Hyper-aware, she spotted a few areas in the uneven ground she wanted the chance to check out. And another spot that looked like the leaves and branches that had fallen into the hole with Kobrinsky and the woman. If she was asked right now if she believed the victims were buried out here, she'd have said yes. There were too many indications of burial spots.

Kenna looped the rope around a nearby tree and tied off the end around her waist. She threw the other end to the hole. "Tie her off."

Kobrinsky said, "Get ready to pull." He used the rope to climb out of the hole and stayed by the dog. Poor guy hadn't stopped whining. Blood wet the side of the deputy's leg through more than one layer of clothing. He grabbed the rope with both hands, no gloves. "Pull!"

She braced her weight and used her body mass and the rope around her waist to lift the woman from the hole.

Kobrinsky rolled the dog handler onto the ground, and

Kenna nearly collapsed. She untied the rope and ran back. "Life Flight will be here soon." She gave the woman a cursory check-over while the deputy felt for her pulse. The tourniquet high on her leg looked like his belt. "It's pretty faint. How long had you been down there?"

"Too long," he said. "The dog got confused. Turned around like he didn't know where to go."

Kenna looked in the hole. "Dead animals. Looks like a couple of cats, and they died bloody. So the dog might've been thrown off by conflicting scents of death."

"Who would—" He seemed to cut himself off, and his face paled.

"Take it easy. Marion set this up to throw off anyone looking for the burial site. She could've done this years ago, just in case anyone searching—or a dog—found her spot."

"All so whoever came to dig up the victims, or unsuspecting people, got hurt?" He spoke through gritted teeth. "She's messing with us. Sending us on a wild goose chase."

"That makes it more likely they're here."

He huffed.

"I'll find them."

"I'll get the sheriff out here."

"I have done work like this before, you know." She didn't necessarily need law enforcement help.

The deputy looked her up and down. "I don't see a badge."

She nearly said, *That's never stopped me.* But a helicopter engine and rotors got close enough he wouldn't have heard it. Still, it would be satisfying for him to know.

The paramedics got the woman loaded, and the deputy went with her.

He tossed her his keys. "Lock it up and give those to the sheriff or someone at the department when they show up."

"Take care of them." Kenna clasped the keys. No one objected when the dog hopped into the helicopter—which was fine with her. She had a dog and didn't need to make friends with another one that she would have to leave when she moved on.

She walked back to the deputy's car and found his evidence collection kit.

Her phone rang. She jogged to her car to get her earbuds out of the cupholder, then stuck them in and answered the call. "Yeah, Maze. What's up?"

"Helicopter?"

She explained about the hole and the two people who had fallen in and reiterated the conversation she'd just had with Deputy Kobrinsky.

"And now you're going back to Forrest's?"

Kenna grabbed the evidence collection kit and turned back to the path.

"You're going the wrong way."

Of course, the teen was tracking Kenna's GPS. She wouldn't expect anything less. Things were generally better for both of them if they knew each other were safe. And if they weren't, they needed to be able to easily locate each other.

After what had happened the last time Maizie went into the field—her first time as part of the "team" such as it was—no one wanted to take more chances. Getting kidnapped by a dangerous corrupt sheriff from Colorado had set back Maizie's healing journey. Kenna wasn't in a hurry for Maizie to join her where it could get dangerous, and they'd end up risking her peace of mind.

Considering the girl was a tech genius, that was just fine. She could stay in the trailer on Stairns' land where she was safe.

"I need to find her," Kenna said. "There's no one here. The scene needs to remain secure until the sheriff or someone else arrives to take control of it."

She eased her way to the edge of a spot she was sure would fall out from beneath her feet. Then grabbed a log that had some weight but wasn't too heavy for her to lift. She tossed it and watched the surface fall away.

"Nice try, Marion."

Maizie said, "Just watch your surroundings. We don't want today to be the day the Walker gets the jump on you."

Kenna patted the spot where her gun was holstered and moved to the next area she thought might be a trap. She got too close, though. Her shoe caught something, and the ground started to slip away. She scrambled and lurched backward, landing with her behind on the solid winter ground.

Maizie gasped. "Did you fall?"

"I'm fine." Kenna rolled to the edge and peered over. "Dead animals." She winced, her heart thumping in her chest. "She wanted to throw off the K-9."

"We already knew she was despicable. But killing animals is..."

"Sometimes I forget the depravity people can come up with—and some even take pleasure in." Kenna shook her head, even though no one could see her. "I spend time with good people, and I forget."

"Better than swimming in it twenty-four seven," Maizie said. "I don't mean me," she quickly corrected. "I mean you working cases. Living in the middle of the depravity because it's all you see. Taking a break from it is good for you."

Kenna had been encouraged to see the lighter side. Now she knew the Light, and had it in her, she understood fully what that meant. Not just finding joy in a sunrise, or a baby giggling—or bringing a child home to their parents. But the goodness of God that had brought her through more than she could even comprehend. A God who had allowed her to survive when it should have been impossible.

Thank You. "I'm not sure I like that it seems to be that much darker now, compared to the light. It wouldn't have been so shocking before."

Maizie said nothing.

"It's how life goes. Things change. You change—hopefully for the better. You adapt. You grow." Kenna dug in the evidence bag and pulled out some markers. She found a notepad and sketched the area, marking the traps. Date. Time. Weather. Everything she'd been trained to do when working a scene.

She made a list of marker numbers and noted where each one was placed.

No way was she about to take photos with her own phone and risk them taking it from her, legally in a way she wouldn't be able to argue with. Thankfully, there was a camera in the bag.

Kenna walked the whole area. She found two more traps on the periphery before she turned to the clearing. Behind the oak, where Marion had told them to dig was where the largest trap had been.

Had their killer really dug those herself? The sheriff's department would have to figure out if she'd paid for it to be done. That would be another piece of evidence against her. They might even be able to add conspiracy charges.

Kenna turned, surveying the grass. "I know why she picked this spot." She glanced at the trees, then the sky. "No shade. The sun soaks the ground all afternoon."

"I thought it was freezing?"

"It is, but this spot on the mountainside acts like a suntrap. Thirty-five degrees feels warm, and the ground probably rarely has snow on it. She isn't just confined to burying them in the warmer months."

"Good for her," Maizie said, sounding fully like a teenager.

Kenna chuckled. "She's smarter than I gave her credit for her. The plan was far more elaborate."

She wasn't sure what she'd thought about why Marion took the girls. Seemed it had been for a housekeeper job, with a note of her pretending as though she were a mother to a terrified child. Then when that child reached her first milestone of womanhood, she disposed of them and found a new victim.

Kenna found the first spot and knelt.

"How do you know they're buried there?" Maizie asked.

Kenna dug out a small shovel, taking a second to check the area around her and make sure she really wasn't going to be surprised by an assailant. No one was watching her.

But that didn't mean the Walker, or whoever he had taking pictures of her, wasn't around.

"There's a depression," Kenna replied. "A difference in the ground because of what is under there. She didn't bury them too deep, so the earth settles around the body and the grass doesn't grow back quite the same."

Kenna dug as she talked, going over some things she'd learned at Quantico. Other things she'd picked up from her father.

These days she didn't know where she got most of what she knew. She simply absorbed things over the years. She still read law enforcement journals, and white papers. Jax sent her stuff, and they discussed it.

She unearthed an area about three feet wide, two feet out from where she knelt. When she had dug down about a foot and a half with the trowel she had to stop and take a picture—

which meant several. She included the evidence marker number in the image, logged it on her paper. Then she cut the fabric back to reveal a small skull and bowed her head. She gave this stolen life a moment of silence and then dug far enough she could see around the neck.

"Not this one." She noted all the conditions she could think to write down, then moved on. Praying she would find Ramon's sister, as much as she prayed she wouldn't and left a chance the girl might still be alive.

The second wasn't so decomposed as the first one she'd dug up. Kenna didn't think too much about the insects. She simply scooped the dirt back over it and left things intact as much as possible.

"Come on." She guessed where Marion might have started and tried the centermost depression.

The first?

Kenna knew she was right when there was no burlap sheet. No covering. And the state of the skull brought bile up into her throat. "It's her." She had a gut feeling, but couldn't prove it until she dug far enough to see the little girl's neck. "Serious head trauma. Her skull is cracked."

"Before or after she died?"

"I'm sure there are ways to tell, but I don't know what they are." Kenna wiped a tear from her cheek, probably smearing dirt on her face. This little girl had suffered. That could not be denied.

"Does she have the necklace?"

Kenna managed to lift it from around the girl's neck—or what remained. She hardly had to disturb anything. Not from a spine severing injury, just decades of decay. "It's time to go home, Meri." She held the necklace in her hand and gave herself a moment.

"Disturbing evidence?" The sheriff stood across the clearing. "Really?"

Kenna rolled her shoulders, slipping the necklace into the back pocket of her jeans as she stood. "It's called evidence collection. The FBI can vouch for my training."

"And I'm supposed to just buy that it's all above board."

She didn't really care what he chose to believe. Sheriff Gingrich would dismiss her or accept her presence here. She tended to wind up with one or two outcomes with local police. They were solid, and they ended up dead. Or they were corrupt, and they ended up coming after her—and ended up dead.

Far as she could see, steering clear would be a better idea.

"Scene has been secure since your deputy left." She grabbed the big notepad and handed it over. "Everything I've done so far has been logged and photographed. But I've barely scratched the surface, so I doubt I'll have to come back and testify."

"Well, there's something to be thankful for at least."

He didn't like things he couldn't control. And he didn't like strangers disturbing how he thought things should be. She was pretty sure this guy also didn't want her presence inferring he should've closed this case years ago—which was, of course, absolutely true.

"I'll get out of your hair, now that you're here, and you can have your scene."

As long as he understood that if anything was amiss in what was made public, she would bring the truth back to bite him.

Sheriff Gingrich sighed. "I'll have to get that K-9 back out when his handler is healed. We need to find all the bodies without anyone falling into more traps."

"The dog's confusion was how they were injured in the

first place." She explained about the animals in the pits. Some are fresher than others. Marion had killed more than humans. "She might've hired someone in town to keep the traps stocked with fresh kills periodically."

The sheriff just looked confused. "I'm not digging up this whole field. That will take days."

"I'd think you have people for that," Kenna shot back. "Or you could call the state police."

He laughed. "And let them take the credit?"

Kenna grabbed a stack of evidence markers. She walked all over the field, laying one down beside where she could be reasonably sure there was a child buried under the surface. She walked back and handed the rest of the stack of markers to him. They tumbled into his cupped hands. "You did a good job, finding them all. Good for you, Sheriff."

Kenna patted him on the shoulder, then strode away to the path and to her car. Leaving him to comprehend the fact she'd handed him this entire discovery. Even if anyone in town might've already heard she'd been behind it. He would be on record as the one to get the credit. She didn't need recognition.

She had what she'd come for.

Chapter Eight

Kenna held on to the hardback songbook as the congregation sang, "Oh, the love that sought me. Oh, the love that bought me." Finally, on verse four of the hymn, "In Tenderness He Sought Me," she'd figured out how the melody went enough to sing along. "I'm sitting in His presence, the sunshine of His face. While with adoring wonder, His blessings I retrace. It seems as if eternal days are far too short to sound His praise."

Her attention went back to the first verse.

In tenderness He sought me, weary and sick with sin. And on His shoulders brought me, back to His fold again.

Forrest nudged her arm, and Kenna realized everyone had started to sit. She settled on the cushioned pew beside her friend.

The preacher wore a buttoned shirt, no collar or robe, with the sleeves rolled down even though the room was warm. His head was shaved clean, and he looked at least fifty. Thick neck, wide-set dark eyes. Pastor Bruce Kilborn had a lightness to his expression but wasn't the kind of guy she'd want to meet in a dark alley.

"Before we get to the Word," he began, "I just wanted to pass on a warning from the mayor about the incoming storm. It's been unseasonably mild the past few weeks, but that's about to take a turn. We're supposed to get a cold front from Canada that will bring down snow and icy temperatures. So get stocked up in the next couple of days and stay safe. We have a list of those in need if you'd like to help a brother or sister who could use some extra supplies or a meal."

Forrest leaned over and whispered, "You should make a few trays of your lasagna and freeze some." Her father's lasagna hadn't lasted one evening even though she'd made a whole dish of it. Forrest had scarfed down several helpings.

"Sure," Kenna whispered back, chuckling.

The lady in front of them turned back and gave them a glare for whispering too loud.

The preacher read a few verses from Isaiah about holiness, talking about the sin nature versus God's instruction to be holy as His people.

Kenna wrote some notes in her phone—references to look them up later, and a couple of questions to ask Jax.

"You are a new creation. So consider yourself dead to the sin nature inside of you. It is dead. It is no more. So live in Christ. Live for God."

Kenna wrote a lot down, because there was so much she didn't fully grasp yet about what it meant to be a Christian. This journey would end up being the most important case of her life.

The case that saw *her* rescued and brought home.

Pastor Bruce prayed, and people started to disburse from the sanctuary. The lady who'd glared saw Kenna's phone in her hand and huffed.

Kenna turned to Forrest and found her making a face. "Did I need to tell her I was using my phone to make notes?"

"I would've, but it wouldn't have been as holy as a pen and paper."

"Do you have stuff you need to get before the storm?" Kenna asked.

Forrest nodded. "Are you going to make sure they get all those bodies out before the snow hits?"

"I can pray they do," Kenna said. But she was pretty sure if the sheriff needed help, he wouldn't ask. She didn't need to wade back into that again today. Not to mention it really was safer for everyone if she didn't get close to the people in the police department. She'd already met her quota of dead or corrupt cops she'd known in her lifetime.

"I'll hit the store on the way home," Forrest said. "You touch base with Kobrinsky. Get an update."

Kenna lifted her brows. Apparently, her friend was getting comfortable enough to give her orders—or wanted an afternoon alone running errands. She then eased along the pew, into the aisle, at the same time Theo and Alonzo exited their row on the other side. She had seen them come in with their wives and waved to them, but they hadn't spoken. "Gentlemen."

Alonzo paused to make way for her. "So you took our advice and ended up saving two more lives to add to the one from before."

Two beating hearts in a field of cold corpses didn't seem like an upside to her. "I'm just glad her dog didn't decide to take a bite out of me."

Alonzo eyed Forrest, like maybe he shouldn't talk in front of her, but said to Kenna, "You showed up just in time, like you did at the house. Right?"

"I guess so." Just like at the house that hadn't been why she was there. She had placed the necklace she'd taken from the body in her RV, in the lockbox with one of her father's old guns. When she saw Ramon, she would be able to give him that small bit of closure.

She'd found his sister.

Theo turned to Forrest. "Heard about your troubles. You think there's something to it?"

Was he really asking about the note?

Kenna didn't want Forrest being harassed. After all, Kenna was the one who'd asked the two men about Forrest's husband and son's deaths. "We don't need to—"

"Want us to take the case?" Alonzo asked, cutting her off. "Find out if there's anything to it. We don't need to trouble you with it unless there's any weight to it."

Forrest pressed her lips together, as though biting them on the inside.

Kenna needed to dispel the tension. "You're stealing my case?"

Theo eyed her. "We know the area better than you, missy."

"So you just cut me out?" She shot both men an aghast look. She'd figured they would offer to work with her, not in competition with her. Would she have accepted a partnership?

Theo grinned. "Them's the breaks."

Kenna fired back with, "Did you find your book yet?"

Forrest gasped. "You lost the book!"

Kenna glanced at her, then back at them. "How come she knows about it and I don't? Someone needs to fill me in on a whole lot of stuff. Pronto."

Theo smirked. "Don't you have a case to work?"

Forrest managed a tiny smile. "I'll let you all know if I need any of it looking into." She turned and wandered to Betty and Charlayne, who were at the back talking to a group of women.

"Why does she know about the book?" Kenna asked.

Alonzo shrugged, but she didn't buy his nonchalance. "She's a smart girl."

"Maybe too smart," Theo added.

Kenna bit her own lips together. *Don't be nosy.* It wasn't cute, even if she had a burning inside that didn't rest until questions had answers.

Over by the podium, and the four carpeted steps that led up to the raised stage, the preacher guy turned to look at the back door.

Kenna motioned with her head. "What's the story with Pastor Bruce?"

"I did some digging," Theo said. "Not sure many folks here know, but Bruce Kilborn did a stretch in state prison for manslaughter."

"Circumstances?"

He shrugged. "I'm sure pastor would rather you ask him about it yourself. Then he can keep a finger on the pulse of who knows, and who is assuming this preacher man has been God-fearin' his whole life."

"People would judge him for his past?" Kenna said. Having been a Christian for only a few months, she had plenty in her history that people would frown upon.

Theo shrugged. "Christians ain't perfect. They're humans who do dumb things, say worse, and we've gotta just hope they're at least trying to do better next time."

Kenna was. Hopefully, that could be said of most honest followers of God.

"Excuse me?" The voice was female and far too soft. "Are you Kenna Banbury?"

She turned to see a couple in the aisle.

"We'll see ya." Theo clapped her on the shoulder. The look on his face said he knew this wouldn't be good.

The couple were both older, maybe in their midfifties, and she wore a long dress. He was slender. Both had on thin wool coats, and the woman had a white cloth securing her hair back. Sturdy black shoes. No makeup and only thin gold bands indicating their commitment to each other.

She turned to face them. "Yes, that's me. How can I help you?" Then someone moved beside her.

The preacher.

"We can talk in my office," he suggested. "If you'd like?"

The husband nodded. He led his wife there. Kenna followed, and the preacher closed the office door behind them all. He brought in a third chair, but the husband stood behind his wife's chair.

Bruce sat behind his desk. "This is Mr. Merrington and his wife. Their daughter Rebekah went missing six years ago."

So not the most recent victim, but the one before that. And she had likely been buried with the others, years ago now, cold in that field and decomposing.

Kenna laid her hand over her heart. She angled her body toward the grieving parents and asked softly, "What was Rebekah like?" She directed the question to the mother, who flushed.

"She was a sweet child. Always so ready to help." Mrs. Merrington tucked her hand in her pocket and brought out a faded photo.

The husband's hands flexed on the chair.

"Rebekah loved to make animal sounds," she added. "She could mimic nearly every bird call or chirp you can think of."

Kenna took the picture carefully and smiled. "She sounds like a lovely girl." Equally as carefully, she'd refrained from using the past tense.

"We had heard in town that you were here. We didn't

know if anyone was even looking for the missing girls anymore." Tears gathered in the mother's eyes.

"We lost hope at times," Mr. Merrington said. "Though it shames me to admit it, I did fall victim to the sin of unbelief that we would never find her."

"Hope can be so fragile," Kenna said. "Sometimes it seems as strong as a bull. Other times it's as fragile as a bird with a broken wing. Hope is a gift we're given. A kind of grace, which we need so much but don't deserve."

The husband nodded. "You're right."

Kenna had been on both sides of it. Since Maizie had been kidnapped in Mexico, she knew at least something of what these parents felt—to an extent anyway. She'd needed to rage until her teen was back and safe, to fight her way to getting Maizie back.

Learning to trust God seemed like it would be a lifelong journey, and she'd end up taking two steps forward and then one back at every time. Then. Now.

Mrs. Merrington accepted the photo back. "We had heard that the police may have found the...the—" Her voice broke.

"Marion Wells is in custody." Kenna nearly mentioned that the woman wouldn't be hurting anyone else, but something held those words back. "She gave me the location, and the police are doing their work at the scene."

"And if they find my Rebekah?"

Behind Mrs. Merrington, the husband's hands flexed again. Controlling his anger, and the frustration he had over feeling powerless?

"You'll be able to lay her to rest soon," Kenna said.

The woman flushed. "She's been with Jesus for a long time. But it would be good to bring her home."

Kenna wondered if they would bury their child on their land, where they could keep her memory close by. "You'll be able to remember her life and find some peace for yourself. At least, that's what I'll be praying for."

Pastor Bruce said, "If you need anything from the church at this time, or anytime, please don't hesitate to ask."

Mrs. Merrington nodded. She rose but paused by Kenna's chair. "After she has been...identified, will you come and see me? I'd love to show you some of the pictures I have at home. Start remembering."

Kenna said, "I would love to see them."

They closed the door as quietly as they lived.

Pastor Bruce blew out a long breath. "Is it always that tough?"

She studied this rough-looking man. "I'm Kenna."

"I used to go by Slim. Now I'm Bruce again, which my mother would be delighted to hear if she wasn't with the good Lord nearly thirty years." He dropped that last piece of information casually, as if let her know he had also suffered loss.

"Yes, Bruce. It is often like that."

"How do you do it?" He leaned back in his chair, and it creaked.

"Letting them talk while you listen is a gift. Another grace, but one we give to each other rather than what we accept from the Lord."

"Huh."

"That's pretty new." She explained a little about what had happened in her heart the past few months. "But not why I'm in Wisconsin."

"So you did come here to solve this case?"

She nodded. "I'm glad I could help."

Bruce shook his head. "Seems like they'd never have been found if you didn't come here."

"We all have our callings. This is mine." She figured she would ask the pertinent question since she was here. "Do you have any reason to believe Forrest Crosby's family were murdered? The police assume they were killed due to an accident, but perhaps it wasn't as it appears to be."

"Don't pull any punches, do you?" He nearly smiled, but this guy was the kind of man who'd learned early how to school his features.

"You've been around this area a while." Longer than they'd been buried, at least. "Have you heard anything you'd consider credible about their deaths?"

Bruce shifted in his chair. "If I had, there would be a problem telling you. There's an assumption of confidentiality in counseling appointments."

"Unless that person committed a crime, in which case you're legally obligated to report the crime, or you become an accessory."

His brows rose. "Guess you feel strongly about that."

"You have no idea." As long as the pastor hadn't knowingly been an accessory to a crime. She was horrified by the idea of church leaders counseling a person and allowing someone to continue to be victimized when they should be removed from a situation for their own safety.

One of the things that her innate need for black-and-white justice had to let go of, so she could find some of that hope. So she could believe God would sort it all out.

All she could do was trust He had it.

"So you can't tell me anything." She stood since there was no point in staying if he could only hedge. Maybe he felt as powerless as she did when she heard about people being hurt, but Kenna didn't need another best friend.

"How about you call if you have any more questions, and I'll let you know if I think of anything."

She eyed him while he wrote something on a small piece of paper. "I don't—"

"Here." He held it up.

For the sake of not arguing, Kenna grabbed it. "Thanks." She didn't say, *See you later*.

On the way out, through the sanctuary, she looked at the note. There was a trash can by the door, and she could simply drop it in rather than make more contacts in this town that would be connections tying her to this place.

She blinked, staring at the paper. The circle hole at the top, that had been ripped free of what held it. The handwriting. The note read,

NICE TO MEET YOU.

Followed by a number that was way too many digits to be his phone, even with the area code.

"What?" The quiet question dissipated fast in the empty room.

Kenna turned back to the door across the sanctuary. His note had the same handwriting as the one left on Forrest's door. Same circle where it had been torn away and used. He'd wanted her to know it was *him* that reached out.

She strode back to his office but found it empty. She checked the storage areas, then behind the church. The pastor's parking space was empty.

He had left.

Kenna headed for her car, parked in front of the building. Chill wind bit at her legs and face. She tucked the collar of her jacket closer around her face, feeling the cold to her soul. Bruce wouldn't have left that note for Forrest if it wasn't possible it was true.

So who had told him the information...

And was that person the killer Forrest was writing a book about?

Her phone rang just as she got to her car, a local number she didn't recognize. "Banbury."

"It's Kobrinsky. I need a ride home from the hospital. And thanks to you, everyone in the department is busy."

"What if I'm busy?"

"Are you?"

She climbed in her car, trying to think of something to say.

Before she could make something up, he said, "I'm waiting in the lobby."

Chapter Nine

Kenna pulled up at the curb and texted the number he'd used to call.

Need me to carry you out?

The lobby doors slid apart a minute or so later, and he came out, walking on a pair of crutches. Kenna opened the passenger door for him.

Kobrinsky said, "As if you could lift me?"

Right. She'd indicated that before. "How is the K-9 handler lady?"

"Her name is Jo Sammers. She's not out of the woods, but she's stable. She lost a lot of blood and there's some swelling on her brain. Once her boyfriend showed up to secure the dog, they could treat her without the animal trying to snap at them."

"I'll be praying she keeps healing."

He glanced over at her. "So you're one of those?"

Did she want to get into that?

Kenna just said, "Yes. Now give me your address so we can get you home."

He rattled off a number and a street.

"That's Marion's house."

He shrugged. "Let's go."

She drove off for the sake of getting out of the lane where she'd been blocking traffic and people going in and out of the hospital. Still, she put no destination in her phone maps app. Her mind was full of implications of the conversation she'd just had with the preacher.

"What do you know about Pastor Bruce?" she asked.

"I know I have a buddy in Appleton who arrested the guy for the crime he went down for."

"And now? I figure if your buddy saw him these days, he'd see how someone can turn their life around."

Kobrinsky huffed. "If that's what happened."

"You think it's a scam or something?" She held the wheel, the interior of the car warm enough she wanted to push up her long sleeves. The fact he would see the scars on her fore-arms stopped her, even if he knew she couldn't lift heavy things.

"It's religion. Of course, it's a scam."

There was a story there, but she didn't want to get into a debate she wasn't ready for. "I think maybe it's not *always* a scam. Hopefully, it's not even a scam most of the time. But there are people in every sphere who will lie to get in posi-tions where they can look good, or have money given to them as part of the ruse. You and I wouldn't be in the lines of work we're in if they didn't. You know, our real jobs."

He huffed. "Knew that would get a rise out of you."

"Good for you." She rolled her eyes. "How's your leg?"

"Didn't hit anything vital. But I'm on desk duty until I'm cleared, which means you're my new partner."

She huffed a laugh and pulled up at a stop light, then glanced over. "Wait. You're serious?"

"Someone's got to pick up the slack. I figure the sheriff won't complain when I tell him I decided it's you, and that out of the kindness of that churchgoing heart, you'll do it pro bono."

Kenna put the car in Park and engaged the handbrake. "Get out."

Kobrinsky busted up laughing. "This is gonna be good. Most interesting thing that's happened all year."

"The year has barely started."

"You know what I mean."

Kenna hit the dash screen and dialed Jax's number. Which she'd been intending on doing before Kobrinsky threw a wrench in everything. She would take him to Marion's and leave him there. He could call a cab to get home. Or walk for all she cared.

"I was hoping you'd call." His warm voice came through the speakers, and it sounded like he was walking. Most likely out of church given the time in California.

"I just have a quick question," she said.

"Uh-oh." He could read her tone that easily?

"Precisely how much would the FBI or Wisconsin State Patrol care if a sheriff's deputy was mysteriously left on the side of the road to freeze to death?"

Kobrinsky shifted in his seat and grunted. "Is that your boyfriend?"

Jax said, "Whatever trouble there is, I'll make it disappear."

As if they really would since that was illegal. But Kobrinsky didn't know they wouldn't purposely conspire like that. What he now knew was that she had protection.

And Jax knew what was going on.

"Deputy Jerry Kobrinsky, meet FBI Special Agent Oliver Jaxon." The name sounded strange to her ears even with her being the one who said it. She only thought of him as Jax. Calling him "Oliver" would be so weird.

"Am I supposed to say, 'Nice to meet you'?" Kobrinsky scoffed. "Take the next right. Marion's house is over there."

Jax was the one who asked, "Why are you going back there?"

Kenna grinned to herself. "I guess he thinks his colleagues missed something."

"I have to interrogate the woman in a couple of days when I'm back at work," Kobrinsky said. "I need something to get her talking."

"I'm not sure it matters." Kenna felt her smile widen. "She'll probably just want to talk to me again."

Jax chuckled through the phone line. "Let me know if you want me to do anything on my end. That could help."

She didn't want him to put his career in jeopardy. Or his life in danger. She'd seen him nearly dead just a few weeks ago.

Not again, thanks.

"Anything new on our mutual friend?" she asked.

"Nothing but quiet," he replied. "Unless you have something."

Kenna didn't like the sound of quiet. When it was just her, it was soothing—until it got boring. With a case, it was never good. "When I do, you'll be the first to know."

"Have a good one."

"You, too."

The phone line went dead.

She had driven to Marion's house, all taped off and locked up. But Kobrinsky wasn't looking at the house—he was looking at her. "So your boyfriend is an FBI agent."

That sounded entirely too much like an accusation. "I guess I have a type."

He snorted. "I do, too. And it ain't PIs."

"Lucky for me. Now get out of my car."

"You're coming inside. I have a key for that lock, 'cause it's mine."

"What are we looking for? Do you seriously think you all missed something?" She stared at him. "Do you?"

"This is the case of our lives. Do you want out of it? Because I don't want to disappear from the reports, or the articles in the newspaper. I could get invited on TV. You could come with me, and someone will probably write a book about us. Or they'll make a movie." He motioned at her. "Given how plain you look, you'll make me look good sitting next to you."

She stared at him.

"I'm kidding! Lighten up."

"You're a pig."

"Then you know what you get with me. Because I don't sugarcoat it." He pushed the door open. "Come on, let's go give the scene a fresh glance."

She'd found the closet and saved a girl's life last time. If he wanted to take credit for spotting the next thing no one else had seen, she would make him work for it. He could work the case of Forrest's family in exchange for her cooperation. Or she could work him up to more than that.

Everything in his life was about what he could get out of it. She was surprised he hadn't hit on Forrest the past few years, since she lived alone now. Not as a predatory move, but she could see him purposely seizing the opportunity to fish in a new pond.

Gross.

She walked behind him as he moved on the crutches to

the door. "Have you thought about running against the sheriff at the next election?"

Kobrinsky handed her the keys. "That would be next fall. It'd take a big case to get my name out there."

"How about the fact a man and his son were killed, and it was ruled an accident? Possibly wrongly." She shrugged. "That means negligent leadership at best."

"You're still on that train?" He didn't look at her.

"Yes, so tell me what you know."

He entered the house, and she followed, closing the front door behind her.

The place had a stillness to it that had a darkness hanging in the air, and almost maleficence seeping from the walls. But she knew what had happened here over the years. Why wouldn't she feel it like it hung around still as a kind of evil presence?

"Look around," Kobrinsky said. "When we're done, I'll tell you." He headed for the living room.

She stared at his back. "I haven't had lunch yet, by the way."

He called over his shoulder, "So you're gonna get all crabby? Look fast. We can order a pizza at my house. All the restaurants will be full of Holy Rollers getting lunch."

Kenna bit the inside of her lip. If he thought she was going to his house...

She wanted answers about Forrest's family, but not even that badly. She also wanted to know if Marion had kept any souvenirs from the victims she held here, so she could remove anything that would lead the police here from the first victim's identity to her family...and then to Kenna now. She didn't want to put Ramon Santiago—or anything he was about to do to get his reputation back—at risk. Like putting him on the radar of the dirty FBI agent who had ruined him.

At least, not before he was ready.

She trailed into the bedroom, remembering a house in Salt Lake City where she'd searched the bedroom of a serial killer with her friend Ryson. The police lieutenant had been there when she met Jax and thoroughly approved of how her life had changed since then. She was proud of how he'd cleaned up his act and took his family to church now—a different kind of pride than what she'd felt knowing she was right about Marion. But even that hadn't been an overblown sense of her own abilities. Just the confidence she had in solving a case like she solved all the others.

She'd been raised the way she had for a reason. The experiences she'd gone through made her who she was today so she could do a job not many people would be able to do.

And she wouldn't wish this job on anyone else.

She wanted to be the one to carry the weight so that someone else didn't.

God knew what He was getting into with her. He wasn't surprised by how she was—the person He had made her to be.

She used her skills, and she saved lives. Justice was found because of her.

And I'll do it for as long as You able me to.

One day, she would be done as a PI. And she didn't plan to regret any of it. Especially not if Jax was there, in person rather than on the phone.

Kenna found a suitcase under the bed. Dark teal colored, hard sided. Like something from the '50s or '60s. She tugged apart the latches, having to push hard to get them to click open. The lid lifted free, and she leaned it against the green crocheted blanket hanging over the side of the bed.

She yelled, "Kobrinsky!" and stared at the contents of the case until he came to the door. She got up, snapping a photo of it with her phone. "I know how to get her talking."

He maneuvered around the bed and swore loudly. "Is that a head...in a plastic bag?!"

"I've never seen him, but I'm guessing that's...Mr. Wells?"

Kobrinsky swore again.

"Do you want me to call it in, or do you want to pretend we were never here?"

She'd rather stay here, so she could ask whoever searched this house why they hadn't looked in the case under the bed. Maybe they'd concentrated on the closet where Kenna found the girl, but that was the worst excuse.

She palmed her phone. "I'm calling it in."

"*I'm* doing it." He shook his head. "If anyone asks, I found the head."

"Of course you did." She folded her arms and waited while he made the call. When he hung up, she showed him the note from the preacher. "What does this number mean to you?"

"That's the sequence state police uses for case numbers. That one is old."

"Get me a copy of the file, and I'll tell whoever shows up that I pulled the case out from under the bed at your instruction. After all, it was your idea to come here." He would get all the credit, and she would get answers. Whoever's attention was on her and Forrest, it wouldn't become a problem for her friend. Kenna would make sure of that.

He stared at her. "You drive a hard bargain."

It would be good for him to remember this. "I can be your best friend, or your worst nightmare."

Kobrinsky laughed. "I'm pretty sure your idea of a nightmare doesn't end with me looking like Mr. Wells here."

He might be right about that, but she wasn't going to confirm either way.

"Let me get that number, and I'll run it for you when I get to my computer." He reached for the paper.

"Type the number in your phone."

"Text it to me."

"Are you going to be difficult at every turn?" Kenna eyed him, then hit Send on the text. "Don't bother answering that. I already know."

"You'd like my ex-wife. The two of you would get along great."

"I don't plan on being in town long enough for that." She headed out first, and they met a deputy at the door. She thumbed over her shoulder at Kobrinsky. "He found a head."

The deputy blinked. Geez, the guy was like nineteen.

"Rayland, go get your evidence kit. You should've known you would need it."

Kenna stepped outside, and Deputy Rayland jogged to the patrol car.

"The kid will probably barf in the suitcase, but at least he knows to hustle." Kobrinsky nudged her shoulder. "What?"

She had a hunch, but wasn't sure she could articulate it.

Kenna stepped off the porch and tried to figure out a direction to go. Toward whatever was giving her this odd feeling. She scanned the street. Marion lived at the end of a cul-de-sac, her neighbors a quarter mile up the road behind their fences.

Movement shifted between two trees to the west. She spotted a flash. *A camera.* Kenna took off running that direction, sliding out her weapon and flicking off the safety with her thumb.

She raced toward the trees, desperate to catch whoever had been watching her. *It's about time.* If it was the Walker or an associate, she wanted to know. Then she would catch another serial killer. Everything from her time in Mexico would be settled and she would finally be able to move on.

Kenna raced between two trees, trying to see where the flash of movement had gone.

Someone tackled her from the side, which felt like getting sideswiped by a Mack truck. She slammed onto the ground, and her head hit something unyielding.

Everything went black.

Chapter Ten

The door opened.

Kenna didn't open her eyes, even if she was trying not to black out again.

"Here." Something cold touched her hand.

She took the ice pack, surprised it was the sheriff who gave it to her.

Kenna sat up on the couch in his office, then winced as pain roiled through her head. "I can't believe he got the jump on me."

Sheriff Gingrich settled on the edge of the desk. "By all accounts you tore off after him. And you're surprised he jumped you?"

"I'm not a rookie. I know what I'm doing." She held the ice pack against the side of her head where she'd apparently hit a rock. Thankfully, it wasn't worse than a bad bump.

"I caution my rookies not to hurry into any situation. I'd think your FBI background at least would've taught you the same. If not the rest of your history."

"I can't usually wait for backup. There often isn't anyone to wait for." She leaned back against the couch so she could look at him without craning her neck. "I'm accustomed to being out there on my own."

Gingrich studied her. "Careful, your jadedness is showing."

He wasn't going to admit she achieved a good deal by herself. Of course not. Because that would only highlight what he hadn't been able to do here. Plus the fact a sheriff would never admit that a private investigator might have a valuable role to play in law enforcement.

She frowned. "Just running on the welcome I usually get."

"With no exceptions?"

"The exceptions are dead." Like the sheriff in Northern California who had known her father.

There were no memories in this part of Wisconsin. She'd never been here with her father, even if her dad had met Forrest here. This man didn't know her dad when he'd been alive, as far as she knew. It was only Forrest who had been mentored by him some when she'd been a young writer.

"You're drifting." The sheriff poured himself a drink that definitely wasn't coffee. "Want something strong?"

"No, thank you." She'd never liked the feeling of being out of control, and she quit drinking after college.

He dragged over a chair and sat, crossing one leg over the other knee. The door opened, and Deputy Kobrinsky hobbled in on his crutches.

Kenna announced, "The man of the hour."

Sheriff Gingrich glanced at her, one eyebrow raised.

Kenna closed her mouth.

Kobrinsky said, "Deputy Rayland is working with the sketch artist and getting us a picture of the guy who hit you."

The sheriff turned to Kenna. "Why did you go after him?"

"He was taking a picture of me." She was going to sound

nuts either way, so she explained about the guy the FBI was currently tracking and how she'd met him in Mexico.

"Who is he?"

"We only know who we think he is. This guy named Parker, former military. It's the only thing that ever made sense as far as identifying him. But he could have a partner, and that could be the one who is here taking photos of me, watching me on behalf of the real Walker."

Kobrinsky said, "El Caminante?"

She tried to nod, but it hurt.

"That guy is bad news."

Kenna closed, then opened her eyes. Enough of a nod that he got it.

"There's a possibility that killer is here?" The sheriff paused. "You don't think you've given us enough work to do already, cleaning up after you? You brought someone else after you?"

She winced. "You don't have to yell at me." And that wasn't what she'd done.

Both men glanced at each other.

Kobrinsky dug a phone out of his pocket and tossed it on the couch beside her. "I called your boyfriend while you were out. Figured he'd want to know what happened."

He'd spoken to Jax. "And?"

"He said you should call immediately." He glanced at the sheriff. "And we need to pass the sketch to the FBI as soon as we have it."

The sheriff shifted in his chair and sipped his drink. "If this is an FBI case and he's got someone watching you, why not just go to the FBI and stay where they can keep an eye on you?"

"It's complicated." Kenna set the ice pack down.

Kobrinsky said, "You want the Walker to find you rather

than let them take him down? Or is this about your boyfriend being on the taskforce, so you don't want to step on toes? Or are you the only one who gets to put yourself in danger?"

An image flashed in her mind. Jax hanging from a hook in a barn in Mexico. Beaten and bloody, dangling there unconscious.

No way was she going to go through that again.

"If I go to California, I'll have to meet his mother."

The sheriff chuckled over his drink.

Kobrinsky grinned. "Didn't peg you for a coward."

Kenna nearly told him to shut up.

Thankfully, the door flung open, and Forrest rushed in. "You can't detain her without charges." She looked around.

Kenna raised her fingers and waved, but other than that didn't move.

Sheriff said, "She's here of her own volition. She ain't under arrest."

Forrest shut the door and came over. She slumped onto the couch beside Kenna. "You don't look so good."

"I'm alive." And they had a shot at getting an image of the man who'd been photographing her. Was it Parker, or someone else?

Forrest said, "What's going on?"

All the events prior to her getting knocked out rushed back to Kenna's mind. "Marion had her husband's head under her bed." And Pastor Bruce had given Kenna a case number.

Forrest's brows rose. "Just the head?"

"In a plastic bag," Kenna said. "It was pretty juicy."

The sheriff cleared his throat. "She's a civilian."

"Yeah, she's a writer, though. It's not like they're normal." Kenna grinned at Forrest, who chuckled.

Forrest's interest moved to Gingrich. "Can I see a picture?"

"Why?" Kobrinsky said. "Are you going to write a book about it after you finish the one you're doing now?"

Kenna figured it would likely be about Marion. After Forrest solved the current mystery she was working on, would she write a book about the kidnapper the police hadn't managed to catch?

Gingrich said, "This department does not provide information about cases, past or present, to those who aren't law enforcement."

Kenna caught Kobrinsky looking at Forrest with a whole lot of longing. *Oh no.* She glared at him and mouthed, *Don't even think about it.*

He just grinned.

Clueless about the deputy, Forrest said, "Maybe the FBI will come here and catch this guy so you don't have to worry about him."

"Right," Kenna said. Not that she was actually worried. And that wasn't why Forrest thought Jax should be here. They'd talked about that at length late into the night over the past few weeks.

Forrest had lost her family. She didn't think Kenna should be wasting her time now that she and Jax knew they liked each other. Kenna's life always seemed to be more complicated than that, but she didn't like the idea of waiting until things "settled down" for them to see where it would go. But that didn't mean she was ready to jump in with both feet either.

A relationship was scarier than the worst serial killer she could imagine.

She had no clue where to put Jax's mother on that scale.

Talk about scary.

If she left Wisconsin now, she'd never find out if Pastor Bruce believed Forrest was in danger. Or who might've talked to him about the accident. If she left, and something happened to this good but lonely woman, Kenna wouldn't easily forgive herself.

Giving in to the pounding in her head, Kenna bent forward and put her head in her hands. Closed her eyes. *I'm supposed to ask for wisdom, right?*

Asking for Jax was far too selfish. He needed to live his life. Protection for Forrest seemed less self-serving. Kind of like her need to keep Jax safe, even if that meant him being far from her.

"What happened to the guy who tackled Kenna?" Forrest asked. "Did you get him?"

Kenna lifted her head and leaned back against the couch.

"The deputy raised his gun," Kobrinsky said. "Apparently, the guy laughed, and ran off." Hence the sketch artist. Deputy Rayland had seen the guy and lived to tell about it. "They should be done soon."

Forrest said, "Good, because Kenna needs rest."

"They're done. He's on his way." Sheriff Gingrich looked up from his phone.

Kenna closed her eyes, trying to figure out how to ask Kobrinsky to get her that file to go. When the artist came in and Kobrinsky said her name, she opened them again.

Forrest said, "Should you be sleeping when you were unconscious?"

Kenna shrugged. "It helps. I don't have a concussion."

Kobrinsky handed Forrest the paper, and she held it so Kenna could see.

The man had a beard. Heavy eyebrows. Wispy hair. Maybe in his sixties.

Her heart sank. This guy had gotten away. She might be lucky she wasn't dead, but the officer would be kicking himself for a long time that an old man had run off.

"I don't think I recognize...," Kenna began. But there was something oddly familiar about the guy. Did she know him?

"I'll send this to your boyfriend." Kobrinsky got up, hopping a little as he grabbed the sketch, then headed to the door.

"Let's go home. I'll drive you." Forrest stood.

Kenna shifted to the edge of the seat.

The sheriff said, "She'll be out in a minute. I just need a moment with Ms. Banbury."

Forrest glanced over but left without argument.

Kenna shot him a look. "Are you going to tell me I messed up again?"

He sat back in his chair. "I'm down a man. Kobrinsky is injured."

"I don't owe you. Call the state police." She didn't want to get deputized, or work for this guy.

He set his drink on the table. "Three days from now, I've got a sensitive detail coming through the county. Kobrinsky was going to be my guy, but he's out. It's only escort. The marshals have asked us to provide assistance. They are bringing a high value detainee through the area and down to Chicago so they can testify."

"That's an odd route." Landing so far north and spending so much time on the ground put them at risk. But then, maybe landing at a closer airport posed the same risk.

"That's the point, I think. No one knows they're coming through."

"And you think I can help?"

The sheriff shrugged. "I think you're here, and you're capable. You're on the side of what the feds are doing, and I'll be busy. All my people are busy doing work you caused."

It was on the tip of her tongue to point out that he could at least be grateful. But she wasn't the one who had two crime scenes to process.

"You want to be thanked." He chuckled. "Don't we all. But while you might've closed one case, you seem to have several more to work now. So I'm not sure thanks are in order just yet."

He thought he could've figured this all out himself? Maybe he should have done that.

"You're the one who let Kobrinsky say he found that head. So he could run against me next year, right?"

Kenna said nothing.

"I'll tell you when and where to be."

"I'll think about it." Kenna got up, which made her head swim. She didn't like it, but she grabbed the back of a chair to steer her way to the door. "Why don't you send me all the information you have on this marshal thing, and the guy they're transporting, yeah? I'll take a look and then decide."

"You'd love to see all that." He made a face. "And if they gave me anything, I would certainly not pass it on. Unless you'd care to be deputized until such time as I decide to release you."

Kenna grabbed the door handle and glanced over. "Don't even think about it." He had no idea how she felt about badges, or things that seemed inevitable.

Gingrich chuckled. "Don't worry. I'd make you go through deputy training, and you wouldn't like it."

Kenna swept out of the room, then strode to Forrest. "He thinks I've lost my edge. Can you believe that? He thinks I've gone soft, and I need training."

Forrest chuckled. "You're slurring your words. You should probably get seen by a doc—"

"Nope. Don't." She lifted both hands. "I'm good."

The lady behind reception walked over, blond curls and a

Bluetooth headset with a red light on the earpiece over her left ear. "Here you go, hon. I left the photos out as you requested."

Kenna turned to Forrest. "Is that what I think it is?" She put her elbow on the counter.

Forrest took the file, as though nervous to even touch it. "I've never read the details." She swallowed, then said, "I've never even looked at the reports."

Kenna touched her shoulder. "You don't have to do this alone." She peered over and looked at the case file. "Kobrinsky!"

He looked over. "Oh. Right. I'll email that paperwork you asked for."

"Thanks." Her head pounded. "Let's go."

As they neared the doors, Forrest said, "I just want to know if there's reason to think it wasn't an accident. Maybe it will feel like someone else's file."

Probably that wasn't going to be true, but they could at least hope. Maybe Forrest was counting on it.

And why was it so much easier to help someone else than to deal with her own fears? Walking through this with Forrest meant giving hope and peace to someone else. And avoiding her problems. Helping a hurt woman to move on and take another step.

If Kenna didn't have Forrest to help, what would she do? She'd have to go back to Colorado and get up in Maizie's business so she could feel good that the teen was healing from the trauma she had been through.

One day everyone would be fine, and Kenna would have to face the fear in her.

She'd been through so much. She'd survived.

God had given her new life. He had given her hope and a reason to keep going, more than just solving cases.

She had people who cared for her and a man who inter-ested her more than anyone had in a long time. Who made her want to believe she could have something of what she had lost.

"Are you having some kind of existential crisis?" Forrest clutched the file and stared up at Kenna.

"Yes."

"Let's go, so you can read it at home where you're not in front of an audience." Forrest tugged on her elbow, and they stepped outside.

Kenna said, "Good idea." Her head was pounding and spinning now. She definitely needed to go take a nap, and a lot of pain meds. With all the surgeries she'd had, Kenna had made sure she didn't lose her tolerance for regular pain meds.

Hopefully, they would work today, and another day in the future she wouldn't wind up with kidney problems because she got hurt more than most people seemed to.

They headed for the front doors.

"Let's order a pizza," Kenna said. "I haven't eaten since breakfast."

Chapter Eleven

Jax stepped out onto the patio, closing the sliding door behind him. His sister looked over from her lounge chair, where she watched her kids goof off in the pool with their dad.

"Everything okay?" Laney waved him to the seat beside her.

"Nothing new since that deputy called me." That had been a surprise, when Kenna's number flashed up on his screen and the caller turned out to be a Wisconsin sheriff's deputy.

For a second he'd thought she was dead, and his heart had nearly stopped.

Everything in him wanted to run. Jump on a plane, and rush to her side. Stand between her and whatever came at her, because a person who had been through what she had didn't need to suffer even one more second. The fact she kept going made her even more amazing than she was just being a survivor.

"What did your boss say?"

Jax settled onto the lounge chair beside her, where he'd left his lemonade. It was warm from the sun now. "We have a witness sketch, so we're trying to ID that person."

She reached over and squeezed his knee. "Kenna is okay, right?"

"I regret telling you the story." He sucked down some warm lemonade.

"As if I was going to let you get away with not explaining why you have all those scars."

The kids had gone to bed, but they'd still been hanging in the pool that day a few weeks ago. Laney's husband was a surgeon, and she was a nurse. Neither of them had blinked at the scars on his chest and back since he got back from Mexico, but they had demanded the story.

Since then, it had been regularly pouring out of him. Apparently, he needed someone to talk to. But with the frustration of wanting to be near Kenna and not being able to go, he was a little worried that when they met, Laney might not like her.

Laney said, "Don't you have secret friends who can find out who it is?"

Jax smiled. He'd explained about Maizie, but never once used her name. "Pretty sure she hacked my phone a while back, so I'd be surprised if she isn't already running it. But it's a risk, with her history. She might know him."

His boss had the guys in the office running the image against Walker's known associates. What he needed was for

Maizie to look in Kenna's just in case she had ever run across the guy before.

"And if Kenna's in trouble, you'll be there?"

He glanced at Laney, curious about her tone.

"I know you say she's worth it. But she hasn't come here to meet us," Laney said, as though she wanted to give Kenna the once-over and check out who her big brother was interested in. "But it's complicated. And she's busy, and you're busy." She waved a hand. "Whatever."

Jax chuckled. If he didn't get them to meet each other soon, he was pretty sure Laney would pack up the kids and her husband in their high-end SUV and go track Kenna down. But if it happened at the wrong time, everyone would be in danger.

"I just hope I can help her and that no one else dies."

She tipped her head to the side. "You've always been a good guy. That's the problem."

"I don't want to talk about Cayleigh."

"Does Kenna even know about her?"

Jax winced. "She knows I have an ex-wife. If she remembers that. It was back in Salt Lake City when I told her. But I don't know if she's thought about it, and it's not like Cayleigh is an issue."

Laney's brows rose.

"What?"

She burst out laughing. "You're such a guy." She waved a hand, still chuckling. "Catch your killer. I'll worry about Cayleigh, and I'll let you know if it becomes an issue."

He grinned around the rim of his glass. "Thanks?"

She shoved his shoulder. After a minute of quiet, she said, "Is Kenna really okay?"

He should've known she would be worried about a

woman she'd never met. Simply because Jax cared about her. "Bump on the head. Knocked out."

She grabbed her phone from under the towel, where it was out of the sun. "I'll send you a list of things she needs to watch out for."

"Thanks, Sis."

"You're—"

His phone ringing again cut her off. It was Maizie.

Jax answered it. "What's up, kid?"

"I know who he is."

Jax shot up. He kissed his sister's forehead and headed for the house. Then his car. "Who?" He closed the patio door and strode through the house.

Maizie made a slight moan sound through the phone.

"Whatever it is, we're gonna handle it. Right?" He climbed into the driver's seat. "Now tell me who he is." He squeezed his fingers into a fist on his knee.

"He was in Vegas." She paused, as though she needed to in order to continue. "With that mystery solving group. Intellectus."

"In the old church," Jax said. "That they turned into a kind of library?"

"Yes," Maizie said, her voice now connected to the car speakers. "His name is Stan Tilley. He was in Vietnam. At one point he was in the same team in the Marine Corps as Malcom Banbury."

"They knew each other?" He had an old friend who worked in military intelligence, who might be able to pull up old records. Find out if the relationship was friendly, or full of animosity.

"After the Marines, Tilley dropped off the map. Rumors in an autobiography on a senator that's been extensively pirated on the internet claims they were part of a secret group that let the government pump them with drugs. They were sent out on missions during the Cold War, and unofficially credited with a few dozen high-profile assassinations."

"So he's a killer." And yet, he hadn't killed Kenna.

He'd been taking pictures of her for the real killer. Which made Tilley the accomplice. Maybe even the mentor.

"And he can tell us where the Walker is."

Chapter Twelve

Kenna shut off her car. "One second." She pulled the earbuds from their case and stuck them in both ears, leaving the sound low and ambient so she didn't miss anything.

It wasn't worth the risk for someone to come up behind her and catch her unawares.

She didn't get out of the car, but closed her eyes for a minute. "Can you hear me?"

"I can," Maizie said. "And this might be crazy, but is it at all possible that Marion Wells is the killer Forrest is writing her book about?"

"You tell me." Kenna's head still pounded from getting knocked out. This had been a long day, to say the least, but she wanted to find Stan Tilley, which was why she'd driven all over town after Maizie called to tell her why that witness sketch looked familiar.

All she remembered about him was an older man, heavy-set, asleep in a tall-backed chair. In a church that had been converted to a sort of library and meeting house, for the mystery solving group Intellectus. The fact he'd known her father was a new piece of information.

Of course, he did.

Sometimes it seemed like nearly everyone had known him. Or read one of his overly sensational novels, or watched a movie based on one. It was a wonder she ever met anyone who didn't know who she was, as his daughter or in her own right. But when she did—like with Marion, who must live with her head in the sand—she preferred to remain anonymous. Shame about the part where Marion was a stone-cold killer with no conscience.

"I can't believe she actually had her husband's head under her bed." Kenna shook her head, not quite able to grasp the fact there had been yet more to this case than she realized.

"You're drifting, I think. Don't you need to sleep?"

"This is the last motel," Kenna said. "I'll just go in, flash his picture, and then head home. How have you been sleeping?"

"I usually have music playing all night, and I leave the lamp on. Sometimes I wake up and think I'm back..." Maizie's voice trailed off. "Then I see where I am."

"That's good." Kenna had done something similar for a while. Then again, the light had been on this morning when she woke up, so maybe she still did it. "So what have you got on the case file number Pastor Bruce gave me, the police ID'ing the head, the witness sketch, or anything else?"

Maizie sighed. "I'm looking. And Jax hasn't heard back from his boss yet about his request."

"It's a Sunday."

If she could find Stan Tilley and get him in custody, Jax wouldn't have to come to Wisconsin. She could ask Stan all the questions Jax wanted answers to, and he could at the most just maybe come here and transport Stan back to California. Then again, there were plenty of people who could do that.

He didn't need to put himself in the line of fire.

She wanted to call his boss and feel the guy out. See if ASAC Clarke was leaning toward Jax staying in California, waiting for the Walker to make his move, or if he was amenable to Jax following up on the Stan Tilley lead and coming out here.

She wanted to see him.

An image flashed in her mind, again. Jax hanging from a hook, chained by his wrists so that his body hung limp. Beaten.

Kenna pushed the car door open and got hit in the face with a blast of cold wind that stole her breath and pricked tears in her eyes. The cold was the only reason for the moisture, clearly. Not the lamp being on and the ready images in her mind of the man she cared about nearly dead.

They'd survived Mexico.

Maizie said, "Your car locks didn't beep," so Kenna went back, grabbed her keys, and locked up the car before she walked to the motel's main office. "Are you okay?" the teen asked.

"Yep."

Maizie went silent.

"I'm okay," Kenna said. Just as long as Jax stayed safe then things were fine. There was a K-9 handler here whose life had changed. There was a husband dead, and multiple children tormented for years before being buried in a clearing.

Kenna needed to focus on the high-stakes things. Whatever was going on in her head, or with this squeeze in her chest, she could figure it out. *You can help with that, right? Get my head on straight.* Except for the fact that facing it meant facing herself. That was the hardest part. She knew her tendency was to bury herself in work. The cliché was true, as much as she didn't like it.

She wanted to spend time with her friends, but she didn't want to *need* to spend time with them.

Which was going to make this relationship between her and Jax interesting. Hopefully not harder than it needed to be since they both had enough going on with work.

She entered the main office, pushing aside those thoughts as she stepped out of the cold. Behind the desk, a woman in her midtwenties pushed glasses up her nose. Kenna peeled off her hat and unzipped her coat because the heat in here was cranked to the midseventies.

"Help you?" The woman had a dark tan, and blank eyes.

"I hope so." Kenna pulled a twenty from her pocket and showed it to the woman, along with her phone. Not the screen showing the call was still connected to Maizie, but the photo of Stan Tilley they'd found. Which Maizie had run through a program to artificially age him to the gray he had now. "I just need to know if you've seen this man around, or if you're even renting a room to him?"

The woman reached out and grabbed the twenty.

Kenna nodded toward the phone. "So, have you seen him?"

"I'm not sure I can remember clearly enough if I've seen that guy."

She was fishing for more money. "You copy guest driver's licenses, right?" Hopefully, they did and weren't the kind of establishment that didn't care who a person was if they paid cash. But given this employee and her attempt at extorting more money from Kenna, this could go either way.

"My boss requires ID with every form of payment. Card or cash." She made a face. "Or I get fired."

Which meant that if Stan Tilley was staying here, his current ID would be in their files. "I need to know if his picture is one of them." And Kenna would pay for the information, but this twentysomething didn't get to know the exact amount up front. "He's bad news, and I need to find him before he hurts anyone else."

"I'm..." The other woman hesitated. "I'm not really supposed to show anyone who comes in the business files or give out people's personal information."

"Want me to come back with the cops and a court order?"

She shifted in her seat.

Kenna leaned against the counter. "I need to know if he's here." She reached in her pocket and flashed two twenties. "Can you check?"

"If you make it worth my while to risk my job breaking the rules."

Now they were speaking truthfully. "See if his ID is in there. I'll pay you for a copy and his room number." Kenna held the money in view and waited.

The receptionist looked through the file cabinet drawer. "Huh." She stiffened. "Room thirteen." Then drew out a paper file.

Kenna handed over the money, then snapped a photo of Stan Tilley's ID with her phone.

In her earbuds, Maizie said, "Got it." Then, "Hello, Marcus Alberton from Minnesota."

Kenna closed the file and handed it back to the girl. "Any idea if he's here now?"

"None of my business when the guests come and go. I don't want to know."

She stepped back outside.

"Are you going to knock," Maizie said, "or just sit in the parking lot and wait for him to come out, or go in?"

"I've got a better idea." Kenna turned on her car so it would heat up and took off her gloves. She texted Kobrinsky with the information so he could pass it on to Sheriff Gingrich, as though from an informant or as an anonymous tip.

All she needed to do was wait until someone from the sheriff's department showed up.

Maizie said, "I have an answer for you about Marion and the killer Forrest is looking at."

"Yeah?" Kenna said.

"The files Forrest collected that she sent to me are all bodies that washed up on the shore of Lake Michigan. The theory was that the killer took them, went out on a boat, and killed them on the water. Then dumped their bodies in the lake. But some washed up—whether intentionally or accidentally."

Kenna had a number of theories about that.

"But Marion has never done anything like that. She has no access to a boat that I can see, and there's no indication she ever has. Plus, the victims Forrest's killer took were never reported missing. No one ever noticed they were gone."

Which, in a way, might be more tragic, except that Marion's victims had been innocent children.

Kenna said, "What about the file number Pastor Bruce gave me?"

"Hopefully, Kobrinksy will send it tomorrow even if he's out sick for a few days. But you could remind him he said he would get it to you."

"I'll go talk to the pastor as well, see if he's willing to tell me anything." Tomorrow. Not tonight. The way her head pounded, she really did need a solid night of sleep. Hopefully, that would come knowing Stan Tilley was in custody.

"Marion's victims were spread out because the media ran each one and people were in an uproar."

"But no one ever put it together that they went to the same school." Kenna paused. "Because there only is one elementary in this area."

"One of the kids was homeschooled, right? What's her name..." Maizie's voice trailed off.

"Rebekah Merrington," Kenna finished.

She needed to pay the mom a visit as well. Take her up on the offer of seeing pictures and talking about her daughter. Again, hopefully after Stan was in custody.

She didn't want to bring danger to innocent people. Especially ones who had suffered enough.

Was that what she was doing with Jax? Following the same line of thinking that kept her apart from people for fear that her decision to go hard after evil and injustice would hurt others?

It sounded noble, and it was a good thing with innocent people. But with Jax? He knew what he was getting into.

"I have to make a call," Kenna said.

"He's on his way home," Maizie said. "He stopped by the grocery store on the way from his sister's house to his."

"Did you put a GPS tracker on my boyfriend?" Kenna chuckled.

"I just have movement alerts on his phone, that's all. He added me to his family on this app that lets you see where everyone is. I put you on there as well."

So if Kenna accessed the app, she could see where Jax was whenever she wanted? That might be *just a tad* stalkerish. But she wanted to, even if all she would see was a little icon of him. Did the sense of connection from knowing his whereabouts help him feel closer to her?

"Bye, Maze."

"Dispatch just sent the deputy over to your location."

"Thanks." Kenna hung up and dialed Jax.

When he picked up, he said, "Is this you, or a sheriff's deputy again?"

She smiled to herself. "It's me."

"How is your head?"

She filled him in on that and everything else, up to why she hadn't pulled out of this parking lot.

"You found him?"

"I hope so. There's a deputy on the way."

"I'll have to push the paperwork through so they know he's a federal suspect, wanted for questioning. Otherwise, they might not hold him."

Tilley had assaulted Kenna, but he could simply be charged and released pending a court date. She would only press charges this time for the sake of the FBI needing him in custody. Normally, she wouldn't have bothered about being tackled or having a stalker. But Stan was a means to an end.

Kenna said, "You can probably get the address of the motel where he's staying from the app you have where you can see my location."

Jax said nothing for a second. "Are you mad?"

"I want to know what it's called so I can get it. Although, it seems to already be installed on my phone without my knowledge."

"Maizie wanted to know where you were," he explained, "and it was easier than putting a separate tracker on you."

Kenna rolled her eyes. "Maybe I want to see where *you* are."

"You can. If you show up in person and visit me, you'll see exactly where I am."

"I'm on a case."

"Funny. Me, too."

"It's a Sunday. You should go home and rest." Kenna shifted in her seat, which was just starting to heat up.

"I could say the same thing about you," Jax said. "And tidy up the RV, because I might be there in a couple of days."

Kenna chuckled. "Who says I'll invite you in? You can stay with Kobrinsky."

Jax laughed. "Wanna go out for dinner while I'm there?"

He really thought his boss would approve of a trip to Wisconsin to secure Stan Tilley in custody, with the hopes of flipping him into revealing the Walker's whereabouts? "There's a grill I've been to a couple of times we could go to."

"Let's make it a date."

She wasn't sure what sounded scarier—Jax being up here, putting his life at risk, or sitting across a table from each other and trying to think of something to say that wasn't about work.

He chuckled. "You're scared of me."

"As if I'm going to give you the satisfaction of admitting that." It was more complicated, but it also wasn't.

"Don't worry so much. God knows what He's doing."

Kenna stared through the windshield at the motel, and the dark room where Stan Tilley had paid for a room. He was right, but letting go and allowing God to be in control was another one of those complicated/not complicated things. "I had questions about the sermon from this morning, but that was before I got knocked unconscious, so I'll have to save those for later."

"Paste your notes into an email and send it over. I'll look."

"Thanks." She didn't get a chance to say anything else to

break up their comfortable silence because a marked police car bumped up the drive into the parking lot. "Cops are here."

The deputy climbed out.

"They sent Deputy Rayland," Kenna said. "The kid barely needs to shave."

"I'm not sure it would be legal for him to be a cop…"

"You know what I mean." She felt her lips curl up. "He reminds me way too much of that cop in Hatchet. The one who overdosed."

"You've met a disproportionate number of police officers who have lost their lives."

"It's the life I chose."

He made a noise that sounded like disagreement. "I'm not sure that's entirely true. You don't control attacks, threats, or the actions of the bad guys you're chasing."

Kenna knew that was true—to an extent. If she didn't show up places and stir the proverbial pot, things wouldn't get better. People would still be victimized. But things also wouldn't get worse first. "I should go help him, just in case there's an ambush or some kind of altercation."

"I'll stay on. Put your earbuds in."

"I didn't take them out." Kenna pocketed her phone and keys, then pulled on her gloves. She had a weapon on her, but winter clothing made easy reach not so easy. "Rayland!" She jogged over, avoiding the patches of ice.

"Hey." He lifted his chin. "Thirteen?"

"That's right."

They squared up on the door, avoiding getting shot through it if whoever was inside opened fire. If there even was anyone inside.

Rayland pounded his fist on the door. "Sheriff's department! Open up!"

Chapter Thirteen

The door swung inward.

Kenna held out a hand, stopping Rayland from entering. "How about I go first, and you back me up?"

He swung around to her, gearing up to argue.

"Because if the department loses another deputy to injury, that's a problem. They need you healthy and working. That makes you more valuable than me right now." She waited for his expression to shift with understanding and then turned to the door. She didn't go inside, but instead looked all around the frame of the door.

Just in case.

"I'm surprised it was unlocked," she said. "About as much as I'm surprised it didn't explode in our faces when you knocked."

"Then why'd you let me knock, what with me being so valuable and all?" There was a note of humor in his tone.

"Rescuer safety first."

He snorted. So did Jax, through her earbuds.

Kenna stepped in. The room was somewhat cramped and

smelled faintly of cigarettes, though it had probably been years since anyone was allowed to smoke in here.

Stan Tilley had a military-style duffel bag on the floor at the end of the bed. A plastic sided crate the size of a long rifle. Another smaller plastic crate on a chair.

Newspaper on the nightstand—actually more than one. She counted three, one local and one from Chicago plus a national publication. Who read the newspaper these days? Though, she didn't have an online subscription to anything either.

Rayland searched the bathroom. She heard the shower curtain swipe back and held her breath for a second. He didn't indicate anything untoward in there.

Kenna looked in the nightstand drawers before moving to the bed, but Stan Tilley had nothing stashed under the pillow or the mattress.

Quietly, so Rayland might not hear, she said, "Could you hear him?"

"Enough," Jax said. "I can't now, though. He's not by you?"

"No."

"Now I know why Maizie has you take photos so she can see them right away. I need you to describe the whole scene to me." Jax sounded frustrated, and she didn't blame him.

It was late, Kenna was dragging, and her head hadn't quit pounding. She let out a sigh he would hear over the phone line.

"Fine. Get it done fast, and get home so you can sleep."

She smiled to herself and flipped the latches on the small case. "Whoa." Before Jax could ask—and since Rayland poked his head out of the bathroom—she said, "At least two handguns. Pistols. He's got a revolver. Extra magazines. Extra bullets for all of them. Three tactical knives and a cutout in the foam for who-knows-what." She paused. "I'm not sure I want to ask, but it would fit a grenade."

Jax said, "Fits, since he's a pro."

Rayland wandered over to look. "I'll log it all and get it back to the station."

She opened the long flat case, part of her hoping it was an electric guitar, but no luck on that. "Sniper rifle." And a nice one. "This guy makes serious money. His gear is top-notch."

"That doesn't bode well."

"But he's taking photos of me? He should've just squeezed off a shot and put a bullet between my eyes. Game over."

Rayland turned around, his face pale. "What? This is the guy who tackled you, right? The old man?"

Kenna straightened. "He's here working for a serial killer. Taking photos of me, so they can try and draw me into coming after *El Caminante*. But why do that if they can just eliminate the problem?"

"Because you're not a problem they need to get rid of."

She frowned at Jax's statement while Rayland pulled out his phone and called the sheriff. Then wandered to the bath-room. "I don't like games."

"Yeah, no kidding."

"Why doesn't he just come here and face me himself?"

Jax said, "And we've arrived at the point the Walker and I agree on."

"That he and I should have a showdown?"

"We both want you to come to San Diego so we can see you." Before she could figure out what to say in response, he continued, "Just for different reasons."

"Sorry." She didn't like that he felt even a slight note of kindred spirits with a killer.

"I put the request in to come to Wisconsin and detain Stan Tilley to bring him back to California."

Not if I find him first. "I have some questions for him myself." Kenna stepped out of the bathroom, but Rayland probably thought she'd been talking to herself. Or praying. But she didn't want to lie and pretend she was more spiritual than she actually was. That wouldn't be good.

"I'd offer to interrogate him together, but..."

"Yeah." Kenna continued wandering around the room, wishing she could haul drawers open and shove stuff aside in a hurry. If Stan Tilley had been in here, they could have arrested him already. She could've escorted him back to California—or to the closest FBI office so he could be extradited between states. But he was still out there.

And from the look of this room, highly dangerous.

"We have to assume he's stocked up with weapons," she added. "Wherever he is."

"So the BOLO says *armed and dangerous*," Rayland said. "That's what I told the dispatcher to report. The night shift deputy is headed here to help out and she's passing the BOLO to the state police."

Her hands might be tied while the police did their thing, but she would still be actively looking for leads. "The sooner we catch this guy, the better."

"Almost sounds like you don't want me to come there," Jax said.

Kenna lifted her brows to Rayland. "Given all this gear, he's highly trained. Someone could get seriously hurt—or a lot of people."

Jax stayed quiet.

Rayland set the duffel bag on the bed. "At least there's not a head under the bed."

"Did you see it?" Kenna asked. She had caught a tone when he mentioned it, and knew he'd taken the suitcase to the coroner. "I don't blame you for not wanting to find another one." She could still remember her first dead body.

How green was this deputy? Even though he was on the younger side, he seemed to know what he was doing. There was a logical progression to the way he searched the room. Like now, taking out items one by one. Laying them on the bed. Taking photos.

Rayland said, "I didn't lose my lunch, if that's what you're asking. The coroner?" He shook his head. "Ran to the trash can and threw up after she unwrapped it. I had to stop the head from rolling across the table."

Kenna caught the flash of amusement on his face, or satisfaction that he hadn't been the one to hurl. "I managed to hold it back. My first dead body. I swallowed hard, and the agent with me gave me a mint."

"Kobrinsky said it's a rite of passage to face it."

"He's not wrong." She just didn't agree with all of his opinions—or methods. "Did the coroner ID the head officially?"

"She wanted to know where the body was," Rayland said. "Like I was hiding it in my car, or something. Maybe it's buried in the field with the kids that—" He cleared his throat.

"How's the progress going on that?" Kenna had been out of the loop since the head. They'd identified the man following her, but that didn't solve the open cases the sheriff had now.

"It'll take a few days. State police is sending up crime scene people to collect evidence and unearth the bodies. Out of our hands."

"It's rough work, but it's what they do."

Jax muttered in her ears, "Should be a federal case."

She'd have agreed. Back when she was an agent herself. However, now that she had a more *freelance* existence, she could honestly say that the local professionals could handle it. Just because it was a high-profile case didn't meant it couldn't be solved by this sheriff's department and the state police.

The feds didn't want to do the grunt work when the suspect was already in custody.

"Tell me," Rayland said, "how'd you know it was Marion Wells?"

"Instinct." She wasn't sure she could chalk it up to anything but that. "I've solved a lot of murder cases, and worked a lot of investigations where someone went missing. I looked where the sheriff didn't, because I had the luxury of following theories without the pressure of time or it being fresh in the news. I could work leads that went nowhere because I had the time to spend chasing them even if it was just to rule it out."

"Huh." Rayland looked over, holding his phone out to take a photo of a plain gray T-shirt. "I thought you were gonna point out what he missed."

"Everyone missed a lot. That's how crimes continue for years, longer than anyone can stand allowing them to continue. But wishing you have a suspect doesn't make one magically appear. You have to knock on doors. Interview suspects. Or pore over every word of the case file that's already been put together." Kenna shrugged. "That means you all did the hard work. I just did the reading homework."

He smirked. "Right. And as soon as you figured it out, you called the sheriff so he could get a search warrant?"

Kenna smiled. "Where would be the fun in that?"

"Shame. I'd have liked to see you confront Marion with the truth."

"I'm just glad I found that girl alive." Even if Rebekah's father wasn't happy with how long it had taken. "At least one was saved."

Kenna wandered to the window and looked out. They didn't need Stan Tilley showing up before the other deputy. What they needed was a taskforce here to find the guy and hunt him down. Not just Jax with no backup except her. She'd be more worried about protecting him, and he would be more worried about protecting her by putting his own life on the line to draw out Stan.

Where are you, Stan?

She tapped her fingers on the side of her leg and watched the parking lot. The odd car passed on the street, then one going the other way. "We need to find out if he gave the manager here his license plate number, or any details on what car he's driving."

Rayland stowed his phone. "I can go ask."

"Hang here until the other deputy shows up. Otherwise, you're leaving the scene unsecured."

"But *you're* here."

"And I'm not a deputy." Even if the sheriff had threatened her with that for his escort detail.

Been there, done that. She had no interest in taking on a badge again, but if it gave her credence when she needed it then fair enough. Sheriff's departments had a lot more leeway with that stuff. She could be deputized for a short time—which had happened in a town a few months ago. Maybe nearly a year. It felt like a lifetime since she had met a man who had been like a brother to her father. A man with an odd file in his safe.

She needed enough downtime to follow that lead even if it went nowhere.

A car eased into the parking lot. Tinted windows, a dark-gray compact. It couldn't be going more than fifteen miles an hour.

Instinct prickled the skin on the back of Kenna's neck. She drew her weapon, just in case.

The car turned onto the lane right in front of them.

"Head's up."

"What is it?" Rayland said. "The deputy?"

"No, and it might be Tilley." She moved to the doorframe and peered out, keeping her body behind cover. What was...

The driver's side window rolled down. A gun barrel rested on the frame, pointed at them.

"Get down!" Kenna turned, already lowering to one knee. She grabbed Rayland's arm and pulled him to the floor beside her.

Glass shattered with the first grouping of shots and sprayed across the room.

Rayland grunted.

"Kenna, you okay?" Jax. That was Jax. "I'll call it in."

All she could do was hunker down on the floor and remember to breathe as pain pounded in her head with every heartbeat.

Gunshots smacked the wall, like fireworks exploding one after each other. A split second between each.

A line of bullet holes appeared on the back wall. Steady aim. A professional.

"Stay down!" she yelled.

Rayland probably thought she was crazy for thinking he might consider getting up. He probably had no intention of doing so, but there was a slim chance he went for a look. If it saved his life, she would keep reminding him to stay down until the—

Everything went silent.

The kind of silence that seemed almost thick. Or as if her ears had quit working.

Dust hung in the air.

She heard the rev of an engine and rolled to look out the door without getting up. The dark compact sped past, between the deputy's car and the one parked beside it.

Kenna clambered to her feet and stumbled. Her shoulder hit the doorframe, and she nearly lost her grip on her weapon. A sheriff's department vehicle on the street flipped its lights on and accelerated down the street. "Your backup is chasing Tilley." She turned to Rayland, now standing. Cold washed over her and she shivered.

"You good?" Rayland brushed off his hair.

Kenna tried to nod.

"I'll tell him to be careful." He stepped outside, leaving her alone in the destroyed room. She heard him call in shots fired, so the deputy would know this wasn't just about a speeding car. Stan Tilley was armed and dangerous and should be approached with extreme caution.

Kenna's left earbud started to fall out. "Jax, can you hear me?" She pushed it back in, having to cough against the cloud of dust created by all those shots on the wall. Through the window, which he'd shattered. In the door. All of it right at the level where her head had been moments before. If she hadn't seen it coming, someone could've died.

Thank You, Lord.

"Copy that. I'll talk to my ASAC," Jax said in her ears. "Get approval to come to Wisconsin. This guy needs to be arrested."

She stared at the room. If Jax came here, then there would be another person for her to safeguard. It had ended well this time, but next? Who knew what might happen.

He could end up practically dead, hanging from a hook again.

She shivered. "Stay in California. I'll find him."

"By yourself?" His low voice rumbled through her. "This isn't your case. It's mine, and I need to work it."

"No." She couldn't go through that again. Not long ago, he'd been in the hospital. Since she'd faced down a dangerous man in his room while he wasn't able to walk. "You'll get hurt again."

She knew it wasn't rational. Just the fear talking.

She expected him to argue, but the line just went dead.

Chapter Fourteen

Kenna gasped awake, tangled in sheets, and sweat. She kicked the blanket off and let the chill air wash over her. Not even a second later, she began to shiver. If she didn't get up, but stayed all day horizontal like this, maybe her head wouldn't hurt at all. She could lie here and pretend it hadn't slammed into the ground when she fell yesterday.

Maybe today wouldn't feel like three days in one.

She rolled over and reached for her phone. The new RV had become familiar, but she didn't want to get to the point where she considered it home. Not if it ended up ruined like the others. She'd been shot in her Class C. And the van she had after that was set on fire. Then there was a classic car, and motel rooms. The car drew too much attention.

Maybe Stan Tilley wouldn't find her in Forrest's garage.

Then again, if she thought he didn't know where she lived, she was probably kidding herself at best. Fear would turn her into an agoraphobic person if she allowed it. Even if that didn't sound like a bad existence since her home had wheels. She could drive wherever she wanted. See the country—or even other countries—outside her windows. Order what she needed delivered to her door. Stay where she wanted. Leave when she was ready.

RVing wouldn't make her feel trapped like her dream had.

Caught. Alone. Jax dead. Maizie gone. Her family destroyed.

Alone was easier. As much as it had been its own kind of hell at times, she'd grown to appreciate the simplicity. Or it was the fact she could control pretty much everything around her when she eliminated the variables.

And then I gave that up to You.

Which meant she needed to pray through the fear and figure out a way to let people into the danger of her world without being terrified by it.

She typed out a couple of texts to Jax, who was probably at his desk already. None of them seemed right, so she left a draft in her messages and got up instead.

Coffee. The morning routine. Some stretches since her neck and shoulders felt like concrete. It made her think of Jax to go through the regular routine. Something he might want to know.

She didn't send that either.

Nothing she could think of didn't sound glib, or like she wasn't dismissing the issue. She'd told him not to come and the call had ended abruptly. Maybe they'd gotten cut off last night rather than him hanging up on her. She figured not, but in this morning quiet where the day hadn't yet been interrupted with reality, she could believe still.

She sat at the table and sipped her coffee. Halfway down cup two, she called Maizie's number. The teen didn't pick up, so hopefully she was sleeping or busy talking with the couple she lived with. Living her life where she was safe, and healing.

She then called the sheriff's department.

"Kobrinsky."

She stared into the empty cup, feeling the pull of a frown. "I thought you weren't working for at least a couple of days." Why was he at work the day after he'd hurt himself?

"Sheriff is in court this morning," the deputy said. "So I came in to cover the office."

He sounded grumpy, which made her smile. "How's your leg?"

"How's your head?"

So he was going to be like that? "What about the K-9 handler?"

"Her boyfriend said she should be released in a couple of days."

"That's great."

Kobrinsky sighed. "So what fresh trouble are you going to cause today?"

She figured that meant she should tell him why she'd called. "I was just looking for an update on the hunt for Stan Tilley." The other deputy had followed him last night, but quickly lost the speedy driver who turned out to be their shooter. She'd seen the deputy when he showed up at the motel to tell them that Stan had gotten away. It only got worse when they explained the background of how he wasn't just a speeding ticket waiting to happen.

"Nada since last night," Kobrinsky said. "And considering the sheriff wants an update when he gets out of court for lunch, you can bet I've got everyone out looking. And the state police."

"Good."

"Wanna help out?"

She figured it would be more beneficial for her to get out on foot than in a car. "Moving aimlessly, hoping to see him?

No, thanks." She needed a more strategic plan than that or she would just end up frustrated if Stan didn't approach her.

Did she want to be bait?

"State police found the gray compact you described," Kobrinsky said. "Abandoned on the side of a street about five miles from the motel."

"So looking for the car is a dead lead."

"And if he's changed his appearance," Kobrinsky pointed out, "we won't spot him easily."

Kenna poured more coffee. "Nothing in the motel room suggested he does that regularly."

Which meant if she saw him, she would recognize him. Especially now she knew it was Stan following her for the Walker. Considering his motel room had been burned, he would either lay low now or he would come after her. Hit back.

Enact the plan.

"Is Marion Wells still in holding?" Kenna wanted to know if she'd said anything about her deceased husband. She should also go talk to Bruce, the pastor, about the note he'd written and left on Forrest's door. Despite the fact she had no leads on Stan, she didn't have nothing to do.

"The sheriff didn't want her transferred to the jail just yet. We might have questions."

"And the file you were going to send me?" Bruce had given her that number. Along with his phone number.

"Right," Kobrinsky said. "I've got to go see the coroner in a while about ID'ing that head. How about you come over and babysit the office. I'll send it when I get back."

So he was going to manipulate her into helping out. At least he was upfront about it. "Can I talk to Marion while I'm there?"

He chuckled. "You drive a hard bargain."

"You could just let me go talk to the coroner. Then you don't have to get coverage."

"I'm going."

"I heard she puked when she unwrapped the head," Kenna said. "I'm guessing talking about the juiciness isn't going to make her wanna say yes when you ask her out."

"But I'm gonna walk in there with the crutches, all injured. She'll have to help me with the door, and she'll feel all sorry for me. And *then* she'll say yes."

Kenna rolled her eyes, grinning. She wasn't going to let him know she thought that might work. "Got it all figured out, don't you?"

He chuckled again. "Worth a try."

"All just to find out if the head belongs to Mr. Wells?"

"Might not be him. Though, I have no idea if he was the first victim, or if the first kidnapped girl might've been the first life Marion took. He might've been dead for longer than kids have been going missing, and the bag just preserved the head really well."

Kenna knew who the first girl was—and she'd seen in the TV footage, and those impassioned pleas for her safe return how they'd felt about losing her. The police had the timeline, and Meri Santiago was the first taken, but she had yet to be identified. And she wasn't from the local area, while the rest of the victims had been.

"What do you know of Mr. Wells?" Kenna asked. After all, the victim could have been another random male, and the husband was alive and well somewhere. Perhaps even with pertinent information on Marion.

"He disappeared years ago," Kobrinsky replied. "I had to hit the paper archives to pull the files from the last time a car was dispatched to the address. The sheriff remembered him, and the paperwork correlates what he said. Marion's husband was a mean drunk, but she never wanted to press charges."

"Question is, did she kill him, or did she have someone else do it?" The possibilities made her wonder if there was a connection between Stan Tilley and this community that went back further than Kenna's arrival here. "Maybe I'll ask her."

"You think there's an accomplice...with the girls?" Kobrinsky asked.

"That's a good question. But there was nothing in the investigation I came up with that suggested she had any relationships, or anyone else who came and went at the house. No family. Barely any friends outside work." And the book club. "No hobbies, groups, or clubs she was part of. She didn't eat out much, she didn't go to church. She got groceries once a week, and she went to the library."

The fact Marion Wells had routinely checked out children's books had been a clue Kenna couldn't ignore. They might have been for her to read, since she was a school librarian, but they also might've been for the children she kept locked up behind her closet.

"What makes a woman with a quiet life do something like this?" Kobrinsky wondered aloud.

"Let me in to ask her," Kenna replied. "I'll find out."

"Fine. Be here in an hour."

He hung up, and it didn't feel like it had when she got cut off with Jax.

Could I have just one quiet day? Do You take requests like that?

She wasn't sure how far God would go to honor a request for a peaceful few hours. In the middle of a case, there were occasionally calmer days or times when things seemed to lull. Normally it didn't bode anything good.

Kenna took a shower and put on insulated pants and a T-shirt. Often she didn't even look at the scars on her arms, but today she paused. Ran her fingers over them. When her mind wanted to twist what had happened in her nightmares, warping her memories, the scars were a reminder of what had happened.

The black-and-white of what she had lost, the fact she'd survived while so many things were gone. Including the life she'd been looking forward to living. When her mind wanted to spin the tale and distort the past, this was a kind of Scripture. Irrefutable truth.

Kenna trailed through the house to Forrest's office. She wasn't there, and Kenna needed to get to the sheriff's station to cover for Kobrinsky. She did feel a little responsible for his injury, and the fact the department was so busy right now. She had the training to cover for them—as long as no one handed her badge. Unless it was life or death she didn't want the responsibility.

"Forrest!" She called out a couple more times, but her landlady wasn't home apparently.

Given someone wanted to stir up trouble surrounding Forrest's family's deaths, Kenna prayed for her that she wasn't trying to take it upon herself to figure things out. As soon as she could, Kenna was going to hit up the pastor and get him to admit what was going on.

Why Bruce had been the one to bring this to Forrest's attention—and Kenna's by default, or by intention—she didn't know. As soon as she got to a department computer she would look up the case file herself and get some answers.

Kenna locked up and drove to the sheriff's office.

Snow was starting to fall, and if the temperatures were any warmer, the forecast would call for drizzling rain. She stopped behind a school bus of kids who had to be going on a field trip. Then signed in at the department.

The fiftysomething bleached blonde receptionist looked down her too-big nose, scowling in a way that let Kenna know she had lipstick on her teeth. She was professionally put together otherwise, with her hair curled and wearing a pair of slacks and a blouse. Reading glasses hung from a string around her neck.

"Is the sheriff in?" Kenna asked.

The scowl didn't go anywhere. "No, ma'am. He's in court all day, probably won't be back until tomorrow."

"Thanks." She was about to ask where to find Kobrinsky when he swung into view on his crutches, behind the desk, down the side hall.

He spotted her. "This way, Banbury. Paulette, did the coroner call yet?"

"Just did, hon. She's ready for you."

"Kenna is in charge while I'm out." He turned away without seeing the look on Paulette's face.

"I guess I drew the short straw." Kenna tried to commiserate with a look.

A moment later, Paulette winked. "Seems like that's how it works with these guys."

"Doesn't matter where I go, the culture of a small-town sheriff's department isn't so different from the next one over."

Paulette's brows rose. "Maybe *I'll* run for sheriff."

"You absolutely should." Kenna smiled. "Give these guys a run for their money."

Paulette smiled back.

"They won't know what hit them," Kenna added.

Having Paulette as the sheriff could be a terrible eventuality that wouldn't do the county any favors. Alternatively, it could be the best thing that ever happened to the people who lived around here. Paulette could run on the ineptitude of the longstanding administration. Create a whole lot of division in town. Point out that having Kobrinksy in charge would be nothing but more of the same.

Paulette eyed her. "Unless *you're* planning on putting your name on the ballot?" Suspicion raced across her face like a mouse running across the room to hide.

"Don't worry. I'm not sure I qualify, even if I was a resident of the county." Kenna knocked on the counter. "But if you need any tips, hit me up."

Paulette said, "Coffee?"

"I would love some." Kenna trailed down the hall with a smile on her face. When she found Kobrinsky at his desk in the open bull pen area, he did a double take.

"What's up with you?" He chuckled. "Everything is nuts, there's a mountain of work, and you're smiling?"

Kenna tugged out a chair at an empty desk and sat. "It's a new day. Things are changing." The fear seemed smaller when she got to banter with acquaintances. When the people she cared about weren't in danger. When the cases she was working had leads, not just a bunch of evidence that made no sense. "Don't you have somewhere to be?"

He eyed her. "The case file is open on my computer. Don't go messing with my stuff."

Kenna raised both hands. "You're the boss."

"Are you sure you *don't* have a concussion?" Kobrinsky settled his crutches under his arms. "No more bodies. No incidents. No surprises. No traps. Two hours. That's all I ask. Got it?"

A distant buzz cut off her response.

Paulette said something Kenna couldn't make out, then a young woman—she couldn't be more than eighteen—raced down the hall in white sneakers. She wore an overcoat over her diner uniform, her hair pulled back into a ponytail. She looked scared out of her mind.

He stepped away from his office door. "What is it, Loretta?"

"The pastor. He had a seizure in the diner just now. Beryl called for an ambulance, but he's gone." Tears rolled down her face. "He died on the floor."

Chapter Fifteen

The faint sound of snoring wasn't Marion. Kenna passed her cell and peered in the one at the end, where she spotted a man on the cot fast asleep. His belly distended with each inhale, and the smell of each exhale permeated the air around him with a musty tang. Kenna's nose wrinkled.

"That's Lance. He's the town drunk," Marion said. "Been there since yesterday and probably won't wake up until tonight. Then it'll be time to go out and do it all again."

Kenna stood by the bars, about a foot back. She wanted to lean against the wall, but coming across as relaxed wouldn't do the conversation any favors. Not to mention the fact she wasn't interested in a rapport with Marion even if it might help.

Bruce was dead.

Pastor Bruce, who'd written that note and put it on Forrest's door. Who had information about her family's deaths, and had provided her with that case number—her next job. She'd wanted to go to the scene, but Kobrinsky called in relief for that. Kenna might have solved a lot of mysteries, but being here in this part of Wisconsin felt like being pulled in fifty different directions.

Where she was—and where she wanted to be.

Who she was with—and who she'd rather be with.

No. You'll get hurt again.

She needed to talk to Jax.

"Just gonna stand there and stare at me?" Marion said, her expression stone-cold.

Kenna shrugged. "Maybe you'll break and confess to something else."

The former school librarian sat straight on the cot in profile staring at the wall to Kenna's left. No wonder no one had suspected her. The woman could hide all the malice and evil under the surface, stuffed so far down no one ever found the truth in her. Like the girl she'd hidden in her closet—and all the ones before that.

"I've been looking into your background." Kenna softened her tone some. "I found the callouts. The times the neighbors had the police come. So they could check you were all right."

Marion huffed.

"Make sure he hadn't killed you." But she'd chosen to stay. And then he'd been gone, and Marion had kidnapped girls to use as housekeepers. "He tried...didn't he?"

"He sure was determined. I'll give him credit for that." Her expression remained impassive.

"Sorry." Kenna paused. "It must be painful for you to think about him. Since he caused you so much harm."

Again, Marion huffed.

"But you got out of that situation." Whatever had twisted her inside hadn't come from only domestic abuse. Marion had been predisposed, probably through many different experiences and perhaps mental health issues. A number of factors, not just one. Otherwise, psychopathy would be easier to spot.

Someone might have saved those girls' lives.

Marion's lips twitched. Who knows what she was thinking.

"We found his head," Kenna stated.

Marion smirked. "Served him right."

"Did you cut it off?"

She chuckled.

This woman was sick. The ways she must have traumatized those girls was unthinkable, even only considering the mental or emotional turmoil.

"Did you kill him?"

Marion let out a sigh of regret. "I should've. I wasn't strong enough to swing it."

"Who cut his head off?"

Marion said nothing.

"What do you lose if you tell me the truth? If you didn't do it, then you can't be charged for his murder." Just as an accessory. "This conversation isn't being recorded, and I could forget we ever had it."

"So it's just because you're nosy?"

"Who killed him, Marion?"

"I did." The woman glanced over, sneering, then got up and came over.

Kenna made sure not to back up even when Marion got close to the bars. It would look too much like a retreat.

"I'm the one who put the pills in his drink to knock him out."

And someone else had cut off his head? "Must've been nerve-wracking, wondering if he'd realize something was going on."

"He thought he was clever. But in the end, who was the clever one?" Evil shined through Marion's expression.

"Had to have been satisfying, stuffing him under your

bed. Keeping him close." Kenna let her lips curl slightly, as if she were smiling.

Marion chuckled a little.

Kenna needed to know if there was someone else in town —an accomplice, or a relative of Marion's—that she needed to be worried about. "Who cut his head off?"

Marion paused a split second. "J. Pierce." She tipped her head back and cackled with laughter, the only sound of humor she could make. A terrible, horrible noise.

The guy in the next cell woke up, sputtering, and fell to the floor by the sound of that thud.

Kenna moved to the side so she could make sure he hadn't hurt himself.

"What the heck is that?" He sat up, breathing hard. Eyes glassy.

"Don't worry about it," Kenna said. "Did you hurt yourself?"

He patted himself and shook his head. "I hafta pee."

"I'll give you some privacy." Kenna moved, and the guy disappeared behind a half wall.

Marion sneered in the man's direction.

If what she'd said was true—though Kenna didn't think the killer from Forrest's book was the one who'd cut off Mr. Wells' head—it changed things. It meant a connection between Marion's case and the rest of what might be going on in this county.

Like Pastor Bruce's death.

"J. Pierce?" Kenna lifted her brows. "You know who he is?"

"What do you care? It's not your case."

"It would make for a juicy story. Forrest's book would probably be a bestseller if she revealed his identity."

Marion snorted. "So you don't care for you. You just

wanna tell Forrest who it is." She shook her head. "Figures. You are a do-gooder after all."

As opposed to being as self-serving as Marion? "Come on, you've got to want to spill the secret. Maybe you could even make a deal with the district attorney. Get a lighter sentence, or some other concessions, and in return you tell them who J. Pierce is."

Now Kenna knew why God had her in this office and not out working the crime scene. Even if she wanted to run out and go see what had happened to Bruce, there were cops working that. She had a lead on a connection to all of this—and maybe even whatever had happened to Bruce.

The waitress had said he collapsed at the diner.

So was it an accident, natural causes...or murder? Seemed entirely too coincidental for it to be an accident. She'd planned to speak to him. He knew something about murder written off as accidents. The guy was candidate number one to be silenced by a killer.

Forrest was on that list, too. Which meant Kenna needed to warn her—as soon as they ran into each other again, or Forrest replied to a text.

"I'll think about it." Marion went back to her cot. "And I'll be talking to my lawyer rather than you. Maybe *I'll* be the one that writes a bestseller."

Kenna said, "All the best with that."

She double-checked on the drunk, who had gone back to sleep, and went out to the main office. No one was back yet. That same restlessness permeated her, making her want to run. Get to work, pursuing a suspect. But with not much in the way of leads, she didn't have much to do but stay here. Look up that case.

Or deal with the real issue that was going on right now.

Kenna wandered to a corner of the office out of anyone's

earshot—which meant the receptionist Paulette. She pulled up her texts and took a deep breath, pushing it out slowly. She held down the button to record a voice message. "You were hanging from a hook. Just dangling there, covered in sweat and blood. I thought you were dead." She had to clear her throat but didn't let go of the button. "I thought I lost you before we ever started."

She let go of the button, sending the message, and had to sniff. Swallow against the lump in her throat.

She stowed her phone.

Relationships suck, You know?

She figured if there was anyone who understood what went on in her head, or how her feelings worked, it was God. *Things were easier when I was alone.* Not that they'd been better, but there was less to work through because there hadn't been anyone else to contend with.

But now that she had family and friends in her life, people invested in her who she cared about in return—and the whole other category that Jax fell into—things would get sticky. She'd have to contend with the fear that came up. With her need to be the one who went in, alone, to save the victim.

She'd done it with Forrest in Marion's house and found that girl, saved her life even. Forrest had backed her up. But Kenna had been full of herself and her own ability to solve a case. Today that felt a whole lot different. The Christian she was trying to be didn't need to be irritated because she had to babysit the office. Or that she had time to process what was in her heart and mind about Jax coming here.

She'd felt free to do what she wanted and go where she felt like going for years. She took cases she wanted to take and left the others. Flying under the radar, making the world better. All that.

This freedom she had now, in Christ, was a whole lot different.

Instead of being alone she had connection—something she'd never sought out or asked for. No wonder figuring it out was proving difficult. Or just uncomfortable.

Kenna slumped into a chair and used Kobrinsky's computer to look up the case number Bruce had given her. The case was old. Far older than Forrest's desire to write this particular book.

"What's that?"

Kenna started. She hadn't even heard Paulette come into the room. "Hey."

"Front desk is boring. Figured I'd see what you're up to." She settled on the corner of Kobrinsky's desk like someone hadn't asked her to check up on Kenna and what she was doing.

"It's case related." Whatever else she said would get back to the sheriff.

"Huh." Paulette slid her glasses onto her nose. She'd cleaned the lipstick off her teeth and had the scent of mint on her breath. "Tamarin... Oh, the coroner. That was years ago." She skimmed the screen alongside Kenna. "Yeah, their car accident."

"What do you know about what happened?"

"Pretty much that. It's been so long, but I could look up some news articles."

"That would be great, thanks." Kenna smiled. "The sheriff might need some context if this becomes relevant."

"Why would it?" Paulette lowered the glasses, frowning.

"You said this person was the coroner?" When she nodded, Kenna said, "And he died in a very similar way as Forrest Crosby's husband and son." She had only briefly skimmed the report, but caught enough of the details. "At a spot called Stevens Point."

"That's a town west of here."

"Okay, so it didn't happen locally." The report was from the state police and had no photos, just the written report. They hadn't done much as far as any evidence collection. "But did this Bill Tamarin guy live around here?"

"The Tamarins lived in town." Paulette's gaze distanced for a second. "Meadow Drive, I think. I used to be friends with their daughter. She moved away for college in St. Paul before the accident and never came back. There wasn't much point."

"Did Bill Tamarin have any connection to J. Pierce or the book Forrest is writing?" It was a hunch. A longshot at best. But she needed something that would help her figure out what was going on.

"Huh." She hopped off the desk. "I need to look something up. Come with me, though."

Because Kenna couldn't be alone? She wondered if Paulette had somehow listened to the conversation with Marion. The receptionist hadn't asked about it.

Paulette's fingers flew across the screen. "Yeah, here it is. It's old, but there's a true crime blog that links to the article." She turned her monitor so Kenna could see. "The coroner, Bill Tamarin, went public with his theory that J. Pierce was behind not just the bodies that had washed up on shore, but other kills also. Apparently, there were connections."

"When was it that he went public?"

"This was put up a couple of years before they were killed in that accident, so it's not like it's some kind of conspiracy." Paulette paused. "More like a tragedy if you ask me."

"Seems like there's a lot of that going around." When was Kobrinsky going to show back up and tell her what had happened with Pastor Bruce? "I know about the bodies that were found on the beach. The theory Forrest has in her notes is that J. Pierce, the killer, had a boat and would take victims out and kill them over a period of days."

Paulette's cheeks pinked. "That was what the media said. I have to admit, when I started working here, I looked up the case files with the state police system. The sheriff caught me, but we talked about it. I was new so he let it go, and I've never looked up a case. Just local media and news reports. Sometimes he has me draft a press release now or send out what he wrote."

"A lot of people get interested in true crime stuff," Kenna said. "But what were the other kills Tamarin referenced?" She motioned at Paulette's screen.

Paulette read down the screen. "I don't know that this makes much sense."

Kenna could have her send links, which she'd pass to Maizie to look into. Nothing else was coming together, and this could be the answer to all her questions.

"It looks like a hit-and-run. A drifter got killed by a guy in a truck who was driving drunk. One of them is a teacher who had a heart attack after school one day, and they didn't find her until the next morning." Paulette worked her mouth back and forth. "Why would he say a killer did that when they're tragedies and accidents?"

"That's a really good question."

One Kenna planned on finding the answer to.

Chapter Sixteen

Kenna's phone started to ring in her pocket. At the same time, the front door opened, and Kobrinsky hobbled in. She ignored the incoming call. "What happened?"

He looked tired, and definitely needed to go home to rest. "He's dead."

Okay, so Kobrinsky wasn't the biggest fan of Pastor Bruce. "I was looking for information I didn't already know."

Then she could get out of here. With him back, she was free to go. How the sheriff chose to relieve his people and get shifts covered wasn't her business, even if she wanted to tell this deputy to rest.

Kobrinsky glanced at Paulette. He didn't want to talk in front of her?

"She's good."

"I know." He shot them a look. "That's not it."

"Worried Paulette will run against you in the next election?" Kenna felt the older woman gently smack the outside of her arm. She just lifted her chin to the deputy. "How about we just worry about solving this case, not politics?"

Probably a pointless intention, but she chose to believe

that politics didn't enter into local law enforcement. At least some of the time.

"He's dead," Kobrinsky repeated. "What case is there to solve?"

She motioned for him to keep going.

"Pastor Bruce keeled over at the diner. His heart stopped. No injury, no assailant."

Paulette said, "Does he have any allergies?"

"She's got you solving crimes now?" Kobrinsky looked at Kenna. "Between you and the true crime so-called experts, my job is becoming more and more impossible. Everyone has an opinion. But this wasn't murder."

"You don't know that." Kenna shrugged. "He could have been poisoned."

"No one was in the kitchen who doesn't work there."

Kenna said, "Is the coroner doing an autopsy?"

He sighed. "The pathologist will run all the tests. The coroner will certify cause of death."

"I know how it works." At least if there was some kind of life-ending substance in his body that ended Bruce's life, the doctor would find it. "Question is, how it works in this county. Like if the medical examiner finds one thing, will the coroner on occasion be inclined to make a *political* ruling and sign off the death whatever way she chooses. Or however she's asked to by the person pressuring her." She remembered Kobrinsky had mentioned asking out the coroner but didn't bring that up now. Might not go down well.

"You mean like natural causes?" Kobrinsky made a face. "It wasn't murder. This isn't some kind of conspiracy. And I'd ask you not to go around town stirring up ideas of a conspiracy. Thank you."

Paulette said, "Right. After all, it was just a tragic accident."

Kenna glanced over, and the two of them shared a look. They'd been talking about incidents like that, ones Kenna needed Maizie to look into in case they were far more sinister than accidents. It might sound like a conspiracy. As in, how the previous coroner did when he claimed other "accidents" were in fact something quite different. Then he'd been killed in an "accident."

She'd barely scratched the surface and still had a lot more questions. She needed to know what he'd seen in the reports and the evidence that indicated as such. She would get the same treatment—unless Forrest put it all in her book.

Could be a great bestseller, turning perceived opinion on its head and proving what people believed wasn't true at all.

Kenna's name wouldn't need to be anywhere in it.

"What's going on?" Kobrinsky glanced between them.

Kenna pushed off the counter. "Nothing. I should go since you're back."

Paulette said, "The sheriff is on his way over from the courthouse."

Then it was *definitely* time for her to leave. "Thanks, Paulette. It was fun."

The receptionist blushed. "Anytime. Keep me posted on that thing."

"Right." Kenna pushed the front door open. "The thing."

She walked out, grinning. Let Kobrinsky think there had been some kind of noteworthy happening while he was out. In reality, she'd been given the runaround by Marion. Or so she would assume until she could prove otherwise. There was no concrete connection between Marion and J. Pierce, and as far as she knew, no one had even ID'd the legendary killer most folks considered to be dead.

Kenna needed to regroup and figure all this out. But first, she was going to check out Pastor Bruce's untimely demise and figure out if there was more to it than health issues.

She dragged out her phone and discovered the missed call had been from Forrest. Kenna called the other woman back while she walked to her car, constantly watching for Stan Tilley.

For a while there, she'd nearly forgotten all about him.

That would be nice.

"Hey."

"Hey, yourself," Kenna said. "How's things?"

"Casual. That's good." Forrest chuckled. "When you're really dying to know where I've been."

"Did I give you the third degree?" Kenna unlocked her car and checked the back seat before getting in the driver's seat. "Did I interrogate you?"

"I'll explain later where I was."

"I would come home now, but—"

"Pastor Bruce died in the diner, and since he left that note, it's suspicious, and you think the two are connected."

Kenna winced. "Yes."

"Catch me up when you get home."

"What's for dinner?"

"Nothing is defrosted, and I have three hours. Could be anything at this point."

Kenna grinned. She'd heard the amusement in Forrest's tone. "Whatever you're in the mood for is fine by me."

Forrest actually laughed. "Risky move, but we already know you have guts." She hung up, still laughing.

Kenna turned up the radio, singing along with the local contemporary Christian music station where she knew the words and humming along when she didn't. If Stan Tilley wanted to make a move again, that was on him. If the sheriff wanted her to do a job, that would come soon enough. Right now she had to work the scene in front of her and not worry about how things would turn out.

A block later she caught a tail.

Kenna didn't bother with her blinker and took a right turn. Not overly fast or at the last second, but close enough the person in the silver Mercedes behind her had to react quick to keep behind her.

The next stop light, she hung around an extra second after it turned green. The car pursuing her stopped behind her, and she saw who was in the front seat.

Kenna drove straight to the church after that, since it was closer than the diner. She parked out front, and when they pulled into the space beside her, she waited by her door. Hips against the car, arms folded. She checked her phone. No new calls or messages. Then sent a text to Maizie.

> I have things for you to do when you're free.

The teen didn't technically work for Kenna, except that she kind of did at the same time. Kenna just tried not to treat her friends like "staff" if she could help it. Maybe one day she would build a whole team. She might not want to be out on the road solving cases forever, and if she found good people, maybe she could have a base of operations and skilled people to do the leg work.

Is that Your idea? Because it never would've been mine.

The chill in the air made her nose cold, and clouds hung low and thick in the sky.

Theo climbed out of the driver's side, though she was pretty sure this was Alonzo's car.

"You're getting rusty."

Theo rounded the hood of the car. "That was fun."

"It's been a while?"

Alonzo just chuckled. "Not as long as you think."

The retirees were such an interesting pair. The only thing her brain could figure is that there was some connection that brought them together in a way they had to do life side by side for years in this frozen tundra. Which was Charlayne's words, not what Kenna felt about the Northern States.

She knew what she thought. Question was, whether she was correct about it.

Kenna said, "Why are you guys following me?" Hadn't she asked them to make sure Forrest was safe, or were they here with her because her friend had gone home?

"You're looking around the church, right?" Theo nodded toward the white clapboard building.

Alonzo said, "Figured we could help."

They cared, and they were nosy. She figured it was an even spread between those two things.

"Let's go." She pulled the front door of the church open, feeling the pull of a smile on her lips.

"Something funny?" Alonzo's dyed black brows rose.

"Nothing about this case."

They stepped into the entryway she'd heard someone call a "narthex" right as a lady walked down the hall in their direction. She had a knee-length corduroy skirt and a knitted sweater, tight curly hair, and glasses, along with sensible footwear.

"Hey, Becky." Theo eased over and gave her a side hug.

"Hi, Pops." Becky gave Alonzo a similar greeting.

Theo said, "Becky was in Betty's Sunday school class for years." He waved at her. "This is Kenna Banbury."

"You met with Pastor Bruce?" The edges of her eyes were puffy. She'd been crying, but not destroyed-life-is-over upset. More of a reserved grief.

"That's right." Kenna nodded. "Is it okay if we ask you

some questions, and maybe take a look around?" She wanted to ask if the police had been through here, or if they'd get to see the scene as is.

"I just got here a few minutes ago, so I need to make some calls. Find out who the elder board wants to pull in to lead the church now." She sniffed. "So I'll show you his office and leave you to it."

Kenna could find it herself but didn't mind being escorted.

Theo walked with Becky in front of them down the sanctuary center aisle, talking quietly. "Did you see Bruce yesterday, or hear from him this morning?"

"He eats breakfast at the diner on Mondays every week. He likes to talk to people in town on his day off, and I drop off his groceries after lunch." Becky wound her arm in Theo's, leaning on the older man for strength.

"How did he seem last time you saw him? Was he upset, or worried about anything?"

That was exactly the line of questioning Kenna would have gone with. Had Theo been some kind of cop? One of her theories—the top one, in fact—was that he was a US marshal formerly, or still, and Alonzo some kind of high-profile mobster. Laying low here in Wisconsin where none of their pals would find them.

Or they were partners. With the book of equal concern to both of them, maybe they'd both gone dark side and were now on the run.

Becky pulled up short. "The door is open."

Theo eased her back. "Stay here."

"Let me." Kenna pulled her gun.

Theo said, "You think you're the only one with one of those?"

"That's between you and the sheriff." Kenna eased up on one side of the door, Theo on the other.

The hand signals he gave her dispelled all doubt that he'd been a cop.

Kenna nodded in reply. She counted to two and eased the door open, then stepped inside. The place was a mess. It had been recently tossed. She checked every corner and the door in the corner that led into a tiny bathroom. As she stepped back into the room, she said, "Clear."

Theo stowed his weapon. "Looking for something?"

"He already gave me a case number, but maybe he had notes or files?" Kenna replied, easing around the room.

Becky started to cry. "What's happening?"

Alonzo touched her shoulder. "Where's your kettle, Becks? Let's go make some tea." They disappeared into the hall.

Kenna said, "US marshal?"

Theo flinched. "Dang. You are good."

And yet it was less satisfying than he probably thought. "Let's figure out who wanted Bruce dead."

"Apart from a mystery killer who hasn't ended a life in years and who everyone thinks is dead?"

"Yeah, apart from him."

Theo grunted, his face in the credenza cabinet. "If it is a him."

Kenna looked around, trying to find rhyme or reason in the way the mess had been made. "We should probably let the police do this. State or the sheriff."

"We're doing them a favor." Theo paused. "Only, don't tell them I was here, all right?"

"And you expect that to work when there are witnesses?"

"A guy can hope."

Kenna opened the first drawer on a file cabinet. "Let me

guess? I shouldn't run your face or Alonzo's through any data-bases in case I flag something? Or will there simply be a suspicious lack of information on the two of you?"

He chuckled. "You probably have someone who could find out whatever you need to know under the radar, but we also paid a lot of money to take steps to protect ourselves."

"And the book you and Alonzo were worried about?"

Theo shrugged. "It'll turn up."

"I thought I had time to speak to Bruce about the case file he pointed me to. I thought Forrest was safe in her grief, working on her book. I figured I'd find my friend's sister, and the killer would get arrested, and that would be the end of it. Not that I'd be here waiting to run into a guy who works for a serial killer trying to get a rise out of me and finding heads under beds."

He didn't laugh because it wasn't funny. "So I should tear up the town in a panic?"

Kenna looked at the desk, now covered in papers mostly strewn from the second drawer of the cabinet. Financial records. Giving statements. Old sermon notes from the previous pastor. "I'm not the one to ask about overreactions. I'm having enough of my own."

Fear was as crippling as worry—or full-blown anxiety.

"And what do you do to keep fighting?"

"Work the case," Kenna said. "And lately, pray."

"There you go."

Movement at the door drew her attention. Alonzo stood there alone. "Anything?"

"Nothing definitive, but we haven't looked over every-thing." And none of it was personal. Kenna said, "You?"

"He saw the only therapist in town. Part of his parole agreement was that he check in regularly with a mental health professional." Alonzo tucked his hands in the pockets of his slacks. "She is making her calls now, but she's pretty upset. Apparently, they were good friends. He helped her husband when he got hurt, and still does. Came over last week to help clear leaves out of her gutters before the next snow."

Someone wanted him dead.

Because of a bunch of deaths made to look like accidents... or natural causes. Tragedies. Loss that was part of everyday life. Maybe she was barking up the way wrong tree and there was nothing to this but coincidence or correlations that only looked like they fit.

"What do you think?" Theo asked.

Kenna didn't like being wrong. "Everything in me is telling me he was murdered."

Chapter Seventeen

Kenna pulled onto the street, ready to be home. Moisture had crystalized on the branches of the trees, and the road was slick in places where water had puddled. The temperature was dropping rapidly from where it had been the past few weeks, during the unseasonably warm spell that kept the temperature hovering almost at freezing.

There had been nothing at the church about Forrest's family, nothing about accidents, or information about any deaths at all apart from funerals the church conducted. Whatever Bruce knew before he died that had compelled him to leave that note on Forrest's door he hadn't written it down. He must have learned the information orally and never made notes.

Or whoever had been in his office making a mess found what they were looking for.

She had looked everywhere, even in his sparse living space. Bruce's residence hadn't been like the last pastor's house she'd been in. The man might've looked like a gangster, but he lived like a monk.

Thankfully, there had been no severed heads anywhere.

But that didn't mean Kenna was happy that a man was dead and she had nothing to go on.

Was it even murder?

If it was because of what he knew, and had been determined Forrest find out?

Kenna gripped the wheel and frowned. Outside Forrest's house, Sheriff Gingrich had parked by the curb. As she pulled up, he got out of his car. Kenna eased hers onto the driveway, feeling the need to stake her claim to being here—something he didn't have—but unsure why she felt the need to do that.

He stayed by his car.

Kenna strode over, making sure she didn't fall on a patch of ice. She didn't need to land on her behind in front of the sheriff. "How was court?"

He had an impassive expression on his face. "Court was court. I'm not here to chitchat."

"Why are you—" Kenna started. Several cars pulled onto the street. Three. "State police?"

Her first instinct was that they were there for her. Kenna's thought spiraled trying to figure out what on earth they might be arresting her for. Could go one of several ways, and even have something to do with the FBI. Or Stan Tilley.

She stood as still as possible. "What's going on?"

"Care to share what you found at the church earlier?" the sheriff asked.

He wanted to know about Bruce? "You think I was looking for something?"

His eyes narrowed. "You expect me to believe it wasn't about searching his residence and his office?"

That entirely depended on whether he'd feel it was interference in his case, or if he'd want a statement he could add to the case file. "A man is dead. It's very sad, the community losing their shepherd like this. I'd like to help out the church if

I can. I don't belong to it except that I'm a family member from out of town."

The look on his face said he wasn't sure what to make of that. "I'll need a write-up. Did you find anything?"

"No. Why are you worrying about it if it's not a case? Just crossing i's and dotting t's, or what?" She studied his expression as she spoke, and saw a shift.

The officers from the state police had suits and wool coats. Most had pins on their shirt collars. How far had they driven to get here?

Kenna said, "What did you need the cavalry for?"

"You've decimated my department and piled on their case load."

"Yeah, sorry about finding that girl still alive." She folded her arms, tugging the back of her coat across her shoulder blades. A piece of fluff from her hood tickled her cheek, but she ignored it.

One of the state officers glanced at the sheriff.

"Kenna Banbury." She lifted her chin. "Nice to meet you guys. Can I help you?" Of the three guys, she spotted one amused and hanging back.

The sheriff said, "You have it?"

The state officer in front pulled a folded paper from the inside pocket of his coat. "Are you the resident? This is a search warrant for the home address of Forrest Crosby and any vehicles belonging to her."

Kenna glanced at the sheriff. "Why do you need to search Forrest's house?"

The state guys got moving, passing her and the sheriff. They headed to the front door, and one knocked.

"Answer the question, Gingrich." She wasn't going to budge until she got an explanation. Forrest's home was a sanctuary. Like home was, or should be, for anyone. And yet, they felt whatever they knew warranted invading the space where she grieved. Where she struggled to keep the memory of her family alive while outside this house the world seemed determined to keep going.

"My office received an anonymous tip. I've directed the coroner to do a series of tox screens to see if we can ascertain what was used to poison Bruce Kilborn."

"You think he was murdered?" And that Forrest had anything to do with it? That was insane, and a serious leap. They would need evidence enough for probable cause in order to get a search warrant. An anonymous tip wasn't enough. What did Gingrich know that he wouldn't want to tip his hand to her on? "I thought the consensus was natural causes, some kind of reaction, or just a medical tragedy."

The front door to the house opened.

The state police officer with the warrant spoke to Forrest, but Kenna couldn't hear it.

Gingrich said, "Are you going to get in the middle of this and make everything more difficult for us...or let the police do their jobs?"

"Funny. Couple days ago, you were asking for my help on that escort thing." She watched his face, and from the look of it, he might still be asking for her help. Or, he planned to and it hadn't occurred to him that she might not want to after this. "I'm gonna go inside, since I'm staying here."

He didn't try to stop her, but he did go with her. Close enough instinct had her walking faster than she would've because it felt a little like being chased.

Kenna found Forrest in the entryway.

Her friend whispered, "They're searching *everything*."

Kenna squeezed Forrest's shoulder and stood beside her. "Did they tell you what they're looking for, or why they're here?"

"They think I had something to do with Pastor Bruce's death!" Forrest whispered the words.

Kenna would be shouting, but maybe that was why Forrest had pulled back so hard on her volume. To get some control. She faced the sheriff. "What evidence do you have?"

Gingrich lifted his chin. "I'm just here to support the state police. It's their case."

She wasn't sure that was true. Not unless it served his purposes to allow them to have it.

Forrest turned and walked down the hall, following one of the officers, even if she hung back.

He went into the office. Another entered the child's bedroom that had been unused for so long.

Forrest whimpered.

Kenna said, "Is it necessary for them to go in her son's room?"

Gingrich looked in there. When he glanced back at them, he almost looked sick. "We have to search all of it." He looked like he wanted to say more, maybe to ask Forrest about keeping her son's room as it was indefinitely.

Kenna gave him a tiny head shake. "What did they take to the judge that got a warrant? Because a couple of hours ago, everyone was talking about a medical issue."

The state police officer who had the warrant brought it over and handed it to Kenna. "Read it yourself."

She scanned the wording. *What on earth?* This was bizarre. The sheriff had to have received that call hours ago, not so long after Pastor Bruce was even declared dead. The warrant would have taken time to get. And yet they were here, and it was barely midafternoon.

Forrest nudged her arm. "What does it say?"

"They have a witness statement that you had motive to want him dead, so your lawyer can get a copy of that and see what it says." And who said it. Was Forrest actually going to be arrested? That was the last thing this quiet woman needed. "But I figure that's the anonymous tip that came in. They have Bruce's phone, on which evidently was a series of texts indicating your intention to end his life."

"I said I'd kill him?" Forrest blinked. "Does it say why I wanted to?"

Gingrich's jaw muscle flexed.

There was a way guilty people acted, even if they were determined to pretend they were innocent. This wasn't that.

Forrest had at least that going in her favor.

The state police officer in the office strode out. "We're going to be packing up everything in here and taking it with us."

"It's not evidence of murder," Kenna said, shifting slightly so her shoulder was in front of Forrest's. So her friend would know Kenna was here for her, standing with her in solidarity. "It's research for a true crime book."

Another one of the officers came in through the kitchen. "There's an RV in the garage, and we need it unlocked."

Oh no, they didn't.

"That won't be happening." Before they could all argue, Kenna said, "The warrant covers the house and any vehicles registered to Forrest Crosby. That RV is mine. And they wouldn't be going inside it."

"We can come back with an amendment." The cop didn't want to back down. "She might've passed something to you to hide."

"Wow," Kenna said. "This is turning into a conspiracy. It's gonna be an even better story for the newspapers to report when you realize you're all wasting your time chasing nothing. There isn't even any evidence yet that Bruce Kilborn was murdered."

"Yet." Gingrich shifted his weight.

"Did you also get search warrants for anyone in the local area who knew him before he went to prison, or during his incarceration?" Kenna made eye contact with each of the cops. "Just to make sure this wasn't the actions of someone desperate for revenge, and clever enough to cover their tracks. Make it look like natural causes."

It almost sounded like the work of a professional killer.

"How about this?" The officer who'd been in Forrest's study disappeared for a second, then came back with a paper file.

Forrest groaned. "You think I didn't look it up after the note?"

Kenna took the papers. "So she has a copy of the accident report." They'd have to work harder than this to prove she had motive to kill Bruce.

The officer said, "I want a statement about this 'note' you're talking about. But the texts on Bruce's phone talk about how he's stirring things up. Blaming Forrest for their deaths even, wanting them out of the way."

Forrest let out a whimper.

"How he was going to tell everyone that she is the one who killed them."

"I have this file as well. And a few others," Kenna said. "Does that make me J. Pierce, because I've been reading acci-dent files?"

Gingrich said, "I don't know. Does it?" He seemed almost amused. Or intrigued by the idea Kenna might be a serial killer.

Being accused of murder? There was something different for once.

She nearly rolled her eyes over the absurdity of it all.

She could explain everything to these cops, but it was

almost more fun to watch them figure out how wrong they were.

Sheriff Gingrich tugged cuffs off the back of his belt. "Forrest Crosby, you need to accompany me to the sheriff's department for questioning."

"You don't even know if it was murder yet," Kenna said. They didn't have the test results. She turned to Forrest. "If you're not under arrest, you can decline."

Forrest glanced at the officer who'd had the search warrant.

Kenna took a photo of the warrant with her phone—which none of them liked, given their reactions. But she got it before an officer snatched the paperwork out of her hand.

"Am I under arrest?" Forrest asked.

"We would like you to come to the station and answer some questions," Gingrich replied. "If there's nothing to this, then no harm done."

Kenna said, "Really? When you've intruded in this entire house for nothing?" Disturbing private spaces, and the memories Forrest held dear. "You're gonna have to work a whole lot harder if you want to effectively ruin Forrest Crosby's life and send her to prison for murder."

They were going up against Kenna now.

Usually, she fought to find the killer. This time she'd be fighting for the accused innocent person.

"You're not a lawyer," Gingrich said. "Forrest, you need to come with us."

Forrest lifted her chin. "I think I'll choose to call my lawyer first."

"We're taking the evidence covered under the warrant for further scrutiny," the officer said. "After all, there's a whole lot about murder in that room."

Kenna almost wanted to show them her RV and what she

had hidden away there, but they'd probably lock her in a facility where she could receive treatment for her mental conditions. Or what they'd think were psychoses. "It's called a *job*," she spat.

Then she glanced at Forrest. She needed to take an honest look at her friend, just in case. After all, Forrest hadn't yet told her where she'd gone this morning. But committing murder? That was so unlikely it was almost laughable.

Which meant someone wanted the spotlight on Forrest. Or even wanted her to go down for murder.

She couldn't make any assumptions, but she could do everything in her power to prove Forrest was innocent if that was the truth. If someone really had murdered Bruce, and his death wasn't a coincidental medical tragedy or an accident, then there had to be justice. It was reasonable that Forrest might've wanted Bruce to not say anything further about her family's deaths. She hadn't seemed to want to deal with it.

But badly enough to end his life?

"Found something!" The cops all left Forrest and Kenna in the hall. One came back with a note in a clear plastic bag. "Care to explain, Ms. Crosby?"

"It's *Mrs*. And I've never seen that."

Kenna leaned over so she could see it. Her phone started to ring in her pocket.

"I d-didn't write this." Forrest's voice shook.

"You're under arrest for the murder of Bruce Kilborn."

Kenna was shoved back while they put cuffs on her friend. She kept her mouth closed while they moved to the door.

Forrest, pale-faced, was about to collapse.

"I'll get you a lawyer." Kenna took a step, but Gingrich stepped in front of her. "Don't say anything without the lawyer!" she yelled.

Gingrich said, "We'll be here for a while, and you don't need to babysit evidence collection."

"Don't worry about me. I'll be helping my friend fight this idiotic arrest." She strode through the house to her RV and let herself in, locking the door behind her. The call had been from Maizie, so she hit Redial and listened.

When the teen picked up, Kenna said, "Clear your task list. We've got work to do."

Chapter Eighteen

Kenna fired off a quick text to Theo and Alonzo on the way back into the house. She stood at the living room window and watched as officers loaded Forrest into the back of a state patrol car. She rubbed the heel of her hand across her breastbone. Her head hurt a whole lot less than it had the past day or so.

She spun around. Gingrich hadn't left yet.

You're unbelievable.

Kenna thought the words but didn't say it. She needed goodwill with the sheriff and his department so she wasn't denied access to be able to help Forrest.

"I have work to do."

Kenna smiled. "Funny, I was about to say the same thing." She strode past him. It wasn't worth getting into a bickering match. He'd realize what a low opinion she had of a man who'd only managed to retain his job for the past thirty-however-many years. He hadn't been required to grow. But soon enough he'd be challenged. She almost wanted to pray he would be ousted.

That gave her the energy to stomp all the way to the

garage, where she unlocked her RV and tried not to slam the door behind her. She called Maizie, who answered immediately.

"I'm on it," Maizie said. "I can't believe they arrested Forrest!"

"You and me both, Maze." Kenna put her earbuds in. She grabbed the edge of her counter at the kitchen sink and bent forward, stretching her back. "I haven't even been to the diner where he died. I haven't seen his body, but I did talk to Marion."

"Does Forrest have an alibi?"

"That's for a lawyer to find out."

"As soon as I read that paper, I did a web search," Maizie explained. "I don't know much about warrants, but it looked bad enough, and she doesn't have anyone that's a lawyer in her contacts."

Kenna straightened. "You found someone?"

"It's a firm in Chicago with a sister firm in New York. They take on criminal cases, and high-profile civil ones. They have a junior associate who can take the helicopter up."

"Some kid just out of law school?" Probably the family member of a friend, some kid whose daddy paid his way.

"It's not what I know you think," Maizie said. "He's won three cases, and as soon as I mentioned your name, they were falling over themselves to call me back. They said he's their brightest up-and-comer, and he will drop what he's working on to come up there."

"Tell them to send him."

Maizie's computer keys clacked across the phone line. "The retainer is a pretty hefty. It's—"

"Doesn't matter."

"You're certain she's innocent?"

Kenna could plead her friend's guiltlessness, but that wasn't always how the justice system worked. "It's not on me to prove she's innocent. It's on the DA to prove her guilty beyond a reasonable doubt. And I've got nothing but doubts right now. There's no way they'd have arrested her unless they know something I don't. It all seems seriously flimsy. Not to mention circumstantial. If this kid is as good as they say he is, he'll tear their case to shreds and have her released before the end of the day."

"Good."

Kenna wanted to ask Maizie what she'd been doing that morning, but their pact was that the girl shared if she chose to. Instead, she asked, "Have you heard from Jax?"

The question came out before she realized its implications.

She bit her lip and straightened.

"From what's coming and going on his phone, something serious is going down in San Diego." Maizie paused. "There's been nothing for an hour, but he's at the office and he hasn't left."

"Okay." Maybe that was it. He was just busy.

"What did you send him? It looks like an MP3 file."

"Voice message."

"Oh. Is that so I can't read it?"

"That isn't why I did it that way." Kenna sighed. "I just wanted him to hear the tone in my voice." So maybe he would understand why she'd reacted the way she did.

Someone pounded on her RV door.

Kenna called out, "Yeah?"

"You have guests."

She stuck her feet into her rubber boots before stepping out but didn't put her coat on. The sweater she had on with her jeans was just fine. She stowed her phone in her back pocket with her earbuds switched to let in ambient sound and the volume on the call turned down.

Gingrich stood in the garage looking at the family bikes.

Kenna locked the door. "How much longer are you all gonna be?"

He glanced at her. "As long as it takes."

Kenna hit the button, and the garage door rolled up.

Maizie said, "The lawyer is on his way. Lucas Amrand, from Creason, Amrand, and Franks."

Kenna said thanks quietly, then watched the car at the curb come into view under the rattling, rising door. Theo and Alonzo came over, moving fast...toward the sheriff.

Alonzo went first. "What are you thinking, arresting that woman?"

Kenna looked at Theo. "Do we need to intervene?"

"Only if the sheriff doesn't let him say his piece." He eyed her RV. "This is yours?"

"Yep."

"This thing is the top-of-the-line model." He whistled. "Must've set you back a few pennies."

"It's my home, it just has wheels. Housing is expensive."

He chuckled. "When you're done, sell it to me for used prices, yeah? You'll make Betty's whole year. She'd love to travel."

Kenna said, "I'll keep you in mind."

She didn't mention that her homes had a tendency to meet grisly fates. If she was going to upgrade, she couldn't think of anyone better to take it off her hands.

Alonzo went on, "...if you even think for one second she could be capable of that. It's idiotic!" Then his rant dissolved into mutterings in a foreign language.

Kenna glanced at Theo and whispered, "Italian?"

The old marshal whispered back, "Don't run his face. Too risky."

She wondered how he had a driver's license, but then Theo had been driving every time she saw them, so maybe he didn't have one. That would be an effective way to stay under the radar.

"Get out of my face, Bernstein." Gingrich shook his head. "Don't tell me how to do my job." He was through the door in a second, back to his so-called evidence collection.

Alonzo spun around. "How do we fight this? No way did Forrest kill Bruce. It's ridiculous."

"We know how you feel on the subject," Theo said. "And we're not the ones you have to convince."

Alonzo lifted his hands, then let them fall back to his sides. "So how do we prove it?"

Kenna said, "Do either of you know where Forrest was this morning? She said she'd tell me, but we didn't get a chance to talk because the sheriff was already here." She didn't think it was anything sinister. And certainly not that Forrest planned to confess to murder.

There might be something in her files, but the police were taking them. And likely her computer and phone as well—unless either one was somewhere other than in the house, or on her person.

"We can find out," Theo said. "I'll see if Betty knows."

"We can go to the diner as well." Alonzo glanced at her RV, not as impressed as Theo. But maybe mobile living wasn't his thing. "Find out what we can about what happened."

Kenna nodded. "I'll talk to Kobrinsky and see if the coroner will meet with me. But I want to be at the sheriff's department when the lawyer shows up." Not just because she wanted to see the helicopter land in the parking lot. Or on the field across the street beside the children's playground. "Who would do this? Who wants Bruce dead and Forrest framed for it?"

That had to be what happened.

Theo scratched at the stubble on his jaw.

"I want an answer," Kenna said. "Before Forrest has to spend a night in jail." She stared at the door to the house, wondering if the sheriff was on the other side, listening. Or if he was somewhere else in the house, touching personal things and being nosy in the process of doing his job.

Were the state police asking themselves if they'd been dragged into something that was going to make them look like chumps?

Who in town was congratulating themselves because their plan to frame an innocent woman and stop her from what—writing a book about J. Pierce—was going well so far?

"I don't understand why Forrest is such a threat," Kenna added. But whoever was behind this would learn quick she was a force to be reckoned with.

Was it J. Pierce himself?

Or someone else entirely?

One of the officers carried a box out to the car. There were a number of further trips, and the three of them shot the breeze, probably speculating. No one was convinced this arrest had any weight. They'd rather believe—even if it turned out to be foolish—that Forrest would be free.

Kenna had set several things in motion, but as soon as the cops were done, she'd be back pounding the pavement.

The search took the better part of an hour, during which she set up lawn chairs for Theo and Alonzo and made them both a cup of coffee. Kenna leaned against the hood of her Subaru while they sat on the drive next to the RV garage, watching the cops haul out box after box.

Then more. Then more still.

Her phone buzzed. "That's me. You might want to look at it."

She didn't react right away to Maizie's statement. Instead, she waited a second before she tipped her hip, up, tugged out her phone, and looked at the new message. Air caught in her throat, and she coughed.

"Everything good?" the guys asked in chorus.

"Mm-hmm. It's good." She didn't look up from her phone.

Theo knew it wasn't okay, that whatever she'd just looked at had significance. He just didn't know she was looking at an epic picture of him in the '80s in the Chicago club scene, dressed in a suit with ruffles on his shirt front. Slicked back hair and a pinkie ring. The undercover federal agent had busted up a ring of drug and human traffickers who were all Sicilian mobsters.

Alonzo wasn't pictured there, but she figured he'd been a part of it. Or another case that put them both up here, pretty much in hiding.

Through the earbuds, Maizie said, "Looks like you were right about the marshal thing. I'll figure out what his last case was before he dropped under the radar, and if we need to worry about this book."

She shot back a text to Maizie that just said,

Sounds good

Alonzo said, "We're just gonna sit here and let them take her stuff."

One of the cops glanced at them on the way to the car, evidently able to hear that.

"It's a legal document," Kenna said. "They're within their rights to take what they deem relevant. If it goes nowhere, she gets it all back." But the damage to Forrest's privacy would be done. "There's nothing we can do without making things worse for her...and for us."

She figured as much as Theo and Alonzo wanted to intervene, they needed to stay off the radar of the sheriff's department and state police. Two men with a connected past who'd stayed safe for years knew how to keep themselves safe. She shouldn't be as worried about them getting involved as she was. But the fact was that after one note, a man was dead and an innocent woman had been arrested.

Kenna turned to the two older men. "She is innocent, isn't she? That's not just wishful thinking." They started to bluster, and she held up one hand. "I haven't known Forrest except for the past few weeks. There's nothing about the time I've spent with her that makes me believe she had anything to do with her family's deaths or Bruce's. There's no way. But before I go all-in to defend her, I have to ask."

Theo said, "She's innocent."

"Okay." She happened to agree, but it was about what she could prove.

Alonzo just looked at her like she'd betrayed the *familia* and needed to learn a lesson. One she wasn't super excited to learn. There had been enough craziness. She should sit them down and tell them her story. Lean on these two men to help her figure out how to get Forrest out from police suspicion.

Gingrich appeared. "We're done."

"Great. Thanks so much for coming. Have a good day." She walked toward him, arms out, ushering him to the curb. "Good to see you."

He glanced over and eyed her. "Don't leave town. And *don't* make trouble."

"Sure, sure. I won't get in your way, but you *will be* releasing my friend." She folded her arms, still not wearing a coat. The warmth from the coffee had worn off. "Have a great rest of your day." She waved as he drove off.

Theo and Alonzo were chuckling, putting their chairs

away, when she strode back over.

"Coroner's office?" she suggested.

Theo said, "I'll drive."

"I can follow you."

Alonzo shook his head. "You can come with us."

After Kenna locked up the house and ended the call with Maizie, they headed out. Theo played country music through the car speakers. Alonzo stretched one leg across the back seat. At least he let her ride in the front seat, not in the back like a kid.

"Is there a reason we can't drive separate and meet there?" She turned to the side so she could see both of them. "Some secret, local thing I don't know about?" As long as they actually *were* going to the coroner's office and not some clandestine location. "Guys?"

"Trust us," Alonzo said, his attention on his phone.

Theo said, "It's safer to stick together than it is being alone."

She had to think on that for a moment, since for so long she'd believed that alone was safer. Why would it be better if people she cared about were at risk just being with her? Sure, they could watch each other's backs. But two were more vulnerable than one.

She couldn't reconcile it in her mind. "Let's just go see what the coroner has to—"

In that split second, she spotted the truck through the driver side window.

Barreling straight toward them.

"Watch out!"

Her words were swallowed up in the crash. The force of the truck slammed into them, sending them spinning. Metal screamed, and she could smell burning from somewhere.

The car went off the side of the street and rolled.

Chapter Nineteen

Kenna sucked in a sharp breath through her nose. She blinked, trying to figure out what had just happened. A fog of powder hung in the air around her that smelled like fireworks. The airbag in front of her had smacked her in the face. She pulled the knife from her right boot and deflated it.

Her face felt like she'd been punched, and she was having trouble focusing.

Crash.

They'd crashed. Because that truck had hit them from the side.

She touched her face, ensuring her nose hadn't been broken. The familiar twinge of pain in her forearms anchored her. *You're alive.* She gave herself the survival peptalk. *You're breathing. You're not done yet.* One day she would be—but not today.

The sun hung in the sky behind the heavy clouds.

The car engine ticked as it cooled, shut off by the force of the truck slamming into the side of their car. Twisting around, she saw the grill in the window on the driver's side. The truck was still right up against them, where it had shoved the left side of Theo's car in at least ten inches.

He lay slumped against the airbag on his side, blood down his face. But if she deflated his airbag, he'd have nothing to rest against, so she left it.

Phone. She needed to call for help, but her phone was… who-knew-where.

Kenna twisted all the way around and let out a yelp. Her chest hurt where the airbag hit her, and she'd probably feel the full force of whiplash tomorrow. But that wasn't all the reason she'd cried out.

Alonzo lay across the back, his leg at an odd angle.

She gritted her teeth and breathed through her nose, which hurt not just her head but also her face. *Move.* Phone. Ambulance. "Hang on." Her voice sounded far away to her ears.

She looked for Alonzo's phone but couldn't see it. Theo's was in the holder on the left side of his steering wheel. Or it had been. She would have to lift up, get her knee in the seat, and grab onto something while she looked over the airbag on his side. The whole time, she'd have to pray his phone hadn't been shattered to smithereens in the crash.

Easier to find hers.

Where had it been before the crash?

She jabbed at the seatbelt button, her finger flashing with pain. When it finally released, the seatbelt whipped across her, but Kenna managed to untangle her arm. She wasn't hurt. At least not apart from the general battering and going uncon-scious again, which wasn't good.

She needed to get help on the scene to take care of these two men.

Ambulance. Life Flight again, like with the K-9 handler.

Kenna pushed out a breath and bent forward. No phone. Where was it? She sat back.

Light flashed from her right.

She twisted to the window. Stan Tilley stood there with a phone, the camera light on. It flashed several times in a row. He was taking pictures of her? Kenna grabbed for her pistol and tugged it free of the holster. It fell on her lap, but she got it back in her hands. Safety off. She opened the door with her left hand across her body and kicked it wide.

Help. Please. She could use some holy wisdom right now.

Kenna clambered to her feet. Everything spun, but she fought back the wave of dizziness and grabbed the top of the doorframe to stand. Gun up. "Taking pictures?" Her voice was stronger now, but she could use even more than that. "Did you hit us?"

Stan Tilley took a couple more pictures, then lowered the phone.

"Give me that phone, and go."

He chuckled. "You think you can aim and actually hit me?"

Kenna lifted her hand from the doorframe to give herself a two-handed grip on the gun. Everything rotated. She leaned back without realizing it and slammed against the rear passenger door. That would help her keep upright, as long as her legs didn't give out.

Stan came over, stomping. He was at least six inches shorter than her, wearing a lined jacket over jeans. Boots. Bushy gray beard and a beanie. His nose was red from the cold.

Why wasn't Kenna feeling the cold?

She gripped the gun. He came almost close enough she could've touched the barrel to his shirt. She blinked. His hand connected with the gun, and she lost her grip on it, crying out.

He slapped it out of her hand. It fell to the ground.

Kenna tried to grab him and toppled over, landing on her hands and knees. Stan swiped the gun off the ground and threw it toward the trees. As if that left her without a weapon?

"Don't." He stood over her, but too far away for her to do anything. "That's not what this is about."

She backed up and leaned against the rear door. "If the Walker wants to talk to me, he can come here himself."

Stan's beard shifted as he moved his mouth. "Nah, this is fun."

"Friend of yours?"

"More like a business associate with mutual interests."

Kenna said, "He's a serial killer." She took them down, and anyone who was an accessory to their actions. Didn't he know that meant him? "And you're his accomplice."

And yet, right now there was nothing she could do about it. She didn't have the physical strength to take him down. Not even her will could overcome the fog in her mind and the lack of strength in her arms. She needed to protect Theo and Alonzo from him and get them to the hospital.

"Just go." But maybe leave the phone.

Or she needed to find hers on the floor where she'd been sitting.

Determination could get her to a result. God could use her consciousness to direct her to the solution of how she was going to get help here. Or He had it already in the works.

Help us, Lord. She meant them right now, but also every-thing else.

Kenna stared at Stan. "Call for an ambulance before you leave."

He chuckled. "Theo's car didn't get in contact with the dispatcher yet?"

Did he have that set up? She hadn't heard anything.

Maybe help was already on the way. If someone was coming, hopefully that included the police. She could keep Stan talking, and they'd be able to arrest him for attempted whatever this was with his truck. Murder. Vehicular manslaughter. She didn't know which it was.

Kenna blinked more than she needed to, so she came across as helpless. Which she kind of was, but that wasn't the point. "They say you knew my father."

Stan surveyed her. Finally, he said, "We all have a story. Mine is classified."

"So you served, and they redacted the good stuff?" She hadn't tried to find out what her father had done during his time in the Marine Corps. She'd always thought more about him as an FBI agent, even though his military service was only part of the life he'd lived.

"They wrote me off. Left me for dead, discarded and forgotten about. Like I was nothing to them. Just trash." He stared at her. "Your father did that to me."

Cold crept over Kenna. She shivered, but inside there was a whole lot of numbness she didn't like. This man had been sidelined. Stan Tilley knew what it was like to be wronged. Maybe she could use that. "An innocent woman could go to jail because you did this."

He barely reacted, but he'd heard her. And he didn't like it. "How about I kill the sheriff for you? That should stall the investigation." Just like that, he offered to murder?

"I don't want you to kill the sheriff." She just wanted him to show up and arrest Stan instead. "Did you kill the pastor? Or Mr. Wells?" He might've been the one who had cut off Marion's husband's head. Or killed him so she could cut off the head after. Whichever it was, hopefully the pathologist could point the sheriff's department in the right direction.

Stan chuckled. "Never been to Wisconsin before a few weeks ago. Don't know the pastor."

"How do you know Mr. Wells was killed before you got here?"

"Because I read the papers." He sneered. "And I listen to the police band. It's not that hard to find out information in a place like this where folks will still talk to strangers. But can't you go somewhere I can chase you where it's warm?"

Kenna wanted to look at Theo. Or Alonzo. Find out if they were still alive. Would help get here fast enough, or were they already dead? Surely one of them would've woken by now.

"Did you hear me, or are you gonna pass out? I'll take some more pictures."

"Chase me? You've caught me now."

Stan looked around for his phone. "This was fun and all, but the instructions are pretty specific." He turned to the left and started to move.

A gunshot went off from inside the car.

Kenna's whole body flinched, and pain pounded in her head. Stan stumbled back a step, blood blossoming on his upper arm on the right side. He moved left, taking a few rushing steps, and grabbed his right arm with his left. No weapon. No phone.

This was her chance to take him down.

But she couldn't move.

Stan ran toward the woods, moving southeast. She followed him so far—straining to keep him in sight—that her head swam and her eyes rolled back in her head.

Before she passed out, she thought she heard a vehicle.

. . .

When Kenna awoke, she still felt numb, but it was a warm numb and she was comfortable. The hard ground and the cold outside of the car were gone. She seemed to be in a bed. Covered in blankets.

A clock on the wall ticked.

She turned her head to it but couldn't figure what the numbers meant. Her thoughts swam, and her mind didn't want to process what she was seeing.

Consciousness retreated, then returned later.

The door opened, and the sheriff entered. "Good. You're awake."

She cleared her throat. "What's going on?"

"Looks like your deal caught up with you." Gingrich stopped beside the bed. "Theo hit his head, like you, but he's awake and giving the nurses grief. Betty is asking them what kind of muffins they want. Trying to smooth things over. Alonzo is in with a doctor having his leg sewn up. They're both going to be fine."

"And Forrest?"

"Maybe right now you need to be more worried about *you*." Gingrich pointed at her, to emphasize that last word, but it just looked patronizing.

She looked on both sides of the bed and found the buttons, holding down the one that raised the back of her head. She didn't like being at a disadvantage, and him standing over her left her uneasy. As her upper body rose to sitting, she said, "I need my phone. Or any phone."

She'd have to remember Maizie's number. Or Jax's. They were saved in her phone.

Could she recall the digits?

He pulled her phone from his pocket and handed it over. The screen was shattered, and the whole device had been bent in half, like someone had been trying to fold it.

"Great."

He sat at her bedside. "I'll get the nurse to bring you a phone. She wanted to know who your next of kin was, but I didn't know who to tell her."

"After all, you arrested my landlady."

"And your RV is locked up, so I couldn't find any personal information on you."

"Good," she muttered. The word slipped out like that before she could work out if she needed him on her good side —or if she didn't care right now.

He let out a sigh, as though she was an imposition he didn't want to deal with but had no choice.

"What's going on?" She shifted slightly and turned her head so she could stay still but facing him. It ached more than she wanted to admit. How long had she been out? The clock numbers made sense this time. She'd been out for hours apparently.

"You're in protective custody as of now, by order of the FBI."

Kenna blinked.

"Yeah, that was my reaction, too. They called not long after my deputy got to the scene. So now you've got a permanent babysitter until their agent gets here and we can get this Stan Tilley business taken care of."

She'd rather he worked on finding out if Forrest had actually killed anyone at all. Then her friend could be released.

"I'll send Kobrinsky to do the overnight shift," he continued. "He needs to rest, but if he can do it on detail, he'll keep from going crazy."

"The way I will with him in my RV?" Maybe he could sleep in Forrest's house. Or in his car on the drive.

"We all have to deal."

"Why? I can just leave."

Gingrich shook his head. "I know you won't do that. You're too loyal to leave town with Forrest still in custody. Which is why I want you on that protective detail. The fed can help. You can draw out Tilley and keep out of the way of my citizens. So no more of them get caught up in your business."

Her mind couldn't even process that right now. Questions popped into her mind, but she couldn't figure out how to get them out.

"We'll get to that." He waved a hand. "You can rest up for now."

"You'd better not rest. I want Forrest out of that cell."

Gingrich sighed again, looking exasperated with her. She was about to call him out on it when he said, "I know she didn't kill the pastor. The profile matches J. Pierce, but that also makes no sense. So right now I have no idea who did."

She blinked. "What?"

He'd let the state police arrest Forrest when he knew she hadn't done it. Why do that? Just so she was out of the picture and he could find the real killer? Everyone had written it off as natural causes, and Kenna hadn't even been to the scene.

Gingrich said, "J. Pierce can't be the one trying to frame her for murder. That's impossible."

"How do you know?" Kenna studied him. "Who else would want her out of the way? All she's doing is writing a book about him. She's not exactly a threat to anyone else."

"I know it's not him because I killed him myself."

Chapter Twenty

Kenna absorbed the information. Her faculties seemed to be coming back online. She reached for the pitcher on the side table, but it was too far away. Gingrich got up and gave her a cup of water that was way too cold. She winced. "Thanks."

He stood by the bed.

"You killed J. Pierce?" She frowned up at him. "Is that why everyone thinks he's dead? You circulated the story, or started a rumor?"

Then there was the issue of the kills attributed to that murderer, and the ones that others suspected were—accidents and deaths that appeared more natural, like Bruce's had originally. Kenna wasn't sure it was one case, or even simply two.

This whole thing was a collection of disparate pieces with no perceivable connection.

Gingrich took his seat again. Kenna hoped the doctor or some other medical staffer didn't come in and disturb him before he got the story out.

The sheriff let out a heavy breath, as though he'd carried this weight for years now. "It was years ago now. Nearly fifteen, maybe? I was chasing him pretty hard since a body washed up on the lakeshore." He winced. "A young woman. The things he did to her..."

Kenna let him process his memories without her opinion coloring how he chose to deal with it.

"Then a young man went missing. A local. There were a couple of witnesses, he took the guy from the parking lot behind a bar that's out of business now." He frowned. "Maybe that's why it didn't survive. Anyway, there were a couple of witnesses, and I had a plate number for the van. I managed to get a sighting, and followed up. The vehicle was parked at the marina when I caught up to it, and I spotted a boat leaving the harbor." Gingrich closed his eyes.

"How did you know it was him?"

"I just knew." He opened his eyes. "I stared at him. He stared at me from behind the wheel. I had no way to chase him. I was so angry, I got my rifle from the truck with me and opened fire. I didn't stop shooting. Watching him duck down like he was scared was so satisfying. You have no idea."

"I probably do." She had emptied the cup now, and needed to get up soon to use the bathroom. But this broken man needed to get his story out.

"I must've hit the fuel tank because the whole boat went up. Kaboom!" Gingrich clapped.

Kenna flinched. "It exploded."

He nodded.

"Did you find the remains?"

"Two bodies, just a collection of pieces that were charred. Most of it was too burned for DNA, but we got one sample that remains unidentified. It didn't give us a familial match on any of the victim's family members, so I figure it was the killer. I never figured out who he was, but it didn't matter. It was over."

Kenna stared at the tiny hospital room. They hadn't changed her out of her clothes into a hospital gown. *Thank You.* She wondered if they'd done tests on her while they hooked her up to the IV connected to her elbow. The bag was nearly empty, all the medicine in her.

"I probably need to be seen by a doctor so I can get out of here," she said. "But I want to know what you think about the accidents or deaths attributed to natural causes. Did you know the coroner, Bill Tamarin?"

"What about him?"

"He's one of the people who brought up the accidents and deaths not ruled murders. Then he has an 'accident.'" She made air quotes. "Seems pretty suspicious if you ask me."

"You talk to Kobrinsky about this?"

She wasn't going to lie to him. "He has the file number."

"Good." Gingrich stood. "I'll take a look. You rest up."

"Because you expect me to work for you, while also in protective custody?" She sat forward, ready to get out of here whether she had a ride or not. There were calls to make, and she was hungry. But the pressing matter would come first.

"I'll keep you posted. If you're gonna pass out in the middle of a favor, you're no good, are you?" He left the door open.

The doctor came in a few minutes later, using words like *probable concussion.* She didn't like that and managed to argue her knowledge of herself. He threatened to make her sign refusal of treatment papers while he removed the IV. She told him there was nothing to treat. It went on for a few minutes.

He warned her what symptoms to look out for and left her to it.

Kenna pushed back the covers and swung her legs over the edge of the bed.

A nurse strode into the room, holding a phone to her ear. Frowning. "Yes, she is. Okay." Older than Kenna, she had the look of someone who'd seen everything at least once and was no longer capable of being surprised. Or so she'd thought until now. She held out the phone. "There's a call for you."

Kenna eased her feet to the floor and tried to figure out where her shoes were. "Thanks." She took the phone. "Maze?"

"No, it's me."

Jax.

"I'm okay." Kenna nearly collapsed to the floor. She heard the nurse say, "Whoa. Easy." But she didn't want to lie down again. "I'm okay." She said again, into the phone. "Really. I'm all right."

"But you won't stay in the hospital," Jax scolded, "and you refuse to admit you might be hurt."

"Just because I've been knocked out twice in the last few days doesn't mean there's anything wrong. I have work to do."

The nurse gave her a look, crouched by the bed. She retrieved Kenna's boots from a cabinet and set them on the floor.

"Tomorrow you'll feel like you've been hit by a truck."

"Probably." She wanted to say more, but the thoughts escaped her.

"Good thing I can see for myself."

"Tomorrow?"

"ASAP," Jax said. "And it can't be soon enough as far as I'm concerned. My ASAC signed off on picking up Stan Tilley, so I'm going home to pack."

"How did you know where I was?" She eased her feet into her boots.

"Maizie called when your heart rate went haywire and she couldn't get through to you."

"My phone was broken." The nurse hung by the door, probably waiting for her to give back the phone. "I'm in protective custody until further notice." Then the sheriff had said she'd be with the FBI. Which meant she'd be with Jax.

Kenna lowered her chin. "Did you get my message?"

"Yes." His voice softened. "We'll talk about it. But for now, can you just trust that we get more done together than we do apart?"

She might need another case—and a lifetime working together—to fully let that sink in. But she was willing to try. "For now."

"All right." He sighed. "I'll see you soon."

"Bye."

The nurse came back over to get the phone from Kenna. "Boyfriend?"

"FBI," Kenna corrected.

"Whatever floats your boat, I guess." She wandered to the door. "You good?"

"Yeah, but do you know where I can find Theodore Campbell?"

"Down the hall to the left. Follow the noise." She disappeared into the hall.

Kenna used the bathroom across from this room, moving gingerly. There had to have been pain meds in that IV bag. She'd refused a prescription from the doctor. It wasn't worth messing around with narcotics, even if she was going to be grumpy tomorrow if everything hurt.

She wanted to feel the pain so she could work with her body, not be clueless as to what hurt and carrying on as per usual. That would only make recovery take longer.

That was her story, anyway. She was going to stick to it.

Betty stood in the hallway, drinking from a paper cup. A little square tag hung over the rim, but Kenna couldn't make out what kind of tea it was. She hadn't laced her boots, and the aglets clicked on the floor as she walked. Betty glanced over. Her eyes filled with tears.

"What's going on?" Kenna pulled Betty in for a hug.

"You look awful."

Kenna barked a laugh. "Thanks?"

"You know what I mean." She patted Kenna's cheek. "I just visited Charlayne. Alonzo is charming all the nurses, and it sounds like his injuries aren't as bad as anyone thought."

"That's good." Kenna didn't like being responsible for other people getting hurt. Even if they were adults who knew the risks. "How is Theo?"

"The worst patient in the world. Yelling like he's in charge, with blood running down his face. They cleaned him up and gave him a shot to knock him out. It was the only thing that got him to quiet down." Betty shook her head.

"Sorry he was there," Kenna said.

"Sounds to me like if he hadn't been, you might be dead or missing. Given how he told the story to the sheriff. He yelled through that as well." Betty rolled her eyes.

"The sheriff knows about Stan Tilley?" He hadn't mentioned it, except the plan for the FBI to take the case. Maybe he thought he had enough on his hands. "What about the fact Theo winged him?"

"He thinks he missed."

"Kenna, is that you?" Theo's roar came from inside the room.

Betty patted her shoulder. "Best of luck, dear." She moved to a chair and sat with her tea, sipping where it was quiet.

Kenna braced herself and peered into the room. Theo sat up in the bed, in a hospital gown, tucked in by the covers. His head had been bandaged, and the rest of his skin was about the same color as the white cloth. She winced.

"Yeah, you look great yourself."

"So Betty pointed out." But they'd let her out. Maybe that was self-preservation on the part of the hospital, though. No one wanted to be sued. Or deal with an irate patient who might go so far as to argue the hospital had kidnapped them. Some people loved to argue about their rights and freedoms being infringed upon.

Kenna didn't have the energy to get worked up. She needed to get back on a solid footing before Jax showed up. Just talking to him had thrown her enough. In addition to eighteen hours of sleep, she needed a pot of coffee, the evidence that exonerated Forrest, and Stan Tilley in cuffs.

So not much.

"Sit down before you fall down, kid."

She grabbed a chair and leaned her head back, eyes closed. The strength and energy she had seemed to sink into the floor. She wasn't sure how she was supposed to get out of this chair and go anywhere, let alone get back to the case.

"Still trying to fool anyone looking that everything's fine?"

She peeled open one eye. "Thanks for taking that shot."

"I missed."

"Did you? We need information from that guy. It would've died with him." Kenna paused. "Instead, you slowed him down, and we might be able to catch him."

"I like the sound of this 'we' business."

"I mean the FBI and myself." She frowned.

His expression turned entreating. "Woman, let me in on this."

She lifted one brow.

Theo cleared his throat. She saw his eyes fill with tears. *Lord, what is going on?* Two emotional men in one day, and a call from Jax? Her heart might not be able to take this. Kenna pushed herself out of her chair and went to lean against the side of the bed. "What's going on?"

He stared at her hand on his arm. "I want to help. With Stan. Fighting for Forrest. All of it."

"Because Stan slammed his truck into your car?"

"I haven't felt that alive in years. I need to work, not live this marshmallow existence. Let me work. Please."

Kenna needed to dig a little more. "That's all of it? You just miss police work."

"Don't you? That's why you're a private investigator, isn't it?"

"This isn't about me."

"I..." He cleared his throat. "I have some symptoms. Betty knows, and she's mad because I haven't talked to the doctor about it yet."

"What's going on?"

"I had cancer about ten years ago." The skin around his eyes flexed. "It's back. I'm sure of it."

"And you want in on my fight?" She scoffed. "How about you fight your own battle?"

"I want to live again before I die." He grunted. "I've had a good run."

Kenna wasn't going to condone what might turn into a complex suicide. He wouldn't make it easy for any of them, least of all Betty. "You want me out there distracted because I have to cover your back, and you're worried about me, when we could be focused on the job? There are already enough things to do. Plenty of leads to run down to figure this out."

He could work on Forrest's case while she and Jax went after Tilley—and did the marshals escort thing. Or Theo wanted the job with the marshals.

"Don't sideline me, Kenna." His eyes entreated her. "Get me outta here."

If she made him stay, that would make her a hypocrite, and she didn't like the idea of that. "There's enough to do that I absolutely need your help."

Theo nodded. "All right. That's enough for now."

Kenna figured it didn't matter if she did object to him effectively committing suicide—or trying to go out in some kind of blaze of glory.

"Tell me how you faced down Tilley like that. You kept him talking, distracting him, like it was no big deal."

"He wasn't there to kill me."

"But the threat is still real. He could've kidnapped you. He might've if I hadn't hit him. So why did you not seem scared when you were in danger, but you're terrified when it's someone else? Like the idea of me going out there with you."

Or Jax being here. In the line of fire, with a chance he might get hurt again like he had been in Mexico. She knew he was still recovering somewhat, but that was a cop-out excuse.

The fear in her was real.

Alive like the memories of her time with a serial killer had been for so many years. The night she'd lost Bradley and the baby she was carrying—their baby. Even just the idea that she might have to face down that kind of loss again terrified her.

So what was she going to do about it?

Theo patted her hand. "People are gonna do what they're gonna do. You can't keep everyone safe."

"I don't like losing people." She swallowed against the thickness in her throat.

"Losing people is a part of life." He left his hand on hers. "But if all you think about is what you have to lose, then you don't ever consider what you've gained enough to appreciate it. Because you're too busy worrying you'll lose it."

Chapter Twenty-One

Two days later
Undisclosed location, northern Wisconsin

Kenna held the phone to her ear, the screen cold on her cheek. Even behind sunglasses, the glare from the sun reflecting off a fresh blanket of snow was nearly blinding.

"Did you think about what I said?" Theo asked.

"About appreciating what I have, not worrying about losing it?" She scanned the sky, leaning back against the sheriff's department cruiser. "I'm trying to do that, but his plane hasn't landed yet."

He chuckled. "I'll distract you then."

"Please tell me you got Forrest's alibi." She bounced one knee, and switched to looking at the small buildings in this tiny airport. Two hangars. One office building, single story that looked like a trailer or portable classroom at best. The air traffic control tower was basically a shack.

"The lawyer told me to leave it alone."

"In a way that makes you confident he's got this handled?" She'd been over to the sheriff's office once, last night. Forrest had been talking to the psychologist who worked in town. Dr. Jennifer Rayland, the deputy's mother. She'd offered to buy the lawyer a cup of coffee, but he'd been headed back to his hotel room to get to work and they'd barely spoken. He'd better be worth every single penny of the considerable amount of money she was paying him.

"But I'm not gonna let this go," Theo said.

Kenna didn't plan to either. She'd been resting physically the past two days, but hadn't quit working. "Did you tell him who you are?"

Theo chuckled. "That would've been fun."

"We need to find someone who saw her nowhere near the diner anytime around the morning. So there's no possible way she could've done it. There has to be a way to prove she didn't do it."

"Beyond a reasonable doubt." Theo made a noise in his throat.

The lawyer, Lucas Amrand, might be fighting it, but it wouldn't be long before Forrest was transferred to jail. She shouldn't be behind bars in the first place. Kenna couldn't imagine what her friend was going through. Having her freedom taken away like that—especially if she was innocent. Forrest lived life on her terms, alone with her grief in a way that meant she could find contentment in what she had left.

Kenna had been the same way for a long time. She had a wider circle now, but Forrest seemed to be stuck where Kenna lived after Bradley's death. Going through the motions settled into routine, which became her way of life.

Peace looked different for everyone.

Healing didn't always mean a person returned to who they had been before life tore them apart. Maybe it wasn't supposed to happen that way at all. Kenna was different now. There was no way she could be who she'd been years ago.

Even God made everything new—and everyone—so He had to understand that things changed. They needed to. The same way they did naturally with new seasons. This snow would melt. Plants would grow. Life went on, and things never stayed the way they were.

An airplane that had been sitting at the end of the runway revved its engines and started to pick up speed, a prop plane that would seat four at most. The kind of thing she'd be scared to fly in because it was so small. She preferred the huge airliners that went across the Atlantic.

Maybe Jax wanted to explore Europe with her. She could show him the places she'd gone with her dad before he disappeared for three days on a case, and she had to stay in the hotel room.

The airplane buzzed down the runway, sliding sideways. She winced, but it caught traction and took off.

"Where are you?" Theo asked. "That sounded like a plane."

"Because it was. I'm running an errand for Sheriff Gingrich. Picking up my boyfriend from the airport." And boy, that sounded weird to say out loud. "And getting a break from Kobrinsky's cooking, his furniture, and the smell of his bathroom, all in one."

Theo should've laughed but didn't. Instead, he said, "Be careful."

Kenna touched the badge hanging in front of her jacket. "No kidding. You could at least call the marshals. Find out who this guy is."

"Operation like that? No one knows except his handlers. Which makes me wonder how your boy got a ride on the same plane."

"The sheriff vouched for him, said he's part of the escort detail." Other than that, she had no idea how this all came together. While Jax was debriefing her late at night, she'd fallen asleep partway through when the pain meds she'd grudgingly taken kicked in. She hadn't asked the next day.

"So they have extra manpower. Probably someone your boy ran into who knows him. Otherwise, they wouldn't take someone's word for it."

"His name is Special Agent Jaxton, not my 'boy.'"

"And that's with an X, not *c-k-s*, right?"

Kenna frowned.

"For when I look him up."

"You need to focus on helping Forrest," Kenna said.

"And finding that guy I winged," Theo added.

"That's *my* job."

"Being bait is never a good idea. Trust me."

The irritating part was that she did. He could be a criminal who turned against everyone, or he'd been burned but Alonzo still needed protection. Either way, he was a good man and she did trust him. "I'll be okay."

A plane came into view. Far enough away she'd never be able to read a tail number until it was almost on the ground. She could barely tell it was a small white plane. Pointed nose. Half a dozen windows.

Snow swirled in the air.

Kenna pushed off the vehicle and looked around. She was on protection detail after all. "I should go. The plane is here."

"Tell your boy I said hey." The line went dead.

Kenna stowed her phone, shaking her head. She took a few steps away from the car, watched the plane for a second, and then checked the ground. The area around the airport was a flat snowy tundra. A huge hill behind her, the runway in the valley. In front was nothing but horizon and a huge sky heavy with more snow.

Nothing out there.

Only a single vehicle passing on the road about a mile away to the east. The buildings had a couple of people working, and she'd checked them out already. Between Gingrich and Maizie, she knew who should be here and who shouldn't.

Like that glint on the roof.

Kenna opened the back door and pulled the shotgun from the lockbox. *Might as well mean business.* She slammed the door, glanced at the plane, and jogged toward the hangar. Beyond that stood a portable office building where she saw something on the roof. Maybe some*one*.

She waited at the corner of the open hangar door. Someone moved behind her, but it was just a guy sweeping the floor since the last plane took off. Heat from the hangar's interior rolled out in waves like the ocean crashing on the shore.

Kenna lifted her chin.

He stopped pushing the sweeper and stared at her. She turned enough to show him the badge hanging around her neck, and he shook his head.

Yeah, you and me both.

Life in a city with departments of hundreds of law enforcement officers was a whole lot different than tiny departments. Places that felt like the edge of the world. Or the vast wild north.

She looked back at the roof and saw a protrusion over the edge on the far side. A rifle barrel? She couldn't be sure until she saw the rest—and the man holding it.

How did he get up there?

She crept up the wood ramp to the door, praying as she eased it open that it didn't even creak.

The plane was coming in to land, miles to the left. Only slightly bigger now than it had been.

She rounded the jam into the office and heard a muffled sound. The door clicked shut behind her. It had to be eighty degrees in here, and she immediately started to sweat. Why did people pump the heat so high? It was below freezing outside, but that didn't mean it should be T-shirt weather indoors.

Behind the desk, tied up and starting to come around, a heavy man lay on the floor. No shoes. Sweat under his arms, dampening the polo shirt he wore. Khakis. Glasses on the floor a foot or so away.

She could help him in a minute after she took care of a bigger problem.

There was no way to get to the roof from in here.

How had he gotten up there?

She stepped out the back door from a storage room, and icy air hit her in the face. A dumpster pushed up behind the portable building. Of course. That had to be how he climbed up. And she'd wasted time going inside when she could've walked around.

Get it together.

She didn't want to believe her recent injuries were affecting her judgment, but she would need to be doubly careful to make sure a mistake or lapse in sense didn't cost someone their life.

Kenna could hear the plane now. She hopped up on the lid of the trash can, got her feet under her, and did the same onto the roof. With a split second to assess the situation, she got the shotgun in front of her and ran across the slick roof to the man lying prone on the front lip about ten feet away.

She skidded part of the way, but managed to keep from yelping.

The plane circled around overhead.

As the shooter twisted around to see who was behind him, she planted her left foot and kicked him in the face.

His finger squeezed the trigger, and a series of shots popped across the open runway.

Finger on the trigger? *What kind of low-budget—*

He launched up at her, letting go of the gun so it fell over the edge of the roof. She twisted her hips and slammed the shotgun into his chest. He grabbed for her, but she kept moving.

The shooter stumbled back two steps.

Their low-rent assassin was maybe five ten and looked like he belonged in a biker bar. Or on the way to one through the snow. He had the gear, so he was a local or someone who lived in a climate like this. Though his jeans were wet from where he'd been lying facedown on the roof.

He balled a fist and punched. She caught it with her shoulder, then came up in a hook with the shotgun in her hands. She slammed the underside of his chin, and his head flung back. Two steps in retreat, he stumbled back.

Kenna kicked him in the stomach, and he fell over the edge of the roof into the pile of snow under the window. The mound created from shoveling snow off the path didn't look soft. She winced and looked for the plane. She spotted it over on the left, making its approach.

A good amount of snow had fallen in the two days she'd been resting at Kobrinksy's. In protective custody against her will. Talking to Maizie. Checking in with Jax and his progress getting on a flight when nearly everything had been canceled.

She went back to the dumpster behind the building and jumped down. She didn't feel as bad as she had a couple of days ago, but she also didn't feel good.

The plane would be on the ground in a minute, so she went into the office and got scissors to cut the guy free. He must've interrupted that low-budget shooter and wound up getting tied up for his trouble. She found a desk phone with dial tone and hit 9-1-1, explaining someone had been hurt. She didn't need this place crawling with cops when a high value federal fugitive was being transported through, but she also wasn't going to leave someone injured with an assailant outside in the snow.

The guy blinked up at her.

He looked like was about to defend himself against an attack, so she lifted the badge she hadn't managed to conveniently lose in the snow yet. "Help is on the way. Just stay here."

She went back to the door and stepped off the porch, watching the plane touch down. The wheels skidded. The plane slipped violently from side to side.

Kenna's breath caught in her throat.

It was going much too fast, or so she thought. What did she know?

The plane engines roared, wind against the flaps. Trying to slow down?

It careened down the runway, hit a berm of snow, and went flying the other direction. Like the ball in a pin ball machine.

Kenna only realized after she'd set off that she was running. The ground turned slick under her feet. Her winter boots had decent traction, but she slipped and slid like the airplane.

Impact hit the plane's right side, and in a split second everything got worse.

A fireball erupted under the plane.

One wing lifted into the air, and it flipped over, landing

on the roof. A wave of snow spurted out from under it as it impacted the ground.

Kenna's foot slipped, and she went flying. Air expelled out her mouth in a cry. She landed with the gun under her and had to get her legs righted before she could push off. *Ouch.* Her ribs had taken the brunt of the battering from the gun and the hard ground beneath it.

Jax.

She had to get to him.

The fact she was witnessing her worst fear right in front of her face wasn't something she could dwell on. How was she supposed to appreciate what she had if she never actually *had* it? They'd barely spent any time together, and now he could be dead?

Kenna cried out as she stood.

She kept running, skidding in spots.

Kenna headed for that open door. She couldn't even make sense of what had happened. Had the guy on the office roof been a spotter for someone else? She couldn't work it out.

She spotted movement in the airplane doorway. A tall man stepped into view, holding on to the side of the opening.

He jumped down onto the snow, lowering into a crouch before he stood up.

Alive.

Unhurt by the look of it, but not even wearing a coat over his sweater and pants. His eyes widened as he saw her tear across the space that separated them as fast as she could. "Did you see—"

Kenna slammed into Jax, and they caught each other.

Chapter Twenty-Two

"I'm fine."

"I'm not!" Kenna screamed the words against Jax's shoulder, then realized she was being ridiculous. She shoved him away. "Go get your coat!"

Jax's white smile flashed in the dark.

"Is anyone hurt? We have to get out of here before anything else happens." They also needed to talk through all of whatever on earth that had been. "Inside is probably warmer, though."

"Not really." He shuddered. "Why is it *freezing*?"

"It's called winter." He wasn't in San Diego anymore. "Do you at least have a base layer on under that?"

"A what?"

Kenna winced. "This is gonna be rough." She looked back at her vehicle. "Maybe I should run over and get the car."

"I'll do that in a second."

She looked down at his shoes, then up at his face. "It's slippery. You're not going to be running anywhere." Kenna climbed into the plane, which immediately looked odd. Upside down meant the seats were hanging from the ceiling, but that meant the men were easier to find. Two marshals and a man in cuffs, all dressed so she'd never have pegged them as anything other than regular men. At least they had coats. "Someone checked the weather before the plane took off."

"I have a coat." Jax nudged her arm as he passed, a gentle and playful jab she liked a lot.

One of the marshals said, "This her?"

"Yes, sir." Jax nodded. "Marshal Pilsborough, Kenna Banbury." Pilsborough had a beard. "And that's Marshal Destain." He motioned to the clean-shaven one. "And their friend here, who you can call Jim."

"Sheriff's department." Kenna indicated her badge. "Deputy Banbury, I guess. If you need that. Kenna is fine, though. What about the pilot?"

Jax shook his head. "We need to get moving." Who knew who they might run into on their way down to Chicago, or wherever she was saying goodbye to them.

On that thought, she went to the nearest window and lowered the shade so she could look out. "Whoever hit the plane could be on their way over." She spotted a car. "In fact, they're headed this way now." Under her arm, she took a photo of the prisoner with her phone.

Maizie would get his image right away.

As Kenna watched out the window, the car fishtailed on the runway. Another plane was coming in for landing. Then she remembered she'd called 911 for the office guy who'd been tied up.

"First responders should be inbound," she said, "but I don't see any sign of lights and sirens." How much longer till they got there?

Jax said, "Got a radio?"

"In the truck." She thumbed over her shoulder. "And there's no time to go fetch it before that vehicle gets here."

"Right." Marshal Pilsborough shifted his weight, rocking back and forth a little before he got the momentum to stand. Behind him, Marshal Destain held his arm awkwardly across his body.

She said, "Dislocated?"

He nodded.

"We'll take care of that after we get somewhere safe." She motioned with her head. "Jax?"

He shrugged on his coat. "I got him."

"Great. Let's roll out. We need some cover before—" Breaks squealed outside, and the car spun on the ice. "Let's go now. While they're busy."

Pilsborough grabbed the fugitive by his elbow and laid a sweater over his cuffs.

Kenna glanced at Jax, who gave her a quick nod and then went to the doorway. She tucked her hood up over her head, even though it would be blown off in a couple of seconds. If she could...

The car had settled on its side over by the nose, but far enough out they'd see the attack coming.

She said to Pilsborough, "Get cover behind that piece of wing." It was big enough to safeguard all of them for a time.

But at some point, they were going to have to make a run for it.

"Copy that."

Hearing them move behind her, she treaded carefully toward the overturned truck. Then spotted movement at the back, a shadow on the ground.

Kenna braced the gun against her body and fired a warning shot so they'd know she wasn't going to just let them kill her. *One down.* She didn't have an unlimited supply of rounds.

"Kenna!"

She started to back up, knowing exactly what Jax meant by that without him even having to ask why she was letting herself be exposed while he got to safety. Maybe it was a shade of the same worry she felt knowing he was in danger.

She took each measured pace carefully and didn't see anyone else at the car, but she knew they were there.

"Move," Jax ordered.

She turned and sprinted around the back of the wing, sliding on the icy snow like she was coming into home base. Shots rang out over her head, followed by Jax's return fire almost immediately.

Pilsborough lifted up and fired two shots.

Kenna did the same, though she had to reload first. Her knees dampened with the cold. The prisoner they were escorting didn't look much happier than the marshal with the dislocated shoulder.

"I still have one arm that works," he said.

"If I could lift up without getting my head shot off," she said, "I'd fix it for you."

Pilsborough chuckled between shots.

Destain said, "You've done it before?"

"You're gonna be picky at a time like this?" The prisoner, Jim, motioned to her.

"Yes, I've done it before." Kenna nodded. "But I'll admit it's been a long time." A bullet sang over her head, and she ducked.

Jim frowned. "Who *are* you?"

Kenna grinned. "Deputy Banbury."

Jax stumbled down to one knee and slammed into her shoulder. "Want the shotgun?" he asked, his face very close to hers. She saw the edges of his mouth curl up, entirely too entranced by the way it looked. "We're going to distract each other and wind up getting killed."

Pilsborough fired, then backed up from the edge of the wing. "That's the last one. I think we're clear."

"Let's go check it out." She didn't want to carry the shotgun, though. It was getting heavy, and she couldn't let that distract her. She needed to put all her attention on being aware of the threats coming rather than her own issues—including the handsome, distracting man.

Just great.

"Let me take that." Jax held out his pistol, barrel down. "Let's trade."

Kenna leaned over as they swapped weapons. "Get out of my brain."

She saw the intention in his eyes, but now was *not* the time for him to kiss her. Hadn't she just been thinking that they needed to focus? Maybe it was just her.

"Let's go." She followed Pilsborough, taking one side of the overturned vehicle than him. "One down here."

The guy lay bleeding onto the snow, staring at her with lifeless eyes.

She kept going and found another with Pilsborough standing over him. The back hatch of the small compact SUV was open. She peered in. "The driver is out, or dead. They've got a case back here." She climbed in and checked the driver's pulse. Nothing. "He's dead. And this is a grenade launcher."

"That must be what hit the plane."

Kenna climbed out.

Jax came over, Destain and Jim behind him. "Let's get to your vehicle. Get out of here."

They crossed the runway, and the plane that had landed a short while ago had taxied into the hangar. A police car and fire truck pulled in, lights and sirens going.

Destain said, "Figures the locals would show up after the danger is over."

"Hey." Kenna glanced over. "You'd better have no filter because you're in pain. 'Cause that was uncalled for." She tossed Jax her keys, and he winked. Then she jogged over to meet the officer local to the airport and the firefighters.

"Never seen you before."

"Deputy Banbury. I work for Gingrich." If they had an opinion about the sheriff, they kept it to themselves. "At least for today. There's a guy in the office. He was tied up, lost consciousness, and possible other injuries. The shooter..."

She glanced around.

"Lose something?" The officer's breath puffed out white in front of his face. He wore a uniform coat, gloves, and a beanie. And, like her, he probably had on insulated pants. A man accustomed to the temperatures where he lived.

Jax had come from San Diego. He'd been wearing shorts not long ago, and was definitely not accustomed to the freezing digits out here. She needed to get him a hot drink, and get their friends under cover.

There was more snow on the forecast.

"There was a man on the roof. Others in that car over there." She pointed across the runway. "The occupants of the vehicle are deceased. The shooter must've run off, but I can give you a description." She glanced casually at her car and saw they'd loaded the prisoner in the back. "I've got an injured man if any of your firefighters are EMT trained."

"All of 'em are. Department policy."

"Great." She called out, "Marshal!" and waved. "Let's take a look at your shoulder."

Jax guarded the car.

Destain took his dislocated shoulder to the firefighters. A couple of others walked the office guy out of the portable building. They let him sit on the hood of the police car, which was probably still warm. He blinked at her and gasped. "I woke up, and she was just standing over me. She didn't do anything. She just left. Then I heard all those gunshots outside, I had to hide!"

Kenna ignored most of that. "The guy who attacked you. Have you ever seen him before?" They wouldn't need her description if this man could ID the shooter.

The guy blinked. "Well, yeah. He's a local. Part of this group that thinks they're big game hunters."

The cop said, "Ramsey?"

"His brother. Not Earl, the other one."

"Doug."

The office guy nodded. "Yeah. It was him."

The cop said, "Got it. I'll get an alert out. We'll find him." It was always better when local cops went after local bad guys. They knew where to look, or who to ask.

Kenna said, "I've got to get back to work, get out of your jurisdiction. Call Gingrich if you have any questions or if you need a follow-up, yeah?"

"Sure. Yeah." The guy looked a little star struck.

Maybe she was his type, or he just liked lady cops.

She patted his shoulder on the way past. "Thanks. You have a good night." Then jogged to the car, not wanting to face any more delays. The quicker this job was done, and they were away from anyone looking for Jim, the better.

Destain joined her, sliding in the back seat. She got in front, since Jax had slid the seat all the way back to accommodate his height and he had the engine running.

Kenna clipped her seatbelt in. "That way, where the gate is. Then hang a right, that'll take you to the highway." As he sped away, she pulled off the beanie, making her forehead itch, then ran her hands through her hair. "They were locals, the guys who hit the plane. Hired guns?" She glanced in the back where Pilsborough and Destain sat either side of Jim.

Pilsborough shrugged. "Fits. Someone hires locals, it can get passed off as random."

"I've got a plate full of coincidences right now. I don't need anymore." She also had someone, definitely not a local, who was here stirring up trouble for her.

Kenna got on the phone, calling Gingrich. When he picked up, she said, "Am I supposed to say that the 'package is en route' or something?"

He chuckled. "No, but that's good to know."

"Well, here's the bad news," she said. "You knew they were coming in. So did I. Who else is on the list? Because someone gave out information, and I'm guessing these marshals keep their operations pretty tight."

"You think one of mine leaked information?"

"That's exactly what I think." Given the state of loyalty— or lack thereof—in his department, she wouldn't be surprised at all at someone angling for a promotion. The idea they might be passing information to a criminal and putting lives in danger, including cops' lives, was unbelievable. "Who else knew?"

"I'll make a list and send it to the marshals."

Because he had as little loyalty to them as they had to him? She wasn't surprised about that. "Figure out who knows. And don't tell anyone where I am. Don't leave any electronic record. I want verbal instructions only."

Visibility in front of the windshield had narrowed to a few feet amid swirling snow that didn't seem to know where to land. Jax held the wheel and kept a good pace on the highway that was thankfully mostly empty at this time of night.

"I know how to keep people safe," Gingrich said.

"So do I," Kenna said. "Now tell me where I'm going, because this snowstorm is starting, and I need a place we can hole up if it gets bad."

"I have a cabin you can go to. It'll be about a half hour from where you are." He told her the highway number, the turnoff, and visual markers only a local would know.

She wrote them on a napkin she found in the glove box. "Got it."

"There's supplies, and you should be good if this lasts a day. Call me when you get there." Gingrich hung up.

Kenna mapped the location where they were supposed to turn off the highway and started directions for Jax. He put her phone in the cupholder to the left of the steering wheel.

Then she turned. "Okay. Now that you know you can trust us, it's time for someone to fill in some details." If she was going to have a clue about what they would face getting Jim to a secure place where he could stay while he testified in Chicago, she needed information. "Who's going to start talking?"

Destain closed his eyes, leaning his head back on the headrest.

Jim grinned at her. He lifted his cuffed hands and patted Jax's shoulder. "Got yourself a keeper."

"I know." Jax didn't sound amused, but maybe he was concentrating on driving in wintery conditions.

Pilsborough said, "You know enough."

"Testifying in Chicago, all very hush-hush." Kenna paused. "Against who? They seem to be going to great lengths to stop it. And despite the secrecy, they knew when you were landing and where. They hit precisely at the right moment."

His expression shifted.

She didn't much care if he didn't like it. This was the truth.

"He's testifying against a dirty federal agent," Pilsborough said.

"Someone with the connections to hire locals and find out

information from a sheriff's department." Kenna tried to think if she'd heard any rumblings but hadn't been in the loop for a long time. "Let's get somewhere safe and warm, and you can practice giving your statement on me."

Jim nodded. "That's fair."

She spotted headlights behind them. "Someone is coming up fast." An idiot who thought they should speed in freezing conditions.

"Everyone hold on," Jax said. "This might get bumpy."

Kenna gritted her teeth. She didn't need to be in another car accident.

She glanced at Jax. "Get us out of here."

Chapter Twenty-Three

"That's the plan." Jax gripped the wheel, the rush of adrenaline making him restless, but the weather outside didn't look inviting. "You've already been in one car accident this week."

The vehicle behind them had to be an SUV. The sheriff's department car was a mid-2000s model. He couldn't outrun them if this was the black vehicle he'd seen in the hangar. Whoever had landed after their jet, they'd maneuvered into the hangar and gotten in this vehicle behind them.

So their pursuers had switched from local hitters to a different team that had flown in from out of town.

Or that was the plan all along, given the timing. Assume the locals wouldn't get the job done—or count on them to slow down the people in this vehicle long enough to be there and scoop up the remains.

Hopefully figuratively, not literally.

The radio on the dash stayed silent. They were a few hours from the safety of that sheriff's department building, and too far north on the peninsula to have anywhere they could make a stand. If they were going to get to this cabin, they couldn't be followed or it would be the worst idea to leave the vehicle and flee inside. They would only end up trapped.

Jax held the wheel tight. He scanned the mirrors.

No one in the back said anything.

Between Jim and his two marshal babysitters, Jax had enough of an idea of what they were up against. Kenna wasn't going to like it—or her connection. But if she did, she'd be even more onboard with getting this guy to the federal courthouse in Chicago than she already was.

Kenna didn't need a personal connection. She went to bat for anyone, anywhere, at any time, if they were innocent or in danger. She fought that fear which lived in her, raging and trying to drag her down. She fought it and managed to keep on moving.

The road up ahead angled to the right, a sweeping bend of the two lanes on this side.

He'd have to...

The SUV sped up angling for his left side, trying to get around them. Or the plan was to side-swipe them.

Three miles until the turnoff, he'd have to take to get to the cabin.

But it looked there was at least a gas station at the next exit, along with a couple of fast-food restaurants. Probably all closed down due to the storm coming through. Perfect time for a clandestine operation—if it wasn't also the worst time for one.

At the last second, Jax yanked the wheel hard to the right and got them over the V onto the exit ramp. The SUV sailed onward, down the highway.

He braked hard, then remembered to pump the brakes.

The sheriff's vehicle fishtailed, but he managed to keep control as he slowed them down and pulled up at the intersection. The SUV on the highway braked.

"Did we lose them?" Pilsborough asked from the back seat.

Jax had met the guy at a training conference for federal agents from all branches, some kind of cooperation thing. Or an attempt at one. They'd been paired up in a door kicking exercise and taken first place rescuing the hostages.

They hadn't kept in touch much, but just enough he knew he could trust the guy.

"Don't count on it yet." Jax headed for the gas station. There was no way to track the location of the other vehicle. Hopefully, they didn't have the means to track the sheriff's department through some kind of GPS. He tapped the screen of the phone and called—

"Maizie?" Kenna said.

"I have a question for her," Jax said. He took a right turn and headed for the gas station. They needed to be gone before the SUV came back around, or they needed somewhere to hole up.

Maizie picked up. "Pablo's Pizza Palace."

"I need the escape special," he joked. Kenna shot him a look, but he'd have to explain it to her later. He continued, "Does this vehicle I'm in have a GPS transponder? Because if it's sending our location, I need to turn that function off."

"Please hold." Music came across the phone line, through the tinny speaker on the bottom of his phone.

"Someone want to explain what this is?" That was Destain.

Jax pulled behind the gas station and parked out of sight, in the shadows. He cut the headlights but left the engine running. A dark-gray cat jumped the chain-link fence out of sight.

Kenna twisted around in her seat. "We need to know if they can track us, right?"

"So you call a pizza place?" Destain didn't sound any happier than he had the entire plane ride. Jax had figured out pretty quickly that the guy was either afraid to fly or nauseous because of it.

Kenna faced forward again. "You have your resources, I have mine."

The music quit. "Sir?"

"I'm here." Jax shifted in the seat and leaned forward a little, stretching out his shoulders. He wanted to crank the heat in the car, but that would only make getting out all that much more brutal of a shock. Why did people want to live in the north?

Not that he was going to admit to Kenna that he was *freezing*.

"Your vehicle is transmitting its location," Maizie said.

"Tell me where the transponder is, and I'll pull it out." Jax would have to dig up a flashlight, but no way a cop car didn't have one.

"I can dig up schematics, but what I'm looking at indicates it might be buried in the dash. Probably so it can't be disabled easily. I'm working on disabling the signal itself. Burying it with so much interference that there's no way they can track you guys to..." Computer keys clacked. "Okay, I'm done."

"We're clear."

"Anything else I can help you with tonight, sir?" Maizie asked. "You'll be getting an email with a survey. If you could give me five stars, then my boss will keep giving me amazing Christmas presents."

Jax chuckled. "Sure thing."

"Oh, and if you can tell her, I'm running *everything*. I'll have a full report as soon as you get to the place."

The call ended.

Jax pulled out from behind the gas station because this was the last place their location had pinged from. It would be the first place someone searching for them would look. He scanned for big black SUVs and made his way to the drive-through of a fast-food place, then behind the building. He backed up next to the dumpster so he could pull out fast if necessary.

Pilsborough said, "Interesting friend."

"She comes in handy."

"But you're not going to tell us who that was?" Destain huffed. "We can still make trouble for you, using resources outside the Bureau."

Except that this wasn't a Bureau operation.

It was theirs, and he'd tagged along.

"You wanna go on record, talking about tonight?" Jax paused. "I'd have thought you'd need to keep it under wraps. For the sake of protecting your witness."

Kenna said, "Head's up."

"Where?" Jax shifted the car to Drive.

"Ten o'clock."

"Great," Destain said. "They found us."

Jax bit back what he wanted to say. If there was a leak, it could be someone in this car. He couldn't decide, if it was him, whether he would come across disgruntled or act like everything was fine. Or keep his mouth shut and go with it like the witness.

The SUV moved away from them, and he couldn't see it between buildings. There weren't many cars around, but a few people were filling up—plus gas cans. Stocking up with supplies from the store.

He pulled out.

"This sheriff's department decal might as well be a neon sign." Kenna bounced her knee.

Jax couldn't avoiding smiling after spending the past few weeks apart from her. He wanted to reach over and squeeze her knee to reassure her, but there was enough to concentrate on. One thing he knew about Kenna—she could handle herself. They'd be safe soon enough.

He pulled onto the road and headed back to the highway, constantly checking to see if they were being tailed.

They made it to the turnoff for the cabin in good time, but immediately he saw the problem. "The lane up to it wasn't plowed recently."

"We can stop and put chains on, or we can walk." Kenna shifted in her seat to face him.

He stopped and did the same. "We'd have to hide the vehicle in case anyone comes this way."

Pilsborough nodded. "Let's get the chains on. We'll leave tracks, but we'll be warm and rested when they get here."

Jax was hoping for some coffee, or soup. So far they were in one piece, and not being followed.

Thank You, Lord.

He didn't know what kind of place this cabin was, but if they could get there, they could at least get warm.

After a few minutes, they got the chains on and began the arduous journey to the squat structure on the hillside. They weren't facing the incoming weather, but snow still swirled in front of the cabin.

Dark. Cold.

Jax got out, wrapping his coat tighter around him. The wind whipped at his ears and nose as he opened the rear door for Destain. "I'll go check it out inside." Jax pocketed his phone and grabbed the shotgun from the floor under the driver's seat, where he'd stashed it.

Kenna met him at the door.

"Is there a key, or a door code?" he asked.

She typed four numbers into the pad below the handle and stepped back, his pistol between her palms. "Ladies first?"

Jax shook his head and stepped in. He flipped the switch, and nothing happened.

"I'll go look for a generator after we clear it." She handed him a flashlight.

Jax clicked it on. "Copy that." She had lived on the road for years, so she knew what she was doing in the outdoors living department. He just wanted to know if the sheriff stocked his place with coffee, and if there was enough room for five people to stretch out and get some rest.

The cabin was a one-room structure with a bed located on the other side of a bookcase with open shelves, so what was on either side was visible. Rows and rows of battered paperbacks filled the shelves. A ratty recliner, old table, and two chairs next to a vintage kitchenette with a yellow refrigerator from decades past. No TV.

He cleared the small bathroom at the back. "We're good. Send them in."

She came over and kissed his cheek. "Copy that."

Jax's fingers flexed. He wanted to pull her in and see where that would go, but they also needed to get the two marshals and their witness inside.

He was still standing there staring after her when Pilsborough stepped in and said, "Cozy."

Jax turned to the kitchen and pulled open the refrigerator door. All he found was a half-empty bottle of tomato sauce and an empty pizza box.

Destain slumped onto the couch with a groan. Jim went to

the wall by the fireplace and sat with his back to it. They all looked exhausted.

Jax pulled open cupboards and flashed his light over a basic kitchenware setup that leaned toward camping. Everything hummed, and the lights flickered on overhead.

"Bingo." Pilsborough sauntered into the kitchen. "Coffee?"

Jax found a cupboard with canned soups and chili, hot chocolate mix, and a jar of instant coffee. "Only this." He pulled it out, wrinkling his nose. Behind where the jar had been, he spotted powdered creamer and nearly threw up in his mouth. He set both on the counter and searched for a kettle.

The stove was electric, so it probably ran off the generator as well.

He turned on one the burners and pulled down four cans of chili and a can of tomato soup, which he dumped in a pot beside a metal kettle heating water.

"Wake me when dinner is ready." Destain settled down on the couch out of sight.

Jim had his eyes closed.

"I should find wood to make a fire." Pilsborough lifted his chin. "Seems like you've got this covered."

"Anything I need to be concerned about?" Jax asked.

"Just get some food in Destain," Pilsborough replied. "He gets hangry."

From the couch, Destain called out, "I heard that!"

Pilsborough grinned in a way that let Jax know he enjoyed getting a rise out of his partner. That was good—it meant they'd worked together long enough Pilsborough trusted him. Jim hadn't seemed scared or didn't show it. Maybe the prisoner figured this was as close as he'd get to a vacation. How long was his sentence?

Kenna appeared in the door but stopped. She kicked her boots against the outside of the cabin, depositing the snow outside before she came in, then bent to unlace them. She left her damp boots by the door and deposited what she had in her hands onto the kitchen counter. "Chargers. Plugs. There's a weapons lockbox in the trunk." She glanced at him.

She couldn't lift it.

Pilsborough was about to remove his coat when Jax said, "Can you grab the lockbox?"

The agent shot Jax an odd look, then nodded. "Sure. Look for wood in that crate. And find matches and a newspaper, or some other kindling."

"On it." Kenna glanced at him. "Coffee?"

"I'm heating water. It's instant."

She laughed. "In some cultures it's considered a delicacy." Jax made a face.

"Agree to disagree, I guess."

"Is it a deal breaker?" he asked.

"You'll have to work harder than that to find something to convince me it's not worth it."

"I thought the exercise might do it," Jax said. She'd been shot not long after they met, and he'd effectively been her physical trainer in the months after. Getting her moving every day so she could heal and not develop too much scar tissue. "But the distance is definitely a problem."

He'd missed her. She knew it.

Kenna shot him a soft look he liked a whole lot. This woman was so different than the one he'd met more than a year ago. She'd given her life to Christ, and it showed. Her gaze drifted to the men in the living room. "You call our mutual friend?"

"Mostly she calls me."

"To rat me out?" Kenna's lips curled up.

Jax shook his head and pulled her close. They could talk about this more later when there was some privacy. For now he gave her a hug, his lips on her forehead. They stayed there for a long second before she squeezed his arm and stepped away.

"I'll find wood and make a fire."

Chapter Twenty-Four

Kenna rocked back on her heels and stood, the fire beginning to flicker to life. Pilsborough could stoke it if he cared enough to tend it constantly. Some people did, but she preferred those logs you buy in a paper bag, where she only had to light the bag and then just watch it.

Gingrich had a beat-up table in front of the couch. Under the surface was a kind of shelf. On it were old dusty magazines and more books that weren't on the shelf. She'd already sent him a text commenting on the amount of paperbacks he had in here. And not the kind that were purchased but never read. *No one asked me about my e-book app.* These had been well-appreciated.

Destain's jaw had slackened, and he was almost snoring.

Kenna took two steps toward Jim to go around the coffee table over to Jax in the kitchen, who was spooning out chili into bowls. Jim's eyes opened, that protective instinct he'd learned keeping him aware so he was never vulnerable.

She spread her fingers out and eased past him. The prisoner didn't move.

Apparently Destain and Pilsborough weren't worried he

would turn violent, or try to escape, despite the fact he had been originally convicted of murder.

Kenna's phone buzzed in her pocket. She'd brought her earbuds from the car, so she put them in and answered Maizie's call. "How's things?" She wandered to the bedroom area and sat down, setting the phone beside her.

"Uh..."

"You can just tell me the update." After taking out her hair tie, Kenna flipped her hair forward and ran her fingers through it, about the best she was going to get right now.

"I mean, I'm fine. I just didn't know you were going to ask me that."

"I'm fine, too." Kenna flipped her hair backward, sitting upright again, and retied her ponytail. "In case you were curious."

"Speaking of fine..."

Kenna chuckled. "Jax?" He was walking toward her with a steaming bowl and a spoon. "I see what you mean."

Maizie laughed. It was a beautiful sound, given all the girl had been through.

Jax handed her the bowl. She mouthed, *Thank you*, and he winked.

As he walked away, she wondered how she'd gotten this far with a man again. At the same time, as it seemed so clearly obvious that she would feel this way, she also couldn't see where she'd taken the steps in his direction. She hoped it was God leading her. And that He wouldn't leave her to despair again like the last relationship. Still, it was a risk she hadn't anticipated.

Kenna took a bite of the chili. "Yeesh, this is spicy and terrible."

Across the room, Jax sat at the table with Pilsborough. Jim

was eating. Destain hadn't woken up yet, and no one disturbed him.

"What's the update, Maze?" She took another bite.

"It's all much easier from a distance." Maizie sighed. "I was talking with Elizabeth about it a couple of days ago, before you got hurt. How it's more like watching a TV show or hearing a story. You, and Jax. She said it does me good to see something healthy that's not moving at warp speed. Apparently, that's a bad thing?"

Kenna swallowed a bite. "Head spinning isn't always a bad thing. Relationships go at all different speeds."

"She said yours was good for me. So I can see normal, even if it's not typical."

"And you have each other's numbers now?"

"Mm-hmm," Maizie said. "Is that okay?" She sounded worried enough.

"It's fine," Kenna said. "You're amazing, and the FBI might not know it, but they *definitely* need your help." She heard a relieved chuckle. "How is Cabot?" There might be work to talk about, but Kenna wasn't going to forget to ask about her dog.

"She's all right. I think winter makes her tired."

"Okay, so tell me what's going on." Kenna dug into the meal while Maizie clicked keys on the other end of the line.

"James Bernard Hauserton was convicted of two counts of murder half a dozen years ago in the state of Arizona. He worked in a gun store, and on paper had affiliation with a local group who liked to stage armed protests outside government buildings. They all live on one ranch on the east side of Arizona in the middle of nowhere. The website indicates they've started their own town, and it's not US territory. It's an independent country. Can they do that?"

Kenna said, "Folks can declare whatever they want. Doesn't make it true."

"The court case files have a lot of redacted parts. Is that normal?"

"No. Any idea what it was about?"

"There are indications he was a confidential informant for an FBI agent." Maizie paused. "Maybe that's why he was with that group."

"Maybe." It was speculation at best, but she wasn't going to begrudge Maizie theorizing. "But it was also years ago. People change."

"I hope so. For both our sakes."

Kenna smiled around a bite. "What about more recently?"

"Prison records indicate he kept his nose clean. It doesn't have the alias he's using, or anything about him talking to the marshals, so I'm not sure I'll get much more. Only that he went to the doctor every week for a shot."

Kenna figured that could actually be meetings with the marshals.

"I can't see who he worked with at the FBI, so I can't tell who he might be testifying against."

"Okay, what about Gingrich's people or anyone else?" She also wanted to ask about the latest with Forrest and her lawyer, but first she had to ascertain they weren't in real danger staying here. No way could they afford to get complacent if they were about to be attacked.

Kenna set her bowl in the kitchen sink and filled it with water. She set the faucet back to a slow drip so the pipes didn't freeze and walked to the window.

"Kobrinsky is up to his eyeballs in debt," Maizie said. "I'm not sure buying that boat last summer was a great idea, but the woman on it with him on Instagram seemed to be having a good time. And all her friends."

Kenna rolled her eyes and peeked out between the drawn curtains. Dust puffed up when she moved the material, making her sneeze.

"Bless you."

She glanced back at Jax, who returned to his conversation with Pilsborough, then tried to see if there was any movement outside. No point being caught off guard as much as any of them could help it.

"Rayland doesn't have much in the way of assets. His personal car is registered to the same address where his mom lives and has her office. So I guess he still lives at home?"

"It's a rough economy."

"Nothing odd in his financials. Gingrich, either." Maizie paused. "Pilsborough is a few days late on this month's child support. He has a four-year-old and a three-year-old, both girls. They live with his ex-wife in Santa Monica."

"And the other?"

"Destain is a little more...hard to nail down."

Kenna's eyes burned from staring at trees outside, so she moved the curtain back and went to make herself coffee. Thankfully, this instant was the freeze-dried kind, not the powder stuff that sucked.

"I've got a rental agreement, and a cabin up in Big Bear that looks like it's been in his family for generations. He drives a hundred-thousand-dollar car."

"Some newer ones cost that. It's crazy." Kenna shook her head.

"And he made a huge payment on it recently, settled the debt. Plus, he opened an account with an online bank based in the Caymans. So he has some money offshore."

Money that Uncle Sam never picked up on him having. "Interesting."

"In all, it was sixty thousand. He was smart, spreading it

out across multiple things so it was broken up. Didn't raise any red flags."

"Huh." Kenna turned her back to the counter and sipped the coffee. "Anything else?"

"I'm working on Forrest's case. The law firm took me on as a contract researcher."

"Really?"

"Yeah," Maizie said. "I sent them some information, and they jumped on it. Stairns verified my abilities and vouched for my integrity. No one's ever done that before. Said I was trustworthy."

"Doesn't mean it's not true."

"I know *you* think it. You gave me access to like... everything."

"You earned that respect," Kenna said. She wasn't going to get into how with other people in earshot. They didn't need to know sensitive family business—everything Jax already knew full well. She wanted to find out if they had boundaries on how they communicated. Not because she was concerned, but just to hear about how he was protecting Maizie's recovery. Because she wanted to know everything and she felt a lot like mama bear with this teen.

"Love you."

"Yeah, yeah." Kenna hung up and wandered to Jax, at the table with his back to her. He twisted his shoulders, and she leaned down to whisper, "Destain's financials."

Jax's gaze narrowed. He and Pilsborough both pushed their chairs back and stood. They seemed to communicate without words, not saying anything. They approached the back of the couch, and in one move flipped it back and onto the floor. Destain's legs swept through the air, and he tumbled onto the floor, waking up sputtering.

"What the flip are you guys doing?" He rolled over onto his backside and scrubbed his hands down his face.

"Funny," Kenna said. "I was going to ask you the same thing. Like how come you suddenly made a big payment on your car. The one beyond your government salary. Or the fact you have money stashed in offshore bank accounts. Care to share, Marshal Destain?"

Destain stared up at the three of them standing around him. Jim shifted to set his bowl aside, on the floor, staying where he was. The marshal said, "You think I'm dirty?" He twisted to the side to face Pilsborough. "For reals? Me?"

"Then you should have a good explanation for the windfall." Pilsborough's expression remained neutral. The fact Jax vouched for him made all the difference, but it didn't mean Destain hadn't been implicated.

With what happened to Forrest, that seemed to be going around. But no way were the two related. At least not connected.

Kenna had either succeeded in losing Stan Tilley, or he would show up at some point. She'd rather be back helping Forrest and the lawyer, Lucas Amrand, clear her name. Maizie was great at what she did, and she could find anything if it was connected to the internet. Any file. Any record. Evidence that would exonerate Forrest, or at least put enough suspicion on someone else that she would be out from under the spotlight.

Jax glanced at her.

Kenna needed this moved along so they could get going. "Talk, Destain. Or we leave you out in the snow." She folded her arms, creating that so familiar twinge ache in her forearms. She'd come so far. Things that used to be familiar felt new again, and her world had shifted. Amid the changes, she found herself struggling to keep up.

Destain shook his head. "Fine. I didn't put the operation in jeopardy." He looked at Pilsborough. "I wouldn't do that."

"I hope not," his colleague said.

"They leaned on me for information, but when I didn't give it up, they said they'd make it look like I was guilty. That huge payment landed in an offshore account in my name. Why not use some of it to pay down my car? They can't take it back if I've already transferred it out. I should get something for my pain and suffering!"

"Being implicated as dirty?" Kenna said. "Seems a little convenient."

"They were going to ruin me! Why not get something out of it?" Destain lifted his chin, but the effect wasn't the same considering he was still sitting on the floor.

Jax said, "Let's get you some dinner, and you can explain the whole thing." He apparently wanted to play good cop in this scenario.

"While Jax gets you some chili," Kenna said, "why don't you tell me who these people are? Because so far we've had locals and another group in an SUV right on their tails. So what is it? Two different groups after Jim here"—she waved in his direction—"or one set of people with deep pockets, or a whole lot of connections?"

Destain shifted and stood.

Kenna took a step back. He clocked her move and didn't like it. Did he think she would allow herself to be vulnerable?

"I don't know who they are," Destain said. "I got an unregistered email on my personal account. They sent pictures of my family. My friends. They threatened to ruin my career. They told me they do this all the time, framing people and making it look like they committed murder." He shrugged. "I'm not going to jail. I can't."

And yet, he'd kept their money. He hadn't gone to his boss at the marshals and explained the situation.

But something he said caught her attention.

...framing people and making it look like they committed murder.

That's exactly what happened to Forrest.

After years of accidents and natural deaths written off as that, despite the few naysayers who argued differently. Then *they* were killed as well. Now this?

An entirely different story.

Or a new chapter in one.

Kenna didn't get it.

Lord, I have to figure this out. There's no way Jim and Forrest are connected. At best it could be the same people, or someone who got the idea from them.

She tapped her fingers against her leg, trying to get her mind to assimilate the information faster than it was. Dumb car accidents, and getting shoved. She'd blacked out too many times this week. It wasn't helping her operate at full capacity.

Pilsborough sat with Destain at the table.

Jax came over and touched her side, then slid his arm around her back. Staking his claim.

Kenna shifted her gaze to meet his, turning slightly toward him.

"Are you okay?" he asked.

"We need to figure this out."

Jax squeezed her very slightly. "We need to get somewhere safe. After that, we can run it all down and figure it out."

"That could be too late." Forrest might not have that kind of time. "Who is Jim testifying against?" Surely he knew.

Given the shift in his expression, he did. And he knew she wasn't going to like it. "Cecilia Warren."

Everything in Kenna iced over like the ground outside. "Why did they let you come along? You could be working with her."

Jax shook his head. "Pilsborough knows me." Maybe the marshal knew he might need assistance—the kind he knew he could trust. "And I explained you'd be the one doing the escort for the sheriff's department."

Kenna squeezed the outside of his arm and left her hand there. Still, she tried not to make it look like she was clinging to him. She twisted in his hold so she could see Jim, who stared at her. "Cecilia Warren?"

He nodded.

The front window exploded, and Jim's body jerked.

Chapter Twenty-Five

The world spun around her. It took Kenna a second, but she realized Jax still had a hold on her. They tumbled together onto the overturned couch.

The arm provided some coverage, but they couldn't stay here.

"Keep low," he whispered.

She shook off the surprise and lifted her chin. The fire in his eyes was part anger and part affection—a whole lot of feeling—and was all directed at her. The force of it was almost overpowering. She had to blink and hang on for a second.

At least long enough for reality to set in.

Someone was shooting at them.

Kenna wrapped one leg around his and rolled them both onto the floor. A shot embedded itself in a book, knocking over a whole row into the bedroom.

"I'll take Jim." He let go of her and crawled across the floor, around the end of the couch.

Kenna clenched her teeth and went for the weapons bag instead.

"He's alive. Whoever is shooting, they just winged his arm."

Pilsborough said, "Copy that." He had crawled to the front window on the other side of the door and lifted up far enough to peer over the bottom windowsill. "It's that SUV. I count at least three guys."

Destain had chili all over his shirt and didn't look happy about it.

"You guys keep Jim safe." Kenna had a score to settle.

She flipped the latches on the weapon case and pulled out a pistol, loaded it, and stuffed an extra magazine in her pocket. The duffel beside it had her gloves on top. She tugged on a hat as well, then grabbed her jacket from where the chair had fallen over onto the floor.

She crawled to the bedroom corner, and through the bathroom to another room behind it, which doubled as a mudroom and rear exit.

Out of sight of whoever was in front shooting at them, Kenna zipped up her coat and took a long breath to steady herself. Adrenaline wasn't always a friend. Sometimes it made you move first before thinking, or shake when you needed to be steady. Plus, these days she had the Lord on her side. She could rely on Him instead of what she was capable of.

Go before me.

She unlocked the deadbolts on the door and eased it open, praying it wouldn't creak. Never mind. That wasn't on the table as an option. She peered out but didn't see anyone.

Visibility was awful. Snow swirled around in thick flurries like a tornado, whipped by the wind. She winced against the icy wet breeze that hit her face. Fog gathered between the trees, creating haze anyone with sense would hide in.

Now or never.

She checked again, saw no one, and went to the back

corner. Peered around, still saw no one. Checked behind her. Gun up, ready.

Kenna went to the front corner and spotted the shooter by the open passenger door, the rifle resting on the bottom edge of the open window. She squeezed off a shot that would've hit the window if it were rolled up. It slammed into his center mass.

She swung with her arms, around to the nearest gunman.

Another squeeze. She hit him before he could aim. His shot at her, where he'd turned to where her shot came from, went wide. *Thank You.* She wasn't sure God would ever condone taking a life—or if he *should*—but that was a big debate she could worry about later.

A shot from inside hit the third man.

The fourth kicked the front door in and headed inside the cabin.

Kenna stumbled as she raced across the snow. Ignoring the cold wetness soaking into her pants above her boots, she squared up on the door, shoulder to the frame on one side. She looked first, then swung in with her gun up.

Blinked.

Pilsborough stood watching. Jax used a towel to apply pressure on the inmate's arm.

Destain grunted. He rolled, holding on to the gunman. They punched each other and grappled, then slammed into a chair, knocking it over. A fork clattered across the floor, and then the man's pistol.

Kenna checked outside again. "I think we're clear. If you're done."

Destain cried out. He lifted the guy's shoulders and slammed the back of his head on the floor. "Now I am." He lifted up, one knee bent in a lunge, and turned to them. "I'm not dirty."

Kenna held up her hands. Right, the gun. She tucked it in the back of her belt. "Maybe the not-dirty marshals could tie up this guy and check the rest of his friends are dead." She strode around the couch and crouched beside Jim.

Jax was on the other side, looking concerned.

She asked Jim, "What's new?"

Jim opened his eyes and groaned. "It's just a flesh wound."

Kenna grinned, not quite able to laugh right now. "We need to get you to a doctor."

Jax nodded. "It's not life-threatening, but he's losing a lot of blood."

She wondered if Jim had faith in God. Maybe he considered the Lord to have saved him, as this could have been much worse than it was. "Let's get him up, and we can head out."

They weren't going to have a fun time all squashed in the back row in the sheriff's vehicle, but it wouldn't be forever. She would drive as fast as she could to the nearest hospital. But first, she texted Maizie for the closest medical facility and told her that their prisoner had been winged so the teen wouldn't worry that something more serious had happened.

Pilsborough went outside first, and Destain helped Jax with Jim.

Kenna followed Jax's friend, scanning as she moved. "We won't get anywhere fast in this weather."

"Maybe we should stick here, hold out and go in the morning." Pilsborough glanced back. "He won't bleed out."

Kenna said, "They already found us once."

"She's right," Jax said from the doorway. "We can't stay in one place. We need to keep moving."

As they crossed the clearing, Kenna noticed something amiss.

Pilsborough reacted first. "Tires are slashed."

She jogged around to the driver's door of the SUV and stepped over the dead guy. "Keys in the ignition here!"

Pilsborough opened the rear door so they could help Jim climb in. Kenna adjusted the front seat and started the engine, getting the rearview adjusted so she'd be able to see if anyone followed them. First, she would have to turn around in this small area, in heavy snow. The other alternative was to back up all the way down the lane to the main road.

The doors all shut, Pilsborough leaned in the open front passenger door. "Hit that button, open the back." He motioned to it, then sprinted back to the cabin.

The marshal emerged a minute later with the unconscious gunman over his shoulder. He deposited the guy in the back.

"Got some way to tie him up?"

"Yeah," Pilsborough called out. "There's supplies back here." His tone was tight.

What kind of supplies?

He got in the front and hit the button to lower the back hatch.

Kenna shivered at the cold air and cranked the heater. "What supplies?"

"Let's just get going, yeah?"

Kenna put the SUV in Reverse. *Here goes nothin'.* Maybe the fact she drove RVs, trailers, and campers regularly would help.

Please, Lord.

She didn't want to be the woman who couldn't three-point turn in the snow, even though it definitely wouldn't be her fault.

"Anytime." Pilsborough glanced over.

Kenna found a dial for four-wheel drive and decided on that. She eased the SUV past the sheriff's department car, rapidly being covered in snow, and reversed behind it while she turned. Drive. Left turn onto the lane.

Easy-peasy.

Her phone rang. She tucked it on the dash and put the call on speaker. "Got me an address?" Maizie would put it together that the others could hear her. Though, Pilsborough didn't seem to be paying attention. He was rummaging through the glove box looking at papers.

"I'm sending it now."

Pilsborough frowned.

"Thanks."

"All good?" Maizie asked.

"Yep." Kenna hung up.

"You have a kid that works for you?" Pilsborough said, leafing through a stack of envelopes.

"Not sure that's your business."

"This car is owned by a guy in Appleton. It's probably stolen, but we can find out."

Kenna held the wheel tight and eased down the lane, careful not to go too slow or too fast. They didn't need to get stuck or start sliding. "Even if they find the guys we just killed back there are the ones that stole it, we still won't know who they work for." Dead men couldn't give statements. "No point busting the guy in the trunk for car theft."

"Oh, I'll figure something out."

She caught a scary look in his eyes, and glanced in the rearview. She couldn't see Jax, but just knowing he was back there helped her keep her wits about her. "You guys good?"

"No, my arm hurts."

Kenna started, hearing all that from Jim in one go. He hadn't said much else.

Destain chuckled. "We'll get you some happy meds when they patch you up."

"No drugs," Jim said.

"Liquor?" Destain asked.

Jim shook his head. "Not if it gets us all killed."

Pilsborough huffed. He flipped his phone end over end on his knee. The fact he hadn't called for help, or a SWAT team of state police to escort them, was interesting. They wanted this operation undercover. Gingrich had received the request and handed it to her without further ado. But he hadn't had a good reason until Kobrinsky was injured.

Far too much coincidence.

But she wondered if Kobrinsky hadn't been injured... would he still have made up an excuse for her to take this escort duty?

Kenna spotted the highway up ahead, after a dip in the lane. She eased down on the gas, and they bumped up the far side of the dip onto the highway. Semi truck headlights rushed toward them from the left. Kenna grabbed the wheel and swung it to the right.

The SUV slid around, out of the way of the semi. Wind rocked the vehicle as it sped past, honking loudly. Whoever it was, they didn't slow down to see if the occupants of the SUV were all right.

Kenna pulled over to the lane the semi was in and followed it south, driving slow until she had her phone giving her directions. There were no other cars around, so she glanced back at Jax. He lifted his chin. *Guess we're good.*

In his expression, she'd seen plenty of indication he was trying to figure out something. He wasn't the only one who could read the other. There was something not right here, and it had nothing to do with the two of them, but she trusted he would figure it out.

"Whoever these people are," Kenna said, keeping her eyes

on the road, "how do we know they won't catch up to us at this medical center we're going to?"

"She's got a point." That was Jax.

But it wasn't like it was them against the rest, as much as she'd prefer it that way. He still needed to maintain his standing with the feds. The last thing she wanted was for association with her to cost him his career.

Destain said, "Keep your eyes peeled, I guess."

Kenna tipped her head to the side. "Jax."

"Yeah?"

"Ask Maizie for an alternate." They could use a Plan B at any moment, and she wanted one figured out before the last second when it might mean life or death.

"On it."

Kenna drove at 35 mph on the highway, trying to figure out where the road lines were, While she held steady on the wheel and peered into the swirling snow, all she could think about was Forrest sitting in a cold cell. The fact Marion Wells was right beside her wasn't right at all. One woman was a stone-cold killer. The other had never killed anyone.

And she was out here, helping a man who could fix something in the FBI that had been broken for a long time.

Cecilia Warren had been Kenna's roommate at Quantico. An agent everyone thought had gone to the dark side during an undercover operation had been reported as missing, the subject of a manhunt that never turned up anything. Cecilia had been his handler, and when Kenna met him in Mexico, the story he'd told her was far different from the official report.

Now she ran into a man who was prepared to testify against this dirty agent.

Because the marshals were building a case against her? They'd have to have brought it to the attention of the FBI's Office of Professional Responsibility. But as much as she wanted it otherwise, some people did live as though they were above the rule of law.

Like it didn't even apply to them.

Kenna's soul-deep sense of justice didn't like it, which was why she'd been so determined to figure out a way to expose the corruption. But had Jax already managed that?

She didn't like the distance between them any more than he did. But on her part, it was more that they had so much they didn't disclose until it was essential. She wanted to figure out how they could do that differently. If she got the chance to remember this later.

Up ahead, she spotted a row of headlights facing them like Christmas lights. "What does she have, Jax?" This was more like a holiday nightmare.

Looked like four vehicles. The row facing her had the semi winding around them, half off the road on the shoulder given how it was tipped to the right. Trying to get past them to continue. It wasn't easy, but the driver got around the roadblock. Kenna didn't figure they would be as able.

"A homestead close by, about a mile. But it'll be rough going in this weather," Jax said. "The owner's name is Merrington."

"We're going," Kenna said. "East or west?"

"East."

She eyed the left side of the road, where a line of cars blocked oncoming traffic. Beyond them, and all around, nothing but white and the night sky with the muted sun rising in the distance to her right.

Kenna hit the gas and the SUV lurched forward, picking up speed. She'd have to time it right, but with no way to figure out when the right moment would be, who knew how this would go.

Guess it's up to You.

The headlights rushed toward them.

At the last minute, Kenna dragged the wheel to the left, angling over to the car on the left-hand side. Headlights flashed across the right side of the SUV, and she felt the impact on the back corner.

The SUV swerved, and the embankment came up way too fast.

Chapter Twenty-Six

Kenna found herself in an odd moment of clarity. The vehicle bumped down the embankment, which turned out to be shallow, and lurched up the far side. Her mind cleared so she had no thoughts in her head to grasp. There was nothing but peace in that moment.

The peace she had in Jesus, permeating through her.

If they all died tonight, she would be laid to rest. And that seemed fitting—to call it "rest."

It would happen with Jax here.

In tenderness He sought me.

The windshield showed her nothing but cloudy, snow-laden sky, then they lowered back down and hit flat ground. Kenna eased down the gas, forcing her foot to not mash the gas pedal and leave them spinning.

Pilsborough gripped the handle above the door on his side. Someone in the back yelped.

She leaned forward so her back was off the seat. Grasped the wheel tight. Drove up the hill on the left side of the highway, the snow getting deeper and deeper. "We aren't going to get much farther."

Was this really Merrington land, or would they fall short of safety?

She also had to wonder if bringing this situation to their doorstep was a good idea. Kenna didn't like the idea of putting innocent people in danger, but right now they needed some serious help.

Whether that roadblock of cars were friends of the local guys from the airport, or colleagues of the men they'd left up at the cabin, she figured they would find out. And either way their intention was lethal.

The vehicle slowed despite her pressing down on the gas pedal. They were wading through deep snow now.

"Jax?" She heard movement but kept her focus on the SUV moving.

Then he said, "I don't see them behind us yet. But it won't take long."

Pilsborough said, "Everyone, guns ready. We get out, and we run over that hill."

"I know the residents." Kenna hoped they'd be amenable to what was about to happen—or they could get some kind of compensation from the federal government for it. She pulled the wool hat off the dash and tugged it on, along with her gloves. "Let's go."

One glance back at Jax, and she caught his nod.

They pushed open the doors.

Kenna led the way, shielding Destain against anyone coming up behind them. He told Jim, "Let's go. Get moving." They'd have to deal with the body in the trunk later.

Free of the car, they ran up the hill through snow now a foot deep. Her face numbed, pounded by falling snow. Behind them she spotted flashlights in the dim light. With no lights of their own, they could disappear into the dark and the fog.

She angled closer to Jax, intentionally or not. And somehow, she nearly collided with him as they stumbled up the hill. "Higher than I thought." Her words disappeared against the wind. She doubted he heard it, but she had to say something. Let the worry out somehow.

We need that peace, God.

She stumbled, planting a hand in the snow, she grunted and clambered back to her feet. Jax grabbed her elbow and helped. She had the wherewithal to give him a reassuring smile before she glanced back. Then gaped. "Run!"

She caught up to Jim.

Gunfire echoed behind them. A shotgun, by the sound of it. They crested the hill, and Destain stumbled. His fall dragged Jim down with him, and the two rolled through the snow.

The house at the bottom of the hill was lit up like a beacon of safety in the night.

Please, Lord.

It was far. They'd have to run all the way down the hill to that sanctuary.

Jax grabbed Jim and hauled him up while Destain scrambled out of the snow.

"Come on!" Pilsborough's yell was barely audible.

Another light came down at the bottom of the hill. Kenna pumped her arms and legs as hard as she could, wondering if God had been thinking about this moment with that future-knowledge awareness when she was running just a week or so ago and came back to the house to find Kobrinsky.

So much had changed since then. She could barely keep track of everything she had going on right now.

And yet, at the same time, there was a desperate kind of clarity with every heartbeat. Every breath she inhaled, laced with ice particles. Every warmer exhale.

The rhythmic swish of her arms and legs.

She found herself out in front. Down the hill she spotted a couple of dark shapes heading up toward them. People emerged from the house and barn. She didn't want them being shot at along with her, the marshals, Jax, and their prisoner. They all needed to get in and hunker down behind cover. Protect themselves from the incoming attack.

Pilsborough broke out in front of her and waved his arms. "Hey!" The word drifted away on the wind. He kept waving.

Kenna waved a little, but they already had these people's attention. Hers was on the two shapes coming up fast. "Dogs."

But what kind of dogs were these?

They looked like missiles hurtling through the snow.

If they were trained to protect their property and the lives on it, they would attack anything they perceived to be an incoming threat. She didn't know how they'd been trained, so she couldn't give a command. Most of the time it was tone anyway, rather than the word.

Kenna eyeballed the one closest to her, coming up fast.

She pulled her fuzzy hood around her neck, holding the sides of the collar at the front, then tucking it close to her neck. As the dog raced up to her, she slowed. Knelt. Turned her head to the side and gave the dog her shoulder.

He slammed into her with a low growl.

The force sent her onto her side, and she stayed there while the dog sniffed and growled. "Hi, puppy." She kept her voice as light and high as she could. "How are you?" The dog didn't bite her head off. "You're a good puppy."

Hopefully, only the dog could hear her, or this would be exceedingly embarrassing.

Destain raced over, looking like he was going to attack the dog.

Kenna raised her hand, palm out to the man. "No!" She

said the word loud and sharp, the way she would with a dog command. Destain nearly tripped over himself to stop.

A gunshot cracked across the night, and Pilsborough went down.

Kenna gasped. The dog hit the deck on its belly, ears up. She didn't pet the dog, figuring she'd get her hand bitten off.

"Down!" The cry belonged to a male.

The men with Kenna crouched, and gunfire echoed up toward the people behind them, firing at the top of the hill.

Jax went to Pilsborough. "He's hit!"

The gunfire suppressed the attack coming up behind them. Multiple figures down the hill fired rifles. The other dog was out of sight. In the snow? The one by her was a heavyset German shepherd. He'd need the body warmth in these freezing temperatures—and that long winter coat.

"Come on!" The tallest male waved them over. "Run to the house!" He turned toward the others. "Help with the injured man!"

Kenna got Destain and Jim. The dog bounded over after them. She eyed the ridge but didn't see anyone coming after them.

The run down to the house was arduous, and she wasn't carrying an injured man. Thirty or so feet from the house, the snow under her rose in a hard-packed mound she had to climb over, then disappeared. Gravel crunched under her boots.

She waited for Jax, who was helping Pilsborough. It was too dark to see the damage, but the marshal had been shot. Jax's expression strained.

They got Pilsborough over the packed mound of snow, where it had been plowed to the edges of the drive, and carried him to the side door of the house.

She watched the ridgeline.

Mr. Merrington's guys spread out around the gravel area.

The dogs stalked as well. Everyone on edge. Merrington came over to her. "Not how I thought I'd see you again."

"Sorry to bring this to your doorstep." Literally.

"We help our neighbors." He nodded. "Get inside out of the cold. We will stand guard."

"Thank you." Kenna stepped inside, to a mudroom not warmed by the home heating system. Rows of shoes lined the floor. Boots and sneakers of all sizes. Flip-flops, sandals, and slides. Kids shoes. Adult work boots. A bench seat was covered with gloves, hats, and scarves, and above those a row of hooks. Sweaters. Jackets. Coats. Snow gear.

She hadn't seen more children with them at the church, but evidently there were a whole team of them. Was that who Merrington had outside, holding guns and defending their property?

She winced. *Lord, keep them safe.*

Kenna tugged off her hat and gloves, then stepped inside.

"There. On the table." Mrs. Merrington had a dark-red sweater over her dress, and slippers with rubber soles on her feet. She glanced over. "Kenna."

"Sorry to barge in like this."

"Let's tend to your friend, and then we can talk." Her tone was all efficiency, and zero irritation about the fact they'd barged into her house, bringing blood and danger.

A slender girl ran in, wearing leggings and an oversized shirt, a similar sweater pulled over the T-shirt. She carried a tackle box, handing it over to her mother.

"Thank you, Lenore." Mrs. Merrington set the tackle box on the dining table beside Pilsborough's hip. "What's his name?"

"Mike." Jax's expression pinched. "It's bad, right?"

"It's certainly not good." Mrs. Merrington pulled huge metal scissors from the tackle box of what looked like medical supplies, slid them up the hem of Pilsborough's shirt, and started cutting.

Jax pulled back the material on his side. "Found it." He bundled up a shirt and pressed it against the marshal's side. Pilsborough's entire body jerked.

Mrs. Merrington grabbed her tackle box. "Switch sides." As she rounded his boots and stepped behind Kenna to where Jax stood, she said, "Kenna, check where your other friends went, please."

Kenna strode through the kitchen, past a wall of bookcases that separated the open dining room and a living room, across the hall to the huge sectional that looked supremely comfortable. Destain watched out the window, and Jim sat on the couch with his head in his hands.

She turned back to the kitchen and saw two little girls down the hall, one a foot bigger than the other. Both of them had nightgowns on, and the smaller one held a teddy bear that looked well loved.

Kenna winked, trying to be reassuring.

She probably looked like a mess, so she pulled her ponytail out and did the hair flip. Secured it back away from her face again. They weren't safe. This wasn't over. *But every woman knows fixing your ponytail makes you feel better.*

The girls stared at her.

Kenna left them and returned to the kitchen. Pilsborough was almost gray, splayed out on the table. Jax handed Mrs. Merrington a fresh piece of gauze.

"How is he?" Kenna asked.

"Almost got it." Mrs. Merrington had a flashlight in one hand, long tweezers in the other. She dug into Pilsborough's side, thankfully where Kenna couldn't see every grizzly inch of it. "Almost...there." She lifted the tweezers, a mashed round between the tips. She dropped it into the metal bowl

Jax held out. "Keep the pressure on that. I need to wash up."

Mrs. Merrington went to the kitchen.

Kenna moved around the end of the table, wondering if she should remove the marshal's boots.

"Whoa," Jax said. "Don't get too close. I know you don't like blood."

She glanced at the wound and her stomach lurched. But despite the mess, he had the injury covered. "I'm good." Then she moved all the way to his side, and he lifted one arm, so she took that as an invitation to slide her arms around him. She tucked her face neatly in his neck, her forehead on his cheek.

They were cold, sweaty, and exhausted, but it still felt good to stand there for a moment. He put his free arm around her back, the other pushing on Pilsborough.

"Is he going to be okay?" Kenna turned her head to look at the marshal.

"Depends on how the next twelve hours goes," Jax said. "He's alive. We have to pray the bullet didn't do too much damage on the inside."

Mrs. Merrington came over, her clean hands raised. A drip of water fell from her elbow. "I'm going to have a look at that right now, before I sew him up."

"You seem like you've done this before." Kenna reluctantly stepped back from Jax.

"After..." Mrs. Merrington gave them a knowing look. "You know..."

Kenna knew.

"We didn't want much to do with government. Police or healthcare. They're all the same, only interested in their own ends or how much money they can make." She gathered supplies from the medical kit. Thread and a needle. A small bottle of something she poured on the needle. "We became a lot more self-sufficient after that. On the internet they call it homesteading, but this isn't fashion. It's survival."

Kenna knew a little about the kind of pain over loss that changed the way a person lived their life.

She moved to a chair that had been pushed back to the wall and sank into it while Mrs. Merrington got to work.

Jax said, "I need to wash up as well." He leaned down and kissed her cheek on his way past. "I'll check on your husband as well, ma'am."

"Thank you, Agent." Mrs. Merrington's full attention remained on Pilsborough and his injury. "Kenna, will you hold the light?"

She stood, taking the flashlight. "I don't know whether to apologize or say thank you. Maybe both."

"The Lord guided you here. I'm thankful we are able to help." Mrs. Merrington jabbed a pair of odd scissors into the wound and opened it up.

Kenna swallowed hard, holding the flashlight and watching the woman more than the wound.

"I needed to talk to you, and I asked God to supply me an opportunity to do that. Now here you are."

Kenna frowned. "Talk to me about what?"

Mrs. Merrington glanced at the entryway. "About where Forrest Crosby was at the time Pastor Bruce was murdered."

Chapter Twenty-Seven

"Mrs. Merrington—"

"It's Alice."

Kenna couldn't believe she might've walked not only to safety, but also into an alibi for Forrest. Could that really be what God was doing here?

Alice ducked her head and made the first stitch.

Blood oozed from the wound, but nothing else did, which was a good sign there wasn't life-threatening internal damage. At least as far as Kenna knew—which wasn't much. Blood needed to stay inside the body. The heart needed to keep beating. Doctors insisted they knew more than everyone, and nothing they did would make her feel better than the chance to get in a car and *drive*.

Alice got to work, moving efficiently but slower than Kenna would've gone. Not rushing wasn't a bad thing, though. The woman seemed to know what she was doing.

Gunshots echoed outside.

Kenna flinched and turned to the window, but couldn't see out. They weren't protected standing here. They had to trust that the people outside would keep them safe. Just like at the cabin, a bullet could shatter the window and take someone's life with it.

Jim needed to be looked at when Alice was done with Pilsborough.

All Kenna wanted to do was go outside and help Jax. Make sure the children fighting this fight for them had someone to watch their backs. That was who had been outside with Mr. Merrington.

His children.

Had he trained them to fight a war?

Even if he had, she didn't like the idea they could lose their lives fighting one.

"Flashlight, Kenna."

Alice focused on her task. She grabbed her lip between her teeth while she pinched the skin together with one hand and sutured with the other. Moving proficiently, like a woman who had done this before. Apparently, she had no issue with the sight of blood or a gunshot wound. And even if she'd never sewn up a person before—just clothes—Alice Merrington didn't give any hint she was even nervous.

Kenna's stomach flipped over just looking at the blood.

A gunshot sounded outside, and Alice flinched.

She was nervous. For her family.

They both needed to be distracted from what was happening around them.

"Will you tell me what you know about Forrest's whereabouts?" Kenna asked.

It wasn't an interrogation. Just a quiet question between two women who would be overwhelmed with fear for people they cared about if they didn't occupy their thoughts with something else. They'd be overwhelmed with the sight and smell of blood, and the grisly injury on a federal agent that could turn out badly if he lost his life.

Kenna continued, "You mentioned an alibi?"

Alice let out a breath, her body completely still. "I don't like lying." She paused. "I have to say that. I don't like the fact that I've been lying. But while husbands might be the head of the family, that doesn't make them a hundred percent correct about everything."

"Okay." Kenna leaned her hip against the table. She touched two fingers to Pilsborough's wrist and felt his pulse. Thankfully, it was still there.

"I love everything about my husband and the life we have. But the horrible truth is that my son is a fantastic writer. He has talent. The stories he creates should be celebrated. Encouraged. Not swept away as if they weren't a part of Reuben's soul written down on paper." Tears gathered in Alice's eyes. "He wrote a poem about Rebekah. I've never read anything that beautiful."

"Reuben was with Forrest?"

Alice swiped her cheek with the back of her hand. "My husband will find out I went behind his back. That I deceived him."

And an innocent woman would go to prison because too many secrets had been kept. Because someone was trying to frame Forrest, and the people who knew the truth stayed silent.

She didn't fault Alice for wanting to keep the peace in her marriage. But the cost on this one would be high.

Kenna had to figure out how to get Alice and Reuben to give a statement that Forrest was with them. They might be the only ones who could give the lawyer what was needed to get the charges dropped. Would it prove beyond a reasonable doubt that Forrest hadn't been able to even leave poison for Bruce to succumb to later in the morning? Or would there still be work to do?

"Reuben and I feel terrible. We know we can help." Alice bit her lip again.

"You can," Kenna said. "There are times when we are powerless in a situation." Like with the gun battle that sounded like it was going on outside, and the fact neither of them could go and help. "And times when we hold the ability to change someone's fate."

Like Kenna had with Marion Wells' latest victim. She hadn't been here years ago to save Rebekah the same way, but one life hadn't been lost.

"Lord, help us." Alice whispered the words.

"Give us wisdom, O Lord our God." Kenna closed her eyes for a second. "Protect those outside. Help us to be a force for truth in the world. To stand for justice."

"To love mercy. To walk humbly, not full of pride."

"Amen." Kenna gave her a gentle squeeze on her shoulder. She didn't know how Mr. Merrington would react to finding out that his son was continuing to write. Getting tutelage from an author. The situation might cause a rift in this close family who stood together against the world.

But the truth would quite literally set Forrest free.

Alice said, "Gauze and tape, please."

Kenna set down the flashlight and gathered the items from the bag, tearing gauze pads out of their packets and readying the tape. As soon as she could, she peered out between the curtains. "How many children do you have, Alice?"

"Eight. Rebekah was my oldest, then three boys. Then two girls, and then another boy and a girl—the youngest is three."

"I saw two, they're beautiful."

"They are precious in the sight of God. No matter their appearance."

Kenna turned to the mother. "It was just an expression." She certainly hadn't meant that ugly children somehow had less value. Who even could be the judge of what physical beauty was? Everyone on earth was different. Kenna had physical imperfections, not just scars. No one was free of something they didn't want to change.

"In this day and age, it's important to be reminded that outward beauty doesn't count for much. Inner beauty is far more valuable. Kindness, empathy. Hope. Grace." Perhaps Alice needed an entirely different kind of distraction from the peril going on outside. She needed to talk about her children, something Kenna didn't know much about.

"I think the shooting stopped," Kenna said.

"Justice."

Kenna frowned. "What about it?"

Didn't everyone want to be judged fairly, or for things in life to be balanced? That was a big reason for her why she believed in God. After all, justice wasn't often found in life. She had to believe that if it was so strong in her to want it, then it had to be found *somewhere*. And she had—by hoping in God and the justice she would find with Him the same way everyone would. Face-to-face. *Oh, the grace that brought me to the fold. Wondrous grace that brought me to the fold.*

"Your heart is evident." Alice paused. "I'm grateful to God that life didn't take that from you." Her voice hushed, she added, "I hope you never know the pain of losing a child."

Kenna stared at her.

Alice's eyes sparked with tears.

"Maybe we are more alike than either of us realized," Kenna said, her voice thick. "But I never got the chance to feel my child grow. To nurture that life. Or raise that person."

"And yet you still have hope?"

Kenna wasn't going to tell her that it had been seriously

touch and go for a while. That her shattered heart nearly hadn't made it.

"Your life has moved on."

Kenna shrugged. Some days she wasn't sure much had changed, others she didn't even remember who she'd been just a year ago.

"The agent seems like a good man," Alice said. "Though, I can't say much more considering I only spent a few minutes with him."

Kenna pressed her lips together.

"You aren't hiding anything."

"I wasn't trying to." Maybe in some situations Kenna would have to keep how she felt about Jax to herself, but that didn't need to happen here, tonight. "He is a good man. Maybe the best." Probably better than her.

But relationships should be between two people who balanced each other, not people who were carbon copies of each other. The goal was to grow closer, not side by side in a straight line with distance between them even if it was small.

Then again, she'd never been married, so she might not be right about that.

Kenna figured they should get this conversation back on track. "If you and your son could make a written statement as to the morning of Pastor Bruce's murder, and the time you spent with Forrest, I'll take it to the sheriff. We might not need more than a follow-up conversation to wrap up the situation. We certainly don't need to ignite the core of your family and send it up in flames."

"I appreciate whatever you can do." Alice squeezed Kenna's arm. "But I'd like to talk to my husband before I take any more actions behind his back. And Reuben will get to decide for himself to write the statement out, if he will come to the station with you, or what he wants to do. As soon as the sun comes up, you can take the plane to town. My cousin owns a ranch close by, and Reuben can land there."

Kenna's brows rose. "You have a plane?"

"It's small, but you all should be able to fit. Though, you may need one trip for this injured man to be taken to the hospital, and another for the rest of you."

Kenna let go of some of the tension she'd been holding on to. "Thank you for offering."

"My husband can work out the details. I need to check on the children."

The back door opened, and she quietly left the room.

Then a young man stepped in, tugging a knit cap off his head, his nose red from the cold. "Did she tell you?"

Reuben—or so she guessed—didn't get an answer to his question. His father stepped up behind him, saying, "Did who tell you what, Son? Be clear with your words."

"Yes, Father."

"I understood the question, thank you." Kenna paused. "Yes, I spoke with your mother. We would like to get this man to a hospital as soon as we are able, if your family can help us with that."

"The drive is two hours." Mr. Merrington removed his boots and stepped into slippers, moving into the kitchen so the others could enter behind him—Jax, and the two sons who had come after Reuben.

All the children had the same coloring and features. Kenna would have connected them right away if she'd seen them apart.

Mr. Merrington said, "Reuben can fly the injured man to town as soon as dawn begins to break."

"Thank you, sir." Jax held out his hand, and the father shook with him.

The two teen boys got a cookie from a jar and hurried to the hall. Kenna spotted Destain there, and said, "All good?"

"Jim is asleep." Destain lifted his chin. "What's going on outside?"

Jax said, "The threat has been neutralized."

And the way it was done hadn't fazed those boys. Had they taken lives, then come in and grabbed a cookie?

"Reuben," Mr. Merrington said, "if you could join your brothers."

The teen didn't move. "I need to talk to you, Father."

"Then we can leave our guests and go to the reading room."

Reuben shook his head. "Ms. Banbury needs to hear it as well."

Kenna nodded, encouraging the boy.

Destain disappeared back to the living room. Jax said, "I can make some coffee?"

Merrington took a canister from the cupboard and set it beside the metal carafe that would sit on the stove. Did Jax even know how to make that kind of coffee?

He stared at the can and the coffeepot as if it would suddenly sprout a heads-up display of instructions in the air above both.

Kenna crossed the room and washed her hands. "I'll make the coffee, if you could stay with Pilsborough."

Jax squeezed her shoulder.

Kenna caught the edge of a whisper, and glanced over her shoulder.

Merrington's jaw tightened. Reuben whispered something else. Then he said, "I need to tell the police what I know, or Mrs. Crosby will go to jail for the rest of her life."

Merrington glanced up to where the wall met the ceiling.

Then he strode from the room.

Reuben looked like he wanted to be sick.

Kenna wanted to tell him he was doing the right thing. Instead, she said, "Your mom says you can fly a plane?"

He nodded. "We have a Cessna in the barn. There's enough flat ground behind the house to take off, as long as it's not icy. I'll get salt down and check the plane." He turned to the door but paused, glancing back over his shoulder. "You're the one who found Rebekah?"

Kenna said simply, "Yes."

Reuben stepped outside in barely a minute flat, geared up for the cold weather.

Jax said, "Something I should know about?"

Kenna wandered over to where Pilsborough lay on the table, still out cold. Did they need to be worried about a head injury? He still hadn't woken up. "Reuben is Forrest's alibi for the time of the murder. But his father was unaware what he's been doing."

Jax didn't look like he entirely understood what that meant, but they could talk about it later.

"What happened outside?" she asked.

"Five guys. All of them in the snow. The dogs are patrolling outside. Apparently that's a thing."

"And Reuben will be okay out there with no one to watch his back?"

"They're all dead," Jax said. "We made sure there weren't going to be any more surprises. Or attacks."

Kenna let out a long breath, fighting to hold it together.

"It's been a night." His eyes widened, flashing with contentment at the thought this might nearly be over.

"Yes, it has." A whole lot of running, and not much talking. Whenever they spent time together, she constantly found herself pushing off conversations until later. "I'm glad we could help Pilsborough in here, and that you all didn't run into trouble outside."

"I wouldn't say there wasn't trouble." He gave her a small smile. "But we took care of it."

And in doing so he—they—had taken care of the family in this house. The people they cared about. Jax had kept them safe, watching their backs like she'd always expect her partner to do.

"You were all right in here?"

"As all right as any of this." Kenna shrugged. "And it's not over."

Chapter Twenty-Eight

"Wakey-wakey, sunshine!" The voice was close to Kenna's ear, but sounded like shouting. Someone squeezed her knee.

Kenna blinked. The noise from the plane rumbled through her head, which she lifted off Jax's shoulder. He still had his hand on her knee, so she wound her arm through his and held on to his forearm to give her an anchor point.

He pulled his hand back to his own lap, her arm still wound in his.

Kenna sat up, trying to work out the kinks, but they were squashed in the back of the plane. Never mind the weight limit, they'd just packed in like sardines in a can, and Reuben had taken off in the dark. The plane racing toward the strip of light on the horizon.

Now it was full daylight, and he'd touched down on a runway that bumped with every foot the tires rolled over toward a farmer in a coat and hat, waving them over.

Jax glanced at her. "Okay?"

Kenna nodded. *Ouch.* "My head hurts."

"We'll get you something."

She wasn't the only person in pain in the small airplane. Kenna wasn't even injured. Jim had been shot, but so far refused treatment. Pilsborough had woken up but stayed on the dining table until it was time to go. Then he'd had Jax walk him to the plane.

The marshal looked a little sick. Pale. Alice had given him a pill, and some tea. Evidently, he was going to push through until he couldn't. Which was exactly what Kenna would've done, so she couldn't really fault him. He had to ensure his man got to Chicago. When he was under federal protection, and maybe even not until after Jim had made his statement, Pilsborough would head to a hospital and get a professional to look at his wound.

The plane came to a stop, and Reuben cut the engine. Destain got out first, shifting the seat in front of them so they could climb out. Jax held her elbows while she found her feet. Kenna gave him a squeeze, then stepped away, scanning the terrain for gunmen.

She didn't believe the danger was over.

But it may not come this time like before. Car chases, gunmen, snipers, roadblocks. This was another farm like the one the Merringtons lived on. The man who'd waved them in had wandered off, and came back now driving a red pickup.

He pulled up close to the plane and climbed out. His features and coloring matched the Merringtons, and he stuck his hand out to Reuben. They shook vigorously but said nothing. He nodded to Kenna, then told Reuben, "Keys are in the ignition," and wandered away.

Strategically staying out of whatever was going on. Ignoring the wounded, letting them use his vehicle and giving himself the standing to say he knew nothing about who was here. Maybe even that he never saw anything, or that his truck was stolen early this morning.

Kenna said, "I'll drive."

Jax chuckled. "Good one. But I'm driving. Reuben, you're in the back with Destain." He pulled out his phone.

The kid strode to the back and flipped the tailgate down, the hinges creaking as he lowered it. Then he clambered into the truck bed.

Destain shot Jax a look.

Kenna got in the back with Jim, Pilsborough in the front passenger seat. Did Jax arrange it that way so she'd be able to talk to Jim with only trusted people within earshot? She slid over, and Jim buckled up. The GPS gave Jax the first direction.

As soon as Jax had pulled onto the salted blacktop, the tension in her head eased. She watched the snowy scenery go by, trying to figure out how many days it had been since she had stepped inside her RV. Or felt like she hadn't been hit by a truck.

Now all this?

She angled her knees to point at Jax in the driver's seat.

Jim looked haggard. His skin pale. Dark circles under his eyes. "It can't be a coincidence that you're testifying against... who you're testifying against."

She glanced through the back window, but it didn't seem like the two people hunkering down out of the winter wind could hear them. "Cecelia Warren was my roommate at Quantico," she whispered. "I have a vested interest in what happens to her, but not because I want to help her skate out from under justice."

"She's the one who framed me for murder."

"You're not the only one whose life she destroyed." Kenna leaned closer. "But this needs to be done right."

"You wanna take over this mission?" Pilsborough spoke

without turning around, which he probably couldn't do with that wound in his side.

"Usually, I'd do exactly that," she said. "Take the whole case on myself, and see it through."

But something in her was missing—the drive to jump in with both feet. Because there was so much to take care of here? She didn't want to abandon Forrest and head to Chicago, take the next case before this one was even finished.

A man was dead, and justice needed to be found.

She continued, "Lately, I'm learning the art of relying on other people and not trying to maintain an iron-fisted control over every tiny little detail."

Jax chuckled, but he didn't turn or say anything. She would've kicked him, but there wasn't enough room in this tiny car.

Jim said, "We may need your help. We have no idea what will happen."

So there was a reason why they hadn't had a huge team of feds with them the whole time. Or why they hadn't called for backup at the first sign of trouble. The pilot had been killed, and there was a trail of bodies up through Wisconsin, but not once had the marshals called their boss and asked for help.

"If I'm available, I'll be there." Nothing would stop her.

The next time Ramon Santiago called, she wanted to tell him that not only had she found his sister and he could finally bury her, but she'd also made progress on clearing his name. Getting his life back.

Plus, she wanted to hear Jim's statement. Find out what evidence there was that Cecilia Warren was dirty. As an FBI agent, she had to be above reproach in her professional conduct. Kenna wanted to know what happened after they'd parted ways—not long after they left Quantico. They'd kept in touch, but that had been sporadic and dropped off completely after Kenna left the FBI.

Where had Cecelia gone wrong?

Kenna had looked at her career, and she'd risen quickly. She'd received accolades and awards and been recognized in promotions. On the surface, it seemed unlikely that Cecilia Warren had been working her own angle on the side—for whatever reason. Didn't have to be money. Until she met Ramon Santiago in Mexico, she hadn't thought about Cecilia in years.

Now, she met a second person who had something to say about the FBI agent.

Is this Your leading?

Jax pulled into the parking lot, and the front door of the sheriff's office opened. Gingrich stepped out, holding a shotgun across his body. He waved Jax into the open space right by the door, then turned around so he could back in.

They all piled out, and she stood by Pilsborough until he had his balance. She walked beside him up the curb to the door. "This guy needs a chair."

"Or a hospital?" Gingrich suggested.

"We'll take a doc on a house call if you've got one," Destain said. "But we're sticking together."

Pilsborough nodded.

Destain spotted him through the door into the office. Jax and Jim made four of them, a protective detail—though at this point she wasn't sure who was protecting who.

Reuben hung back. Kenna motioned with her head toward the sheriff. "This young man would like a word in private with Forrest Crosby's lawyer."

Gingrich rolled his eyes. "That guy has been driving us crazy. Hounding us with all kinds of attempts to get her released, then leaving to meet with the county judge at the country club of all places. Then he comes back and demands to know where he can find a Michelin star restaurant where he can order food to be delivered." The sheriff shook his head.

"Turns out I have a way to get them all out of your hair." Kenna held the door for Reuben, who seemed nervous. "Let's go find the lawyer."

Gingrich's department smelled like fresh coffee.

Kenna's stomach rumbled. "Then we'll figure out breakfast."

Jax pulled out his phone. "I'll do that. You get him in with the lawyer."

Across the room, Deputy Rayland stood up from his chair, pushed it back, and leaned both fists on his desk. "What's this?"

Kenna didn't like the way he asked that. She touched Reuben's shoulder. "Private client, lawyer business. That's all."

Rayland shook his head. "Doesn't matter. State police are transferring Forrest Crosby to the jail this morning."

Not after this, they wouldn't be. She wanted to say, *Unless the charges get dropped*, but kept her mouth shut.

Just then, Lucas Amrand stepped out of the conference room. Total big-city lawyer, and he looked about twenty-five at most. Slick brown hair, neatly cut. His suit, tie, and shoes probably cost more than her car if she'd added in his Italian leather briefcase and the coat he'd draped over a chair.

"Mr. Amrand"—Kenna gestured to Reuben—"this young man would like to speak to you about Forrest's alibi the morning of the murder."

The lawyer's eyes lit. "Is that so?"

She turned to the teen. "Reuben Merrington, this is Lucas Amrand."

The kid flushed, tugging off his wool cap and holding it in his hands like he wanted to wring it dry if it'd been wet.

She continued, "And those men would like to talk to your boss"—probably his father—"about borrowing the helicopter."

Pilsborough turned the rolling chair to the right, flashing the silver star of a marshal's badge on his belt, and Destain did the same. Jim had his jacket off, and was peering at the wound on his arm, his shirt sleeve rolled up.

The lawyer said, "I'll have him call this office." He waved Reuben into the conference room. "Let's talk."

The door closed.

Kenna turned to Rayland, feeling the pull of a smug smile on her face. "Tell me, Deputy Rayland..." She crossed the room to his desk.

The deputy looked seriously unhappy.

She'd thought he was a good guy back when Stan Tilley had been taking photos of her, and she'd been tackled. Maybe she'd hit her head too many times the past few days, and she'd lost the instincts she had when she had her wits about her. What else had she missed? Despite that worry, it seemed as though God had it all in hand.

Reuben was here. Jim would get to Chicago. To her left, Paulette walked in, already removing her coat. "Let me guess, I missed all the good stuff."

"Maybe not." Kenna glanced at Rayland. "Why are you so convinced that Forrest is guilty? Did the test results on the pastor's body even come back yet? Is it confirmed he was poisoned, or definitely murder?"

"She's guilty." Rayland stared her down, despite the room full of feds and his boss watching.

"Says who?" Surely not his crackpot detective work.

"All those books about murder. Of course, she's going to kill one day!" Rayland's voice rose. "She probably thought she committed the perfect crime and she was going to get away with it."

"I'll admit, it was clever making it look like natural causes. And her being across town when it happened." She spoke calmly. As if this kid wasn't unhinged and nuts. "That was smart."

"You both probably planned it together." Rayland pointed at her. "All your knowledge of investigations and murder. I bet you're guilty, too!"

"Son." Gingrich stepped between them. "Get in my office. Now."

Destain smirked, watching Rayland stomp like a kid called to the principal's office.

Kenna headed to the coffeepot and poured a healthy amount. "What's for breakfast?"

Jax grinned. "Don't get hangry. I have to pick it up."

"There better be bacon." What had he even ordered?

"You think I don't know that?" His tone softened, as did his expression. "Twenty minutes, I'm heading across the street to pick it up. For all of us."

Paulette glanced between them. "Oh, is this him?"

"Huh?" Kenna nearly sloshed coffee over the side of the mug but managed to save the day.

"I'm telling Kobrinsky. He wanted to meet your guy if he showed up." Paulette headed for the front desk.

"Anything else?" Destain asked. "Or can we talk about how to get to Chicago?"

Kenna sat on a desk over by Jax. "Hopefully, the lawyer's father calls soon and he can get you guys a ride."

Destain headed for the coffee. "Already got an email. They're sending the chopper in an hour, so we're here until lunch."

Kenna glanced at Jax. "We need to talk about Stan

Tilley." Which would at least distract her until she could go tell Forrest that she would be released soon. Right now, she wouldn't be able to temper her hope with doubts enough to keep from getting her hopes up.

Not a bad favor for the sheriff when it netted her a result on not just Forrest's case, but also the upcoming battle to reveal the truth about Ramon being let go from the FBI and written off as a traitor.

Kenna was ready to close all her open cases.

"I'll check in with my ASAC." Jax pulled out his phone. "Find out the latest and if they've heard from the Walker anytime in the last couple of—"

A loud crash from inside the sheriff's office had them all turning. Kenna ended up behind Jax.

The door opened before he reached it, and the sheriff appeared, red-faced and breathing hard. "He just collapsed. Paulette!" He screamed her name in their faces.

"Step out. Let us in." Jax moved to get around the sheriff, who didn't budge.

Pilsborough and Destain just stared, blinking. Jim studied his coffee cup like it had something in it. As if any of them needed something else to happen today? They'd been through enough the past couple of days, and this was their chance to start setting things right.

When is this going to end?

Paulette appeared from the hall. "Sheriff, what's going—"

He cut her off. "Get an ambulance! He's dead."

Chapter Twenty-Nine

"Right here." Destain ushered Jim into a holding cell at the end of the line, where the drunk had been when Kenna came by to speak to Marion. He unfastened the man's cuffs, and the marshal took a chair in the corner, so Jim would be within his sight at all times.

Kenna spotted movement in the middle cell. "Is Marion gone?" She moved to the bars and bit her lip to keep from reacting. Forrest's hair was wild, as though she'd dragged her hands through it a hundred times.

Forrest said, "The state police escorted her to jail, so the DA could talk to her."

"Did Deputy Rayland know anything about the case you're writing the book about? Anything like what Bruce thought he knew, about the deaths ruled as accidents?"

Forrest looked at the wall beside her, shaking her head. "How am I supposed to know?"

"He never said anything to you about it?" She'd figured it was more likely Kobrinksy on Forrest's side, working to break such a huge case so he could be the next sheriff. Rayland had been combative, adamant that Forrest was guilty.

But was it strong conviction...or something else?

"Why are you asking about Rayland?" Forrest asked.

"Tell me what connection he has to you, or any of this, aside from him being a police officer?"

"His mother?" Forrest shook her head.

"What about her?" Wasn't his mom the town shrink?

"The only connection I ever had to anything close to Deputy Rayland was through his mother's therapy practice." She answered Kenna's questions as though being cross-examining on the witness stand. Evidently, Lucas had been prepping her for just in case. "Now tell me why you're asking about him." Forrest pinned Kenna with a stare.

"Because he's dead."

And in the half hour between that moment of insanity and now, Jim had been hidden out of sight, Kobrinsky had shown up for desk work, and an ambulance came and went. Taking the body to the hospital so he could be officially declared deceased, and the cause could be found.

Kenna explained what happened with the reaction, and their going into the sheriff's office. When they'd gotten in there, Jax had tried valiantly to get the kid's heart to start beating again.

It hadn't worked.

All the while, Kenna had tried to figure out how to do that with no strength in her arms. What if she had to perform CPR? With the injuries to her forearms, she had no chance of rendering aid.

"At least I was down here," Forrest said. "So I can't be blamed." And yet, Kenna saw actual fear in her eyes. Not surprising.

"You aren't going to be framed for this." Kenna crossed her arms. "Just like you aren't going to be framed for Bruce's murder."

"How's that?" Forrest asked. "Seems like I already have been, and then you left to work for the sheriff upstate. Now you're back, and the case is moving again." She shrugged.

"I brought in Reuben Merrington to talk to your lawyer."

Fire flashed in Forrest's gaze. "Why?"

"I'm thinking you know why."

The writer looked aside. Another shrug.

"You'll go to jail just so his father doesn't find out he wants to be a writer? His dad already knows about the stories."

"Does he? He could be one, you know. He's got some serious talent."

"My father managed it without a whole lot of skill." Kenna stepped closer to the bars and tucked her thumbs in her pants pockets. "But I don't actually know if he wants to be a writer. Maybe he doesn't. Maybe he wants to journal and be a farmer, but he can do that still...after he's done writing out his statement corroborating the one you're going to give. He's going to help you fight this."

"His idea, or yours?"

"It should be *your* idea," Kenna argued, "to not go to jail for a murder you didn't commit because you were nowhere near the diner when Bruce collapsed."

Destain shifted in his chair. The guy might be looking at his phone, but he was also listening to every word they were saying to each other. Maybe he was currently running a web search on Forrest Crosby, looking up who she was and the book she had published. Articles about the accident, and more recent ones about her arrest.

Forrest let out a loud sigh.

Shoes clipped the floor behind Kenna, and she turned to face Lucas, who was striding toward her. He lifted his chin, then to Forrest said, "I'm going to meet with the judge and the district attorney assigned to your case. The state police are refusing to return my calls, so the sheriff will log the statement the boy gave me, and I'll get the DA to drop the charges."

"That's great," Forrest said. A knot in Kenna's stomach eased.

"The state police can go jump off a bridge," Kenna muttered.

Forrest's brows rose.

Lucas waved a hand. "My father says that a lot. I guess I've picked it up." He held his hand out to Kenna. "Thank you for bringing that young man here."

She shook hands with him. "I'm glad I could help."

Inside the cell, Forrest sat on the cot.

Lucas didn't leave.

Kenna looked over and spotted his attention on her. "Help you?"

"No one else dies," he said. "Got it?"

She lifted both hands. As if she had control over that? Why did people think she could have such an effect on what was meant to be? She'd learned the long hard lesson that she had no control, and what she did have she needed to give to God so He could be in control. Otherwise, she was only wrestling with Him the whole time.

Resting her forearms on the bars, Kenna looked at her friend again. Forrest would be out soon. This inaction would go back to not putting her freedom at risk. Forrest could retreat back into her house and go back to working on her book. "You should get a dog."

But something had triggered all this. More than Kenna being here, or the pastor leaving that note on the door. There had to have been a moment or event to kick it all off.

Forrest was going to have to face that if she wanted this to be over.

"Even if you're released," Kenna added, "you could still be at risk."

Forrest glanced over. "No one has tried to kill me."

From her expression, it almost seemed like Forrest had been expecting that. But why would someone frame her for murder just to kill her in a jail cell. Sure, they might want to get rid of her. That could've been solved by killing her not Pastor Bruce. Not framing her and killing her as well later.

Seemed like an overly elaborate plan.

"You could still be a target," Kenna said. "Whoever put you here might not be happy when you're released. It'll mean it didn't work."

Like Rayland's reaction to the arrival of a witness who could provide Forrest's alibi.

Was there someone else out in the community who was currently reacting the same way, or who would when they found out? If that person had also killed Rayland, then they couldn't have known about the alibi...unless it was Sheriff Gingrich.

"Kobrinsky is here."

Kenna flinched and spun around, nearly jumping out of her skin. "Jax." She laid a hand on her front. "Thanks."

Destain chuckled.

"He's here?" Forrest asked. "Great. The boyfriend shows up, and I'm behind bars. I'd offer you coffee or a piece of my amazing coffee cake, but I haven't been home in three days. I've been peeing in public, and I'm seriously sleep deprived."

Jax moved to stand where Forrest would be able to see him. "Sounds like good time to go home, shower, and take a nap."

Forrest huffed in agreement.

Kenna tapped her fingers on the bars. "Just hang on a little while longer, okay?"

"I don't have much of a choice, do I?"

Sorry this happened to you. She should say it out loud, because for a lot of years she never would have identified with the wrongly accused. These days she had a whole lot of empathy flexing its muscles inside her heart and mind.

Jax laid a hand on her shoulder and squeezed. "The sheriff needs us to go find Rayland's mom and do the death notification."

She followed him out of the hall of cells back to the main office area. The sheriff stood with Pilsborough, who had a lot more color in his cheeks. Whether from the adrenaline, or from something the EMTs had given him, she wasn't sure.

"We're heading out," Jax said.

Gingrich lifted his chin. "Paulette has the food."

Kenna told him, "Keep an eye on things while we're gone."

The sheriff flushed. "Just find her before she finds out through a rumor." He'd seen a subordinate he probably felt responsible for die right in front of him. A terrible way to kill someone if it turned out the sheriff was the one who slipped Rayland the substance that killed him—and his emotional state was just an act. She didn't think he was a criminal mastermind, but also refused to assume.

As they headed to the front desk, Kenna said, "We need to know if Bruce and Rayland were killed with the same substance."

Jax nodded. "And my ASAC wants Tilley in custody in forty-eight hours, or I have to report back to the office."

She blinked. "Two days?" Unbelievable. "I'm going to sleep for that long just to build back the energy to figure out how to draw him out."

Jax's eyes lit with amusement.

Kenna heard a sniffle. "Paulette." Jax went around to the

other side of the counter, but Kenna moved to stand by the receptionist. "Hey." She tugged Paulette to her side. "It's been a rough day already, and it's barely nine."

"Don't tell Kobrinsky I'm crying, I'll never hear the end of it." She dabbed a tissue to her eyes and sniffed.

"Where is he? I haven't seen him."

Paulette frowned. "He said he'd take your food to you, and he took Jax's and Reuben's." She flushed. "The diner waitress thought I was nuts balling my eyes out, but I needed some air so I told the fed to stay put. I'd get it. The sheriff told me not to say anything until we notify Dr. Rayland about her son."

"One sec." Kenna strode back to the office and walked through it, looking around. She spotted Kobrinsky and his crutches at the conference table, two seats down from Reuben. They were watching local morning news on the TV. Both of them were eating from Styrofoam containers. She caught his attention in the window and raised her hands, like, *What?*

He lifted his chin, saluted with his fork, and mouthed, *Thanks.*

She pressed her lips together. They looked to be eating three breakfasts between them. She stomped back to the front desk. "Let's go."

Jax followed her out.

They stepped onto the sidewalk, and she turned to him. "We don't have a car."

Jax held up a set of keys. "The sheriff is letting us use his vehicle."

She snatched the keys from his hand. "Great. Which car?"

"It's a truck. And you're gonna let me drive."

"It's a car, it's a truck. Same diff. One way, anyway. You

don't call a car a truck. But who doesn't refer to their truck, or their SUV, as a car?"

Jax shifted close, facing her. Maybe too close.

"We need to go do a death notification."

He nodded. "But first you need to tell me how you're doing. Apart from being hungry."

She gripped the keys so hard she pressed a button by accident. Across the lot, lights flashed on a white truck. *Bingo.*

Jax laid his hands on her shoulders. "Nope. I want honesty."

She pushed out a long breath, watching it puff white. "I really am hungry."

He waited.

"And exhausted."

"And your head?"

"Probably no worse than yours. You were in a plane crash," she said. "I should be asking you this!" Why hadn't she thought of it? Kenna gripped the sides of his jacket, slipping the keys into his pocket so she didn't have to hold them. She could get a hug instead.

He tugged her to him so they were flush against each other. Kenna just breathed, standing there. Taking that moment to be still. They didn't get to touch each other much, not like a regular couple who saw each other all the time. Missing, longing, and then suddenly being near each other? That could get risky fast.

Good thing there was a case to solve.

She continued, "When Forrest is released, I'll sleep on her couch. You can take the RV. We can all get some rest, and then we'll figure out how to get Tilley to come to us."

He nodded against the side of her head. "We could hang out and watch a movie."

"That's...oddly inviting." Kenna could hardly imagine just

doing something so normal with him when most of the time they spent together had been about working cases, catching killers. Saving lives and escaping dangerous people.

Would they even agree on what movie to watch?

"I'll make dinner," he said.

Kenna leaned back and grinned.

"I see it doesn't take much with you."

That's where he was wrong. "Actually, the bar is pretty high."

She sauntered to the truck. Let him figure out that she meant he was one of the few people—two men in her life—who had proven they were good men. She hadn't had a perfect relationship with Bradley. Jax wasn't perfect, but neither was she. But she knew to her soul that she could trust him to have her back.

That kind of confidence was worth more than anything else.

He hit a drive-through coffee place on the way across town, buying creamy coffees and breakfast burritos that were clearly premade but surprisingly good. Not long after, they got to the office complex where Dr. Rayland worked. After this, they'd head to her house, but it was working hours, so she was probably here.

Jax looked around. "Nice place."

The whole complex was new. Custom lease buildings for office-based businesses. An insurance broker. A mortgage lender. And the offices for Dr. Jennifer Rayland.

Kenna pushed through the front entrance and checked the directory. "Second floor, to the right."

They headed up the stairs, shifting out of the way of a delivery guy coming down with an oversized phone in one hand.

She rounded the landing at the top. "Door's open."

Kenna drew her weapon, hearing the snick of Jax doing the same behind her. She stepped to one side and let him go first.

They squared up on the door, one on each side of the opening.

Jax indicated he would go right, her left.

She nodded, falling back on the procedure that had been ingrained in her through training so it was sometimes as familiar as breathing.

Jax knocked on the doorframe. "Doctor Rayland, this is the FBI!"

Chapter Thirty

Jax stepped in, swept left to right, and checked behind the door. He opened it wide as she followed him in, covering him and helping clear what turned out to be a tiny waiting area. A few single chairs, and one couch style. The cabinet to the left came up below the chair rail and had a coffee setup on it, one of those single-cup makers that uses pods.

Over by Jax was an entry table with a stand for an iPad, though it didn't have the tablet in it right now. The whole place smelled like vanilla candlewax. And the temperature in Rayland's office was warmer than she kept her RV, making Kenna want to immediately start unzipping her outer layers and peeling off her gloves and hat.

"She doesn't have a receptionist. They just sign in electronically?" Kenna glanced around. "This is a simple setup."

"Works for a small town, and this space." He stood by the interior door. "Ready?"

Kenna nodded, and they repeated the same procedure to get into the doctor's office. Again, they found no one. The only thing amiss was a lamp that had been knocked over, the shade crumpled on the floor where it lay.

One overturned lamp wasn't sign of an altercation. It was just an overturned lamp. Might've been knocked over and missed when the doc left last night.

Jax circled one side around the desk, so she moved between the single chair and couch setup. The tiny end table was the only place where a person could set their cup. She hadn't had a coffee table in her life, and figured mostly they were places to put your feet up rather than place clutter on it.

The open corner seemed inviting.

But right now wasn't the time to think about getting a house. They were trying to find a woman. Only, she supposed she'd always assumed she would have a house at some point. Why not think about what she might want to have in that house. It wouldn't come with all the furniture like her RV that she still hadn't been to.

"You good? I need to check in here." Jax pointed to another interior door, behind the desk.

He'd noticed her momentary distraction?

Not surprising.

The guy seemed hyper-attuned to her while she just tried not to get distracted by how good-looking he was. She sighed.

"You're not okay, Kenna."

"You're the one who was in the plane crash."

He eyed her. "I got you a burrito."

For once this wasn't about her being hangry. Kenna pointed to the one on her left, at the end of the couch. "This one probably goes out to the hallway. You think that's a bathroom?"

"I'm gonna find out."

Kenna stood where she could cover him and waited, pushing all the exhaustion-induced thoughts out of her head.

The last thing she needed was for this relationship to turn her into a ridiculous schoolgirl, daydreaming about a guy.

She wasn't going to tell him it was easier to focus without him here. Did he feel the same way about her?

When he turned back, she thought she saw the answer to her question in the intention of his expression. That look in his eyes.

"Clear." Jax holstered his weapon on his hip, then flipped the open side of his jacket over it so it was out of sight.

She set her hand on her hip. "Did you bring a change of clothes with you?"

"We left all that on the plane, which blew up."

"There's a store in town we can go to if you need a clean outfit in the meantime."

His brows edged toward each other, just a flicker. "Let's find Doctor Rayland first and tell her about her son. That's the priority, right?"

She wanted the priority to be sleep, but as always, there was far too much going on. At least Forrest would be released as soon as Lucas could get the paperwork pushed through. The law firm chopper would take Jim to his appointment in Chicago.

Things would settle down again.

Kenna wasn't looking forward to the conversation with Dr. Rayland about her son—who would enjoy that part of the job? This was taking far too long. The mother was going to find out about her child from someone on the street, or a phone call from a concerned friend who'd heard it from another friend who worked at the hospital. "It's a weekday, and it's office hours. Where is she?"

"And did she leave in a hurry last night? Maybe we should check the local hospital. Make sure she didn't have an accident."

Kenna tipped her head to the side. "If she did, you'd think Deputy Rayland would've known about it."

"I just don't get why he's dead." Jax shook the mouse for the computer on the desk, the kind with the monitor and hard drive in one unit. "This thing needs a password."

"If we need in it, I can call Maizie." She needed to do that anyway. And figure out where this woman was, sooner rather than later.

Jax straightened, rolling his shoulders. "Let's hit her house first. She might just be off today, or she doesn't have clients until later." He, too, was pushing through until this was done and they could rest.

"That could be true, except that Doctor Rayland has an appointment with me." A woman stood in the door, jeans below her overcoat, and white sneakers. Her hair had been pulled back into a ponytail, and she held a paper cup of coffee in one hand. The woman looked at the clock on the wall. "In five minutes."

"So she's on her way in?" Kenna checked her gun was out of sight. Thankfully, she'd returned that deputy sheriff badge. *No, thank you.* It had given her credence with the marshals, but now they knew they could trust her there was no reason to have kept it.

"Normally, she's here by now," the woman said, worry etched on her face. "And if she was ever going to be late, she would text me."

Jax wandered around the desk to stand by Kenna. He flashed his badge. "Special Agent Jaxton. This is my associate, Kenna Banbury." He gave her a second to absorb that.

"Lacey Andrews. I'm a nurse at the hospital. I work nights."

"Can we ask you a few questions about Dr. Rayland?" Jax kept his tone professional, not that it muted the effect of him.

Kenna had seen enough women succumb to it, even though that wasn't his intention and never would be. Mostly she found it amusing. Though, she figured one day she wouldn't.

"Sure." Ms. Andrews shrugged and took a sip of her coffee like it was no big deal. But Kenna spotted a flash of interest in her expression. The kind of person who'd love to be part of a true crime story—so long as they also weren't affected by it.

Jax pulled out a little notebook. "Has she seemed different lately?"

"Huh." The woman lowered her coffee cup. "She's been kind of touchy. Like being short with people, you know? Getting frustrated easily."

Kenna said, "When did that start?" A change in behavior might indicate stress, which could have an underlying cause that related to the deaths—murders—in town. She didn't even know what this case was, let alone how far it stretched. There hadn't been time to collect all the information. If Forrest had, it was in the boxes the state police had confiscated from her house. All that work she'd done. Which they were going to have to give back to her if the charges were dropped.

Ms. Andrews looked to the side, thinking for a moment. "Maybe a couple of weeks ago. I came in for my appointment. She was on the phone, and it sounded like she was yelling. When I asked her if there was something wrong, she just said it was a package she ordered that got lost in the mail. But that didn't really seem like what she'd been yelling about." She shook her head. "I'd forgotten about that."

"Anything else you can think of?"

The woman shrugged, going back to her coffee.

Kenna nodded. "Thank you, Ms. Andrews." They needed to get to Dr. Rayland's house, so they could clear up what was happening here exactly.

The woman shrugged, already turning away. "Sure, whatever." She glanced over her shoulder at Jax, interest in her eyes.

Kenna glanced at him as well. More like stared.

He turned to Kenna. "What?"

She studied his face, and the dark-blond hair. His blue eyes. It was ridiculous, really.

He blushed. "What?"

Kenna shook her head and headed for the door. In the front seat of the car, she texted Maizie while Jax drove across town. She wanted a full rundown on Dr. Rayland as soon as Maizie could gather it together. They might find the woman safe and sound at home, and they might not.

"That coffee she had smelled good," Jax said, his eyes on the road.

Kenna finished the message. "We can get some after."

Dr. Jennifer Rayland lived in a modest house set back from the street. Single level, not unlike Forrest's house. Built probably in the '80s, but the windows had been replaced at some point in the past few years.

Kenna's phone buzzed. She looked at the screen while she followed Jax to the front door. "Maizie says our GPS location is the same residence where Jennifer Rayland grew up."

His brows rose. "She's lived in one house her whole life?"

Kenna shrugged, pocketing her phone. "We can ask her about it after we explain what happened." Though, likely she would be too grief-stricken to want to answer questions on her living situation. "Let's find her first."

Jax knocked on the door.

And knocked.

And knocked some more.

Kenna wandered to the front window and peered in—because she wasn't a cop and the blinds were open. "I don't see anything." She went back to the front door. "Turn away or something."

Jax didn't move.

"I'm so glad you've decided to be an accessory. That's just great." She didn't reach for the door handle, or her lockpick, but she was about to.

"We're either in this with each other, or we're not."

"No." Kenna spun around. "Not if it's going to destroy your career, or get you put in jail."

"You worry too much."

"Maybe you don't worry enough!"

Jax's expression softened. "You freaking out is kind of adorable."

"This isn't the time." She wanted to put her hands on her hips, but her jacket was too bulky for that. It wouldn't have the same effect. "Now *turn around* so I can break and enter solo. Who knows, maybe you'll see Stan Tilley in the bushes taking photos of me and those will prove you had no idea I was behind you picking the lock."

Jax chuckled. "I'm only looking for Tilley. I can't say I had no idea what you were doing because you just told me."

"You're very irritating."

"It's called integrity."

Kenna heard the lock click and continued turning the two pics, rotating them around. She shoved the door handle down and put everything away before it fully swung open. "Hello! Anyone in here? Dr. Rayland, can you hear me?"

Jax closed the front door.

They walked through the whole house but didn't find her. Just a master bedroom, a second bedroom that seemed like an updated one that would've belonged to the deputy, though he didn't live here anymore, a sparsely decorated living room, and a dining room converted into an office on one side and a home gym on the other.

"This place seems normal," Kenna said. "She's just not here."

"Car, either. So we can put out a BOLO on that."

Kenna looked around. "She's probably just at the store."

Jax peered at the board above the desk. "She's got appointments listed here, with their last names. First one is Andrews."

"Car accident on the way in? Maybe she was hit with the same thing as the deputy. Maybe they shared breakfast, or met for coffee this morning, and they were both poisoned by the same thing that killed Pastor Bruce."

"Or there's nothing going on but a whole lot of coincidental deaths." He shrugged. "Is this the case you've been working?"

"Two people are dead, and my friend got arrested for it. So yes, this is the case I've been working." Kenna wandered around, looking at things but without opening drawers or cupboards. Or the fridge. "I've got years of accidents, or deaths attributed to natural causes, plus all the deaths that J. Pierce is said to have been responsible for. Then I've got the people who tried to make noise about the accidents not being accidents. A coroner, for one. Maybe more than just him."

Pastor Bruce was dead for the same reason.

Jax said, "So who wants it to look like coincidence or accidents?"

Kenna found a door by the fridge and opened that to find a small hallway, washer and dryer on one side and lined shelves of a pantry on the other. At the far end was another, door probably to the garage. She pushed the heavy door open and fumbled on the wall beside it for a switch. A bare bulb popped and flickered to life. Kenna stared at the interior of the garage.

Jax shifted behind her, close to her back, and peered over her shoulder. "What. The. Heck."

Lining the garage walls were blown-up images that depicted graphic scenes of murder. Torture. Victims bound and bleeding.

She managed to say, "We should call Gingrich."

Who were these people? And why did a psychologist have them displayed around the room like she'd turned her garage into an art gallery? And her son was a sheriff's deputy who had no idea?

Jax froze. "I think I should call the FBI."

"This is my case, Jax." She turned and saw movement behind him. "Watch—"

A heavy figure with a dark stocking pulled over their face slammed into his back before he could turn. Jax slammed into Kenna, and she stumbled back. She fell to the concrete floor, and he landed on top of her. She managed to keep her head from slamming back onto the ground, but didn't move right away. Except to lift her hand and touch it to the back of her head, which she then laid slowly on the freezing concrete. Her gun dug into her hip.

Kenna gritted her teeth.

Jax pushed off her and turned, moving swiftly toward the door. It slammed in his face, and he let out a cry of frustration. He pounded both fists on the spot where the door should be.

They'd have to break down a wall to get out of here.

Chapter Thirty-One

Kenna stared at the ceiling. The bare drywall had been taped but never mudded and painted. She closed her eyes and pictured the figure she'd seen. Dark. Dark jacket, dark face covering. No skin visible, or hair. No discernable features.

Shorter than Jax. Maybe by three inches. So that put the person about five foot nine or ten, close to her height.

"Did you hit your head?" His boots shuffled across the floor, and she felt him crouch, one hand on her shoulder.

Kenna eased her eyes open. "I don't think so."

"Land on anything?" He moved her elbow across her body and slid his hand under her. "Roll over. Let me look."

Kenna held out her hand. "Help me up. The floor is cold."

He grasped her elbow and hauled her up without putting strain on her forearms. Taking care with her, understanding her weaknesses, and not counting them against her. Just adapting to get the work done anyway. The way she did.

The room rotated a little around her. Kenna hung on to his belt, trying not to look at the walls. The scene was pretty gruesome, and she'd need to survey each one to see if the victims in each image were related to a case—any case, or this case—and whether she recognized them.

At least, none of them appeared to be children.

Kenna shivered.

Jax pulled her in for a quick hug, rubbing up and down her back. "It's freezing in here."

"So lets find a way out." She pulled her phone and called Gingrich. He didn't answer, so she left a message and then called Kobrinksy.

"Yo."

"I could use an assist. Jax and I are locked in Dr. Rayland's garage, and there's a metric ton of evidence in here with us."

"Sheriff has me watching the office. State police are on their way, since we're another man down now. And the relief is coming in. Everyone's pissed 'cause they're gonna have to work different shifts. It's a whole thing. The phone hasn't stopped ringing."

"So you're gonna just leave Jax and I to freeze to death?"

Jax glanced over.

"No," Kobrinksy said, "I already sent out the alert. Fire department will be there soon. I'll text you when the time stamp comes up that the truck has been dispatched and let you know their ETA."

"Oh. Thanks."

Jax's lips curled up. Kenna rolled her eyes.

"You said evidence?" Kobrinsky emphasized the last word.

"I left the sheriff a message. Radio him and tell him to call me."

"Copy that."

The call ended.

"So who shoved me?" Jax flipped up the collar of his

jacket and rubbed his hands together. "Did you see their face?"

"Male, my height." She paused to frown. "Actually, I'm just guessing based on body shape. Maybe it wasn't a man, but a woman with a heavy coat on or lots of layers to disguise her figure."

"Or Tilley."

Kenna shrugged. "Right. I couldn't see face or hair color. They'd covered both, as well as any visible skin."

"So just a dark dressed figure." Jax scratched his chin, and the stubble growing there. "Any idea what this sickness is about?" He waved at the room in general.

"Guess we should check out each piece." Kenna glanced around. "It's like a gallery, but why keep all this in your garage?"

"It isn't the first place I'd look." Jax moved ahead of her, wandering around like a gallery patron. "I'd search the whole house, assuming the garage is just boxes of junk. Storage. If her car is on the drive, I'd think it's too full in here to use as a garage."

"And it's locked from the hall side with a padlock, so she'd be able to keep people from straying in here if she has guests." Kenna shuddered. "This is some kind of...what? Fetish room?" She'd met people obsessed with death like that before. Crime scene photos were just images, they weren't art. This was an attempt at art for the discerning fan.

"Easier to burn everything if the authorities are here. She probably kept nothing on her computer or phone. That's the first place anyone in law enforcement is going to look for evidence these days."

She went to the door and tried the lock, as if Jax hadn't done something as basic as turned the door handle.

No tools. No stuff most people collected in their garage. Nothing she could use to pry the door open.

Kenna drew her weapon and aimed at the lock.

Jax slid his arms around her, his arms stretched down hers. His face close. His finger alongside hers so she couldn't squeeze the trigger. "You won't break the lock. The bullet will ricochet, and most likely it'll hit one of us."

"Then stand behind me so it's me that gets hit."

He eased around and pushed her back gently. "Not gonna happen." His expression went completely neutral. "You're not the only one in this relationship scared the other will get hurt."

It wasn't like she was out of control and reckless. She could listen to reason. "I won't shoot out the lock, but the fire department better get here soon." Kobrinsky hadn't texted yet. How long did it take to dispatch a truck in this town, anyway?

"Call Maizie. We need to ID all of these people and get her started working out how Dr. Rayland got these images."

"And where the printer is that produced ones this big," Kenna added.

"That's a great point," Jax said.

She wanted to roll her eyes. He thought she was freaking out so he was being overly encouraging? Usually she didn't have anyone around to give her reassurance. Partnerships didn't usually go well. Especially when it was a man she cared about.

Kenna moved to the first image, zoomed in on the face, and took a photo. She had long hair and a gag over her mouth, but maybe they could get something off the nose and eyes shape that could get Maizie a facial recognition match. She took a photo of the man in the next image, which appeared to have been postmortem given that faraway look.

Lifeless eyes.

She walked all around the room, snapping images of their faces so that they uploaded to the file storage Maizie had set up online. Her phone rang a minute or so later, and she put the call on speaker. "Is there any way for you to see if the local dispatch has sent a fire truck my direction?"

"Hang on. I was looking at those photos." Maizie paused. "You need a fire truck?"

"We're locked in."

"Oh, okay." She sounded relieved.

"They can free you if you're trapped."

"Hmm. Maybe I should've tried the fire department."

Kenna started. She turned to Jax, who was also staring at the phone. He lifted his gaze to hers, his brows raised. They both shrugged. The teen was joking about that? Or at least talking about years of captivity lightly.

"There's nothing on the log they have online."

Jax said, "I'll call Paulette or whoever is on duty, have them transfer me to the dispatch supervisor."

Kenna took the call with Maizie off speaker. "Thanks for checking."

"What about these people?" the teen asked. "Or the work-up I have for Jennifer Rayland?" For a second, she sounded younger than she was.

"Anything interesting in her background?" Kenna didn't want to think or talk about the images in this garage anymore than Maizie probably did.

"The house is paid off, and Rayland has been paying her money every month. Transferring it into her bank account. It covers the taxes and the utilities. She uses it to pay those bills."

"You got into her online bank account portal?"

"If she didn't want me to access it," Maizie said, "she

should've made the password something other than h-e-a-d-d-o-c."

"Head doc?"

"Yeah, it didn't take that long to crack."

"I was thinking more like you'd find out if she has any other properties in her name, in case she's at one of those rather than at home or at work." They were only trying to find the woman. "Even if she's got some kind of bizarre murder fetish, that doesn't mean she killed her son. Or Bruce. Or did any of this other stuff."

"Well, she doesn't have another house. But she does have a boat. It's registered in her father's name still, but he dropped off the map years ago. There's a newspaper article online about how the police were trying to find him. They questioned the family, but Mom and Jennifer had no knowledge of his whereabouts. Looks like his boss is the one who reported him missing."

"A boat." They could check that out, for sure. "Any idea where it is?"

"I'd have said it would be in that garage most likely or..."

"No dice." The garage wasn't wide enough, or tall enough, depending on the kind of boat. "And there are no external structures...unless Jax and I missed an outbuilding in the yard." She glanced at him.

He stowed his phone and strode over. "Kobrinsky is with the state police, says he forgot to follow up. Paulette called the fire chief herself and confirmed the truck was dispatched. They say five minutes."

"Okay." That was good. "Did she say anything about Forrest?"

"Release is in the works. Gingrich is meeting with the coroner about the pastor and Deputy Rayland."

"Before the fire department drags us out of here in a

rescue, we need to figure out who these people are." She motioned to the walls and caught a glimpse of something on the back of a photo that bowed in the middle. "She should've framed these if she wanted to keep them nice."

Jax took her phone and put it on speaker.

"What's she saying?" Maizie's voice came through, all crackly.

"Dunno, kid. Looks like she's onto something. What's up with you, kid?"

"It's been good with Elizabeth," Maizie said. "She signed me up for a women's gym, and we go a few times a week to walk on the treadmill. She said I need to get exercise and drink water."

A women's gym was a great idea. Kenna figured that would be a lot less daunting than a gym with random men walking around, setting off whatever instincts Maizie had randomly and without her being able to control it. Plus, going to a local gym meant the girl didn't spend all her time in one trailer. Health and healing went hand in hand. Kenna had learned that.

Maizie continued, "Anyway, Jennifer Rayland's mother disappeared as well later on. She did all her degrees online, it looks like. And when it came to getting licensed, she had the previous Door County psychologist sign off on all her hours. That guy retired right after she started practicing."

"Maybe he was just waiting for someone to take his patients," Jax said, "and it was a convenient time to be done working."

"He disappears like the parents did. There are photos of his retirement party on Facebook. And right after that, his posts and interactions just...stop."

"Like he's dead. And her parents are both dead. And her

son is dead…" Jax paused. "Because I'm sensing a serious pattern here."

"Is she the kind of person who could've done that?" Maizie asked.

"I've never met her," Jax replied. "Right now, we're just trying to find her."

"Me either." Kenna peered at the under side of the loose photo. "Huh." She tugged the image off the wall. On the back someone had sprawled in pencil. Gibberish or… "Chemical compounds?" She pulled the whole page off and held it with both hands. "Ideas, dates, plans. Notes. Reminders."

"Like Elizabeth's vision board?" Maizie said.

"Or collecting ideas before that, writing notes to herself so she could do that later. Set all her dates and tasks."

Jax surveyed the room. "We never would've noticed that if you hadn't seen it."

"Anyone who came in here would be distracted by this horror show. They'd have missed what was right in front of their faces." Just like they would have if one page hadn't been loose and bowed in the middle on one side. "We need to turn everything around so we can see what's on the back of all the pages."

Someone banged on the garage door from the outside.

She turned to it.

"The fire department is there," Maizie announced..

Jax frowned. "Why didn't we hear the sirens?"

"And we should be able to hear them yelling," Kenna said. "They'd better not try to open the garage door."

"There isn't even a mechanism. They'd have to cut the door out."

"Which I would totally do if I was a firefighter because that sounds awesome. But they'll destroy evidence." She went to the door that led to the house and banged on it. "Hello! Can anyone hear me? Hello?"

Jax turned. "Is this room seriously soundproof?"

"If it is, then that garage door is lined with something." And she didn't like the sound of whatever happened in here being inaudible to anyone outside. A place purposely made to keep screams within the walls.

Jennifer Rayland had a list of things to answer for.

And before this was over, it might grow even longer.

Jax pointed. "And it's sealed like no garage door in history has ever been sealed. Because those things are always drafty."

"I could shoot the lock," Kenna said.

He glanced at her, then handed her the phone to hammer on the door and kick it with his boots. One leg. Then the other.

Someone hammered on the door from the other side.

Jax stepped back. "Give them some room."

Kenna pocketed the phone, not sure if Maizie was still on the line. She started at the garage door, tearing everything down off the walls. She made her way around the room, piling the collection of papers in one hand. It got heavy, and awkward, so she set it in a pile. When she had everything, she rolled it up, noticing more writing on the back. Most of the pages were covered.

If they wanted to figure this out, they needed to know what was in Jennifer Rayland's head.

Lord, what did she do?

The door to the house flung open. A hulking firefighter barreled in, along with a cloud of smoke.

The house is on fire.

Kenna scooped up the papers and put the roll on her shoulder. "Time to go?"

The firefighter looked between them. "That door is solid

metal." His voice came through the mask, sounding faraway and tinny, but loud enough.

Jax grabbed the door before it bounced back and hit the firefighter again.

"Time to go." The first responder stepped back into the hall and waved them out. "Ma'am, you don't need to bring those papers. They aren't worth it."

"They're evidence of murder."

The firefighter stared at her. Then Jax. "Who even are you guys?"

Chapter Thirty-Two

Kenna held her breath until she stepped outside. The first inhale she took ended up in a cough.

The firefighter peeled off his helmet. "This way, ma'am."

Jax, ahead of her, glanced back and smirked.

She sent him a smirk right back. "I'm not going to the hospital."

"Ah," the firefighter gave her a knowing nod. "One of *those* is she?"

Jax grinned. "Yes, sir, she is." He flashed his badge. "Special Agent Jaxton."

Kenna strode past him, across the grass holding her bundle of papers. She set them on the hood of the sheriff's truck that they'd driven here. Before she'd really thought about it, she had her phone in her hand. Who even realized how often they pulled out their cell these days?

The call was still connecting, the strip of green across the top of the screen.

She put it to her ear. "Maze?" She coughed, her voice little more than a croak.

"You need to get checked out. Is there an EMT there?"

Kenna looked around. "They just pulled up."

"Go see them. Let them help you." Maizie paused barely a second. "It is okay to let someone help you."

She glanced at Jax. "He was there. He saw it all, like it was normal." All those images tacked up on the walls, and he'd just...absorbed it. She looked from him to the photos. "Or he'll cry later, in the shower."

"Do guys do that?"

"I have no idea. Maybe? They should if they need to." Kenna had to cough in order to catch her breath.

"Seriously, go see the EMTs. You don't want to mess around with smoke inhalation."

"Says who?"

"Uh, only everyone on the internet. I've been reading articles for the last ten minutes, firefighter testimonials, medical websites." Maizie paused. "You don't want your throat to get all swollen and close up. They'll keep you overnight, you know?"

Kenna's chest shook. Nearly a laugh, but the nascent expression died back to where it had come from. "There's something seriously wrong with me."

"But you have work to do, so you're going to ignore it. Maybe you'll tell yourself that you'll deal with it later, but are you really going to do that? Or will you just shove it down and pretend it's not that big of an issue."

Kenna set one hand on the papers, so they didn't slide to the ground, and closed her eyes. Took a moment to let her mind settle, so that she could at least process what had just happened. It was when she moved too fast to the next thing that she forgot key parts of what she'd witnessed.

A description. Something she'd seen.

Jax, shoved toward her. The gallery of murder. Jennifer

Rayland's perfectly civilized life, hiding a dark and twisted secret.

That firefighter, asking if she was one of *those* people.

"Everyone is probably annoyed by me never wanting to see a doctor," Kenna said. "I probably sound like a broken record."

She didn't usually care what people thought, and she could brush off the idea of another opinion of how she lived or something she'd said or did. The combination of Jax being here and them both being past exhausted made a mess of her thoughts.

What she needed faded back into the case. Worry for Forrest and the question of whether her friend had been released—and if they were even still friends. The issue of where Jennifer Rayland had gone.

"You don't have to grow as a person just because you think people are annoyed by you." Maizie paused. "You grow because it's what you *want* to do. What people should do if they don't want to keep the same issues their whole lives."

"When did you become this sage of wisdom?"

Maizie chuckled. "I'm trying something new."

"I'm not sure I'm prepared for you to have all the answers to my problems." But was that only because, like with what they'd just been talking about, it would mean she was too aware that Maizie could see what her issues were?

She'd know that the teen saw the truth. The *lack* in Kenna.

The things she should do but didn't. Or what she could be but might fail to attain. Ways she could've grown and fell short.

Wondrous grace that brought me to the fold.

"Don't worry, I still have a lot to figure out."

Kenna felt the pull of the smile on her lips. "Love you, kid." She felt someone move close and opened her eyes.

"Love you, too."

Jax stepped into her space and kissed her forehead. "Bye, Maizie." He took the phone and ended the call.

"I need to have the ambulance people check me out." She cleared her throat and gathered up the papers. Then she got a look at his face. "Well, you don't have to look so surprised." She breezed past him and got herself ten minutes with an oxygen mask on. Or whatever they used to give her clean air to breathe.

The EMT shined a light in her eyes.

"Don't use the C-word." Kenna made a face. "Concussion."

"Whether I choose to use it or not may not change reality."

"That's exactly what I'm afraid of." Kenna didn't want to be slowed down. She didn't want to not be able to work. Or worse, miss a threat that came at her because she wasn't at a hundred percent. She could put an innocent life at risk because she failed to spot something.

She held on to the mask, the papers clutched to her front, and laid back on the bed. Eyes closed. She inhaled slowly, then pushed it out at half the speed. She could talk without coughing. She did *not* have a concussion, thank you very much.

Please.

She continued, "If we're going to the hospital, the sheriff should meet us there."

Jax touched her shoulder. "I'll take the truck. Meet you there."

"Find out if Forrest is being released. And tell Kobrinsky we need help finding Doctor Rayland." She glanced at him.

Jax grinned. "I'll call them."

She drifted a little. Aware of the EMT talking to the driver but didn't track what they were saying. Someone tried to take the papers, but she held on to them. The ambulance pulled up to a stop, and Kenna tugged off the mask. She sat up.

"We can wheel you out. So sit tight, yeah?" The woman gave her a polite smile. "Why walk when you can let someone else carry you, like those ancient kings who laid on a bed and got carried around?"

"Hmm. I see what you mean."

The back doors opened at the hospital. A nurse stood there, and the other EMT came around to help. Kenna didn't like even the feel of other people moving her. It brought back far too many memories of being shot. Of the night she'd lost everything, and they'd wheeled her into the hospital covered in blood. Everyone around her had tragedy on their faces.

Today was a lot different. It was freezing, not a warm night. It was daytime. The medical professionals were pleasant and polite.

But I'm going to carry those memories forever, aren't I? It's going to live inside me and jump up at any moment to remind me.

Kenna glanced over at the parking lot for Jax, wanting to see the sheriff's truck. Instead, she spotted someone beyond the pillar holding up the overhang roof that would've protected her from falling snow. A man standing between rows at the edge of the parking lot. A heavy gray beard and an overcoat, topped by a blue-gray wool coat. Staring at her.

Kenna rolled to the right, nearly shoved the ambulance driver down, and swung her legs onto the ground. She managed to catch her knee before it hit the ground and straightened with all the leg strength she'd amassed with those runs she and Jax had been going on.

"Hey!"

"Watch out!"

"What are you doing?"

"Kenna!"

She tore across the ambulance lane, jumped the bush, and realized she still had the papers clutched to her front. She held them tighter and raced toward Stan Tilley.

He turned and ducked behind a car.

"Kenna!"

She heard tires screech.

A car pulled out in front of her and turned sharply. Horns honked. Kenna slipped between two and narrowly missed Stan as he hurtled at her in the car.

She stared at him.

He stared right back.

A siren started up, and dash lights on the sheriff's truck flashed red and blue—as did lights in the grill on the front.

The car swerved around it, and the engine revved.

Kenna ran to the passenger side and hauled the door open. She climbed in while Jax watched the car. "Go. Get him!" She slammed the door, shoved the evidence on the dash, and grabbed the seatbelt.

He yanked the wheel and turned the truck around, bumping the curb in the process. "Care to share why you tore across the parking lot just to escape getting checked out by a doctor?"

Kenna grabbed the handle on the door. "That isn't what this is. It's Stan! We need to get him!"

She spotted the medical staff, staring at the truck like Kenna was a crazy person. Which, okay, to be fair she probably looked like one after that. But she had been prepared to get checked out and actually admit she wasn't all right. That she might need help, because it was okay to admit that. Just like Maizie had said.

Was it her fault when a lead presented itself right in front of her?

"Where did he go?" Jax looked both directions.

She'd been so in her head she didn't know where Stan had taken that car. "Did you get a license plate? I think I remember a couple of digits."

"At least you didn't hit your head." He shook his. "You in a hit-and-run is something I don't need to see again in my life."

She looked around for the car. "Where did all this traffic come from?"

"Looks like school just got out." He took a turn, then circled back around weaving through traffic. "We should go back to the hospital so you can get looked at—and apologize for running off before they could see you."

Kenna spotted the time on the dash. "Aren't we closer to the sheriff's department than the hospital now?"

"You're avoiding the staff."

When she'd just run off like a crazy woman? Uh, *yeah.* "I'll send them a gift basket or something. Maizie can find a good one. We have work to do."

"You think people are in danger being near you?"

"Generally, yes. Specifically today?" There was no way she could explain all of it. "Probably. But I can't help Forrest, find Jennifer Rayland, or trap Stan Tilley in a hospital room." Just lying around made her feel powerless, like the days after surgery when she was on restriction. Unable to move even if she wanted to. "I don't like it."

"I know." He glanced over, heading for the sheriff's department now. "It's not something you need to get over. But it is something you'll have to face periodically. You just won't have to face it alone."

"I prefer to avoid my problems and just work instead."

"Considering you doing that has a tendency to save people's lives, I'm not sure I have much of an argument."

She shifted in the seat. "It's all part of my charm."

Jax pulled into the parking lot of the sheriff's department. Paulette was at her spot when they walked in. She took one look at Kenna and said, "Coffee?"

"You're an angel."

Paulette beamed. Kenna and Jax walked through to the main office.

Kobrinsky rocked back on his chair, tipping it so the front two feet lifted off the floor. The crutches were leaning against the wall beside him. "What did I tell you about causing fresh trouble every time you go out?"

"It's what I do." He was probably just irritated that she'd run across more evidence, and he hadn't been there. "Don't worry. There were no severed heads." She dumped the rolls of paper on the desk. "Just a ton of gnarly photos you won't want to tell your mother about."

She glanced over her shoulder but didn't spot Paulette. Jax shifted the papers out across the table. "I'll see if Maizie has identified any of them."

"Good."

The sheriff came out of his office. Kobrinsky got his crutches and came over.

Kenna said, "What's the latest on Forrest and her release?" She folded her arms, then took off her coat because it was too bulky to make her look threatening. She looked between them, and neither spoke. "Do I need to call the state police?"

"Probably." Kobrinsky slumped to sit on a desk. "They

sent the paperwork over that they're going to take her into their custody and get her to jail. She'll be arraigned in a few days."

Kenna shook her head.

"You might not get a say in this, Kenna." Gingrich huffed. "Even with one of my badges. Sometimes things happen, and there's nothing we can do about it."

"Like sending an innocent woman to jail?" Kenna waved at the photos, because Jennifer was out there and at least Forrest was safe here—for now. "Or knowing people died in your county and you never found the person who did it. You had no clue Jennifer Rayland was mixed up in this. Did you?"

Gingrich's expression shifted.

Jax moved to stand in front of Kenna's left side, between her and the sheriff. "Do you have something you'd like to share, Sheriff Gingrich?"

Kenna looked at Kobrinsky. "Did you have any clue Rayland was mixed up in something like this, Jerry?"

He only looked at the sheriff. "I always wondered what you two had between you. Were you protecting him?"

Sheriff Gingrich blanched. "I've always kept this county safe."

"By killing J. Pierce?" She wasn't entirely sure his boat explosion story meant for sure the killer was dead. Maybe it hadn't been what he thought it was. "Now Jennifer Rayland has a boat. People are mysteriously dying. Forrest is blamed for it. The deputy dies in your office."

"And you're being chased by the lackey of a serial killer," Gingrich said. "What's your point?"

"Too many coincidences." She didn't like that, or the "too many people dying" part.

"Maybe your pal Marion can give you some more information."

Jax lifted his hand. "We need to keep this constructive. We need to find Jennifer Rayland and get to the bottom of this." He waved at the photos.

Kenna flipped one over and showed Kobrinsky the notes on the back.

"Hang on." Kobrinsky leaned over one of the images. Then he shifted to another.

"What is it?" She hoped he didn't have an odd desire to stare overlong at these grotesque images.

Kobrinsky grabbed his crutches and swung over to his desk. "I'll pull up the cases. You can tell me if I'm right and it's the same people." He glanced at them. "The victims J. Pierce killed."

Chapter Thirty-Three

K enna started turning pages. "All of them?" Cold washed over her, as if she'd been doused with cold water. Or tossed in that snow outside. She slumped into a chair and shuffled it toward the desk. The legs didn't really roll, but the struggle used some energy that needed burning. "How did she get these?"

Photos of the victims meant that J. Pierce had taken souvenir shots during the murders. In some cases, after. It meant adjusting the criminal profile to include whatever drove him to document the killings. Share those snaps.

The whole thing reminded her too much of the case where she'd met Jax. Executions online, used as a training for prospective killers. Some seasoned murderer teaching a class and sharing his knowledge. Only it had all been a ruse to draw her out with a complex crime that involved hiring dangerous killers to take out victims and confuse everyone with the methodology and the motive.

Jax shifted in a way she could tell he wanted to offer a word or gesture of comfort. He glanced between Gingrich and Kobrinsky. "How does a psychologist have photos of the J. Pierce victims?"

"Good question." Kobrinsky said. His chest expanded. "Can we get the paper tested? Find out where they were printed. Or have the images themselves analyzed? There could be something in the background that tells us where they were when they were killed."

"Don't we already know that?"

Kobrinsky frowned. "The boat thing?"

A phone rang in another room, the kind of office sounds most people got used to and ignored. Apparently, Paulette answered it from the front desk, because it stopped. Like the coffeepot had stopped gurgling and permeated the room with the roasted scent of that dark nectar of life.

Kenna unzipped her coat and draped it over the chair behind her, brushing back her hair. "I want to know where that came from. There's nothing that looks like a boat in these pictures." She glanced at Gingrich. "You told me a boat story, but where did that information come from?"

"The investigation into J. Pierce's kills." Gingrich folded his arms across his chest. He'd even told her how he chased the killer and one of the victims, and how both had sadly perished.

"I want the reports from the night of that boat explosion," Kenna said.

Kobrinsky glanced at his boss. "What explosion?"

Gingrich's lips shifted.

"The sheriff here"—Kenna waved a hand—"was tracking J. Pierce and one of his victims and managed to destroy the boat. Sadly, both the killer and the victim lost their lives."

"Along with the crime scene and all the evidence?" Jax folded his arms. "How convenient."

She hadn't believed at the time Gingrich told her the story

that it was a flat-out lie. Maybe a shade of the truth at least. "So where are the reports and the evidence test results?"

Gingrich grunted. "What was the point testing anything? It was done."

"Seems interesting to me that you ended the life of a notorious killer and didn't run your campaign on that alone the last...how many years?" Kobrinsky stared at him. "You seriously killed J. Pierce?"

Gingrich shrugged. "There didn't seem to be reason to shout it from the rooftops when I couldn't corroborate anything. All I had was a few charred pieces of wood." He dragged over his own rolling office chair and sat, looking older now than he had when they met. "Half the people who heard it would've dismissed it five minutes later, and the other half wouldn't have believed me."

Kenna had never in her life been so focused on other people's opinions. She cared about who she cared about, and they mattered to her. Their views mattered. Everyone else? She didn't need to win mass approval like the sheriff did every election.

Jax shuffled through the papers. "We still need to find this shrink. Figure out what she's doing."

Kenna shifted the chair side to side as she thought. "Shame we can't ask Rayland about her." In fact, his death was looking more and more convenient. "If she killed him with poison, or something like it, did she kill Bruce as well?"

Kobrinsky's expression darkened. "She was in the diner at the time of his murder. I interviewed her, and she said she didn't see anything. She was reading a book on her phone."

Gingrich said, "We have an alert out for everyone to watch for her and report in. And this county is crawling with state police right now." He shrugged. "What else is there to do?"

"For starters," Kenna said, "you can explain what you're hiding."

"You'd like to think I'm hiding something."

He was hiding a lot, so it wasn't thinking so much as *knowing* he was hiding something. She didn't say that, though.

"Probably want to oust me, just so you can carry on your 'justice' thing, taking down corrupt cops." Gingrich stared at her. "Killing some. Landing others in jail."

"No one that didn't deserve it." Except Sheriff Joe Don Hunter. He'd known her father, and she'd nearly had the chance to have another good man in her life. One who had known both her parents from the stories he'd told. And she'd lost him in a devastating fire. The chance had been gone before she'd barely realized what she had.

Jax touched her shoulder, and she blinked against the burn of tears in her eyes.

Kenna sniffed and turned to the papers. She flipped over a couple of the photos, her mind too seared with the horror to absorb any more.

The writing on the other side really was plans, and ideas. Horrible plans for horrible ideas that most people wouldn't want to think about, but which she saw on a regular basis. Kenna's job was to protect innocent people from ever seeing it. So they never had to contemplate the awful things some people did to others.

Rather than read a story Jennifer had written about a little boy mauled by a bear, which this one seemed to be, she looked over at the clock on the wall. "Is Forrest still downstairs?"

Kobrinsky said, "The lawyer said he had to wait for lunch with the judge and the DA. He wants to be back by midafternoon."

"She doesn't need to sit there," Kenna argued. "We know she's innocent."

"Do we?" Gingrich lifted his chin.

"You have Reuben's statement."

"One child's word?"

Kenna pressed her lips together. He just wasn't going to cooperate about anything, was he? The man was going to drag his feet and be downright combative about every single thing. Forrest was innocent, but were they going to be friends when she was released? Kenna might have to get her RV out of the garage and find somewhere else to park it before this case was done.

Jax spoke up. "Good thing it's up to the DA and the judge to drop the charges, then. You're only the one responsible for gathering enough evidence to prove guilt, and the decision as to how it turns out for the accused isn't up to you."

"Team Kenna?" Gingrich snorted.

"As an FBI agent, I can appreciate your position. It would be difficult for reelection you holding an innocent woman in your cells for days. But on the heels of the arrest of Marion Wells, it'll look pretty good for Kobrinsky, I'm guessing."

"Especially with him being the one that found the head under her bed." Gingrich shot Kenna a knowing glance.

She had to worry about Stan Tilley. "You think I care about who is sheriff in this town when I *don't*. I care that Forrest isn't all right. I care about my family and what they need." If there were victims to save, she'd be going after them. "Bruce is dead. And for what? Same with Deputy Rayland? Why did they have to die? Because Forrest is writing a book?"

"Who says they were murdered? Right, Sheriff?" Kobrinsky shot his boss an accusatory look. "Probably they were just accidents."

Kenna picked up the conversation right away. "Like the

victim who died when that boat exploded." If that was even what had happened. "Did you write that up as an accident?"

"You're gonna interrogate *me* now?" Gingrich said, firing the words like an intentional shot.

"Someone should." Paulette strode in with a stack of Styrofoam containers.

Jax got up and took the containers from her, all except one as she instructed. "What makes you say that, Paulette?"

"Seems like a lot goes on not many people know about." She shrugged one shoulder. "Maybe it's all above board, or maybe it isn't."

"You want transparency in leadership. What a novel concept." Kenna found a burrito in her container and wrapped a napkin around the bottom end. She got up and held out a hand for the other container. "Forrest?"

Paulette nodded, wincing slightly. "She asked me not to let you in."

"But you're taking that to her."

Nod.

"And she's all right?"

"Just not so happy with private investigators in general right now. Apparently she'd rather have a friend."

Kenna slumped back into her chair and bit her burrito. Instead of sticking by Forrest here, she'd galivanted across Wisconsin.

While she ate, she scanned the papers on the table and processed everything Gingrich had said. Paulette came back through, no container. She gave Kenna a little nod, which she took to mean that Forrest was all right.

But she didn't need anything from Kenna.

Just freedom Kenna might have been able to offer her, by working tirelessly on finding evidence. Instead, from Forrest's perspective, Kenna had left.

We need a way to find Stan Tilley.

She wiped her mouth with a napkin. "No one has seen the car that nearly ran me over, right?"

Jax shook his head.

Kobrinsky said, "Is that why the hospital called to say a female patient jumped out of an ambulance and ran across the parking lot like a crazy woman before taking off in the sheriff's truck?"

"Probably." She squeezed the bridge of her nose. "And the marshals left with their prisoner?"

"That's why the lawyer's chopper came and went?" Kobrinsky glanced around.

Gingrich nodded.

"I miss all the good stuff."

"Like severed heads?" Kenna said.

Gingrich barked a laugh.

Kobrinsky didn't seem to think it was all that funny. He glanced at his boss. "How did Rayland die again?"

Now there was an interesting statement. The tone he used to ask the question suggested it was something that had been bothering him. Kenna turned in her chair, expecting the sheriff to at least defend himself. Brush off the accusation.

"I didn't kill him, and it wasn't an accident." The sheriff took a bite of his sandwich.

Jax dug his fork into his salad and speared a big piece of steak, watching the interplay like it was a new sitcom that had recently become popular.

"So what was he dosed with, and did it match the substance Pastor Bruce was killed with?" Kenna had no idea if the coroner was done, or if tests had been run. She looked at Kobrinsky. "Can you ask the coroner?"

"Maybe on Friday night." He winked.

Kenna chuckled.

"I'll make the call." Gingrich moved to the corner of the room, the phone to his ear.

Kobrinsky motioned to the pictures. "So what do the pros think Jennifer Rayland's connection is to J. Pierce? There has to be a connection between them since the doc has these photos."

J. Pierce had killed people on a boat, and Jennifer had one that belonged to her father. Kobrinsky also owned a boat, so that didn't mean anything conclusive. But it could be a serious indicator of a problem they'd need to resolve in order to save lives. Kenna couldn't help wondering if Gingrich knew the answer to her question about the psychologist and J. Pierce. It would mean she didn't have to speculate.

She pulled up what Maizie had sent about Jennifer Rayland and her parents. "She's got a boat. We might find her there if she's laying low. Or she could've checked into a motel under a fake name."

"Or she fled to Canada." Jax pulled over a page and stared at the pencil notes. "This is not a stable woman. It's a woman who incorporates her patient's darkest musings with her own. They aren't responsible, she's disturbed under the surface."

"She went into therapy because she wanted to understand herself." Gingrich tapped his phone on his palm.

"Because of her upbringing, or her issues, or both?" What had Rayland told him? Or did he somehow know she was connected to a killer and he'd done nothing.

"She was good. She had it handled."

Kenna stared at him. Maybe that was what she'd *told* him. "And Deputy Rayland? Was he good?" Gingrich said nothing, so she looked at Kobrinsky. "Any insight? We need to find her. Even if she's done nothing, which is debatable, we have no evidence of what she *has* done." Unless they were hiding more than she realized.

Kobrinsky looked at the sheriff.

Gingrich let out a heavy sigh. "Jennifer didn't like the way she was raised any more than any of us do. She became a psychologist to try and understand why some people are the way they are."

Kenna saw something in his gaze. A deep kind of knowing she understood as well.

"Understanding why her father was the way he was?" she asked. If Jennifer's father had been J. Pierce, the timing and a few other details made sense. How did Gingrich feel a kindred spirit connection with that?

Kenna figured she might as well share. It could be the thing that got him to open up. "That's what got me to apply for the FBI. Making sense of what my life had been helped me figure out who I was supposed to be."

Let them think she didn't believe the psychologist was a stone-cold killer.

"But that means Deputy Rayland grew up under the shadow of it. So what inspired him to become a police officer?" Kenna eased her tone, as if musing aloud. Processing the case. "What did he need to make sense of? Evil? Injustice?"

Gingrich sat forward. "He didn't know anything. She was doing fine."

"This disagrees with you." Kenna waved at the papers. "Did you hire her son so you could keep an eye on them both, maybe?"

"Let's just find her," Kobrinsky said. "Then we'll know if she killed Rayland."

"Sheriff!" Paulette strode into the room, breathing hard and flushed, followed by two officers from the state police Kenna recognized from Forrest's house.

She stood to face them as they entered, trying to figure out if this was good or bad from their faces. "Can we help you, gentlemen?"

Gingrich passed her, shooting Kenna a grumpy look. He held out his hand, and one of the men shook it. The officer produced a paper from his inside suit jacket pocket.

"We're taking Forrest Crosby to the jail."

No, you're not. Kenna took half a step.

Jax grabbed her belt at the back and whispered, "Easy, tiger."

"They're *not* taking her." Everyone heard her whisper. She shook her head and said louder, "She's about to be released."

"You'll be arrested if you try to stop us."

Chapter Thirty-Four

Arrested? As if she cared.

Kenna pulled out her phone and called Forrest's lawyer, who was supposed to be with the judge right now. She listened to it ring, and told them, "Just because you didn't get the memo yet doesn't mean you need to rush and take her to jail."

They did seem to be in a hurry. Maybe it was the weather, or they needed lunch—maybe at the same place where the judge was with Lucas Amrand. That would be good.

"We're leaving in five minutes." The state police officer strode to the door that led to the cells, where Paulette had just delivered food for Forrest. Had she even finished eating yet?

The lawyer didn't answer, so the call went to voicemail.

Kenna ended it. She heard the door open, her attention on the phone. She sent the lawyer a series of texts, wondering if this absence would turn out to be intentional. Getting more and more frustrated over the whole thing, but mostly that Forrest hadn't wanted to talk to her.

Kenna didn't like that her friend had refused her support.

Standing on her own showed strength, but leaning on people who cared about her might help for Forrest more than dogged independence. She couldn't withstand this all by herself. The lawyer might have supplied a helicopter to get those two marshals and their prisoner to Chicago—assuming they arrived—but if he let Forrest go to jail, they were going to have a serious problem.

Kenna would make it her life's work to ensure he understood they had a problem.

She turned to Jax. "Forrest can't go to jail."

Over his shoulder, Gingrich said, "She'll get released. Don't worry so much about it. We need to find Jennifer Rayland and figure out what's going on."

Kenna said, "Where do we find her?"

He was the expert on the psychologist, so he should have some idea where they could look. She only knew about the boat. That would be the first place Kenna went. After that, she'd be drawing a blank without Maizie's help.

She sent her teen friend/assistant/ward—whatever she was—a text.

> Does Jennifer have a phone we can track?

Then stowed her phone. "I'm not ignoring Forrest's situation. Okay, Sheriff? You created this Jennifer Rayland problem. Whatever it is. Maybe you're the one who should clean it up."

What skin in the game did *she* have?

Jax was here, and they needed to draw out Stan Tilley.

She cared what happened to Forrest and would do what she could to help that situation. A woman who might be sick, but only guilty of having gross images in her house, wasn't her highest priority right now.

Jax set his phone on the desk. "Our friend gave his statement."

Well, that was something that had gone right at least. Jim did what he'd journeyed to Chicago for, facing all that danger. Getting shot, along with Pilsborough. And they'd managed to succeed.

"I need to call *my* friend." Kenna huffed. "Or figure out how to get him to answer the phone."

Kobrinsky said, "What are you guys talking about?"

"A different case." Kenna needed a copy of the report from Marion's burial site. "Did all the victims' bodies get exhumed yet?" She motioned to his leg.

"They're pulling the last one today," Kobrinsky said. "There's a whole team here from the state police."

"Whole county's crawling with staties." Gingrich grumbled. "Can't turn around without bumping into one."

His deputy said, "And whose fault is that?"

Jax shifted, leading her away from them for a sidebar. But before he could say anything, the door flung open and the state officer stomped out. "Where is she?"

Jax stepped toward him, slightly in front of her. "Excuse me?"

The guy looked slightly confused, like he didn't know who Jax was. They hadn't been introduced, so that wasn't surprising. Plus, local guys didn't always want the feds getting in their way. About as much as they didn't want to believe they *ever* needed the help of a private investigator. Which was why Kenna tried to take cases that had nothing to do with them.

"It's a simple question," the officer said. "Where is she?"

"Who?" Kenna had no idea what he was talking about. "Forrest is in her cell."

And Kenna was not happy about that. She was downright irritated, in fact.

"Except that she isn't." He turned to face the sheriff. "Where's the computer that will show us your camera feed?"

Kobrinsky snorted.

"There's no feed," Gingrich said. "We have no cameras."

"How do you keep an eye on the cells?"

"I have a call in to get it repaired, okay? They haven't called me back." Gingrich's cheeks pinked. "It's only been a day or so."

Kenna glanced at him. With everything that was going on, he didn't think that was relevant?

Gingrich shifted, like the male equivalent of an eye roll. "It happens intermittently, and I call them. Usually by the time they show up, it's working again! It's not like I plan it that way!"

Jax moved. "Kobrinsky, where's the camera? I want to look at your wiring." He was thinking the camera had been messed with. If so, it was possible someone turned it off and on whenever they needed to. That meant someone in the office had regular business in the cells they didn't want anyone seeing.

Kenna closed her eyes and let out a breath.

One of the guys—she didn't know which—asked, "Where is she?"

The question swam around her. She opened her eyes, blinking to clear the disorientation. She needed to go and see for herself.

Lord, what is going on?

God knew this situation was a mess of bits and pieces. Neither she nor Jax were at a hundred percent. What was new there?

Kenna pushed through to the cells and walked down the hall. Her boots thumped the floor. Forrest's cell was empty.

She looked in the next one.

"Lance." Kenna hammered on the bars. "Lance, wake up! The trailer's on fire! Wake up!"

He started awake, rolled on the cot, and thumped onto the floor with a grunt.

Kenna winced. *Ouch.* "Lance, you good?"

He rolled to his back and blinked. "Where am I?"

"Where do you think?"

He lifted his chin and looked over his mountain belly at her. "Who are you?"

"Doesn't matter right now. Where's Forrest?"

"Who?" He blinked at her.

"The woman in the cell next to you. You must've seen her when you were brought in. Or when you left the other day?" By her count, he'd been here more than once this week. They couldn't hold him longer than twenty-four hours before they had to charge him or cut him loose. If this was his rehab, it wasn't working.

But he might've seen something.

She turned to the state officer who'd followed her into the hall. "Go grab a cup of black coffee. The stronger the better."

Lance said, "Sheriff makes it in his office. That's the one I like, not the swill in the pot."

Kenna turned back to him. "Tell me what I want to know, and I'll get you the good stuff. Otherwise, you drink the swill."

"You're a mean woman."

Kenna bit the inside of her lip to keep from grinning. "Don't you forget it." She leaned both palms on the bars. "Now tell me, who was in here a bit ago?"

"I smelled food, but Paulette's meaner than you. She didn't bring me nothin'."

"But she brought a container for Forrest?" Kenna went over and looked in. The container was on the floor. She reached through the bars and flipped the lid open. "It hasn't been touched."

"So?" The state officer strode down the hall, a steaming paper cup in one hand. "You didn't want her going to jail, 'cause you think she's so innocent."

"And that means somehow I connived to let her out?" Kenna straightened. "It's easier to just let the lawyer do his job. That way she gets to be free, rather than on the run and labeled an escaped prisoner." She took the coffee and went back to Lance's cell. Just a couple of steps to the left, and she could see him again.

He hadn't got up, but still lay on the floor—now with the pillow from the cot under his head.

"Comfortable?" She held the coffee.

He stared at it.

"Who else was in here?" There was a door at the end, a fire exit. Whoever came in or went out—with Forrest in tow—must've disabled the alarm. "Other than Paulette and the food?"

"Give me the coffee, I'll tell you."

"Tell me, and I'll give you the coffee *and* Forrest's food."

The skin around his eyes flexed. He wanted it.

"What's the deal in here?" Kenna glared.

"You'll ruin the good thing I got going."

She lifted the coffee cup like she was going to take a drink of it. "What's that?" Of course, things for him in here wouldn't be the same, but she wanted information.

He sat up, his shoulders slumped forward. "When I need a break from the old lady, I get drunk and Gingrich brings me in. I don't have to go home, and I can sleep with no interruptions."

"Okay..."

"Paulette's brother can get you whatever you want. But I only like beer."

The state police officer moved into view. "You're saying the receptionist in this department has a brother who deals drugs?"

Lance's expression shut down.

Kenna crouched and set the cup on the floor inside the cell.

Lance pretty much crawled across the floor in her direction, which she figured was less energy than standing, then crouching, and then standing again just to get coffee. He sucked it down even though it was piping hot.

"Why'd you give that to him?"

Kenna picked up the container of food, ignoring that ridiculous question. She'd been about to get information, and his question shut the whole thing down. Lance didn't want to talk to a cop. Especially not one who seemed to be more concerned about the department following the rules than real people.

She raised the container a little. "Lance."

He looked up from his coffee.

"Paulette's brother comes in here?"

He shook his head, his mouth an inch from the edge of the cup. "Nah, but if you need somethin' but you're locked up, he'll get it to her. She'll give you whatever, so you don't have to be without." He huffed. "Won't bring me beer, though."

Kenna handed the container to him. "Thanks."

"Tell Gingrich I'll be ready to go in an hour."

"Right." She followed the state police cop back to the main office area, where she said, "Paulette."

Jax moved first, jogging that direction. She followed, but the reception desk was empty. She explained what the drunk had said. He frowned. "The cameras were disabled. Looks like someone just disconnects it whenever they need it shut off."

Kenna folded her arms across her chest. "I really liked Paulette. This is disappointing."

"She's gone," Jax said. "Forrest is gone."

"What on earth happened?" She headed for the door. Icy wind hit her in the face the moment she stepped out.

Kenna looked around the front parking lot but didn't see Forrest. Or Paulette, or Jennifer, or Stan Tilley—because that was a possibility. She strode around the building, all the way around, even though it was freezing, looking at everything. The cells led out to a sidewalk path tucked close to the building, and then nothing but trees and piles of snow that had been shoveled off the walkway.

Fresh footsteps in the snow could be Forrest, and definitely belonged to more than one person.

Kenna tracked them to the rear, and a set of tire tracks. But it could've been anyone since the last snowfall. Even one of the deputies currently out on patrol who'd left this direction. Just because there were footprints didn't mean Forrest had escaped.

Her coat landed on her shoulders.

Kenna smiled at Jax and slid her arms in the sleeves. "She really just walked out?" She had to raise her voice so he could hear her against the blowing wind. "Why would she do that? She should've made a ton of noise and called us in there if she thought she was in danger."

Had Forrest been kidnapped, or had she escaped?

Jax snagged her hand and walked ahead of her to the front door. Kenna checked the parking lot, but since she didn't know what vehicle Paulette drove, she had no idea if it was still here. A matter of minutes, and Paulette had done what she'd done. Now Forrest was gone.

All while they were trying to figure out the Jennifer Rayland issue.

He ducked inside, holding the door open for her.

Everyone was in the lobby, and they *all* saw the hand holding. Kenna let go, but stepped up beside Jax so they were shoulder to shoulder. "Why would Paulette allow Forrest to escape?"

Or allow her to be kidnapped.

Which was it?

Gingrich lifted his hands, exasperation on his face. "Seems like you know more about my jurisdiction than I do."

The state police officer glanced at him. "You worry about your own problems. We'll worry about Ms. Crosby." He turned to his colleague, who hadn't said anything. "Call the office. Tell them we've got a manhunt on our hands."

Kobrinsky said, "Shouldn't it be a *person*hunt?" Then shifted on his crutches and leaned against the wood-paneled front counter. "*Man*hunt seems a little sexist."

Kenna stared at him. The clock on the wall ticked a couple of times.

He shrugged. "What?"

"We have more important things to worry about than you trying to one-up the staties." Especially when she knew what he was like. "What's the plan?" She was the only person in this sheriff's department lobby without a badge, so she figured that at least they didn't think she was in charge.

State patrol glanced at sheriff's department. "Split up?"

Gingrich said, "You wanna go after an innocent woman caught up in a bad situation, be my guest. I've got bigger fish to fry up."

State patrol looked genuinely intrigued about what that might be.

Her phone buzzed in her pocket.

The door swished open behind her. Lucas Amrand rushed in, a paper in his hand. "I got it. She's free to go." He grinned.

Her phone buzzed again. Since she *could not even* with this lawyer kid, she stepped away and pulled it out. He really thought he'd been doing the right thing being unreachable so she couldn't update him. She planned to email his boss—the partner, not his father.

She had a text from an unknown number. Kenna unlocked her phone and opened the message. A photo filled the screen.

Forrest, tied up with a cloth gag in her mouth.

One hour. Address forthcoming.

Chapter Thirty-Five

Kenna had dried off and gotten dressed in just a couple of minutes after stepping out of the shower. No time for anything longer, not that she was a bathroom lingerer. Taking a shower wasn't better than a full night of sleep, but it wasn't nothing.

Jax had opted to use the bathroom in Forrest's house.

As Kenna stood in the doorway of the tiny RV bathroom, wearing insulated pants and a short-sleeved T-shirt, he sat at the table with a cup of coffee. The back of her neck felt a little damp, her hair wet at the edge where she'd pulled it up in a bun.

Maizie's voice came from his phone on the tabletop. "Jennifer doesn't have anything other than that boat, so I called the main office for the place where it's stored, and they told me she never comes by. The last he knew, that boat was in need of repair. He thinks it doesn't even run, and he made a point to tell me no one has any business being out on the water in this weather."

She closed the bathroom door.

He glanced over. "That's probably smart." As she moved

toward him, stepping from carpet to the faux tile of the kitchen area, he gave her a long appreciative look that she liked a lot.

The oddity of having a man in her RV wasn't lost on her. She barely let Forrest in here, and her friend hadn't made a habit of intruding on her personal space. Jax must've let himself in after he was done with his shower. He'd made coffee. Comfortable in the place where she tended to hide from the world.

Maizie's voice jogged her from her thoughts. "So what do we do?"

Kenna smiled at Jax. He smiled back. They'd been staring at each other.

"She's there, isn't she?" Maizie's tone sounded like teenage exasperation.

Kenna grinned. "Is there someone else I should know about? Some other 'she.'"

Fire lit Jax's eyes. "You'd know."

Okay, then. He felt strongly about that. No need to joke about him and some other mystery woman. Probably because everyone in his life thought *she* was the mystery woman.

This flirty thing they had going on right now was nice, but didn't solve their list of problems.

Kenna leaned closer to the phone. "Maizie, did we get the address yet?" She'd ask Jax, only he looked a little distracted. She wanted to get Forrest back, and if whoever took her wanted a showdown, then she planned to be early.

"No." The teen huffed. "So call me when you do."

The call ended.

Jax chuckled. "Not a fan of us?"

Kenna liked the sound of "us" but had to say, "Relation-ships will probably always be a bit uncomfortable for her. Until she learns there are healthy ways to be together. It might take years, though." And Maizie might never get to the point where she could have a long-term romantic relationship. That didn't mean she wasn't healed. It would simply be a choice she was able to make for her future.

"I hadn't thought of it like that."

"But you're still great with her," Kenna said. "She's comfortable talking to you, which I thought would take a lot longer."

He shrugged one shoulder. "I have a sister. It's not that hard."

Just like that? She got a cup of coffee. Leaned her hips back against the counter at the sink. "How long are we going to have to wait for this address?"

She'd never had a sister. Girlfriends were few and far between. And like her relationship with Cecelia Warren—or Taylor, her former therapist and former friend—things tended to not end well. She was trying not to get a complex about the fact that she was the common denominator.

Jax sat back against the bench seat, his steady gaze on her. "You realize it's a trap."

"Yeah, I'm the one springing it."

"How's that?" He frowned.

"You're here. Obviously that's like...the whole plan. We go in, and we catch whoever it is. My trap. They're the one caught." Did she need to explain it?

She couldn't decide if Stan Tilley had taken Forrest to draw out Kenna—or if Jennifer Rayland had arranged it with Paulette so she could finish this a different way. Which would have to mean that Jennifer knew Forrest was going to be released. Her plan to have Forrest go down for murder didn't work.

He chuckled. "Ah. We catch *them*. Of course, why didn't I think of that?"

Kenna lifted a brow. "Unless you're planning on ditching me anytime soon."

Jax got up and came to stand in front of her. Wide shoulders. Taller than her in a way that was nice but didn't mean she had to be up on her tiptoes. He braced his hands on the edge of the counter on either side of her but didn't touch her. His nearness was enough. Like inhaling a potent drug.

"For the record," he said, "even when I get Tilley in cuffs and take him back to California, I won't be 'ditching' you." He made air quotes with one hand. "That's not in my five-year plan."

"Good to know." She inhaled, then sighed out the innate scent that was pure Jax. "You know, it's a lot less distracting when you're in another state working your own cases."

"You mean sitting at my desk, wondering what you're wading into with every new day, and how hard I should be praying about it?"

She scowled.

"I shouldn't pray for you?"

"Oh, you definitely should." She sighed. "It just sounded a lot like what I do."

"Worring about me? Praying?"

As if she was going to let him know how much she thought about him.

Letting him in her life was one thing, but being vulnerable about everything wasn't a switch that could be turned on and off. It was more like a slow leak, and the more that got out, the easier it was for the next trickle to come after. "What goes on in my head is none of your business."

Jax chuckled. And before she could figure out he wasn't looking at a call or text, he'd switched his phone to selfie mode and snapped an image of the two of them. That's how easily he could reach his phone without moving.

"What was that?!" She tried to grab the phone.

His arm slid around her waist. "My sister wants to meet you, so I'll try appeasing her with a photo first."

Kenna held on for dear life.

"What?" His expression softened.

"You have a sister." Somehow she'd never processed that fact. He had a brother-in-law and nephews as well. "And a mother."

He didn't say anything.

Kenna clenched her stomach and admitted the next little trickle of what was in her heart. "I never had either. How am I going to know what to say?"

"You did fine with Forrest, right? And Elizabeth Stairns. Taylor, way back in Salt Lake City."

She didn't need to admit to him that she felt a lot more comfortable in work situations rather than personal ones. Or that talking to men would probably always be easier.

She'd been raised by a single father.

She'd never had a "girl" moment in her life. Unless this counted as one. But since she was so unaccustomed to it, she had no idea what the scale was. She thought maybe this was more like deep insecurity than just being female.

Did every woman feel strong and broken nearly in the same moment?

Jax tugged her against him and held her for a moment. "Like I said, I'm not going to abandon you. Okay?"

Kenna nodded against his shirt, even though *okay* didn't really apply here. It never did. Life was life and being "okay" wasn't a good descriptor of the nuances of human experience.

Bradley had killed himself to escape the horror they'd been in. He'd left her and their baby she'd been carrying alone in that situation because he'd given up hope.

She wasn't going to compare them, even if she believed

Jax would never do that. The past was the past, and it had forged in her all the confidence and all the fears she carried.

Jax was a different man. Their situation would always be different.

Life moved on.

Each case was new.

She'd accepted the truth of what God had done for her, and now she was new as well.

Kenna's stray tears damped his T-shirt. She was supposed to be stronger than this, but the truth was, the more time she spent with him, the more she would feel what she was feeling right now. It would grow. She would fall deeper into it. And then she would never want to wade back into danger when the alternative was to be here and feel safe.

She leaned back, sniffing and swiping the heel of her hand across her face.

"It's okay, you know?" Jax said. "You're exhausted, and that makes anyone's emotions closer to the surface." His eyes did look a little red. "It's been a rough few days."

"At least not wearing a badge means I don't have to do cleanup."

He shook his head. "Thanks a lot."

She grinned. "Sucks to be you, I guess?"

Jax snorted. "One day you're going to say something, trying to be funny at completely the wrong moment, and it's going to sink like a ship."

"Let's face facts, it'll probably be in front of your mother." And wasn't that a nightmare waiting to happen? She wanted to meet his family. Maybe dragging it out this far was making it worse not better, and she should simply tear off the bandage. Show up at his parent's house one day and introduce herself. But who did that?

He slung his arm around her neck and kissed her forehead. "You'll survive her. The rest of us will help you. We're pros."

Kenna got another cup of coffee and refilled his mug. She had just lifted it to her lips when her phone chimed—loudly, because she'd turned it up to take a shower so she wouldn't miss anything. "Is it them?"

Jax tipped her phone up so she could read the screen. "Looks like it."

She gave him her pin code, and he unlocked it.

"Another picture," he said. "Can't see where she is. But there's an address."

"And Maizie couldn't get anything from the number?"

"Before you came out of the shower, she told me it was unregistered. And it seems like it's being turned off between uses."

She pulled open the closet door and dragged out a smaller sweater so she could start layering up. "Where are we going?"

Ten minutes later, Jax pulled over to the side of the street, down from the church.

"I can't believe this was the address." She stared at the building, some lights on inside—mostly in the basement levels, given the lit windows down by the ground. The main sanctuary seemed dark.

"You still think we should hold off calling this in?"

"We don't know if it's Stan or Jennifer." That didn't make much sense as far as a reason not to call anyone. But Kenna only realized that after she'd said it. "You and I can sneak around easier than an entire team. If they jump the gun and go in, they could get her killed."

"So it's recon first?" He flicked off the headlights but left the car running.

She twisted in her seat to grab her hat and gloves off the back seat. The extra layer of a bulletproof vest he'd insisted she put on since they had two wasn't comfortable. She'd been shot in the chest once while not wearing one, so she didn't argue. "You thought I'd just walk in the front door?"

"Isn't that normally in your top three of plans?"

Kenna chuckled, even though inside she was a bundle of worry for Forrest. At least she didn't have to do this alone—or partnered up with someone she didn't trust. "You could take the back door."

"Yeah, no. Together or not at all," he said. "And don't argue that splitting up covers more ground. It would be a waste of you trying to deflect with humor to avoid your feelings."

Too bad her response to that would've been humorous. Now he would never know what she'd have said—and it would've been funny, thank you very much. How was the fact she had been crying in her RV not that long ago avoiding her feelings? They were so close to the surface right now, it was any wonder she wasn't crying again. Or laughing so hard she was crying, which would've been the same thing.

Kenna sighed. "Let's just go."

He grabbed the door handle, a beanie over his hair now. "You think there's a chance this trap is for me?" Stan Tilley would have a clearer run at her if the FBI agent hunting him was out of the way.

"You think there's a chance I'm going to let anything happen to you?" Now he knew why they were sticking together. It just wasn't *only* about him hanging from that hook.

Jax grinned. "You're so romantic."

He shoved the door open, and she got hit with a blast of cold air. Kenna finished tugging on her gloves and got out on her side. She met him at the trunk of her car, and they loaded up. She didn't want to have to hold a gun for an extended period, so she opted for a holster that attached to the Velcro on the front of the vest over her sweater.

Coat open.

Hat on.

Not ideal, but there was also no point being caught outside with no coat after dark in northern Wisconsin with the wind blowing and another six inches of snowfall in the forecast.

She'd put warmers in her boots, and had extras in her coat pockets, but that wouldn't keep the rest of her from freezing.

How was Forrest?

The quicker they got in there, the better, as far as Kenna was concerned. But they needed to be concerned about an ambush or some kind of trap. As of yet, she didn't know if this was Stan's doing or Jennifer's.

Or both.

There was a terrifying thought.

Kenna heard another set of car doors open behind them and waved over the two men who climbed out. Alonzo and Theo were geared up like hunters. While Alonzo had brand-new gear, and a distinct limp that told her he might've needed crutches, Theo's outfit looked worn and broken in, as though rescue missions were a regular hobby. Neither looked like they were at a hundred percent physically, so this was pretty much a ragtag team of exhausted, banged-up heroes.

"So these are your friends." Jax came over and shook both men's hands.

"Their wives are in my book club." For some reason, she thought back to their conversation about her difficulties with relating to women.

"This your boyfriend?" Theo lifted his chin in a nod.

They introduced themselves while wind blew against her, the sides of her coat flapping around. "Let's go, it's cold."

Kenna kept one pistol in the holster in her vest, which left her hands free until she neared the back door and slid it out. Checked it.

Jax glanced at her.

She nodded.

"We'll meet you in there," Theo called over his shoulder. He and Alonzo tromped through the snow toward the other door.

Jax eased the handle down and pushed the door open but didn't go in. He waited. When the door stopped he nudged it open with his boot and checked the area inside before he took that first step.

Kenna held her breath the entire time. She glanced back to make sure no one had come up behind them.

And followed him into the church.

Chapter Thirty-Six

The sanctuary was shrouded in a darkness that didn't seem natural. A shaft of moonlight lit the carpet and a stretch of wood-backed pews. No Forrest.

Kenna took one side of the room, Jax the other. They had to sweep every row. There hadn't been anyone in the hallway on the west side, which acted as a side exit. In order to reach the offices, a person had to walk through this expansive room that seemed to echo with silence.

She stopped just short of the door in the corner and waited. Jax finished on his side, and she pointed at the door.

He nodded.

Kenna waited until he'd crossed most of the way to her and proceeded through the door. She knew parts of this building, but not all of it. There was both an attic and a basement as far as she could tell—the fellowship hall was downstairs. This time of the afternoon there might be lots of people here, using the space. Except that the pastor had been killed, and the weather kept most home. No one wanted to be stuck out in the freezing.

Which was better for her and Jax, as they didn't have to

worry about innocent people hanging around. Or getting in the way.

Her phone buzzed in her pocket, starting to ring, but she ignored it and continued.

Finding Forrest was their priority.

Kenna had looked at that photo she'd been sent, and the first. She hadn't run off in an effort to escape, and the evidence on Kenna's phone would prove it. Empty kids classroom, then another. Empty storage room. Empty bathroom.

Theo and Alonzo stood in the pastor's office, which had been cleared out of all the papers. One drawer wasn't quite shut. His bathroom was empty.

No signs of life.

Theo said, "Basement?"

Kenna kept her focus on the hall, not looking at Jax or the other two men. The last thing she needed was to get distracted by her "boyfriend." They'd had some nice moments earlier. He was figuring out what being with her was going to be like, and she was getting a handle on her hangups.

"We're left," Jax said. "You guys take right."

Kenna said, "Got it" as Theo and Alonzo took off in the other direction.

"Nice guys," Jax commented.

"Yes, they are."

"And the story?"

Kenna felt a smile edge up the corners of her lips.

His voice rumbled behind her. "Okay, I figured by now the trap would've sprung."

"Me, too." They needed to be quiet, though.

Gun ready, Kenna swept another room, one that just seemed to be plastic chairs all stacked on shelves, round tables with fold-down legs between the two sides. No one. She turned out of the room.

Jax stood by the doorway, covering the hall. Before she stepped out, his eyes flashed. "Stan." He set off, and she jogged after him. "He went in here."

"Are we going to be jockeying for who gets to go first our entire lives?"

He grinned his acknowledgement and continued.

Kenna held aim around his shoulder as best she could while he descended the stairs down to the lower level. Every second she figured would be their last. He'd get hit by something, and she would have to watch him die.

And for what?

He stepped off at the bottom, into the foyer. She moved beside him so they could stand together.

"See him?"

"No," Jax said. "Where'd he go?"

"Doesn't matter. We'll find him."

The lower level appeared to be a maze of rooms and hallways, though under one side was the fellowship hall with huge columns holding the roof up. Sunday school classrooms lined the other side. They swept each and found nothing.

With every step, her frustration mounted. "This is getting irritating. I wouldn't be surprised if the doors lock and he tries to burn us alive down here like sticking us in that garage."

Jax pulled out his phone. "No signal."

"How do we even know Forrest is down here?"

"Keep going. Finish the sweep."

His calm allowed her to take a deep breath and continue. Kenna kicked the next door open. It fell off the hinges into the room.

"Huh."

She walked by it to the next one and did the same. It felt good to vent some of her frustration. This door didn't fall in, it just swung open.

Inside, Jennifer Rayland held a knife to Forrest's throat.

Kenna registered the blade, then the fact Forrest was tied to a chair. "Drop it." She moved into the room while Jax covered her and the hall. Then trained her gun on the doctor. "Drop it now, Jennifer, or I'll shoot."

Forrest whimpered.

"It's over. Put it down."

Jennifer's face twisted with anger. "I'll kill her!"

"No, you won't. You're not the hands-on type." Kenna paused. "There's still a chance to argue with the judge that you've never taken a life with your own hands. That you had the chance to, but chose not to. Because something in you knows it's wrong."

Her expression faltered.

Forrest stared, wide-eyed, breathing hard.

"Don't jump from poison to this."

Even though there was no way she would get a reduced sentence. She'd killed a list of people at best, one of whom had been her own son. Not doing this would be a good thing—but probably wouldn't play in her favor in the long run.

"Put the knife down, doc. You're better than the savagery of it." Kenna stepped all the way into the kidnapper's space.

Dr. Rayland backed up around the chair.

The movement eased something in Kenna, but she didn't lower her weapon—she kept coming.

Rayland took another step back, then launched at Kenna. Swung down with the knife.

Kenna planted her foot and swiped at the forearm coming down, cutting it off and shoving the knife aside before it could make contact with her. She leaned on her left leg and swung her right knee up. Caught Rayland in the stomach.

The other woman doubled over. Kenna hit the forearm

with her gun hand, and her wrist smacked Rayland's arm. She dropped the gun.

Pain tore through Kenna's arm enough she couldn't keep herself from crying out. She dropped her gun, and Jax said, "Got it."

Kenna got the kidnapper face-first on the floor and pulled her arms behind her back. Jax kicked her gun over, and she slid it in the holster on the front of her vest.

"Let's get you free." He tossed some zip ties on the floor by Kenna, and she secured Dr. Rayland's hands. It wasn't easy, but it would've been impossible if her wrist was broken.

That was good news.

When she had Dr. Rayland's hands secured and she'd checked the woman for weapons, she turned her around. "Stan Tilley was here. Where is he?"

Dr. Rayland lifted her chin. Midfifties, she had some age lines, but she'd kept up her skin regimen and maybe even sprung for the more expensive stuff. Not that beauty products weren't pricey enough already. She'd made an effort to be noticed, but not stand out.

After all, she was just the town psychologist. Not a famous person.

"Who?" She stared at Kenna, her nose a little too perfect.

"Stan," Kenna repeated.

"Oh, you mean the man who locked us in here?"

"You're the victim?" Kenna snorted. "I've never heard *that* before."

"Me either," Jax said. "Let's get them out of here." He helped Forrest by her elbows, and she gingerly stood. She wore only jeans and a knitted sweater, with tennis shoes. She was going to freeze outside.

Kenna wrapped her coat around Forrest's shoulders. "You know I've got six layers on."

He friend *almost* smiled. "Getting out of here sounds good."

"Were there two of them?" Kenna asked. "Dr. Rayland and a man?"

Forrest nodded. "You showed me Stan Tilley's picture." She paused. "I almost thought it would be Theo and Alonzo who tracked me down."

"They're here," Kenna said. "They're our backup." But she didn't think Kenna would've come?

"Let's go, doc." Jax grabbed the woman by her elbow. "We can call the sheriff to come pick you up. Then you're going straight to jail."

Forrest glanced at Kenna.

"We can get a real doctor to check you out. Make sure you're not hurt." She just looked cold and freezing, but she might be injured. "Do you know where Stan is?"

"They were working together. But he did lock her in here with me. She was threatening to cut off my ear when you came in, but she hadn't done it yet. I think you were right about her. She couldn't do it herself."

"But she killed her son and Pastor Bruce?"

"She told me she did." Forrest frowned. "She was laughing."

Kenna put her arm around her friend and walked her to the door. "What made you say they were working together?"

Forrest stepped out into the hall, moving with jerky nervous strides. She wasn't going to relax until she was safe. "He said something about setting fire to her house just like they planned. Because you found her garage?"

"That's right. It must've been Stan in that mask who shoved Jax and me into the garage and locked us in." Apparently the plan to work for El Caminante and draw her out had changed to helping a local murderer try to kill them?

Maybe Dr. Rayland made him a more lucrative offer...or another reason caused him to want to do what she agreed to.

Kenna didn't need that much information.

The cops, sheriff, and the FBI could figure it out. She only wanted the Walker behind bars, where he couldn't take any more innocent lives.

"I really thought you might not come to find me." Forrest looked at her shoes, then folded the sides of the coat tighter around her.

"I wasn't going to let you die."

"So you were just doing your job."

"Of course, I was, along with the fact I care about you. We're friends, aren't we?" Along with the adage she'd lived under for years. "Forrest, every case I work is personal. Every missing person I look for becomes part of my journey. No way would I have let anything happen to you without me doing anything and everything I could to get you back."

"Thanks, Kenna." Forrest looked up at her with tears in her eyes.

"Anytime." She hugged Forrest to her side.

They carried on walking behind Jax and Dr. Rayland, all the way to the stairs that led up to the main level.

"She's crazy." Forrest winced. "I thought I knew who J. Pierce was, but it was wrong. She tried to get rid of me anyway, because I was too close to the truth."

Kenna bit her lip. "Did she kill your family?"

Forrest nodded, a sharp movement. She cleared her throat. "She killed them because she thought I had figured it out. She didn't want the book to see the light of day."

"But you actually hadn't?"

"I thought it was her father." Forrest gasped. "When it was her mother."

Kenna glanced between the two women. "Really?" That was an interesting one. Not the normal profile for a killer.

"She liked carving things up. Passed the interest onto her daughter. Thank God she didn't decide to completely follow in her footsteps or become a surgeon or something." Forrest shuddered. She almost seemed numb, which might be for the best. Not just because she was cold, but because she had faced head-on the person who killed her family.

"Instead, she chose to try and resolve what her childhood had birthed in her." Kenna had assumed as much, though Gingrich hadn't mentioned Rayland's father. "And her son did the same thing being a cop. But it couldn't have been enough, or she would never have started killing to protect her secret."

Taking the lives of Forrest's husband and son for one.

"I'm sorry you had to face her." Kenna hugged her, and they went up the stairs. She called Gingrich on the way.

"What?"

"How about you swing by the church for a pickup?" Kenna said. "That's what."

He huffed. "Who?"

"Dr. Rayland and Forrest." Kenna hung up and tucked her phone away, ignoring how her wrist hurt. It looked like her detainee was about to bolt. Kenna shook her head. "Don't even think about it. You've caused enough grief."

"And people like you think you're the law." Rayland seemed pretty satisfied by that, as if she'd been pondering who might come against her and the kind of person they would be. And, considering she was a psychologist, she probably thought a lot about human behavior.

Well, so did the cops. "Better than thinking it doesn't apply to you. Or knowing there are rules, and yet completely disregarding them."

 Lisa Phillips

Jax turned. "Where are Theo and Alonzo?"

Kenna's wrist smarted, but she pulled her gun and scanned the hallways she could see. She could call them, but they probably had their phones off. Did their wives have any GPS on their devices? Maybe they'd be able to tell her which part of the church they were in.

She hoped they had run into Stan and were taking care of that situation as much as she hoped they hadn't. The last thing she needed was a professional killer getting the drop on two retirees—even if one was a former US marshal.

"I can look with you." Forrest's voice sounded so small. "We should find them."

Kenna took a step, already shaking her head to decline.

A gunshot rang out through the church. She froze, the dread of grief a real thing that cracked like a whip inside her. *Lord Jesus.*

Someone cried out, a male.

Two more shots.

Kenna started running.

Chapter Thirty-Seven

Kenna tore down the hallway, aware of Forrest right behind her. She drew her weapon as she ran. Following the sound.

"No!" he cried out. "Hold on! Hold on!"

"Theo!" Forrest ran faster, almost coming up alongside Kenna.

She shifted around the corner, partially cutting off the other woman but also making sure that any bullets aimed their direction wouldn't hit Forrest.

They would hit Kenna. Hopefully in the vest.

Down the hall, Alonzo lay on the floor on his back. Theo whipped off his jacket and swayed. He caught the fact they were coming toward him and twisted around, nearly toppling off balance.

"It's okay," she said. "It's just us."

Theo had blood running down the side of his face. A lot of blood.

Kenna and Forrest scrambled to him and knelt.

Forrest took the jacket from Theo and pressed it against

the blood on Alonzo's chest. "Pressure. Pressure. We need an ambulance."

Kenna slid out her phone and held it out. Forrest took it from her. Kenna touched Theo's cheeks. "Where did he go?"

Glassy eyes that couldn't focus. Blood coating her left hand. He'd been shot, but it grazed the side of his head front to back.

"Shot him," Alonzo muttered.

Kenna frowned. "You did?"

He shook his head and caught his eyes before they rolled all the way back and he passed out. She watched the whole thing, wincing. Wondering if she'd have to lay him on the floor. Maybe he should lie down anyway. He didn't seem like he should be conscious right now.

Theo said, "You."

"Where did he go?"

"Behind... Sorry." He seemed sad, or disappointed in himself.

"Don't worry. I'll get him, and you'll have a wicked scar." She winked. "Lay back." Kenna helped him onto the floor, all the way down, then spotted the door behind Theo. Slightly ajar.

Cold wind whipped down the hallway, whistling through the gap.

She grabbed her phone. "Yes, I need an ambulance at the community church. A man has been shot." Then glanced at Forrest for a second.

If she wasn't okay, she was at least going to hang on until help came.

Kenna hauled the door open left-handed, the gun in her right. Only after she'd hit the salted back step did she realize she'd given Forrest her coat.

Wind whipped against her.

"Yah. Cold." Kenna gritted her teeth and looked for Stan.

She spotted movement between two trees, and thanked God she'd put on boots that came up to her knees. She jumped off the bottom step and raced through the snow up what might be a path, or it might not. No one had shoveled it. The snow was at least four inches back here, probably where it never got sun so it never melted.

Stan Tilley had shot Alonzo, and he'd tried to kill Theo as well.

He really thought she wasn't going to come after him for trying to murder her friends? He would realize quickly that she didn't let things go.

Kenna ran to where she'd seen him, spotting footprints in the snow. The stride was shorter than hers. Especially with her running. The cold blasted her from the outside, creating a pleasant numbing sensation that prickled her skin. Enough to distract her from how much her right wrist hurt.

Until she felt, more than heard, someone behind her and spun to meet the threat. He slammed into her, grunting. She fell back into the snow. It hurt. A lot. Kenna cried out, and all the air in her lungs expelled in a rush. He was on her.

She kicked with her legs but forced her mind to stay put. To hang on to reality and what was happening to her rather than go blind with rage and become mindless. All she could do was pray, *Lord...don't let go.*

But that was enough to keep her under control.

She lifted her hips, but his weight didn't allow her to move.

"I always wished I was the one who got to kill your daddy."

His voice rumbled through her. She shoved against him, but he weighed too much and her arms would never be able to shift that much. Not with all the physical therapy in the world.

New plan.

Kenna twisted her body to the side, got one leg out, and kicked him left while she shifted right. He grabbed her. She gritted her teeth and kicked again.

The move shoved her upper body farther away from him, giving her enough clearance to kick again. She unleashed all her frustration into the blow.

As soon as she felt him let go, Kenna rolled away and kept going until she came up against a tree. He grabbed for her leg but didn't latch on.

Her leg.

She scrambled to her feet and slid the tiny flashlight-sized stun gun from her boot as she straightened out to standing and faced him.

She wasn't going to let him get under her skin, or use her past to distract her. Sure, her mother was dead. So was her dad. Just because he was a contract killer didn't mean there was anything off about how either had died.

She wasn't going to let him make her lose her cool.

The Lord bless you and keep you.

Stan shook off a bunch of snow and eased up straight. "I had to settle for just killing your mama."

The Lord make His face to shine upon you and be gracious unto you.

She had no idea if he had a gun, or where it was. He'd tackled her instead of shooting her. Was he not supposed to kill her? That would certainly work in her favor.

A split second later, she realized she was soaked nearly to her skin. Her gloves were wet, but her fingers were still sort of warm from the hand warmer in there. The cold was like an old familiar friend, however, and the lack of pain had a way of crystalizing her thoughts and her will.

Stan Tilley wasn't going to get the better of her.

He rushed at her, and she lifted the stun gun. Pressed the button. Jabbed it against his neck, since that was one of the only places she'd find bare skin. It hit the collar of his jacket. He tried to swipe her hand away, but the pain in her wrist was nonexistent thanks to all this cold.

Kenna planted her feet wide enough he wouldn't knock her down and grabbed him around the ribs with one hand. He battered a fist against her back. She grunted, found skin, and hit the button.

Electricity crackled. Stan's body jerked, and she could feel the sizzle. Maybe it was hitting her, too, or maybe it wasn't. She couldn't quite tell.

"Kenna!"

She kept a tight hold on Stan until he went limp and passed out. She let him drop to the ground, and stepped back, ready in case he was only faking it. Then she yelled, "Over here! And I need more plastic ties!"

Jax raced over. "Are you okay?"

She shivered. Given the tone of his voice, she wasn't the only one who worried in this relationship. "Please tell me you didn't leave Jennifer alone?"

He squeezed her shoulder. "The state police showed up and took custody."

"Great." As if she trusted them. "As long as they don't drag off Forrest as well."

He tightened the plastic ties on Stan's hands. "Let's get him inside then." Jax glanced at her but said nothing else.

He was worried about her? "I'm fine. Just wet."

This was it.

"What is 'it'?"

She frowned. "Huh?"

"You said, "This is it.""

Oh, she'd said that aloud? "It's the end. Jennifer. Stan. This is the moment where I could walk away and it's all done. I can decide if I should say goodbye or just go." She stared in the direction of the back of the church. "I've got everything I came for. If I leave, these people can pick up their lives and continue on. I'll become a memory."

"And you won't have to do any paperwork."

Kenna tried to laugh, but nothing came out. "My hand hurts."

"And you're freezing enough your teeth are chattering." He hoisted Stan over his shoulder like a firefighter. "Go ahead of me so I know you didn't fall behind. We're going inside so you can say goodbye instead of disappearing and becoming a memory." He sounded disappointed.

What was the big deal?

She didn't have to make lifelong friends everywhere she went. That would get exhausting. She could call Forrest later, make sure everything was all right. If she stuck around, there were several people she'd end up having choice words with.

If Alonzo lost his life, she'd be intruding on the grief of people who'd considered him family for years. She was only an interloper. A latecomer.

Kenna had to think pretty hard to get her legs moving, but she found a rhythm and soon enough they were at the door. Her fingers didn't want to grab the handle.

"I've got it." Jax opened the door, and she went in.

Her face immediately flushed. Why was it so warm in here?

"Come on." He nudged her back gently.

Just a pool of blood remained of Alonzo. "Is he..."

"The ambulance is loading them both now."

As soon as she could see the lobby, she looked for Forrest. She didn't care that much about Dr. Rayland. What she needed to know was that her friend wasn't being arrested right now.

The two state police officers had Dr. Rayland in cuffs. And thankfully, she was being quiet.

Kenna's head pounded. Her wrist was starting to hurt again. Did she need to go to the hospital and get checked out by a doctor?

Forrest flushed. "Kenna...maybe you should catch the ambulance before it leaves."

That sounded like running, which she definitely didn't want to do right now. She held out her hand, and Forrest clasped it, immediately tugging Kenna over to a bench seat in the lobby.

"You're soaked," her friend said.

Kenna shivered. "Don't give me back my coat. It'll be all wet."

Jax looked at Forrest, and they had some kind of silent communication. He had already laid Stan Tilley on the floor, hands secured with plastic ties behind his back. Breathing slowly. When he woke, they'd be able to get answers about Walker. *El Caminante.* Who they'd thought was a guy named Parker that she'd met in Mexico briefly.

She had no idea why the guy had latched onto her enough to send a hired killer to...what? Annoy her? Stalk her? Kidnap her?

Kenna's lips puffed out, and she inhaled deeply.

And shivered again, Tilley's words flooding her thoughts.

I always wished I was the one who got to kill your daddy.

What he'd said wasn't true. It couldn't be. Kenna's dad would have never rested if his wife had been murdered. He'd have made it his life's mission to bring down the people responsible.

There was no way.

"Who is this guy?" The state patrol officer waved at Stan on the floor.

Jax folded his arms. "Federal business you don't need to worry about."

The front door opened, and Sheriff Gingrich stepped in. "What have we—" He spotted Dr. Rayland. "She goes with me."

"Great." The state patrol officer nodded. "I'll follow you. Just to make sure it all goes smoothly."

Jax said, "I'll bring this guy to your cells. First thing tomorrow, I'll have an FBI team pick him up for transport back to California."

"I want to go to California."

Kenna twisted to look at Forrest. Her head pounded, her muscles hurt, and she had to gasp a breath. "You do?"

"And by the look of things, I'm driving." Forrest flashed a slight smile. "I'll get Kenna to the hospital."

Gingrich walked to Jennifer Rayland. "Come on."

"This is your fault." She glared up at him. "You were supposed to protect me! We're family, and that means *nothing* to you."

Kenna gaped. *Family?*

Everyone stiffened.

Gingrich's jaw muscle flexed. "Just because we were cut out of the same woman doesn't mean we're family. I didn't grow up with you, I don't know you."

"But you tried to take my son from me, all about your *nephew* and how impressionable he was."

"'Cause you're messed up. Thank the good Lord he

wasn't messed up like you. Growing up in that house, listening to your horror stories."

Jax glanced at Kenna, his brows raised.

She returned his expression.

Forrest said, "Oh my gosh."

The state patrol officer said, "I'm definitely coming with you. And you're going to give me your badge and your gun. Because you're no longer the sheriff."

Gingrich looked like he didn't even care. "I didn't do anything wrong. I'm the one who *killed* J. Pierce. Does it make any difference that she was my mother?" He shrugged.

"I guess we'll find out." The state guy held out his hand, motioning for the sheriff to hand over his weapon and his authority.

Kenna closed her eyes. *I had to settle for just killing your mama.*

She didn't know how long that roiled around in her mind before Forrest patted her arm.

Kenna blinked at an empty foyer, red and blue flashing lights hitting the frosted glass window. The air in the church lobby seemed overly cold. Her clothes had gotten stiff. Even her toes were damp. She'd lost her hat.

She tried to find her phone, patting her pockets and twisting one way then the other.

"This?" Forrest was the only one here with her now. She held out Kenna's phone.

She tried to take it, but her fingers wouldn't move. She used her other hand to hold the phone against her leg, too tired to even process what the words on the screen meant. "Jax left?"

"Don't worry." Forrest chuckled. "He said he'd come and find you at the hospital."

The door opened, and two paramedics entered. She recognized them both and winced. They were the ones in the ambulance when she'd rolled off the gurney and run after Stan, then nearly got run over, and took off with Jax in the sheriff's truck.

"It was..." She wanted to say *police business*, but that wasn't exactly true. She should apologize, but her brain didn't seem to want to work enough for the right words to form.

He crouched in front of her. "Are you gonna run off this time?"

"Does it look like I can run?"

Forrest said, "But we're gonna try standing on our own two feet."

He wrapped a space blanket around her, and they headed outside. She hung on to them even though she couldn't feel her fingers. Forrest was talking, but Kenna couldn't make out what she was saying. As long as she was alive. Everyone who had hurt someone was in cuffs.

Her cases were done.

Solved.

The Lord turn His face toward you and give you peace.

Chapter Thirty-Eight

One day later

Kobrinsky shook his head, leaning back in the chair beside Kenna's hospital bed. "Apparently, she was going to start up again, after she'd killed Forrest. She was going to be 'Jennifer Pierce' and carry on the family business."

"That's crazy." Kenna looked at the door, wondering how long Jax planned to be before he came by. According to the nurses, he'd been there the previous day, and she'd been asleep. They'd passed on the information that he'd told them to tell her when she woke up—that he was staying in her RV. Forrest had asked him to stay there so she wasn't quite so alone.

Kenna planned to order a full security system ASAP.

"Is Forrest okay?" Kobrinsky asked. "Do you know?"

There was something a whole lot like genuine concern in his eyes. The guy presented a good ole boy image, but there just might be a genuinely good guy deep down inside. Would

Forrest always see him as the cop who'd been the one to tell her that her husband and son were dead?

Kenna smiled. "Maybe after you've healed up, and settled into your new role as interim sheriff, you should swing by and check on her?"

The town also needed a new pastor. That would be a transition for a lot of people.

Someone knocked on the door. Betty opened it and looked straight at Kobrinsky. "He wants to know if you have said everything you needed to say."

Theo called out from the hall. "No, what I *said* was, 'Is he done?'"

Kenna bit her lip.

Kobrinsky stood, adjusting his crutches.

She looked up. "If you need anything, give me a call."

The interim sheriff nodded. "Thanks, Kenna."

Betty held the door for him, and when it was clear, the orderly pushed Theo in. "Maybe *I* have something to say"—Betty put a hand on her hip—"about her putting you and Alonzo in that much danger. And when Alonzo was in danger."

Theo rolled his eyes, his face pale and head bandaged. "Woman, she didn't twist our arms."

Betty put her other hand on her other hip. "Just because you're a grouchy old man doesn't mean you get to talk to me like that. If your head hurts, ask the doctors for some medicine instead of yelling at everyone." She turned and walked out.

Kenna gave him a second, then said, "She's right."

He sighed. "I know."

"Maybe while you're asking for pain medicine, you can talk about treatment options." He'd told her days ago that his cancer had come back. At least, that's what she assumed he'd been sick with.

"I'd rather take her on a three-week European vacation and then come back and meet my maker on my own terms. Like in a fiery go-kart accident."

Kenna frowned. "That sounds horrible."

"But it'll make a cool story in the paper. All the people hunting Alonzo and me will think I spent all the money we stole. They'll chuckle and turn the page and go on with their lives. Betty will buy a condo in Key West and live like a queen."

"What was the book?"

"Oh." Theo waved. "A list of the places we buried the money. But he found it. Charlayne tidied up, and she moved it. It's all good."

Kenna wasn't sure that was entirely true, but he and Alonzo were allowed their business. If anyone cared about the money they'd stolen or bringing justice, they were going to come here and find two old men. Justice would feel pretty much like paperwork, a hollow victory.

"Unless you're going to tell someone that you found us."

Kenna chuckled. "I wasn't looking for you."

She didn't know anything about the case. Anything she heard wasn't corroborated—it was just hearsay at best. Unless she dug into it to figure out who in the marshals service, or some other agency, cared about finding them.

"Is there someone looking for you?" she said.

Theo sniffed. "Only the crime boss Alonzo worked for, and he died fifteen years ago. I doubt his kids or the cops trying to nail them back then care now."

"How did you get involved?" She moved her hand across the bed, and the IV needle in her elbow shifted. *Ouch.*

"I was undercover. Alonzo and I became friends enough he told me he was thinking about walking away. So we figured out a plan for him to write a letter to the captain above the cops, trying to nail them by any means necessary. Including breaking the law." Theo grinned. "Two weeks later, all those cops were fired and Alonzo's boss was arrested."

And they'd taken off with the funds to start over. Enough money to set them up for life. They didn't live large—that would have been too noticeable. Instead, they'd become part of a community, cared about the people who lived near them, and stepped up to lend a hand even though it got them hurt.

"So no one at the marshals knew you left?"

"I didn't run off. I resigned."

With a nest egg for both of them and their families. Ill-gotten gains.

Kenna squeezed his hand. "Thanks for helping out."

Theo nodded gently. "Anytime. I mean that."

He rolled his way out, with the help of the orderly. Kenna settled down in the bed and closed her eyes, listening to the hustle and bustle of the hospital hallway outside. She was slowly getting accustomed to the idea of a hospital not being a place where terror mixed with pain and the memories were so close to the surface she couldn't breathe.

She started to hum the hymn they had sung at church. One she needed to look up and copy the words down into her journal.

Someone knocked quietly on the door, and she heard it click.

She forced herself to wake up. Had Jax left because she...

"Hey. Easy." He settled onto the edge of the bed, covering her hand with his.

"I'm not sleeping."

"I heard you humming." He slid his fingers across her palm, making her shiver. "Rest is good."

"I'm here, aren't I?"

He smiled, but she spotted something there.

"What?" Kenna said. He should just tell her whatever it was. She already knew she wasn't going to like it.

"I have to go. My ASAC wants me and Stan Tilley back in San Diego as soon as we can get there. We're supposed to fly out tonight."

She turned her hand over in his.

"Come and see me in California." He said it so carefully, as if concerned she would turn the offer down.

"So your boss can co-opt me into working the case? Or arrest me on obstruction?"

"You think he'd be able to find you?" Jax lifted his brows.

Kenna grinned. "I'd find him first."

He leaned down and kissed her, sweet and soft. Kenna wanted to close her eyes and start humming again, but then she would miss all the Jax happening in front of her. He pulled back a fraction. "Come and see me."

"Okay."

He chuckled. "You had a valid point about getting more done not being around each other all the time. But that's not what I want. Regardless of what people think, I'll just do my job to the best of my ability and be there for you when you need it."

"I'd prefer it if you didn't have to choose," Kenna murmured.

"Because you don't think I should choose you."

"You shouldn't have to give up your career!"

Jax shook his head, half smiling. "Let me worry about my five-year plan."

"Are you going to share what it is?"

He motioned closing his lips and turning a key. "Need to know." She was totally going to get Maizie to find out.

"Fine." Kenna squared her shoulders. "Keep your secrets."

"It'll be the most interesting case you ever solve." Jax kissed her again and stood. "See you soon."

She waved. "I hope so."

He looked like he wanted to give her an ultimatum, but just settled for a wink. And then he was gone. Taking all the flirty banter with him. Off to go back to his job, keeping his obligations to the FBI—the same agency that had burned her.

Then again, she worked with the man who had betrayed her. Kenna would never consider Stairns to be a bad guy. Otherwise, she never would've left Maizie with him and his wife.

If he wanted to maintain his loyalty and have his career, she wouldn't do anything to jeopardize it for him. They could be partners in life but not in work, and that would be fine.

For now.

The doctor paid her a visit and ordered another X-ray on her still swollen wrist. How she'd managed to come through everything without a concussion was a miracle. She watched the marathon of a terrible soap opera on TV for a while, then begged the nurse for coffee. It was terrible, but she drank it anyway.

A while later, Kenna was just dozing off again when her phone buzzed on the side table. She managed to twist and reach far enough to grab it, keeping her head tipped to the side so she could lay her phone on her ear and not have to hold it. "Hello."

"It's just me," Maizie said. "How are you feeling?"

"Obviously, I'm fine, or you'd be sitting next to me, worrying in person."

"Stairns made me ask. After I told him it would be a waste of gas to drive up there."

"Jax wants me to go to California," Kenna stated.

"If you do, I think Stairns will volunteer to drive the RV for you so you can rest."

That wasn't a bad idea. "Don't tell him I'm interested. Make him ask me himself." She wanted to spend a couple of days with Forrest, and make sure Betty and Theo—and Alonzo and Charlayne—were all right. Last she'd heard, Alonzo was supposed to be waking up from his second surgery, to resolve complications from the first one.

Maizie chuckled. "Good to know. Heaven forbid I just tell either of you something straight."

"Where's the fun in that?" Kenna's humor bled away fast. She needed more energy if she was going to convince the doctors that she could leave. Hopefully later on. "Can you ask Forrest if she'll pick me up when they release me?"

"Sure. I also sent you some information that came in from someone called Jim? It's got a password on it that I don't know. It was sent anonymously through the website, and I can't figure out where it originated."

"Don't worry about chasing it down." She had no idea about a password, but if it came from Jim, then it was likely about Cecelia Warren. "I'll figure out what it means."

"Okay," Maizie said.

"Anything else?"

"I was looking into Jennifer's mother. I found birth record for another child, about four years before Jennifer. She had a son by another man who ended up being one of the first victims."

So they'd been telling the truth about being siblings. Half-brother and sister whose lives had diverged after birth and gone on two different paths, while they had remained connected.

Maizie continued, "The state police have logged the name

of every victim Marion Wells buried in that field and made all the death notifications. So they've officially released the information." She paused. "Our friend likely knows we found his sister."

Usually, when someone said *our friend*, it was her or Jax protecting Maizie's identity. This time she was referring to Ramon, the former FBI agent Kenna had met in Mexico. He'd disappeared and had yet to resurface. When he did, she could actually tell him that they'd finally solved the mystery of what happened to his sister who had gone missing years ago.

"There's one more thing I need you to look into." Kenna didn't even want to say it. Months ago, she'd found an autopsy file in a safe belonging to Sheriff Joe Don Hunter. And when her van burned down, she'd lost all the information. Maizie probably couldn't find anything, but Kenna needed to ask anyway.

"What is it?" Maizie asked.

Kenna's stomach clenched. "Stan Tilley said he murdered my mother. Can you—" Her voice broke, and she had to clear her throat.

"I can find anything that's out there. If you can give me any...details you have."

"I'll send you what I know in an email."

"Okay," Maizie said softly. "If there's anything to find, I'll find it. Did you tell Jax? Maybe he can—"

"He has work to do. I don't want my stuff affecting his case. So until we know it was more than Stan just mouthing off to throw me for a loop, let's just look into it, okay?"

"All right." She didn't sound exactly happy.

"I should go."

They hung up, and she stared at the wall for a while.

Did she really believe what Stan Tilley had said? If he'd actually worked with her father in the military, perhaps they had been at odds enough for Stan to develop a grudge. Enough to want her dad dead? She'd have heard his name before, surely.

And now he wanted her to believe he'd killed her mother?

Some kind of contract. Or simply because he wanted to?

Night fell in the early evening.

Even though she was supposed to leave today, it might be a couple more hours before the nurse brought in the discharge paperwork, which the doctor needed to sign. He wanted her to follow up with an orthopedic specialist in a few days to make sure her wrist wasn't fractured since the tests were inconclusive.

Forrest had texted that she would come whenever Kenna needed picking up.

Not bothering to turn the light on, Kenna dressed in the clothes she found in the backpack Jax or Forrest must have brought. Sweatpants and a T-shirt, with a sweater. Sneakers and socks and her coat. Nothing she'd have to struggle with her wrist to get on.

The door opened.

"I'm almost ready to go." She toed her first shoe on.

"I see that."

She whipped around to see Ramon Santiago in the doorway, dressed in heavy clothes with a hood over his hair. He had to have snuck in here without anyone seeing him. "I hear you found my sister." His face stayed impassive, but she could guess what that meant to him.

His mother would be able to bury her finally. Lay her to rest.

Kenna nodded. "I'm glad I found her."

Marion would face justice, and the last victim would live her life.

She toed on her other shoe, trying to figure out how to tell him about Jim and his testimony against Cecilia Warren—the FBI agent who had destroyed his career.

"Your sister is coming home." She glanced at him. "How about you?"

"It's too late for that. But it's not too late for revenge."

Kenna shook her head. "That won't set things right."

He walked to the door, tugging it open. "Don't try to stop me, Kenna. I do what I do."

"That's not how to resolve this. There's a case."

He left.

Kenna rushed to the door. *Ramon.* She didn't want to call his name aloud for anyone to hear. But when she looked for him out in the hall...he was gone.

"Did you need something?" A nurse stopped by her.

"Yeah, I need to get out of here."

She had work to do.

Also by Lisa Phillips

Find out more about Brand of Justice at my website:

https://authorlisaphillips.com/product-tag/brand-of-justice/

Book 1: Cold Dead Night (Aug 2022)

Book 2: Burn the Dawn (Nov 2022)

Book 3: Quick and Dead (Feb 2023)

Book 4: Over the Limit (June 2023)

Book 5: Skin and Bone (August 2023)

Book 6: Dust and Ashes (November 2023)

Book 7: Long Road Home (February 2024)

Book 8: Dead to Rights (August 2024)

———

For Lovers of Romantic Suspense check out

-Benson First Responders-

———

Other series by Lisa:

Last Chance Downrange

Chevalier Protection Specialists

Last Chance County

Northwest Counter-Terrorism Taskforce

Double Down

WITSEC Town (Sanctuary)

———

For other titles including several with Love Inspired Suspense, you can find the complete list here:

https://authorlisaphillips.com/all-books/

About the Author

Find out more about Lisa Phillips, and other books she has written, by visiting her website:
https://authorlisaphillips.com

Follow Lisa on Facebook and Instagram, and subscribe to her newsletter to stay up to date and be the first to find out about raffles and giveaways!
https://authorlisaphillips.com/subscribe

facebook.com/authorlisaphillips

instagram.com/lisaphillipsbks

bookbub.com/authors/lisa-phillips

www.ingramcontent.com/pod-product-compliance
Lightning Source LLC
Chambersburg PA
CBHW021339310726
48971CB00001B/205